STAR MONEY

STAR MONEY

KATHLEEN WINSOR

New York

APPLETON-CENTURY-CROFTS, INC.

Certain quotations are reprinted in this book by the kind permission of the
publishers and copyright owners on the following pages:

11, 16:   lines from *Bless 'Em All,* by Al Stillman, Jimmy Hughes, and Frank
            Lake. Copyright 1941 by Sam Fox Publishing Company, New York.
            Used by Special Permission.

76, 77:   lines from *I'm Waiting For Ships That Never Come In,* by Jack
            Yellen and Abe Olman. Copyright 1919, renewed 1947, by Forster
            Music Publisher, Inc., Chicago, Ill. Reprinted by permission of
            copyright owner.

130, 131:   lines from *You'd Be So Nice to Come Home To,* by Cole Porter.
            Copyright 1942 by Chappell & Co., Inc., New York, New York.
            Used by permission.

400:        lines from *If I Loved You,* by Richard Rodgers & Oscar Hammer-
            stein II. Copyright 1945 by Williamson Music Inc., New York, New
            York. Used by permission.

PRINTED IN THE UNITED STATES OF AMERICA

TO MY MOTHER AND FATHER

Tua res agitur
Horace: *Epistles* I, *18, 84*

"It is you who are discussed here."

PART I

Chapter 1

It was a woman's bedroom, actually a boudoir, and no man belonged in it except by invitation.

But, somehow, it had not occurred to her when she looked at the decorator's plans that Ed might have other tastes or wishes for a room he was going to share. Dallas had suggested this but Dallas did not know Ed, and he criticized almost everything she did anyway.

"Ed will love it," she had told him firmly, shutting down her annoyance at his smile and the sly secret way in which he had questioned her. "I know what I'm doing."

What business was it of his?

And Mr. Hastings had made it exactly what she wanted and believed she had always wanted. It was what she would have done, if she had been able to trust herself to do it at all: The colors were those she loved and which became her best—several tones of white, deep plum, and bright fresh green. A tremendous double bed stood against one wall, still covered with its raw-silk ivory spread. She had sent the maid out when she came to turn it down because she had a horror of the servants overhearing a quarrel. Opposite the bed a pair of French doors opened onto a terrace and across it the uptown buildings looked almost black; it was so late that only a few windows were still lighted. The chiffon curtains hung quiet and undisturbed by the hot August night.

Everything in the room had been made to order and all the pieces were big, impressive, reassuring. The desk and chest of drawers were finished in what Mr. Hastings had called "antique white." There was a white faille chaise, smoked glass tables, big lamps, and vases filled with flowers. Cut flowers were a luxury she had always promised herself, once she could afford them.

It was all so clean, so meticulously arranged, even the magazines laid in a neat line on the low table at the foot of the bed, that it seemed the decorator had just left and no one had yet moved in. She hated a look of clutter, in rooms or clothes, and though she had lived in this apartment for more than a year she had insisted that it keep the original perfection Mr. Hastings had planned for it. Even small changes made inadvertently by the servants gave her a nearly frantic sense of loss and bewilderment.

She walked around it now, mechanically closing the drawers Ed had left opened, thinking somewhere underneath that with him gone there would be more room for her own clothes.

The ashtrays were full of cigarette stubs and she crushed out the one she was smoking but immediately lighted another. As she stopped in front of the desk to pick up a lighter she glanced down at a framed snapshot someone had taken of Ed and her after he went into the Navy. She looked at it a moment, reached out to turn it face down, and then decided not to.

Not just yet. I'll change it later—if he doesn't come back.

If he doesn't come back? What's the matter with me? Of course he's not coming back. He can't. This can't go on and on forever. It's over, it's finished. This time for good.

And I'm *glad*.

But she was tired and felt a sudden almost sickening restlessness.

Whether she was glad or not, his going had left an empty aching place in her life that would have to be filled someway, and very soon. A terror of being alone began to rise. She turned swiftly and looked around the room, and hated it. Without this room and everything that went with it this might never have happened.

Oh, but you couldn't even be sure of that.

It could have happened another way. Any number of other ways. Given her and what she was, it had to happen sometime. And it hadn't been Ed's fault. It was hers. She was the guilty one. She always had been. No one else was to blame. Only her.

She drew a quick gasping breath and was almost surprised she was able to do it. For a moment she had felt she was being smothered. And then she ran out to the terrace, as if she had left someone or something valuable out there. Nothing was there, only the neat and symmetrical arrangement of white iron Victorian furniture, covered with magenta and lemon yellow and ant-poison green cushions. But for once she was not thinking about the pleasure of owning these things. She was trying not to think at all.

I *won't* think, she insisted.

It's done and there's no use thinking about it.

You're only sure through action, not when you stop to think. That was the thing she avoided, and had always avoided. Now, sometimes it seemed she would avoid it all her life; she might have to. Because the greatest peril lay in her own mind, close enough to the surface that she could catch at it—like something in a pool—and if she pulled, it would begin to come up, out of the darkness, something terrifying she did not want to see or know about.

She remembered what Johnny had said to her that afternoon. "You've finally got everything the way you want it, haven't you?"

"I suppose so," she had told him, but of course it was not true.

And it never will be true. Because we can't go back to the beginning

4

and take out everything we wish had never happened. It's all there—everything I ever saw or did or wished for, all the lonely fears and the words that hurt, all the bewilderment and all the regrets. Nothing ever leaves you, and forgetting is no cure. For even forgotten it will still be there, from the very beginning—changed a little, maybe, as you change yourself—and the way you feel about it may no longer be the same as when it happened, but that's part of what you are, too.

> One need not be a chamber to be haunted;
> One need not be a house;
> The brain has corridors surpassing
>   Material place.

How did I happen to remember that?

I remember so much—too much. It can't do any good now; why does it still matter?

She went and stood at the railing.

And then, after a few moments, she leaned over and looked down. Seventeen stories.

Then she leaned even farther, until she could see where the wall of the building met at right angles with the sidewalk. Her hands held the railing hard. Her heart beat fast and she felt a cold weakening terror. Some external force seemed to speak quietly and insistently, like a voice just at her shoulder:

It would be so easy to give up. And why not? What can you gain by going on? Nothing. It would be so easy. You want to. What are you afraid of? They say you lose consciousness anyway, falling. In three seconds it would be over—there'd be nothing more to fear, nothing more to fight. It would all be over; and you'd be at peace. Otherwise there's tomorrow and the next day and the next and all the rest of your life. You'll be alone. What will you do? How will you live? You can't. It's nothing to be afraid of. . . .

She felt as if she were caught in a web of ropes that closed tighter and tighter and the more fiercely she struggled to free herself the tighter it pulled. It was like waking from some nightmare of drowning where she had to fight for a gasp of breath—the night opened out vastly around her, offering some promise of escape that seemed to be almost hope.

It would be so easy.

Yes . . . but you've felt this way before.

She had stood at the window of her room in the Hotel Pennsylvania one morning three years ago and wished that she were dead and could never be forced to make any more decisions, never commit another falsehood, never again know loneliness.

But Johnny had come that night.

Well, he wouldn't come tonight. No one would. She was alone.

5

really alone. And the one thing she had feared most all her life—isolation—she had finally brought about.

She turned away quickly and went back inside. What if you were sorry the moment your feet left the railing? You couldn't decide then to go back. She heard herself laugh contemptuously.

You coward!

You don't dare live—and you don't dare to die.

She walked straight through the room to the mirror that covered the wall behind the bed. She stood and looked at herself, trying, as she had tried hundreds of times in the past, to tell what she really looked like. She had been told that she was beautiful often enough, but she could never feel sure of the men who told her. What did they want? Why this flattery? She had never believed them, because she doubted herself too much.

The girl in the mirror had black hair, parted on the left side and swinging in heavy curves to her shoulders. Her eyes were clear blue-gray and her mouth, both sensual and stubborn, was rounded out with deep red. Her features seemed to have been carefully worked and her face in repose was cool and a little sullen, making her look something like a well-bred gypsy. She was taller than average and built according to American standards—small waist, pointed breasts and round hips, and slender long legs, finely shaped. She wore a gown of silver-gray jersey, molded and clinging, as if it had been wrung out and put on wet.

I really am beautiful, she decided. Maybe I wasn't once, but I am now. And as she looked at herself she thought with scorn of what a fool Ed had been to leave a woman as beautiful as she. Not only beautiful but everything else, too. Money and success and youth and talent.

And what was he? What had he ever done that his father had not done for him?

But when he had gone, he had looked at her as if he no longer knew she was beautiful. Maybe he didn't. Maybe he had forgotten that, too. The way they had both forgotten a lot of things.

"What are you going to do?" she had asked him, while she stood and watched him pack.

He had not turned to glance at her or stopped for even a moment. "I think I'll go back to L.A."

She had felt a burst of fury at that.

Why *should* he go back? He had come from there! She had come from there. Why in the name of *God* go back once you had managed to get away? But of course he hadn't wanted to get away, and she knew that too. Back there he could take up his life where the war had broken it off, and where she had broken it again when he had come home and found her living in this elegant New York apartment.

6

There was security for him back there, and the kind of life he—not she—had wanted.

"Coward!" she had said to him.

But even that had seemed no shock. He was more free of her than she had imagined could be possible. "I don't think so," he had said quietly. "New York isn't the only yardstick for measuring yourself."

And what could she say? Oh, yes it is too? It's the only one for me, anyway, so it must be for you, too? That wouldn't hold up any longer. Now that he had finally escaped her. Funny word to think of when a man leaves his wife, but that was what it was and she knew it.

"Don't go, Ed," she had said so many times. "You can't get along without me. You know you can't live without me." She had believed it was true each time she said it, but what she had never known until now was that she could not get along without him. Even while she knew it wasn't Ed Farrell. It was just someone. Maybe almost anyone. Just not to be alone.

So it wasn't Ed who had been cowardly. She had married him for his peace and confidence, thinking she could somehow acquire it herself by living with it, possessing it and being possessed by it. And if it was any cowardice of his that had kept him from leaving her much sooner, that no longer mattered.

It's me, Shireen Delaney, the person I've got to live with, the one person on earth I can never get away from, the only one I can never leave or somehow get outside of and forget about. The only one I can never drive away from me.

Oh, God, she thought wearily. It's so late. I'm so tired. If I could only sleep. Sleep—that was the thing she had counted on all her life to solve every problem. "I know just what I want," she had once told her mother. "And when I've had enough sleep, I'm sure I'll get it." Sleep changes everything.

But there was one thing it couldn't change this time; she would have to wake up alone in the morning, or in the afternoon, or whenever she woke up. And that day would have the prospect of sixteen hours to go through knowing that at the end she would be alone again at night.

But I can call someone, anyone! I'll do it right now. I won't stay here alone. By tomorrow night I'll be more used to it. The first night's the hardest to spend alone.

She walked to the bedside table and as she reached down to pick up the telephone she saw the book he had been reading, lying opened at the place he had left it last night. It was a copy of *The Lost Weekend*, and she remembered what he had said to her as they turned out the lights to sleep. "This poor bastard—living in a world that doesn't exist. Well, maybe all of us do it." She slammed the book shut and threw herself on the bed, trying to cry, filled with self-pity.

7

How has this happened to me? I've tried so hard all my life!

But no matter what I do it turns out wrong. Every time. Always, always, always. Nothing ever comes out right. Nothing. The men you love. The work you do. The friends you make. It all goes wrong! But how and why? Where did it begin? What was the first mistake? How has it happened?

She sprang to her feet again, sweeping her hands up through her hair.

Where did it come from, this terrible mess a life could get into by the age of twenty-nine? And that stopped her again with a new terror. Twenty-nine. That means thirty next July—not quite one year. And thirty means old. The difference between twenty-nine and thirty seemed vast. At eighteen she had thought she never would be thirty at all, or that if she was she would be too old for anything to matter very much. And now it had almost come. And then thirty-one and thirty-two, and before she knew it she would be really old. The years went by so subtly and so slyly, taking time away from you and you didn't even know it was going. Until, in the end, you must die.

Die.

I'm so afraid!

And suddenly she realized that she had said it aloud. She stopped quickly, as if the sound of her voice were still echoing in the room. There was an unexpected sense of relief. She had heard herself say it, bring it out from inside her and put it into spoken words. I'm so afraid.

There was no beginning and no end to fear: the primitive fear of the dark and of hunger, of growing old or falling sick. Of being alone. The fear of pain. Fear of death. Fear of being laughed at. Fear of failure. Fear of doing or saying the wrong thing. Fear of embarrassment. Fear of poverty. Fear of work and of play. Fear of not knowing enough. Fear of not being beautiful, as beautiful as someone else. Fear of others, fear of yourself. Fear of being asked to do something you can't do and letting it be known you can't. Fear of the past, and fear of the future. Fear of making enemies and fear of making friends.

That's been my whole life, she told herself. I'm terrified!

And now he's gone and left me alone!

While all along it had seemed so easy, little by little forcing him to leave, stripping away his self-respect, mocking him subtly, using all the petty cruelties that must have finally made him hate her. All the great and small crimes she had committed against him, for which she hated herself, which she had promised herself and him over and over she would never repeat. He would have stayed with her, if she had not made it impossible, until the end of her life or his—barring her way to some obscure freedom toward which she strove. She *had* to be free of him. But her fear of this freedom was as great as her desire for it;

8

she had even asked him once more, this time, to wait at least until morning.

"But Ed, honestly, I don't think this is sensible," she had said. "You know how hard it is to find a hotel room in New York now. And certainly you won't get a train or plane tonight. Why don't you just wait until morning?"

He had looked at her and smiled. "What's the matter? The bogey-men crawling out of the wall already?"

All at once she hated him with an intensity she had never felt for anyone. She rushed across the room to grab his photograph, hurling it against the wall and rejoicing at the crash it made and the sound of breaking glass. As it struck the wall the thought went through her mind: Someone else will have to clean that up, not me. Thank God.

She turned around again, ashamed of the mess she had made. What would the servants think? Oh, the hell with them! I'm always worrying about what someone's going to think! What *difference* does it make?

But what will I do now?

I'll go out, she thought, and take a walk. It's two o'clock. I can go to Georgia's. No, I can't. Jim might be there. I can call her first. No, it's too late. You can't disturb people at this hour—even good friends like Georgia. They might not like it. They might get mad.

No—

She was immobilized, unable to make a decision. She couldn't go to bed, because she couldn't sleep. She couldn't go to see anyone, because it was too late. She couldn't call anyone, because they might not want to be disturbed. Her fear turned back into hatred of Ed. God damn him, why didn't he leave during the day? He *knows* I'm afraid to be alone at night! I'll never forgive him for doing this to me! Never never never. No matter how he crawls and begs. But that was false solace too. Because he never would. He had really meant it when he left.

"I can't keep it up any longer, Shireen. I've lost all the respect I ever had for myself—and now I'm losing respect for you, too. We're no good for each other any more. We've gone on already long beyond the time we should have stopped."

"Are *you* going to divorce *me?*" she had asked him furiously.

"I don't know what difference that makes." He had smiled. "You get the divorce if you want to."

"How can I?" she had demanded, building in her mind a structure of difficulties that made this move impossible, aware of how she would feel once he had actually gone out the door and she had to close it and turn and be alone with herself. "I can't leave New York, you know that!"

"Get it in New York then. They have divorce courts here."

9

"I will not! I'll go to Reno! I'll be damned if I'll get it on grounds of adultery!"

He had smiled again, but only for a moment and she could have no idea what he was thinking. That her pride was too tender? Or that it was funny for her to be concerned about adultery when it was she who had committed it, not he? But he couldn't know that. How could he?

Now she wished that he did. She wished she had told him. That was the one way left she could still hurt him, make him pay a little more for having left her alone and terrified.

If I had only known it would be as bad as this, I'd never have let him go.

But *he* knew, damn him! He knew better than I did and he still went and left me to face it by myself. His protection was gone, the one thing he had had left to give her he had taken; all she could do now was hate him.

But she found that the hate came back to where it had begun. Though it wound through her mind it always returned to what she had been trying to escape—a fear infinitely greater than any she could have believed she had. She had run from it, so hard and so fast and had almost thought she had left it behind, way back somewhere in her childhood or girlhood, lost it in success and money and a swarm of possessions and a groping driving ambition for the future. . . .

But she had not lost it at all. She had only buried it and hoped she would be able to forget where, and now it had sprung out of hiding and stood face to face with her and she saw that during all the years she had kept it hidden it had grown to monstrous size and a horrible ugliness. As if a freak child had been born and locked away in some distant room of the house, and fed and nourished but never seen until many years had gone by.

Suddenly she burst into sobs and covered her face with her hands. Go away! she wailed. Oh, please go away and leave me alone!

Chapter 2

Shireen and Ed stood in the doorway of the bar at the Officers' Club, searching among the confused pack of Navy uniforms and colored dresses for the people they had come to meet. The room, jammed with men and girls, was boisterously noisy and seemed overcharged with frantic bursting vitality. Something about it frightened her. She hadn't wanted to come in the first place.

"It'll probably be boring," she had told Ed. "You know how George is."

But it wasn't George she was afraid would be boring. It was herself. A "party." That meant a lot of people, new people, and she was afraid to meet them. She might not measure up to their expectations of her, whatever they could be.

Ed had pleaded with her. "Please come, Shireen. Even if you don't like George, there'll be other people there. Some of them are bound to be nice. And I'd like to do something different for a change—I don't get in very often. Can't you do this for me this once? I promise you we won't have to stay late."

So here they were.

After all, wasn't that what she was in Miami for?

Over the talk and laughter a juke box played loudly and a man's voice sang, with a heavy thrump of basses behind him:

> "There'll be no more promotions
> This side of the ocean
> So cheer up, my lads
> Bless 'em all!"

Across the room someone got up from a table and waved, beckoning to them. "There he is," said Ed. His hand closed reassuringly on her arm. "You look beautiful, darling. I'm so proud of you."

They made their way among the tables over toward where George and his party were sitting, and the men stood up when they got there. George shook Ed's hand and greeted Shireen and began making introductions. Shireen stood with her white-gloved hands folded before her and smiled and said how-do-you-do, nodding her head politely to each in turn. Chairs were shifted around and Shireen and Ed sat down, side by side.

"What'll you drink?"

"Bourbon and water. Shireen will have a coke."

11

And the talk began again, apparently where it had stopped when Shireen and Ed arrived. They had learned, just before leaving the ship this afternoon, that they were to be sent out to the Pacific—probably within a couple of weeks, or three at the most. Whatever connection had been left with their peacetime civilian lives was ended.

The Caribbean assignment had been too good to be true for long, they all agreed on that. It had been almost like going back to college. And, just as in college no one had really believed that life would catch up with them until the day of graduation, they had not quite believed the war would ever catch them either. Even while they had talked about not wanting to be stuck in some godforsaken spot like the Caribbean and never see action at all.

Now here it was. And it seemed to have come very suddenly, catching them off guard. The women, too.

"What happened to Denison?" someone wanted to know. "Wasn't he supposed to be here tonight?"

"Denison's in the hospital again."

The men looked at each other, smiling. "That guy will be in the hospital the day we ship out."

"Maybe that's where we'd all be if we had good sense."

"What in the hell are you talking about? You couldn't do that and you know it!"

"Maybe I couldn't. But maybe it takes more guts than going out and getting yourself killed, too."

"Who's going to get killed?" They all laughed.

"You couldn't pay me to miss it. It's the biggest thing that's ever happened—"

"That's about like saying you wouldn't miss a nice juicy train wreck—"

The men went on talking about war and about going overseas, about something which left women out of their lives completely. And it gave them some strange alien meaning. Death would be their preoccupation now and it was hard to think of them any longer as fractious little boys—they had put themselves beyond the reach and control of women.

Shireen sat quietly, listening to them. She still felt stunned, for she had never been able to believe, even after Ed left for training, that the time would come when she would actually lose him. And part of her held it against him even now. She believed he could have stayed home if he had wanted to; she felt he had no right to let himself be taken from her when she needed him so much. For she was sure that this was the end of her life and there could never be another beginning. The shock had been almost stupefying.

She looked around the table at the ten or twelve other people. There was one very pretty girl—maybe prettier than she was. The

12

rest of the women did not count, since even she could recognize that she was better looking than any of them—and their faces became blanks to her. But she looked at the men as separate individuals, summing each one up, automatically, without being aware she was doing it. She saw that none of them had anything to do with her, and that there was nothing more to think about as far as they were concerned.

The pretty girl, who sat across from Shireen, leaned forward now and smiled. They had been elaborately polite to each other—exchanging smiles whenever someone made a joke—to convince each other there was no enmity and no jealousy. She was George's wife, Shireen had noticed, and her name was Barbara.

"Have you been here long?" Barbara asked her.

"Almost four months."

Barbara looked sympathetic. She pursed her lips and frowned. "You must have had a terrible time finding a place to live. George told me it was simply impossible."

"Well, it practically is. But another girl and I finally found a little house and we rent it together. But the first couple of months we were in boardinghouses and auto courts."

Barbara shook her head. "I don't see how you stand it. What do you find to *do* with yourself?"

There was something about Barbara which roused a strong and rebellious sense of inferiority in Shireen—a quality of sureness and confidence which came out of her and fed itself from its own spring. She must have proved herself conclusively sometime and knew she could do it again.

Shireen glanced uneasily away. "We really just wait, I guess. For the men to come home."

Barbara gave a little shudder. "I couldn't do it. I simply couldn't do it—as much as I love George."

George, who had apparently been listening to his wife while he carried on his own conversation, glanced at her now with a look of quick cynicism. Shireen noticed it but Barbara did not.

So that's what *their* marriage is, she thought. He's going to war and knows she doesn't love him. It made her feel virtuous by comparison, for she had insisted on being where she could see Ed, even if he only got in once a month. But the envy was still there for she saw that Barbara did not really need George and would be just the same with him gone. Whereas everything seemed to be over for her.

The two girls talked a little more, about Barbara's job as secretary for some big advertising man, and Shireen listened wistfully. She said that she had wanted all her life to live in New York and asked her what it was like.

"The war has ruined it. It'll never be the same again." And then

13

she apparently realized they had been talking only about her. "Where do you live?"

"Los Angeles."

"Oh, how wonderful! That's where I've always wanted to go! Don't you love it?"

"No," said Shireen. "I don't. I've lived there all my life—or in Southern California, anyway."

"Oh, well, of course," agreed Barbara sympathetically. "That spoils anything. That's the trouble with me and New York. Other people—" She stopped and glanced at her husband as he made a sudden interruption.

"Well—Keegan finally got here." He looked around the table, nodding significantly. "Wait'll you meet this guy. He's a fabulous character." He stood up now and signaled across the room and they all looked curiously in the same direction.

Shireen turned to Ed. She reached out to touch him and he responded swiftly, grasping her hand and pressing it. Her face was wistful and pleading and sad, and her eyes had filled with tears. "Oh, Ed—" she whispered.

"Darling, don't look like that. You're killing me." He kissed her cheek and took her hand beneath the table, to hold it.

"I just can't believe it, Ed. I can't make myself believe it will really happen—"

"Johnny Keegan," she heard George say then, with a kind of pride in his voice, as if he had produced something unusual for his party. She looked up to see who this "fabulous character" was, thinking he wouldn't be much. No one else was supposed to be fabulous at all when Ed was around.

He had on the uniform of the AAF and Shireen noticed instantly—since that was the way you judged a man nowadays—that there were captain's bars on his shoulders and a double row of overseas ribbons on his chest. It was too early in the war to have seen many men who had come back, and there was something almost awesome about a man who had been where war was, knew in himself whatever it meant, and was back here again with that knowledge as part of him.

He stood easily and smiled at them, one after the other, as the introductions proceeded round the table. When they came to Shireen she looked at him and smiled back, inclining her head a little, and saw his eyes change.

He thinks I'm pretty, she thought, surprised.

She looked at him a little longer, curiously, and with a sense almost of discovery. She knew she had never seen anyone who looked like him before, and yet it somehow seemed that she had. Or was it only that he was what so many American girls were looking for? He was tall and rather slender, dark-haired and brown-skinned, and he had a

14

spectacular picaresque good looks. There was some rushing vitality in him that created an instant excitement, but also a great pervasive tenderness that seemed to reach toward her and every one of them. It was almost as if he had been tailor-made to specification, like his uniform.

She found herself thinking: Are there really men like this in the world?

And then was ashamed of the thought, and the sense of wonder behind it. Anyway, she had always been scornful of those girls who had an "ideal" and who kept looking or waiting for him to show up. She knew better than that. You take what's around, whether it suits you exactly or not. Life, she thought, was like a game of musical chairs and if you weren't quick enough you might find yourself with no place to sit.

For a moment everyone was quiet. George asked him what he would drink. The others sat as if waiting for something more to happen or to be said, and apparently it was expected to come from Johnny. He had somehow thrown the group out of balance. They began self-consciously lighting cigarettes.

"Johnny was in the Philippines when the Japs hit Pearl," George announced, and looked around triumphantly at all the embarrassed faces.

There was another moment of silence. Some of them took swallows from their drinks. Two or three cleared their throats. Shireen's glance flashed by Barbara and saw her watching Johnny, her face open and gleaming; she wished she could snap her fingers and make Barbara disappear from the earth. Johnny seemed perfectly at ease with all this nervous attention and nothing in his manner indicated he was aware of having disturbed them. He leaned back comfortably in his chair, one hand in his pocket, and went on smiling.

Barbara broke the silence first. She bent forward, her hands balanced lightly on the table top, and looked at him. "George says you flew the first bombing mission of the war, or something, isn't that right?"

Johnny gave a slight nod. "That's right," he said, as if admitting to nothing more interesting than that he had been for a swim during the afternoon.

"Well, don't be so modest about it!" she cried. "Tell us what it was like—what happened, and how you felt about it!"

"Barbara, for God's sake," protested George. "Leave the guy alone. Maybe he doesn't want to talk about it."

"There's nothing to talk about," said Johnny. The sound of his voice was soft and a little husky, and laughter ran beneath it.

"Then tell us what you got all those medals for," Barbara insisted. George scowled but picked up his drink and took a big swallow.

15

Shireen glanced around the table at the other women and saw their faces, meek and slightly ashamed about something, watching him. He was the only man there who was not with a girl, but he had somehow made every woman in the group belong to him. It was easy enough to see what would happen if one of them should strike his fancy.

Now he shrugged and smiled again. "There wasn't much to it," he said. "Every time we got back from a mission the colonel would tell us to muster for air medals." They all laughed, relieved by his modesty, and the tension was broken.

"How much longer do you think it will last?" someone asked.

He shook his head. "A long time, I'm afraid."

"Oh, don't say that!" cried one of the girls, and caught hold of her husband's hand. "It can't!"

Johnny made a spreading gesture. "I'm sorry," he said. "You asked me."

"How *much* longer, Johnny?" That was Barbara again.

"My guess is four or five years. Maybe longer."

"In four or five years we'll be old," moaned one of the girls; and all at once everyone was talking again, back and forth across the table. Shireen stole an uneasy glance at Barbara and saw her looking at Johnny and laughing about something, giving a toss to her side-slung blonde shoulder bob and then shaking her wrist with a quick nervous gesture to free the two gold chains that had tangled.

She *is* prettier than I am, thought Shireen.

Or, if she isn't, she's more interesting. She knows what she is. And I don't. I never have. I've been looking for myself all my life and I've never found me. I'm lost somewhere. But where can it be?

And then the juke box began again the song that had been playing when they first came in.

> "There'll be no more promotions
> This side of the ocean
> So cheer up, my lads
> Bless 'em all!"

It was loud and brash and almost defiant, but to Shireen it had a sad and lonely sound. It meant, and she knew it always would mean, the end of her life with Ed Farrell—the first night she had let herself realize that she could lose him. She felt as if she had been standing on a floor she thought was solid and it had suddenly collapsed beneath her feet.

Unexpectedly she glanced at Johnny again and found him watching her, smiling faintly, with some look of intimate appraisal. She wondered guiltily what expression there had been on her face to make him speculate about her, and then she turned quickly to Ed, linking her arm through his.

16

Chapter 3

After an hour or so they went to have dinner, and now Shireen found herself with Ed at her left and Johnny next to him, at the head of the table where it was difficult to keep from looking at him. She began a conscientious study of the menu, found she was reading it over and over, and glanced at Ed in surprise when he asked if she had made up her mind.

But she smiled and leaned a little toward him, tipping her head back slightly, then put one elbow on the table and ran her fingers into the ends of her hair. She told him what she would have to eat, speaking softly and confidentially and never quite closing her lips, as if she were telling him that she loved him. She wondered if Johnny was watching her, but did not look at him to find out. Ed whispered: "You're beautiful," and she laughed, as if they had some wonderful secret between them.

Johnny and Ed began to talk and now Shireen pretended to be interested in the man who sat on her other side. But when the soup came, she found an excuse to turn and listen to them.

Johnny smiled at her, and passed a dish full of celery and olives. She took a celery stalk thoughtfully and thanked him. And she sat a moment, wondering what it could be, that light poignant quality he had kindled somewhere inside him. But she could not tell. There was some mystery to it, or magic.

He's very interesting, she decided. And wanted to know everything she could about him. How, exactly, did a man get to be like Johnny Keegan?

"What did you do in real life, Johnny?" she asked him suddenly. And both he and Ed laughed at the way she had put it.

"A little of everything. Worked my way around the world one year on a steamer. Flew for Pan Am in South America for awhile after college. Went to East Africa on a natural history expedition, and then off on a wild-goose chase for a buried city in Yucatan. When it looked as though war was really coming, I joined the AAF. Guess I'm kind of a jack-of-all-trades—with the usual penalty."

Shireen listened with awe and wonder, seeing in his smile and the sounds of his voice, the way he moved and the gestures he made, some final essence of his life. "Oh," she said wistfully, "it sounds fascinating. It's amazing you've had time to do so much." He looked about her age—twenty-six—or possibly a year or two older.

17

"There's always time enough for anything you really want to do, isn't there?"

"It's never seemed that way to me," said Shireen doubtfully. "I never seem to have enough time."

"Maybe you just don't know what it is you want yet." He said it very gently, kindly, almost carefully, as if to be sure not to hurt her.

"No," she said, and looked down at her plate. "Maybe I don't."

But she had always thought she did. She wanted exactly what everyone else wanted: money and success and fame. And how could she think farther until she had that much?

"Where do you come from—I mean, before you went away?" she asked him.

"Roanoke, Virginia."

"But you haven't any Southern accent."

He smiled again. In fact, he never really stopped smiling, and there was something caressive in his expression, giving her encouragement. "No," he said. "My mother came from Connecticut and she didn't believe in Southern accents. So she sent my sister and me away to school, and we spent our summers in Litchfield."

"What do you want to do after the war?"

He laughed softly. He seemed to have some secret inside himself at which he was perpetually amused and she wished she could learn what it was. How he could be so happy all the time. What it was he found in life to be so goddamned happy *about*.

"I haven't really thought much about it. When the war ends, if it ends, I'll see how I feel then. And what kind of shape I'm in. If I'm still in one piece, it'll be one thing—and if I lose a leg or an arm, then it'll have to be something else. And of course I may not come back at all."

"Oh!" cried Shireen. "Don't say that!"

"Why not? It's true, isn't it?"

"But you shouldn't *say* it!"

He looked at her for a moment and his eyes narrowed slightly; there was the same look of speculation in them she had noticed earlier. Then, all at once, he turned to Ed.

"What do you do, Ed?"

"I'm in my father's business. Selling insurance." He looked a little ashamed.

Well, thought Shireen, and suddenly she was almost angry with him. He should be ashamed. She had tried to make him see that he should not go into business with his father just because his father wanted him to, but should decide for himself what he wanted his life to be.

"Good," said Johnny, and he made it seem as if Ed had made a wise and interesting choice. "My father's a lawyer. He was in the

18

House of Representatives for a couple of years once, when I was a kid. I guess he thought maybe I'd grow up to be a politician. But I could never go along with it. A lawyer deals in other people's grief and a politician does the dirty work for business." He shook his head. "Life's too short."

"Johnny!" That was Barbara again, and he turned to her. "Tell me something. I've always wanted to learn to fly, but I've never been able to figure out how you make a landing without going straight into the ground. Is it hard?"

There, thought Shireen. That's the way I should be. How does she do it? It sounds so simple. And it looks so easy. And everyone knows but me.

There was a lull while Johnny explained, with gestures and that same smile, how you brought a plane down, and when he had finished Barbara clapped her hands together. "Wonderful! But I'm sure it's not nearly so easy as you make it sound. You're much too modest, Johnny. But it's marvelous—I hope you never let yourself be spoiled."

"He won't. Don't worry about it," said George, and seemed rather peevish. "Will you excuse us, please? I have this dance with my wife." The orchestra had begun to play and other couples were getting up. Ed turned to Shireen.

"Would you like to dance, honey?"

She smiled and nodded. If she danced with him now, then later Johnny might ask her. The floor was filling and they moved out among the dancers. But as soon as Ed's arms were around her, she forgot Johnny Keegan completely. All her fear of loneliness and of losing him had come back in a rush. Her eyes closed and she let her head fall against his shoulder.

"What's the matter, darling?" he asked her tenderly.

"Oh, Ed—I can't stand it! I can't let you go! The war may go on for years—we'll be old, we'll have lost everything!"

"We've already had seven years together."

"I don't care about the past! That's over and it doesn't count any more. Ed, there must be something you can do, someone you can talk to, *someway* you can get out of it—"

He shook his head. "No Shireen, there isn't. You know I couldn't do anything like that. And you'd have no use for me if I did." Shireen looked away, ashamed of herself, and hating to be reminded that she had no patriotism. "I don't want to leave you, but I couldn't stay here. You must have seen how the guys felt when Keegan showed up—what do you think it would be like if I never went at all?"

She sighed. "I know. I'm sorry. But I don't know how I can ever get along without you."

Then, after a few moments, she said: "Ed, will you tell me something honestly?"

19

"Of course."

"Is Barbara prettier than I am?"

He showed a moment's surprise and then laughed. "Whatever made you think of that? She's only a pretty girl. You're beautiful. Don't you know that by now?"

"No. I don't."

"Well, my God—you are."

"Really?"

But she looked at him skeptically. Ed didn't know. How could he? After all, he had never really known any other woman but her. She wondered what someone like Johnny would think. He'd been all over the world and met women everywhere and they must all have fallen in love with him.

"Really," repeated Ed, gently mocking. "The trouble with you, Shireen, is that you've never been able to see yourself the way other people do. It's hard to believe, but I guess you honestly don't know what you're like. You could have anyone or anything that you wanted."

"You just say that because you want to believe it."

"I certainly do not. Don't you think I know I've got a damned good chance of losing you one of these days?"

"Oh, no, Ed! You mustn't say that! You know I've never loved anyone but you, and I never will."

"I hope not, darling—because you're my whole life."

"I know," she said, and looked away.

When the music ended they went back to the table and sat down. Johnny and Ed got into a conversation about East Africa, and Shireen listened while they talked eagerly together, paying no attention at all to her. Johnny told him how the country looked, the wild animals that were there, the kinds of guns you used, the plantations in Kenya and Tanganyika and the people who lived on them. Shireen listened jealously. It seemed that Ed was always charming someone away from her, making them think that he was nicer and kinder and better than she.

"It's a hell of a wonderful country," Johnny said.

"It sure sounds like it," said Ed wistfully. "I wish I could see it sometime."

"Why not? I've always wanted to go back. Let's go—after the war."

"And what about me?" demanded Shireen.

"We haven't gone yet," said Johnny, smiling. And she felt a little ashamed for having let him see the jealous selfish part of her.

The music began again and Ed and Johnny went on talking awhile longer. But finally Johnny turned to her. "Would you dance with me, Shireen? Do you mind, Ed?" He looked completely guileless, almost like a boy for the moment. He had the quality anyway of so many

20

American men who continue to look young and eager and unspoiled—sometimes until they are middle-aged.

Ed said that of course he did not mind and she got up and walked ahead of Johnny. But she was suddenly nervous and felt herself trembling inside, hesitant and unhappy. She stood before him a moment, laid her left hand lightly on his shoulder, then took a backward gliding step away from him. But she could not look at him. Somehow he seemed much closer than she had expected and she felt unexplainably frightened.

"You're a very good dancer," he said after awhile, and then all at once she flung back her hair and looked up at him with an eager smile.

"Ed and I don't dance very often—but it's nice of you to say so anyway."

"But I mean it."

"You do?"

She looked at his mouth and the shape of his teeth and then, as if she had been caught at something forbidden, lowered her eyes quickly and glanced away.

A couple of minutes went by and then he asked her: "What do you do with your life? Do you work, are you a housewife—or what?"

"Well, I guess I'm a housewife. But I work, too. That is, I write. I'm trying to write a book."

She felt embarrassed to make this confession but made it anyway because she did not want him to think she was a parasite, living on Ed. She had so much contempt for women who were only wives that she was sure everyone else felt exactly the same way.

"No kidding?" He looked genuinely surprised, as if he had made a discovery. "What kind of book is it?"

Shireen hesitated a moment before answering. She didn't know how much she should tell him—or how much she could tell him, before he would get bored.

"Well, it's a historical novel, about Jamaica around 1700. The central character's a woman who goes there because she committed a crime in England. And she meets a man—of course."

"Sounds very interesting," said Johnny politely.

But she knew it could not possibly have sounded interesting, told like that. And maybe it wasn't anyway. She couldn't tell. She had worked on it for so long and no one but Ed had read it and now she had no idea what it was like.

"You must've had to do a lot of research," he said.

"Quite a bit. I read four hundred books—or not really four hundred. Three hundred and ninety-two, actually."

Johnny laughed. "You're very accurate. I don't think I'd have known the difference. When are you going to finish it? Will you send me a copy—when it's published?"

"Oh, I haven't the slightest idea if anyone will ever *publish* it!"

"You mean to say you've done all that work and haven't lined up a publisher yet?"

"I don't know any," said Shireen.

"But my God, you could have written some of them and probably gotten a contract and an advance. They do that all the time."

"They do?" How was it everyone knew all these things and she never even heard about them? "Well, anyway, I don't think it would be a good idea. I'll send it to someone after it's finished."

"How long have you spent writing it?"

"Four years and a couple of months." Johnny gave a soft whistle. "I'm almost through."

"Good God. I should hope so."

He held her back a little and looked at her, smiling. Then he shook his head. It was a habit he had, shaking his head every so often as if there was no way of putting into words what he felt.

"You're an amazing little chick," he said softly. "Who'd ever have thought it—to look at you?"

She smiled at him, and all at once felt warm and pleased; the fear was gone. He liked her. Maybe even admired her a little. By his surprise and approbation he had given her a sudden sense of counting for something, and she wished she could tell him how grateful she was.

Chapter 4

Shireen was in the garden behind the bungalow she and Peggy Melrose had rented. It was late afternoon and Peggy was out—doing the shopping, perhaps, since this was her week to attend to that, or rolling bandages at the Red Cross. The day was hot and windy but it was quiet where she was, stretched out in a faded green and gray striped hammock. She lay there, back in the half darkness with a book propped against her bare legs, holding her fingers spread wide while she waited for the nail polish to dry.

Ed had left early that morning and though he hoped to get in once more, no one knew how good the chances were. There was nothing to do now but wait, and perhaps say good-by one more time.

"The world's changed, Shireen," he had told her last night, when they left the party and were driving home. "And you'll have to change with it. You've got to stop counting on me."

Well . . .

In her feelings, he had gone already. Every end was also a beginning and she would find some new life for herself. She knew one thing for sure and that was that no matter what happened, she would not be like Peggy and the other women she had met in Miami, who would simply go home in hysterics when their husbands left and wait for them to come back.

For though sometimes, it was true, she felt almost envious of girls like Peggy who, since they did not expect much from life, accepted whatever they got—she was much more scornful than envious.

Because what became of people like that in the long run?

Nothing at all.

And something *would* become of her. She was sure of it. She insisted upon it. She would somehow grab hold of life and force and twist it and finally break it, stamp on the shell and crush it to pieces—and then she would see what was inside. And she would take it out, whatever it was, and have it for herself.

For as long as she could remember Shireen had had some dim belief that something extraordinary lay in store for her. But now she was getting frightened, for here she was twenty-six years old and still merely existing. Whatever this great thing was to be, it had not happened yet; so far as she knew it had not even begun to happen yet. And she wondered if she could have been wrong. Suppose it should always be like this, the days passing swiftly but bringing new ones

23

exactly like all the others? Suppose she should go on, day after day, months going by, and years, and finally die without ever having lived at all?

Oh, but that couldn't happen to *her*.

Surely sometime, not too far distant, she would really begin to live.

She might get her book published—that would give her a new life. But even the thought of finishing it scared her, for then she would find out for sure. Now she alternated between thinking she would become very rich and famous, and absolute conviction that it would never be published at all and she would be trapped where she was.

She could picture herself going to apply for a job, and a man sitting behind a desk asking her what she could do. "I can type," she was saying to him. "But what else?" "Nothing else. That's all. And I make plenty of mistakes, too—I always go back and cross them out with dollar signs."

Fine. That would get her a job, wouldn't it? But she might as well tell the truth, because he would find her out sooner or later anyway. "What's your education?" this man behind the desk was asking her now. "I went to college. I got an A.B., a B.A., whatever you call it." "In what?" "Anthropology." "We can't use you," he said then. "Sorry." And Shireen was going off, refused again.

What will I do *then*?

Well—I can't figure it all out now very well.

She got up out of the hammock and stretched. She glanced at her watch. Five o'clock. Six more hours until it was time to go to bed.

She picked up the book and bottle of nail polish and walked into the house, through the tiny kitchen and dining room and into her bedroom. Peggy would be home pretty soon and get dinner and Shireen would do the dishes. They had mapped out a careful schedule, dividing the work between them and alternating the chores from week to week. After dinner they'd sit around and talk or read or visit some other Navy wives who lived nearby or see a movie.

If this goes on much longer, she thought wearily, I'll die of boredom.

She began to move around the room, peeling down her bathing suit and slipping into a white beach robe, starting the water running in the tub, setting a pair of slippers back into the closet, and then she went to the dressing table and stood looking at a framed picture of her and Ed. It was a snapshot someone had taken just after she got to Miami and she had liked it and had it enlarged. He was in uniform and they stood side by side, Ed with one arm around her, both of them smiling off toward some distant point.

All of a sudden she wanted to cry.

She turned away, and thought of Johnny Keegan instead.

24

She could remember the way he looked, the expressions on his face, the sound of his voice and what he had said, more vividly than she could remember Ed. He had come into her mind, off and on, all during the day. Even while she had been writing. She had sensed in Johnny something she had never found in Ed, and though she had no idea what it was, he had made her suddenly curious and alert.

It occurred to her for the first time that there is a difference in the accessibility people have to each other and that one will touch parts of you another won't, or can't—Johnny had somehow made her aware of him and of facets in the whole relationship between men and women which she had never known existed before.

And this interest she had in the behavior of men and women, the motives behind it and the possible goals, was like a temple in her mind containing something secret and unknown, to which every path led ultimately, though it might wind and twist and cross innumerable other paths in getting there. But, until she had found what the temple contained—or if it was, after all, empty—her only interest was some-how to get in and see what was there. Johnny, she felt, could take her nearer, perhaps even into the temple itself.

Except, of course, that she would most likely never see him again, and anyway she had no right to such thoughts when she was married to Ed. And he was going overseas.

That's typical of me, she thought. I never have had a real sense of decency.

She smeared cream on her face and wiped off the make-up and got into the bath, playing with the suds, lifting the bubbles up in her hands and blowing them out.

After awhile she heard the front door open and then Peggy's voice. "Shireen! Are you home?"

"I'm in the bathtub!" This woman, thought Shireen. I'm going to tear her apart if I have to keep seeing her much longer.

She came in, holding a big paper bag full of groceries in each arm. Peggy seemed to Shireen a drably typical young American woman, and as such Shireen had no use for her. But Peggy didn't know that, and they seemed to be good friends; at least they had confided to each other everything that had happened in both their lives.

Shireen looked up at her from where she lay in the tub, snipping idly at the suds with her thumb and forefinger. "Hi. Have a good time?"

"Well, you know. Same thing. Those women down there. How they gabble. And gossip—all day long they gossip. Sue's got her hair done up and it doesn't look as good as when she had it down and why do you suppose she did it that way and shouldn't someone tell her? You know how it is. Maybe you're better off staying home and writing."

"No doubt about that," said Shireen.

25

"I've got to dump these things. My God, do you know how much this butter cost? Ninety-five cents! I'm afraid we're going to run over our budget this month—" Shireen could hear her talking as she went to the kitchen and she rolled her eyes and gave her head a shake. Then she began to climb out of the tub.

The phone rang.

"Oh, my God!" cried Peggy.

Every time the phone rang now both of them were sure it was either Ed or Bert calling to say good-by. Shireen, drying herself with a towel, listened carefully.

"Hello? Who? Yes, she's here. She's taking a bath—let me see if she can come to the phone—*Shireen!*"

Peggy came running in. "It's for you and it's a man—but it isn't Ed. Do you want to talk to him?"

Could it be Johnny?

"Must be one of Ed's friends," she said, pretending to be very casual. She wrapped the towel around herself and went out to the kitchen.

"Hello?"

"Shireen? This is Johnny Keegan—remember me?"

"Well," she said, "for heaven's sake," as if he were the last person in the world she expected to hear from. "How *are* you?"

They talked a little about how they were and the weather and then Johnny said: "You know, I did a damn fool thing last night. Left my trench coat in your car."

"Oh, did you? I didn't see it, but it must still be there. Can I send it to you? Or I could bring it out—"

"No, I don't want you to go to all that trouble. I thought maybe I'd stop by and pick it up and take you and Ed to dinner this evening—if you're free."

"Oh." She felt suddenly disappointed. She could have seen him again, but now Ed was gone and she couldn't. "That's very nice of you and I'd love to go and I know Ed would, too. But he had to report back this morning."

"Tough luck. I was hoping we could get together. Well—maybe some other time."

She felt as if she had been picked up and then dropped. He didn't like *her* enough to ask her anyway, without Ed. It was something that seemed to have been happening all her life; she never could just get by on her own.

"How about you?" he said then. "Could you knock off a few hours from that book you're writing? I know a good joint that still serves steaks—if that's any bribe."

"Oh, but it really isn't necessary, Johnny."

He laughed. "Of course, I know that. What time shall I pick you up?"

They arranged for him to come by at seven o'clock and as Shireen put down the phone and turned around she took care to close her face, for she was aware of Peggy still in the kitchen, putting groceries away.

"That was Johnny Keegan," she said. "He's a good friend of Ed's and he left his trench coat in the car last night and has to come to pick it up. He wanted both Ed and me to go out to dinner with him but since Ed isn't here he was nice enough to ask me anyway. Are you sure you won't mind having dinner alone, Peggy?"

"Of course not, Shireen. You go ahead."

Shireen wondered if there had been some slight suspicion on Peggy's face, but told herself she was only imagining it and anyway it was none of Peggy's business what she did. She walked back to the bedroom, wondering how she could keep Peggy from mentioning this to Ed and then realized that Ed would not object at all if she had dinner with Johnny Keegan. He trusted her completely and, after all, there had never been any reason not to. She would tell him about it herself and he'd be glad that something had happened to break the monotony for her.

She sat down to make up her face and was surprised at how happy she felt. As if her life, which had been grinding slower and slower these past seven years, had suddenly changed gears, given a hitch, and begun to move again.

By the time she was dressed it was almost seven and she tried for awhile to read. Peggy was out in the kitchen getting dinner. But she couldn't keep her mind on the book and finally tossed it aside and called to Peggy: "I'm going outside for a minute, Peggy!"

It annoyed her, these apologies and explanations she kept making to Peggy. What was she trying to hide? Nothing, obviously, so wasn't it silly?

"Okay!" Peggy called cheerfully. "I'll let you know when he gets here!"

She went back to the little garage and found his trench coat wadded in a corner on the back seat and she took it out and held it, trying to sense what he might have left of himself in this garment he had worn. Then all at once she turned guiltily and went outside again, paying careful attention now to the flowers and noticing how their colors had intensified in the early evening light.

She glanced at her watch and it was ten minutes after seven.

But it did not trouble her that he was a few minutes late. He would come—since there was no way he could guess how disappointed she would be if he did not.

She walked slowly toward the front of the house, pausing every

27

step or two to concentrate with elaborate interest on the carnations she and Peggy had planted. Yes, they certainly were growing. She was very absorbed in her inspection of the flower border when Johnny's car stopped and she heard the soft brief sound of his horn.

She turned quickly and smiled, as if she were surprised to see him there. And then suddenly she felt that he should not have found her holding his coat and began to wonder nervously what she could do with it. He grinned and waved his hand, got out of the car and they walked toward each other.

"Hello, there," he said softly and she lowered her eyes, away from him. His handshake was brief and firm, but seemed nevertheless to give her something of himself and take back something from her in return.

"Hello," she said uneasily. "I'm awfully sorry Ed couldn't be here."

"So am I." He was smiling faintly and she wondered if he had seen through her and was laughing at her. "Here—" he said, and held out a white florist's box. "Do you like these things?"

Surprised, she took it from him in exchange for his coat and pulled the ribbons apart, gently lifted off the cover and found a spray of lilies of the valley. "Oh, they're lovely—" She lifted them out of the box and held them against her lips, feeling the cool chaste moisture, taking into herself some of their fragile fragrance. Then she pinned them to the neckline of her dress, in between her breasts.

He watched her, a little anxiously, but still with that faint smile.

"You didn't need to do that." She spoke to him shyly, and was almost painfully pleased that he had brought them. They had a significance different somehow from anything Ed or anyone else had ever given her.

"They're nice on you. I figured white should go with just about anything. Well, ready to shove off?"

"Will you wait just a minute? I want to get a jacket. I'll be right out." She did not want him to go in with her and meet Peggy so she turned quickly and ran back, picked up her jacket and handbag and hurried to the door. "Good night, Peggy!" she called. "Don't get up— I'm just leaving. See you in the morning!"

"Good night, Shireen. Have a good—"

"Thanks! I will!"

She closed the door and half ran toward the car, smiling at him, and for an instant was aware of herself as she must look to him. Then they started driving and though she had worried about finding something to say, they began to talk easily and naturally.

She had not planned it, but found herself telling him about Ed— how wonderful he was and how happy they were together and how much she would miss him when he went overseas. That seemed to be something she must have understood between them immediately.

28

Johnny listened soberly, as if he was both interested and impressed, and then asked her what she would do after Ed left.

"I'll finish my book—if it isn't done before then. And then I'll get a job and take a Nurses' Aide course and just get along as well as I can until he comes home."

He shook his head. "The war's really harder on women."

She was shocked. "Oh, no, Johnny! How can you even say such a thing, after what you've been through?"

"What I've been through isn't as tough as you think. Anyway, it's always harder to wait than to do something, and it's always harder to stay behind than to go."

"I don't think so. I don't see how any man gets up the courage to go to war—there'd be no way on earth I could make myself do it. And how you could ever make yourself go back again—" He had mentioned last night that he was expecting his orders to come through any day.

He glanced at her briefly and smiled. "Where else do you go—during a war?"

"But you've taken enough chances. You might—"

"I might take one too many?" He laughed softly. "Sure. I might. But if I do, I've had what I want out of life."

Shireen was looking at his hands. They were big and square, with thick blunt fingers. She had noticed them last night and been vaguely disturbed, for they looked powerful and, she thought, a little cruel. But how could you ask a man to explain the shape of his hands, why they should be that way, and whether they were perhaps a better indication of him than his face was?

"Then you've been very lucky," she said.

"Lucky? I don't think so. Because the things I've wanted have been so simple that anyone could have had them. Except that most people are so busy knocking themselves out trying to do everything they think they should do, they never get around to what they want to do."

For a moment longer she looked at him—a curious intuitive look, as if she could find out all at once just what he was. It was true, as she had thought at first; he knew all the things she had to learn. But how had he learned—and what, exactly, was it that he knew?

She was about to ask him another question. But then he swung the car into a parking lot before a low white stucco building that had lights flaring out from every window, and brought it to a stop in line with several other cars. He turned the key and as the motor died it became suddenly very quiet. A burst of music, straining saxophones and a drum, swept across at them. The sound struck her with an almost physical pain.

Johnny sat a moment staring down at the dashboard, not moving.

29

And then he took the key out of the lock and turned to her. She was watching him with a questioning anxious look. He shook his head, smiling, and then lightly he touched one corner of her mouth.

"Come on," he said. "Turn 'em up on the edge a little."

For an instant she did not understand what he meant and then, obediently, imitated his smile. She sensed that he had felt the music, still pouring across them, loud and brilliant, in the same way she did—but was assuming responsibility to ignore it for both of them.

He got out of the car and came around to open the door for her and they walked toward the lighted building. She had a strange sense of helplessness, as if she had given up some vital part of herself and no longer exercised control even over the steps she took. They went in and she stood waiting while he checked his cap and then came back toward her, reaching up to smooth the sides of his hair with his palms. Then he was beside her again and she smiled as his hand touched her elbow lightly.

The headwaiter came up to them.

Chapter 5

"Well!" he said briskly. "If it isn't Captain Keegan! I haven't seen you in such a long time I was beginning to think maybe they'd sent you back again." He shook his head confidentially. "They've got no right to take everything out of a man, you know. War or no war."

Johnny was standing with his hands in his pockets, grinning at him. "I'm shoving off again in a few days."

"No! I can't believe it! Or did you ask for it, captain? I'll bet you did—you're a brave man—" He looked almost as if he would choke on Johnny's bravery.

Johnny laughed. "Bravery's got nothing to do with it. Just too damned many rules and regulations to this stateside duty."

Both the headwaiter and Shireen gave Johnny looks to indicate they knew how brave he was and he wasn't fooling them for a minute.

"You're much too modest, captain." He looked slyly at Shireen. "He's a pretty nice fella, this one—isn't he?"

"I think he is, too," said Shireen softly, and blushed. She felt Johnny glance at her quickly, but did not meet his eyes.

He and the headwaiter talked a little longer while Shireen listened and watched in fascinated admiration. How wonderful it must be to go through life like that, sure of yourself and unafraid of others. She could see it in every smallest thing he said or did, every time he laughed, each movement he made and every gesture. She knew there could be no hard twisted knots inside Johnny Keegan; while she was tied and gagged with a thousand complications of her own devising.

My God, but he makes Ed seem dull!

She was instantly horrified. What's the matter with me? Ed isn't dull. He's good and kind and sweet and I love him.

The headwaiter was laughing and patting Johnny affectionately on the shoulder. "I'll bet I know what you came here for, captain— that steak I promised you last time." He became confidential. "And I've got it for you, too. The nicest tenderest juiciest filet you can imagine. And one for the young lady, of course. Now, captain— where would you like to sit?"

"How about one of those corner tables? Back against the wall. We want to talk."

The man glanced knowingly at Shireen. "Of course, captain. Will you come this way, please?" He led them to a table back away from

31

the five-piece orchestra, and turned and glanced at Johnny for his approval. Johnny smiled and nodded his head.

"Fine," he said. "This is just right."

They sat down and he hovered a little longer, asking if they wanted to order drinks, telling Johnny he would see to everything himself, he would not be disappointed. "I hope you're going to enjoy it, captain."

"I know we will," Johnny assured him, not carelessly, but as if the headwaiter's concern to please had become his concern to be pleased. And then, with a little bow and smile to Shireen, he left them.

"Good Lord! I never saw such bowing and scraping in my life. Did you by any chance finance this place?"

Johnny laughed. "I've been here several times before."

"I know. But—look how well he remembered you."

"Why not?" Johnny handed her a menu and looked at his own. "Everyone's trying to sell something, and if you're a customer he pays attention to you. Even if he's got nothing to sell but himself."

"But most people never get such—"

"Most people don't know what they want, so how can they get it? Know what you want? Food—I mean," he added, with a faint smile and a quick glance at her.

Shireen immediately began to study the menu. She felt some baffling elusiveness in him, as if he were a sorcerer guarding his secret formulae. But I'll find out, she thought. It's nothing he can hide for long. Pretty soon he'll say something that he thinks doesn't mean anything at all, and then I'll know.

She told him what she wanted to eat and while he gave their order, sat looking around the room.

It was dark, lighted by small orange-shaded lamps on each table that cast up a faint glow, shadowing the faces above them. The orchestra was playing a rumba and couples stood packed together on the floor, moving their hips, holding each other close. Most of the men were in uniform and they looked young and cocky, sure of tonight at least. The girls wore pretty, short-skirted dresses, their legs were bare and their faces tanned and they had clean wavy hair cut in long bobs and caught back with pink hibiscus blossoms or gardenias. They were proud, pliant, eager, frightened. And they filled her with pity and nostalgia. She could see herself and Ed in them—if this had happened four or five or six years earlier. And she felt a little lonely, watching them, as if she had been left out of some cosmic scheme.

But I mustn't think such things, she told herself. I love him just as much as I ever did. The war had made it almost immoral for a man and his wife not to be in love. It was part of your patriotic duty, like buying bonds and donating blood.

So she began to think, instead, of how the men had two separate wars: The one here at home, heavy with all the lush and subtle emotions, now become urgent and highly charged. And the one overseas

32

which must forever—in spite of books, newsreels, articles, communiqués—remain as mysterious to the women they left as death is to the living.

Johnny finished giving the order and the waiter left. "What's the matter?" he asked her. "Something's troubling you."

She shook her head. "I'd hate to be as young as they are."

"Why?"

"I guess because everything that's happening to them is so big—and so much more than they're ready for. And nothing can give them more time. A lot of them won't ever have any more time."

Johnny was leaning back, one hand in his pocket, easy and relaxed. "Most of them wouldn't anyway. If they live fifty years longer they'll never be any more alive than they are right now. How many people do you think ever live more than a few days out of their lives?"

"Not many, I suppose."

"Then why feel sorry for them? That's one thing a war does—it hurries you up. Whether you like it or not you've finally got to stop standing around on one foot and then the other, trying to make up your mind. Look at you. The war's done something for you already."

"I can't imagine what." She felt a little offended. When her whole life had been ruined he was telling her it had done her some good.

"Didn't you say the other night it was the first time you'd ever been away from home? Well, you've seen a little more of the world now and you've met some people you wouldn't have met otherwise."

"But I never intended it to happen this way!"

Then she was suddenly embarrassed. For how was it that she pictured herself in some dim recess of her mind as a kind of fairy princess, destined to wear mink and satin and sleep on a feather bed through which she would never feel the hard kernel of life?

Johnny laughed. "So a war came along and fouled up your plans."

"I didn't exactly mean that the way it sounded."

"Of course you did. You're a spoiled little girl. But why apologize for it?"

The waiter set down plates of soup, hot and oily with rings of onion floating in it, and they began to eat.

"I'm not concerned for myself," she insisted. "It's only because of Ed."

"Sure, I know. But war is part of the life of practically every man who's ever lived. This isn't the first one—and you aren't the first woman to send a man away to fight."

"I didn't think I was," she said primly.

"Every woman thinks she is. Or feels she is, anyway. We're all sure that we're absolutely unique and the last thing in the world we'll ever admit to ourselves or anyone else is that we're not."

"I'm not unique," said Shireen proudly. *"I'm* the completely typical American."

33

"What?" He gave a burst of laughter.

"But it's true. I really am, only I just began to realize it lately, coming across the country on a train, I guess." As she talked to him now her eyes lightened and her face seemed to shimmer. "I mean that seriously, Johnny. Name any typical American trait you like—I've got it. Or throw them all together, every one you can think of, and that's me. There's only one thing about me that's unique at all—and that's that I'm so goddamned typical."

She made a face and a quick gesture with her hands, and they both began to laugh. All of a sudden she was feeling much better. He had been in control before, giving her his ideas, and now she had asserted herself, let him know that someone existed back there behind the pretty, distracting face.

The waiter took their soup plates and served the steak while they both watched admiringly. It was thick and crusty on the outside, burnt a little round the edges and a melting square of butter stood in the center of each. He worked busily, dishing out French fried potatoes, green peas, setting down the romaine salad that gave off a faint garlic smell. While Johnny shook his head, nonplussed, until even Shireen could almost believe this was the first decent meal he had had in many years.

"Will you tell the captain I'm beginning to regret that overseas assignment?" he asked the waiter.

Shireen hoped that what he meant was that he was beginning to regret it because he had discovered her. But how could a man like Johnny, who was some embodiment of all the men ever loved by women, find in her his own requirements? The wish was absurd.

She asked him about the war and he answered her quickly and willingly but did not talk about his own combat experiences. He told her instead about the people of the countries he had been in and, though she listened carefully, he somehow conveyed the impression there had not been any interesting or beautiful women among them. She felt relieved and refused to let herself realize that this was only one more evidence of his deliberate conscious gallantry: there were no women in the world but the one he was with.

And she noticed something else. He had strained out, even in talking about war, all the ugliness and sordidness. What he left were elements of beauty: courage, tenderness, selflessness. Apparently he had some ability to see only that which he felt worthy to be seen. And Shireen was sure this was some superiority he had over her. For ugliness always cut through to her, and invariably made her feel abashed and guilty.

"Can you speak French?" she asked, when he made a reference to the summer he had spent in France.

"Sure."

34

"Speak it for me, please. Say something—just anything. I want to hear you." She wanted him to display his accomplishment, so that she could admire him for it.

He looked at her, smiling, and then spoke several rapid sentences, watching her as he said them:

> "—Ta main se glisse en vain sur mon sein qui se pâme;
> Ce qu'elle cherche, amie, est un lieu saccagé
> Par la griffe et la dent feroce de la femme.
> Ne cherchez plus mon coeur; les bêtes l'ont mangé."

Shireen listened intently, convinced he was talking to and about her, wanting so much to know what he was saying that it seemed incredible she should not be able to understand it. But she could catch only a word here and there. She felt as if he had spoken to her, not in a language known to millions, but in some private magic tongue.

She clasped her hands delightedly. "It sounds beautiful. Tell me what it means."

"Nope." He shook his head. "Anyway, it was just a few lines of poetry."

"You won't tell me?"

"Not now."

"But why?"

He looked at her with an expression that was part amusement, part tenderness. "Eat your dinner. Like a good little girl." Shireen hesitated a moment, then did as he had told her.

"I took French for a couple of years," she said. "But I don't remember it. I always hated languages—I guess because I never had any immediate use for them."

"You mean to say there's got to be a use for everything?" His voice was gently mocking, but Shireen answered him seriously.

"Of course. One way or another."

"Of course, she says. There are some pretty goddamn wonderful things, you know, that are no use at all."

"Oh—those. It's all useful, to anyone who wants to write."

They both laughed.

"Is that what made you become a writer? Because you could find a use for everything?"

"Maybe it sounds funny, but it's true just the same. Nothing's lost that way. You never waste any time. If you're bored out of your wits, someday it will be handy to know what boredom means. And if you're miserable, you're not just miserable. You're learning something useful." She nodded her head wisely. "Life is really very interesting. It's such good material for writing." And suddenly she threw back her head and laughed, pleased with herself as it seemed she had never

35

been before. She felt this was the first time she had been completely alive, as if she had been becoming herself in preparation for this moment when Johnny Keegan sat watching her with wonder and amusement.

"Anyway," she said, "I never decided to become a writer; I just started writing. I haven't the vaguest idea why, but I've done it all my life, since I was about eight years old. But I'm not a writer yet, you know. No one's a writer until they've had something published, and I never have."

"You will. I'm sure of that."

"If I don't—I'd as soon be dead."

"What!"

They looked at each other suddenly and Shireen realized with dismay that she had made a blunder. She began, in confusion and alarm, to try to take it back. "Of course I didn't really mean that. I only meant that it's a lot of years to gamble with and I'd hate to think of it being wasted—that much of my life—"

"How could it have been wasted? You're happy with Ed, aren't you?" He was watching her closely now.

"I'm very happily married," she said, talking quickly to cover her panic. "So's Ed." What did I say that for? So's Ed. Why shouldn't he be? "We think a great deal of each other. I mean—we're very much in love." But now her face was hot and she could not look at him.

He was shaking his head again, as if she had surprised him. "He seemed like one hell of a fine guy to me. I've met a lot of people, knocking around the world, but very few I've had any real respect for—and he's one of 'em. I'd say you're a pretty lucky girl."

"Oh, I know I am! No one could have a better husband than Ed. It's just that—well, after all, if I made some money it would be nice for both of us, don't you think?" She felt a little sick at her stomach.

For now he knew too much about her, and he wouldn't like her any more. He knew that she was different from the way women were supposed to be and that it wasn't enough for her to be happily married. And since that threatened his own position as a man, as well as Ed's, he'd defend Ed in order to defend himself. She felt wretchedly nervous and disgusted with herself. She must try to patch it up someway, weave quickly over the tear she had made in the fabric and persuade him it had not been torn at all.

"There's never been a finer man than Ed," she said. "I wouldn't trade the years I've spent with him for anything in the world."

But was there never a time and never a person ready to accept you as you were? Did you always have to hide and pretend and only be liked or loved for qualities that were not so much your own as those someone else wanted you to have?

Chapter 6

The waiter came and set the dessert before them: sweet crisp meringues with ice cream in the center and a spiral mound of thick whipped cream on top, streaked with strawberry sauce. Shireen began asking questions again; it seemed better to talk about him, since that way she could not inadvertently let him find out something she should conceal.

"What do you think of women in other countries, Johnny? As compared to American women, I mean. A lot of men say they like European women better, because they're more pliable. Brought up to please men."

"Like them better? No, I don't think so. After all, the typical American chick is pretty hard to beat anywhere, isn't she?"

She smiled at him, assuring herself that by indirection he meant her. "You're not married, are you?"

"No. How could you tell? Does it show much?"

"All over you. Why is it you never got married, Johnny?"

"What would I do with a wife? I'm a guy who's got sand in his shoes—I have to keep moving."

She felt a little disappointed. Probably she had been expecting him to say he had never married because he had never met anyone like her. But that was pretty silly of her, wasn't it? Since this was only the first day of their lives that they had shared—the first day they had existed for each other.

"Well," she said, "I guess you're wise. Marriage is an institution for women. I never have been able to see what men get out of it."

Again he gave her that look of faint surprise and shook his head. "You see what Ed's gotten out of it, I hope."

"Nothing much, when you come right down to it. Of course, I'm a good cook. Otherwise, he just supports me while I write a book. Though certainly if I make any money, I'll pay him back."

"Pay him back? What for, for God's sake?"

"For all the years he's worked and taken care of me. I figure that roughly I've cost him a couple of thousand a year—for seven years."

"You can't be serious."

"Oh, but I am. I really am."

"You're amazing."

"Me?"

"Yes, you."

Then he looked out on the floor, where the dancing had begun again, and neither of them spoke for several moments. She was not sure that he had liked what she had said then, either. But why couldn't anyone see that she had a sensible attitude toward this business of marriage, while almost everyone else took things as they were without ever thinking about them?

Then she heard him laugh a little beneath his breath.

"What?" she asked him.

"Those guys out there. Every one of 'em wants to turn around and take a good look as he goes by—then they see me watching 'em and don't dare."

She felt a quick keen sense of primitive pleasure at what he had said, letting her know that she was desirable to him and to other men, too, but that he would tolerate no sharing. It was as if he had touched her, with one light stroke made her receptive to him. She had a sense of helpless drifting carrying her closer and closer to him, but warned herself that this was dangerous, and wrong.

She had only one responsibility in life now and that was to Ed Farrell.

"Was North Africa very fascinating?" she asked him anxiously, determined to get them back on an impersonal basis.

"Not very. Why?"

"Well, I don't know. I thought maybe I'd like to go there sometime. But you don't think I should?"

"You should if you want to. That's the only way I know of to decide about anything."

He looked at her closely and she began to feel that he was searching for something he knew was there but which she had hidden from him. It gave her an uneasy sense of being in reluctant flight. Then he looked away and back to the dance floor again, as if he had decided to let her keep whatever it was hidden a little longer.

He seemed to be moving, even when he sat perfectly still, and she felt his restless need of taking in more and more of life. Now he began an impatient beat of his fingers on the table.

Shireen put down her coffee cup. "I've had all I want. I'm ready to go."

He gave her a momentary puzzled frown, as if he did not understand what she meant. "Oh. I'm sorry. That's a bad habit I've got. I'm not going any place—you know that."

"I thought maybe you had to get back to the post."

"I've got nothin' but time. For a day or so."

"A day or so?"

"Maybe a little longer. Depends on when my orders come through."

"But that won't be for at least a couple of weeks, will it?"

She had been taking it for granted that he would come out to see

38

her and they would go swimming together, or have dinner again, or go driving in the evening.

He shrugged. "They could come tomorrow. I've been expecting them for quite awhile. I never thought I'd be here this long—but that's the Army."

She might have missed him!

"But you won't go overseas right away, will you?"

"I'll have a couple of weeks leave, I suppose."

She gave a little sigh of relief. "That'll be nice, won't it? What are you going to do?"

"Go up home."

"Up *home?*" It would scarcely have occurred to her that anyone would voluntarily go home.

"Sure. Got to see my family before I shove off."

He smiled at her and she began to feel uncomfortable. She was acting much too disturbed at the prospect of his leaving.

"There are a lot of people I'd like to see," he explained.

"Oh."

Shireen looked down at the tablecloth where she was etching a pattern with her fork. His words had changed in her ears. *There are a lot of people I'd like to see* had become *There's a girl I want to see.*

"I suppose," she said, replying to what she felt he had said.

He watched her a moment longer, still smiling, but she could not look at him. They sat silently then for several moments watching the dancers. Finally she glanced back at him, scarcely turning her head, looking from the corners of her eyes.

A painful yearning ache swelled and took her by the throat. She longed desperately to reach out and touch him, feel the texture of his face. He seemed to her just as he should be, with some unity and perfection completely his own. But it was not only that, or not really that at all. There was something else—he was every beautiful evanescent thing she had ever seen and wanted.

He evoked the same emotional qualities there were for her in glistening sunlight, lilacs, a flaunting butterfly, certain quiet clean magical moments in a forest, the fainting time of twilight, early fall, a low red autumn moon.

Everything that she found most beautiful. And most painful, because they could not last and could never be possessed.

It was a longing that seemed to come up out of a buried time in her life, and was fraught with strange lonely significance. Some promise of frustration, defeat, despair. She watched him: admiring and eager as a child, wistfully anticipatory. But knowing at the same time something more, which might have warned her. Except that she could not let herself be warned by this old hidden knowledge. She had to

39

believe there would be some time when she could catch that perfect evanescent beauty and make it permanent. Hold it forever.

Feeling her watching him, he glanced back again with a look of questioning. "What?"

She quickly found something to say. "I was thinking about how lucky you are. You've lived exactly the way you wanted to, and most men never do. They get married too young and have kids and then spend all the rest of their lives catching the eight-forty and keeping up payments on frigidaires and insurance policies."

He shook his head. "The thing you don't realize, I guess, is that my life sounds a hell of a lot more exciting than it's been. Most of it I've spent alone."

"Alone?" she repeated doubtfully.

"Of course. Oh, hell, I've met hundreds and thousands of people in all kinds of places. But it hasn't been what you apparently think. It's got advantages, sure, and I guess I couldn't live any other way. But it's pretty lonely, too." He looked back at the dancers again. "And sometimes the loneliness is pure hell."

The sound in his voice surprised her. She had suffered from so much loneliness herself—alone or with other people—that she had wanted to think he knew nothing about it at all. But then, after a moment, his admission of loneliness became even further cause for admiration. It was that much more of life he knew about, and knew how to deal with. It gave him one further dimension.

They sat quietly a moment longer, watching the men and their girls as they moved slowly by, close in each other's arms. There seemed a frightening urgency about them. Time was the element they had lost, and they must make up for it in other ways. The room had darkened further now, giving each couple a private anonymous world in which they could feel alone and unseen—under this mass hypnotism, acted upon and reacting to the heavy throb and pulse of excitement and the music's seething rhythm. There was an almost palpable atmosphere of intense, yearning sexuality.

A couple moved slowly past their table. The girl threw back her head and looked up at the man, her face passionately serious, and he drew her tighter against him, his eyes closing, his mouth against her cheek. They moved on by and were blotted out by other couples coming between them. But the same wild abandonment was in all of them, simple and crude and elemental, like some ancient rite for springtime and fertility.

Shireen glanced uneasily away, and began to look around for some distraction. She opened her bag, took out a cigarette and put it in her mouth. As she picked up the book of matches Johnny took it from her, struck off a flame and held it. She kept her eyes down, but as he was blowing out the match she glanced up at him and for an

40

instant they seemed to see each other nakedly, with mutual awareness that there was something in this room they were trying to ignore which had finally got through to them.

Johnny gave a soft laugh, and again that slight wondering shake of his head.

"But in spite of the loneliness," persisted Shireen, determined to keep some kind of conversation going, "I still think you've been luckier than most people."

"Why?"

He asked it as if he had no special interest in why, but would keep up the game she was playing. She was unhappily sure that he knew exactly how she felt and was amused by her helpless yearning toward him. *Every woman he's ever met has been like me.*

"Maybe because you didn't take half your life to get started living," she said. "The way most of us do."

He shrugged. "I found one thing out early. There's only one way to live: decide what you want and then get it. Or you're likely to be dead before you've made up your mind."

She had done that herself; but it wasn't moral, was it? And certainly you should never admit it. You should feel, as she did, guilty—and then keep on the same way.

"That sounds pretty ruthless, Johnny."

"Maybe I am," he said. "And so are you."

"I?"

"You always get what you want, don't you?"

"I always try."

He stood up. "Let's dance."

They went out among the dancers and found themselves completely alone now, much closer together than when they had sat side by side at the table. She wished he would say something. But he was quiet, moving slowly with the music. And then, to her complete surprise, he bent his head to kiss her. She moved her face quickly aside and looked up at him with bright angry astonishment.

"Johnny!"

He was still smiling. "I'm sorry."

But she felt somehow hurt, invaded. It outraged her sense of personal integrity and renewed the old resentment of the female against the predatory male.

"You shouldn't have done that! I thought I'd made it clear to you that Ed and I are very happily married. Because I came to have dinner with you—I assure you I'm not looking for excitement!"

"I didn't think you were."

"Then I can't imagine what made you do that."

"Just an impulse. Looking at you I forgot my manners for a minute, that's all."

41

"It can't have been only that. You must have thought—"

"I didn't think anything, Shireen. I wanted to kiss you. You shouldn't find anything very strange in that. Should you?"

He seemed amused, but she was nervous and quivering and desperately determined to make him understand that she had not been flirting with him, that she did love Ed and would never tolerate such behavior.

"You certainly must know by now, Johnny, that a kiss is meaningless—if that's all there is to it. We're not kids any more, necking in rumble seats."

"Suppose we knock it off."

She became sulkily quiet, but he did not release her or suggest that they go back to the table. She moved along with him, but resentfully now, as if he were forcing her to obey him each time he took a forward step from which she must retreat. She felt something close to hatred, as if this were part of a long-standing disillusionment. She neither spoke nor looked at him again until the music ended and then she made her way as quickly as she could back to the table. When she reached it she did not sit down but turned and looked at him, unsmiling and frankly hostile.

"Want to go?" he asked her.

"I think we'd better."

On the way out she stood sullenly, while he talked a few minutes to the headwaiter. She pulled on her white gloves, nervously smoothing up the fingers, and when the headwaiter asked if she had enjoyed the dinner she smiled sourly and said it had been very nice. They went out and got into the car.

For several minutes they drove in silence. She had decided simply to sit there, ungraciously, until they got back to her house—and let him know how much he had offended her. She crossed her legs and lit a cigarette and stared out of the window.

"Mind if I put the top down?" he asked her. "It's a beautiful night."

"Not at all."

He started to release the levers and was reaching toward the one on her side, when Shireen did it herself. "Thanks," he said softly, but she did not answer. He pushed a button and there was a whirring sound as the top folded back. "That's better, isn't it?"

"I suppose it is."

She looked up at the spread of stars in the sky and thought he should never have spoiled this evening, which had been so nice until then.

Johnny drove along silently, not trying to force her to talk, and slowly she began to feel more kindly toward him. He turned on the radio and a hearty ingratiating masculine voice burst out: "Do you suffer from fallen arches? Do you come home at night with that tired,

42

achey feeling, out of sorts, with no pep left for anything? If you *do*—"

"*My God,*" muttered Johnny, and spun the dial. Shireen laughed, and found that she was no longer angry.

She was the one who had been silly, getting so upset about nothing. It was certainly no irreparable insult and she should stop behaving like a child. She gave him a quick surreptitious glance, and found that he looked to her once more exactly as he had earlier in the evening. Nothing had really been spoiled after all. He passed one station after another until he found an orchestra playing, and then he turned it low.

Shireen sat far on her own side of the car, but now she slid down in the seat and let her head fall back, her hands lying open and relaxed beside her. The warm gentle evening, the sky and the feel of the air came through to her with great sensuality. The moon swept along beside them, hurrying to keep up with the car.

They had been driving for three-quarters of an hour when he stopped the car. She sat up instantly, before the motor had quite died, and opened her door.

"Let's go for a walk," she said.

She bent down and unstrapped her sandals, tossed them into the car and came toward him barefoot, smiling happily; the increased difference in their heights gave her a sudden sense of exhilaration, some delightful composite emotion of playfulness and dependence.

They started down the beach, Shireen taking a little half skip every so often, and now they were talking amiably together. They walked half a mile or so and sat down on a log, Shireen bracing herself with her hands, scrubbing and spreading her toes in the sand. And now they were quiet again, watching the ocean as it bore up to them and then fell back, with a sweep of white phosphorescent flame running swiftly along the breakers. After awhile she turned to him.

"You love the ocean, Johnny, don't you?"

"Sure. I guess it's part of me—I've spent a lot of my life on it."

"And I've spent most of mine between four walls. I've never been anywhere or done anything or known many people."

"You've got plenty of time."

Johnny was sitting with his hands in his pockets, staring out toward the water. Finally he turned his head and looked at her—Shireen met his eyes for a few seconds and then, helplessly, she glanced away. To cover her embarrassment she bent down and scooped up a handful of sand and let it run slowly through her fingers.

"How many guys have you slept with?"

She glanced at him in quick surprise. "Three—counting Ed. That's not very many," she added apologetically.

He laughed. "I'd say it's enough, considering how young you got married."

"Anyway—one of them I don't count."

"How's that again?"

"Well, after all, it only happened once—and it didn't amount to much, that's all. It was a disappointment and I never spoke to him again."

"Did he know why?"

"What's the difference if he knew? I did." And then all at once she laughed.

"What's the joke?"

"Nothing. Something I remembered."

"Tell me."

"Well, when I was in high school I used to think it was pretty clever to say: My past isn't all that it will be. And then, after I got married to Ed, I told him one day: 'I used to say my past isn't all that it will be. But, goddamn it, it was.' " She shrugged. "He never thought it was very funny." She was smiling at him innocently, and now she opened her hand and let all the sand fall at once.

Johnny laughed softly.

"Poor Ed," said Shireen. She shook her head. "Think how long he's been married to me."

"Yeah, poor Ed. The lucky bastard."

"But you said you would never—"

"I wouldn't. But I can see where it would be fun, being married to you. Come on, let's go back."

They walked side by side, silent again, and Shireen was making up her mind to ask him something. All at once she cocked her head to one side, looking at him curiously.

"Haven't you ever been in love, Johnny?"

Chapter 7

"Sure," he said. "Once."

"Once? You still are, then?"

"It was a long time ago—I was about eighteen. She was a very sweet little girl, a wonderful little person." He shrugged lightly but his face was serious, intent, his eyes squinted, as if to help him look back into the past. "It was a very simple thing—not even physical. In fact I only kissed her once, the last time I saw her. But it's nothing I could explain to anyone—just a kind of feeling that happens sometimes between two people. I guess I don't really know what it was she meant to me, but I've never forgotten her and I never will."

As he talked Shireen found herself growing jealous of the girl and of Johnny's feeling for her; she was analyzing it scornfully. Why, it sounds like nothing but a romantic adolescent idyl. How can he still be taking something like that seriously? It's ridiculous.

"Have you seen her recently?"

"No. I went away to school and she died while I was gone."

"Oh, Johnny! I'm sorry. I'm sorry I asked you."

"Don't be. You couldn't very well have known that. It's strange, though—that little girl had some quality I've never found in any other woman. I don't know just what it was. Maybe a kind of innocence. There was something very light and lovely about her that I think would have lasted all her life, if she'd been able to live it." Then the sound of his voice changed. "Anyway—you asked me and that's what it was."

"And that's all? That's the only time you've been in love?"

"That's all."

"I'm sure she must have been a wonderful girl." She tried to sound sympathetic.

Of course she had some quality you've never found again, she wanted to say to him. She's dead, so she can never do anything wrong. And you didn't even really know her. You're not being fair. It had hurt her to be told about this girl. For he still had with him one thing which was perfect and unbroken and could never change. And she had nothing like that at all.

She had been too energetic in her relationships. She had grabbed at them one after another, like a child with a toy it does not understand or an animal it is too young to know has life and the capacity for pain. She had always clung too long, wrenched at her friendships

45

and love affairs too hard. Until finally she had spoiled them. And Johnny had held this one thing lightly and delicately, as it must be held if it were not to be smashed. So that now, though the girl was dead, he had it still. He was careful, apparently, with people as she was only careful with inanimate objects: like the little set of dishes her aunt had given her, which she had kept wrapped in tissue paper in case there should be an earthquake. But she had never been so gentle with a human being.

"She was a wonderful girl," he repeated. "I'll never feel that way about anyone again."

"Oh, now, Johnny. That's not quite fair, is it? If you make up your mind to that, you're not giving yourself a chance. Why, I'm sure you must have met all kinds of interesting girls since then."

"Sure. I have. None of 'em like Patty."

"But what was it that made her so different?"

"It's not a thing you can define, Shireen. You know that. Suppose I asked you what there was about Ed that made him different enough from all the other men you knew for you to want to marry him. Could you tell me?"

"No," she said softly. "I guess I couldn't."

"Well, then—"

They walked on, quiet again, or only speaking briefly about the night, the phosphorescence on the waves, the birds flying home over the water.

"Look," said Shireen, lifting her arm and pointing to a gull. "Isn't it strange how they seem more silent at night? It's almost as if you could see the absence of sound."

They had stopped and were standing side by side. For several moments they looked at each other.

"You really are a beautiful girl, aren't you?" he said to her now, speaking slowly and reflectively. "Everything about you. The way you walk, the way you talk—the way you laugh."

She glanced up swiftly, incredulously, and found him watching her with the first look of absolute seriousness she had seen on his face. And then, bowing her head a little so that he could not look directly at her, she began walking again. He kept beside her. She repeated the words to herself, so that she would never forget them.

Back at the car he found a cloth in the glove compartment and, while she wiped the sand off her feet and fastened her sandals on, he twisted the radio dial. She shook the cloth out hard, wadded it back into the glove compartment, and slammed the door. She looked at him expectantly, waiting for him to start the car, but he was sitting with his hands in his pockets and looking up at the sky. Her heart had begun to beat desperately and the music brought up a sad sickened faintness. But she did not suggest that they start back. She waited for him.

He turned so that he was half facing her, and his arm rested along the back of the seat. Shireen sat far on her own side and they looked at each other in the vague glow from the radio, questioning, watching, and now both of them seemed to be waiting.

There was only one thing to remember: Ed loved her and depended upon her and would soon be going overseas. Nothing else but that. Johnny didn't count, and neither did she.

A sudden splash of music came at them, chords struck quickly and violently on a piano, and then the orchestra surged in, seized the melody and took it over, leaving the piano as a faint rippling background.

"That does it—" And he reached for her.

Shireen started to move, stricken with panic, but there was nowhere to escape to, his mouth pressed hard on hers, his arms held her bound to him. There was no tenderness now in the kiss or the way he held her, nothing of the quality she had trusted, and she was suddenly as terrified as if she had been captured by a giant. She tried to push him away, full of the anger and fear of a child the first moment it discovers it has been locked in a closet. He had taken her freedom and she had a sense of outrage at the betrayal—luring her toward him with his smile and the soft caressive sounds of his voice; and she hated herself for having been such a fool, and him for having tricked her.

For several minutes he held her so that she could not move. His mouth had forced hers open and his teeth pressed painfully against her lips. But she refused to relax or give herself up to him. And then gradually her rage began to dissipate itself in slow mounting wonder, admiration, and a final sense of primitive female satisfaction. At that moment he released her ever so little—and instantly her fear and guilt leaped up again.

"Johnny! Please—don't! This isn't right!"

"It's right for me."

"No! It can't be!"

She was almost crying now, hurt and ashamed at what he had said, implying that no one else mattered, reducing herself to something inconsequential. He was alone with his emotions, then, and she was no integral part of them; it made her despise them both.

"It is," he insisted.

"But it can't be!"

His hand took hold of her face roughly and held it, his mouth touched hers, and she heard him say: "It is—because I love you."

And it seemed as if a magic door had been opened. She relaxed all at once, her arms went eagerly around him, her mouth became pliable and responsive, and the tide poured over them both. She

47

blotted Ed out, like drawing down a blind, erasing the past and denying the future. Somewhere, far in the distance, she could still hear the music, now mounting and surging, falling away, then returning upon them with furious force, triumphantly, as if to rise up like a giant, seize and destroy them. And then, while they still clung together, the music roared upward and away; and suddenly stopped.

A few moments later he let her go and her head fell onto his shoulder. She gave a deeply breathed long-drawn sigh. "That's something I'll never forget," he said softly. She laughed, pleased with herself. Some sound in his voice convinced her she had eliminated every other woman he had ever known.

His hands moved over her slowly and caressingly, with infinite sensitiveness, drawing with them waves of warmth and delight. But at last she forced herself to move away from him and this time he let her go, as if he had already proved that she was helpless and now was willing to give her the right of choice. She took out a comb and began pulling it through her hair, her arms lifted, and he watched, her captive now. For awhile she pretended to be so occupied with what she was doing that she had forgotten him, and then all at once she looked at him and smiled. He shook his head, wonderingly. She put the comb back and clicked the latch on her bag.

"You've got to take me home now, Johnny."

"Not yet."

"It's late. It must be after two."

He smiled, as if he knew she was being coquettish, and reached toward her, but she put out her hands against him.

"I couldn't do that to Ed."

"Ed wouldn't know anything about it."

"I would, though. No, Johnny—please, don't. You'll only make yourself feel worse, and me, too. We can't."

"How much difference do you think it really makes?"

"A great deal."

"You know better than that, Shireen. There's no real difference between kissing someone like that and making love to them. You meant the same thing by it."

"No, I didn't—I—Johnny, *please* take me home!"

Something had gone wrong somewhere and just now she could not seem to tell what it was. But she must get away from him, get home and not trust either of them any more. She had an intense, frightened feeling of despair and disappointment, not so much with him as with herself. It had shocked and dismayed her to have finally found the woman Ed had been trusting all these years.

"Shireen—" His voice was warm and beguiling and he drew her back against him, his hands on her breasts. She closed her eyes and for a moment did not breathe.

48

Then she shook her head. "I can't, Johnny. I can't. I'd hate myself for the rest of my life. There'd be that much more to regret—"

"What?"

Instantly he had released her and one hand took hold of her shoulder and turned her to face him.

"What did you say?"

She looked at him in alarm, as if his movement had let a sudden cold wind blow between them, depriving her of some primal source of comfort and security. His face was angry and perplexed and she frowned a little, wondering what had caused the change. And then she smiled, tenderly, and her fingers touched the side of his face.

"No, Johnny. Nothing like this has ever happened before. It's a lot of other things—"

"What other things?"

"I'd have to tell you too much to explain it. And you can't possibly want to know about my marriage, any more than I want to hear about Patty."

"No, I guess I wouldn't. But I can't believe you've ever done anything very bad in your whole life. To Ed or to anyone else."

"I have, though. A lot of things—"

But, if he had asked her exactly what they were, she could not have told him for sure. That she had a bad temper and sometimes flew into rages? While Ed always behaved like a perfect gentleman. That she was selfish and egotistical and never cared about anyone else? While Ed merely thought she was cute and childlike and never accused her for it. Those things were bad enough, but the real truth was down even deeper somewhere, and she had better leave it alone. Johnny would never love her if he knew—neither would anyone else. Ed knew her so well that she sometimes thought he was a fool for ever having trusted her at all; but of course she had tricked him into it, by now and then pretending to be better than she was.

"Well," he said, after there had been a long silence. "I guess you're right."

"About how I've treated Ed? Or about us?"

"I'll take you home."

He started the motor and Shireen heard, as if it had just begun again, the swelling roar of the ocean. The wheels ground on the sandy pavement and slowly he swung the car around; then they were driving down the highway once more.

The forward rush of the car gave her some sense of safety and deliverance. It was all right. Nothing had happened. Only a kiss. That was all there was to it, and that was all there would ever be. She had not realized yet that her feeling for Ed had split off from the main section of her emotions, like the cracking of an iceberg.

They were back on the little street where she and Peggy lived much sooner than she had expected. And as the car stopped she glanced uneasily at the house, hoping that Peggy was asleep and would not wake up when she came in. She turned and looked at Johnny questioningly, as if waiting for him to tell her what to do.

He smiled and touched her cheek and again she was assailed by the great tenderness that seemed a part of everything he did. But she had no understanding of it, for Ed was always gentle—she might have got that from him. But she never had. Ed's gentleness seemed a negative quality; Johnny's tenderness was positive, as if it came from some magical, almost poetic, knowledge of women, or from some primitive sympathy with everything that grew and breathed.

"Do you love me at all?" he asked her.

"Of course I do, Johnny."

"You hadn't said so."

"I know. I guess I was afraid to. I don't know why I didn't. I—" She was going back in her mind, searching for the reason why she had not said it, and he watched her for a moment, smiling at her troubled perplexity.

"Come on," he said softly. "Turn 'em up on the edge a little." She looked at him, raising her eyes swiftly, and then all at once her face broke into a free brilliant smile. "That's better." He started to get out of the car, but her hand reached automatically and touched his arm; he turned back. They sat and looked at each other.

"You were right," he said. "It's better this way. Ed's too nice a guy."

Shireen shook her head. "He is—he's always been so good to me." Tears came into her eyes.

"No, Shireen. Don't blame yourself. You can't change anything by regretting it, don't you know that?" He smiled again. "I suppose you think you can." And then he got out, came around and opened the door for her.

As they walked slowly toward the house Shireen was fishing in her bag for the key. He took it from her and opened the door, ever so slightly, then handed it back. And though at every move, handing over the key, watching him put it in the lock, taking it from him again, she kept believing that something would happen to keep her from leaving him, she finally saw that they were going to part. In a few seconds. For they could not stand here and talk. The house was small and sounds carried all over it.

"Good night, girl," Johnny said. "Sleep well."

"You'll call me tomorrow?" she asked him anxiously.

"Yes—"

"What time?"

"I don't know. Whenever I can. Good night."

He kissed her lightly on the forehead, then turned around and went

50

back down the walk. In the house it was very quiet and she felt sure that Peggy was asleep. From the front windows she watched him get into the car, heard the motor start, and then the car moved away from the curb, picking up speed, and he was gone. She went into her own room and closed the door and locked it.

But when she had undressed and got into bed she found that she could not sleep. She began waiting for him to call her. Ed had become vague and unreal, someone she had known a long while ago. When she first made the discovery she was surprised, but after that he did not enter her mind at all. She lay there thinking of Johnny, not caring whether she slept or not.

Chapter 8

Shireen sat at the typewriter, staring at the blank sheet she had rolled in. Every few seconds she glanced at the clock across the room. It had a noisy tick she had never noticed before which seemed to be getting steadily louder and louder. Peggy was in the living room and Shireen was aware of each move and sound she made: she ruffled the pages of a magazine, she struck matches to light cigarettes, she wandered around, once she dropped a book.

Peggy was waiting for one of the girls to pick her up to go to the Red Cross. It was not quite noon.

Shireen had been up since eight—though she had slept only a few hours—because she did not want Peggy to think anything had happened to make her change her usual routine. She was convinced Peggy's mind would be full of devious thoughts if she did one smallest thing out of the ordinary.

Even so it seemed Peggy had looked at her rather oddly this morning when she had asked: "Did you have a nice time last night?"

"Oh, it wasn't too bad," Shireen had said, and she got up to turn on the gas under the coffee again, so that Peggy could not see her face.

And what, exactly, had Peggy meant when she said, "I'm sorry I didn't get a chance to meet Johnny." The girl was so goddamned suspicious.

All morning long Shireen had been sitting there. And she would not have written a word—only she was afraid Peggy would think it strange if she didn't, so that she forced herself to type a few paragraphs now and then, copying something she had done the day before.

She sat on the edge of her chair, ready to spring, her fists clenched —if the telephone rang she must answer it before Peggy did. But she prayed that Peggy would be gone before he called. How could she possibly talk to him with Peggy in the house, listening to every word, trying to make something of it? As she sat waiting she began to hate Peggy for being there and the hatred increased with her anxiety that he might call before she was gone, until suddenly she wanted to rush out of the room, grab Peggy by the throat and knock her dead. The violence of the image scared her and she got up and went into the bathroom to wash her face with cold water.

If you're not careful you'll make a complete fool of yourself and then she'll know it and so will Ed—

Ed.

She put him out of her mind immediately. Ed has nothing to do with this. This is another part of my life, it doesn't affect him.

There was a short blat from an automobile horn and she jumped and started to tremble. The next moment she heard a rap on the living-room window and Peggy's cheerful voice. "Be right out! 'Bye, Shireen! Back around five!" The front door slammed.

Shireen waited for a moment and then ran into the living room, saw the car full of girls go off down the street, and rushed out to the kitchen. She called the number Johnny had given her last night.

It was several minutes before he could be located. But finally, after she had been transferred from one place to another, they found him.

"Johnny—this is Shireen."

"Well." He seemed surprised. "What d'you know?" He had obviously not been expecting her to call.

"Peggy just left—she's going to be at the Red Cross until five o'clock. Can you drive out? I've got to see you."

There was a slight pause and then he said: "I can't do it, Shireen. My orders came through this morning and I'm taking off late this afternoon."

"This afternoon! But Johnny, that's impossible!"

"I told you last night this would probably happen."

"But I didn't know you really expected it to happen! I thought you only thought it might!"

"That's right," he said. "And now it has."

"But you don't *have* to go tonight! Come and see me first. Johnny! You weren't going to leave without even seeing me again, were you?"

"I was going to call you—later in the day. I thought you'd be working."

"Working? I can't work. I can't even think about anything but you!"

"Oh, Shireen—" The smile was gone from his voice now, and then, after a moment's hesitation, he said: "You mustn't let that happen."

"I mustn't let it happen?" she cried incredulously. "What are you talking about? It's happened already—there's nothing I can do about it now! What's happened to you, Johnny, since last night?"

"Nothing."

"You don't sound the same."

"I'm talking in a room full of guys, remember."

"Oh." Of course. She should have thought of that. How would she have sounded, if Peggy had been there? That explained everything, and she went on eagerly. "If you can't leave, Johnny, I'll drive out to the base."

"I don't think that's such a good idea."

"Yes, Johnny. I'm coming. I've got to see you. Tell me how to get there."

He gave her the instructions, told her how to get a pass, which gate to enter by, and where he would be. Then he added: "I haven't got much time. I'm taking off at six-fifteen."

She ran in to start the water for her bath and while the tub was filling she rushed around the room, getting out a dress and shoes, searching frantically for things that seemed to have got lost, throwing off her blouse and linen shorts as she went, doing everything with the rabid haste of someone who has determined not to think at all.

Driving out, everyone seemed to be in her way, the streets seemed more crowded and the other drivers stupider than usual. She thought she would never get there. And, when she did, the men sat around as if they had the rest of their lives to decide whether or not they would admit her to the post.

Johnny was not there yet and she sat down to wait for him, folding her hands in her lap. After about fifteen minutes he came through the door and she recognized his dark silhouette against the bright light. She jumped to her feet quickly, but when he got there he did not kiss her. He stood and looked at her for a moment as she watched him with quizzical childlike eagerness. Then he shook his head.

"Pretty impulsive little chick, aren't you?"

"Johnny, where can we go?"

"I can't go anywhere. I haven't got time. Let's just sit here for a few minutes."

She was surprised and hurt by his casualness, but refused to accept it. "Even if you haven't much time, we can at least drive a little way, can't we?" She glanced around. There were a few men in the cool dark room, playing cards or writing letters. "We can't talk here—there's no privacy at all."

He continued looking at her with that same amused smile, as if he had detached himself completely and had no part in this, but still found her behavior entertaining—like that of a small child who does not quite know what it's doing. It made her want to shake him. She had a maddening sense of groping in fog, trying to pick up mercury, running to catch a chimera. He seemed to have left her, but she could not imagine where it was he had gone to.

"We can't talk here, Johnny," she repeated.

"Why not?"

"You know why not! Please—my car's outside." She started to turn away but he stopped her, not by touching her but by the expression on his face.

"All right, but remember—I've got to be back in half an hour. No more."

54

"I know, I know," she said impatiently.

She walked ahead of him, got into the car and waited for him to come around and drive. Shireen sat low in the seat, close beside him, and now she felt happy and content once more, restored by the mere fact of his presence. She was intensely aware that these might be the last few moments they would ever have together. He might not even have the rest of his life to live, and all the years they had lived already were lost to both of them. They had only some undeterminable fragment of the future left. She turned and looked at him, and for a moment it seemed she had never seen him before. Then she reached out and touched the side of his face. He glanced at her and smiled, and shook his head.

"Even with a couple of hours' sleep, you're beautiful. God must have had to cheat a lot of women—to make you."

Nothing was any different, then, between them. She felt relieved and grateful. But she wanted to hear him say it.

"And everything's all right, isn't it? Nothing's changed?"

"Changed—how?"

"I mean—over the phone and at first, you seemed to be—Well, I was afraid you'd forgotten."

He gave a light sigh. "I haven't forgotten anything. I've just had a little time to think. That's all."

"Think about what?" She began to get anxious again. "Have you been thinking you don't like me?"

"What an idea. You know what I mean."

"I don't know. How can I know? Didn't you mean what you said last night?"

"That has nothing to do with it."

He swung the car off the highway and stopped it and she turned to him eagerly, expecting him to take her into his arms; she moved a little toward him. But he opened the door and got out.

"Johnny!"

"Come on. Let's walk."

"I don't want to walk!"

"Come on."

He looked tired and, in some sense, almost helpless. She got out and stood facing him, as if that might make it easier to get from him what she wanted and felt she must have: reassurance that he loved her.

He stood with his hands in his pockets and looked down at her. She was vaguely aware of the quietness of the little curved beach where they were alone, the motion of the water, lifting and sinking, and the feel of the hot hazy day.

"What have you been thinking about today, Shireen?" he asked her finally, his voice soft and wondering.

55

"You, of course."

"What about Ed? Have you thought about him?"

"I don't want to talk about Ed!"

He shook his head. "There's something about you I don't understand."

"There's only one thing about me you need to understand. I'm in love with you. Last night you said that you loved me—and today you act as if you'd never seen me before. So I don't know if you were amusing yourself last night, or what the hell you were up to. But I do know about myself and I can tell you this: I've found out that I've never been in love before at all!"

"You shouldn't say such things, Shireen."

"I shouldn't say them! Who started all this, anyway?"

"Oh." Now he was smiling again, aloof and amused. After a moment he said, "We were both pretty foolish."

"Is *that* what you think?"

"Of course. What else? You'd think so, too, if you'd let yourself stop feeling for a minute."

"But I have thought about it. I haven't thought about anything else. And all I can think is that I love you."

"Okay. But we can be sensible about it, can't we?"

"How can you be sensible about a thing like this?" The wind blew her hair across her face and she reached up with one hand to fling it back. "Oh, Johnny—" She glanced around, as if she could find some solution out in the water, or hidden somewhere on the sand. "How's this going to end?" She sounded plaintive and looked up at him like a bewildered child, hoping he could tell her.

"It's ended now."

"You know better than that. You can't set an emotion like this going and then just decide you got on the wrong streetcar and want to get off and take one going in the opposite direction. I know you don't feel as indifferent as you're pretending to be. You can't!"

"The way I feel about you has nothing to do with it. The way you feel about me shouldn't, either."

They stood looking at each other, Johnny still with his hands in his pockets, Shireen's dress blowing around her, her hand reaching up again to throw back her hair.

"Shireen—haven't you ever in your life done something for someone else?"

"Of course I have!" Then she looked away. "No, I don't know. Maybe I haven't. Johnny, there's got to be some answer to this, or I'll go crazy!"

He smiled at her, tenderly now. "Life's really very simple, Shireen—if you don't make it hard for yourself."

She looked at him in complete incomprehension. She could imagine

56

only one reason for him to behave like this: last night had lost its meaning for him by morning. "I don't understand you at all," she said.

"Shireen, look here. You love Ed, don't you?"

"Of course I do. I always have. I must."

"Well, then, just remember this, and you won't be so confused any more. He's going overseas. And right now he needs you more than he ever has before, believe me. A guy can get pretty lonely at a time like that."

"What about you? You're going, too."

"Forget about me." He made a quick gesture. "Come on, I've got to get back. Got a hell of a lot to do."

Driving back to the base she asked him where he would be during his leave, if he would write to her, if she could write to him. "Maybe you'll come back here—before you go."

"Not a chance."

"You will write to me, Johnny?"

"Sure." The sound of his voice meant nothing, neither that he would write nor that he was saying it to keep her still.

"Promise me."

"I promise."

"But Johnny—"

"Shh—"

They were back at the base in only half the time, she was sure, it had taken them to drive out. They passed the gate, Johnny and the man inside exchanging salutes again, and then he parked the car. He turned and smiled at her.

"Well, girl—good-by and God bless you." He started to get out.

"Oh, Johnny, you're not really going! I can't let you go!"

He came around and stood beside her, leaning both arms on the car door. "Good luck with that book of yours. I know everything's going to come out right for you."

There were tears in her eyes. "Johnny, I—"

"Don't say it. Don't even think it any more. That's a good man you've got, remember that. And you can't have everything you see. Didn't your mother ever tell you that?"

"Don't make fun of me."

"I'm not. But just remember—nothing's ever as bad or as good as it seems." He touched her face. "And someday you'll be glad you *didn't* know me any better. I don't wear so well, Shireen. Good-by."

He bent and kissed her lightly and then, with her eyes still closed, she realized that he had gone. He turned once and waved, turned the corner of a building and was gone. She sat for several minutes staring off into the distance, unable to believe there was nothing for her to do next—just go home. With no time when she would see him again for her to begin looking forward to.

57

Chapter 9

Shireen got off the train and looked around for a porter.

People went swarming by her on every side and apparently they were all in a hurry and had some special important place to go. The station looked dark and ugly, as if it were located somewhere far underground, part of a horror story of the future when all warmth and growth have disappeared from the top of the earth and mankind must retreat inside the planet. Even the voices around her had a different sound, quick and strident. She wondered if it was true, as she had heard, that New Yorkers were brusque and rude and indifferent; it seemed as if she had got into some alien world where she was even smaller and less significant than she had ever been before.

She had wired the Hotel Pennsylvania for a room, after she read Johnny's letter and made up her mind to go see him.

Dear Shireen:

Had a fine week at home and saw a lot of old friends, some of them still around though most of the guys are gone, of course. I'm in New York now—as you can tell by the stationery—visiting Betty and my two nephews. Bob's overseas, as I think I told you. I hope Ed's been in again since I saw you and that he won't be shipping out as soon as he expected. Be sure to give him my best regards and tell him how sorry I am to have missed him that night. Maybe we'll run into each other somewhere out West one of these days. I'm sure you're fine and hard at work and just in case I forgot to mention it I want to tell you what a hell of a job I think you've done—it takes a lot of guts to work like that and not know what you'll get for it in the long run. But I know it'll come out right for you. I hope you'll be as happy as you should be—you've got everything to look forward to. Good-by for now. I'll be shoving off from here this time.

Johnny.

She had not wired him she was coming. She would surprise him.

The people around her were identifying their baggage for the porters, and she could not continue to stand there waiting. She must assume some initiative herself. No one was going to come and take care of her. Finally she found a porter and went up to him, smiling timidly.

"Would you mind taking my bag to the Pennsylvania Hotel, please?"

He picked it up and started off and she followed him, taking a

58

quick extra little step now and then so that he would not get too far ahead of her. At last they emerged into a long narrow tunnel lined with white tile, which looked to her like some weird never-ending bathroom, where you might wander eternally in a dream searching for something lost in childhood.

She followed him through the crowded lobby and, as she saw how many people stood in line at the desk, was convinced that there was not a room for her anywhere in New York. She wished she had never come, and felt sure that Johnny had gone already—perhaps only two hours ago. To her great surprise, they gave her a room, but told her she must check with the desk clerk in the morning if she wanted to keep it for another day.

"Oh, thank you very much," she said. "It's really very nice of you."

Going up in the elevator she thought of what she would do. She would call Johnny immediately, of course. And then, while he was on his way over, she would take a bath and get dressed. She could even have breakfast sent up to her room. It began to seem like a great adventure again.

The room was on the fourteenth floor. It was small and looked all dull blue and gray and brown, with a painted metal bed and worn carpet. She tipped the bellboy and closed the door and then went over and sat down on the bed, flipping through the telephone directory. Her heart had begun to beat hard and her stomach was churning. She could scarcely believe that in a minute or two she would hear his voice and in an hour or less she would actually see him.

She picked up the phone and gave the number. And while she waited she sat and swung her foot, smiling to herself, remembering something she had said to her mother the last time she was home: "All I believe in is this minute—right here and now. I don't think you can ever be sure of anything else. And I damned well know you should never count on anything else. Take what you can get—and grab it, before it gets away. It's *always* later than you think."

Her mother had not approved of that, of course. Her father would not, either. But then they never had understood her. She had often looked at them and wondered who they were and how she came to be among them.

A woman's voice answered the phone now, repeating the number.

"May I speak to Captain Keegan, please?"

"May I ask who's calling?"

"Mrs. Edward Farrell."

There was a silence while she anticipated the pleased sound of his voice, how amazed he was going to be, and how delighted. Then he spoke to her.

"Hello," he said. "Is that you? What the hell's going on?"

"Johnny—I just got here. I'm at the Pennsylvania Hotel."

"You mean Ed's gone already?"

"No. At least I don't think so. I—"

"You don't *think* so? Shireen, for God's sake—what are you up to?"

This was not the greeting she had expected, and she began to feel frightened. She had intended telling him immediately that she had come only to see him, but now she did not dare.

"Well—I had to come up, Johnny. I wanted to see a publisher about my book. It's almost finished."

"But what if Ed ships out while you're gone? Shireen, you never should have left Miami now."

"But Johnny—"

She slumped back, feeling suddenly tired. How could she make him understand? How could he *not* understand? Didn't he know Ed had seen her every day for years and it could certainly make no great difference for him to see her once more? She had known about the chance that he might go while she was away—and had decided to risk it.

"Take my advice, girl. Get on a train or a plane or whatever you can catch first, and get back there. You can see all the publishers you want in a couple of weeks, after he's gone."

"But I can't see *you* in a couple of weeks!"

"Oh." He sounded like a man who has been hit.

"You know that's why I came, Johnny. I had to see you again. I couldn't let you go—the way we parted. Oh, Johnny, please don't be angry with me. Please come to see me. *Please.*"

After a long moment he said: "Shireen, I can't do it."

"You can't do it? But you can't be that busy! When I've come all this way—you wouldn't let me be right here in the same city and not even see me?"

"Go on back."

"I won't go back! I'll stay until I see you."

"Shireen, don't talk like a child. Go back where you belong."

"Who says that's where I belong? Johnny, I love you! Can't you understand that?" She was suddenly furious with him, for denying her something she had taken such a risk to get. But she still believed she could talk him into coming.

"I tried to tell you, Shireen, that has nothing to do with it."

"It has everything to do with it! Nothing *else* has anything to do with it!"

She heard him sigh. "God," he said softly. "The mess things get into."

"Life isn't always so simple, Johnny," she reminded him.

"No. I'm beginning to see that."

He was silent a moment and she began to grow hopeful again. He

60

would come. He would not refuse her. He couldn't, when she loved him so much. But why should he make her beg him? Why had he become devious when he had been so straightforward in the beginning—as if he had gone confidently into a strange country and then begun to fear it and now was trying to escape. After all, she was the one who was taking the risks and she was the one whose life would be affected, not his.

"Look, Shireen. It can't do any good for us to talk any longer. Betty and the kids are waiting breakfast for me—"

"When will you come, Johnny? Soon?"

"I'm not coming. Don't wait for me. See your publisher, if you think you must, and go on back."

"Johnny!"

"Good-by, Shireen, and good luck. Maybe we'll meet again somewhere sometime."

"Johnny!" One hand went out in an involuntary gesture, as if to catch him.

"Good-by."

"No! Wait! Johnny—"

His voice dropped away. "Good-by." She heard him hang up.

"Johnny!" she cried again.

There was a moment's silence, and then a woman's voice said, "Operator. Your call, please."

She put the telephone back and sat there, slumped over. After a minute or so she reached for it again but then drew back her hand, shaking her head. No. It wouldn't do any good to call him again. There was no way she could argue him into coming, or force him to see her. She pushed her hat off and stood up. She walked slowly across the room and sat down and stared at the floor, unable to make herself believe that she had talked to him and that he knew she had come this long way to see him—and still he had refused to see her.

For a long while she sat, staring at the floor. And she began to realize, for the first time, exactly what she had done.

Since the moment she had started packing her bag yesterday morning she had refused to think about Ed or her marriage or whether she was right or wrong or what the consequences would be later when she had to face herself. She had flown part way, been put off the plane and got on a train, and all the while had felt sure of herself and convinced that what she was doing was inevitable because she loved Johnny and he loved her.

But Johnny was not coming to see her. He was not impressed by her devotion and her willingness to put everything else out of her life for him. She felt that he despised her for it, and now she looked at herself with loathing and contempt. She threw herself on the bed and cried, until she had worn herself out.

61

Finally she sat up, throwing her hair back, went into the bathroom and splashed cold water over her face and then she raised her head and looked at herself in the mirror. Her eyes were red and swollen and she stared at herself as if at the worst enemy she had ever had. Suddenly she made the ugliest face she could.

You look like hell! she told herself. I hate you!

But she could not cry any more.

She went to the window, pushed it halfway up and stood looking down. A swift vivid image of herself plunging through the window and hurtling downward rushed before her eyes and she stared at it in horror, watching herself fall, turning over and over in the air, screaming. The scream wailed louder and louder and then stopped as her body struck the pavement and was smashed into pulp. She gasped and one hand covered her mouth; she closed her eyes and turned away.

But after awhile she moved back and stood there again.

The street was full of people and there was a continuous roar to the city, as though a sinister machine had been set going which could never be stopped. She felt that it could pick her up like a monstrous thresher, whirl her around and grind her to nothing. She had an intense absolute conviction of her own doom—as if she had been living under some tremendous inner pressure of which she had just become aware. And now that she could no longer hide from it, she knew that it was intolerable. She seemed to know at last and finally that she would never be able to learn to live.

She should die. And it would be so easy that way—her body would explode in a miraculous and complete and final release.

She turned away, full of infinite self-pity, and went over to the bed. She lay and stared up at the ceiling and when she woke later could not be sure at first that she had slept. She looked at her watch. One o'clock.

She leaped up. What if he had called? Or come and knocked, and she had not heard him?

That must be what had happened.

She picked up the telephone and asked if anyone had called for her. She waited. No messages. She threw herself face down on the bed again, staring at a seam in the carpet.

But he may come later. I'd better get cleaned up. I wouldn't want him to see me looking like this. She got up again and looked at herself in the mirror, running her hands through her tangled hair and holding the sides of her head.

Look at you. How ugly you are. You look like you could board a broomstick and take off. She laughed, sneering at herself.

But then she took a bath and made up her face, unpacked her clothes and hung everything in the bathroom to steam. She put on a dressing gown she had bought before she went to meet Ed in Miami, black lace over flesh-colored chiffon with a couple of big red roses stuck through the belt. She strapped black sandals on her feet and looked at herself in the mirror; her face seemed incredibly sad and she tried to smile a little, as she would smile at Johnny if he came. The smile disgusted her and she turned away.

The afternoon passed.

She thought of having some food sent up but could not imagine herself eating it, so she did not order any. No use wasting the money. She could not afford it. She could not afford to be here at all, so she must not spend anything she did not need to spend.

Ed's money, at that.

Well, she'd pay him back someday.

What a ridiculous thought! Of course she was never going to have any money of her own, to pay off her sins with. Why was it she could not give up this hopeless hope? Her book would turn out the way everything else in her life had.

She stayed there, waiting, and it did not once occur to her to call the airport or the railway station. She knew she would not leave New York today and maybe not tomorrow. She would call him again at six o'clock, if he had not come by then.

At six o'clock she was told, by the same voice that had answered in the morning, that Captain Keegan had gone out around noontime and left no word as to when he would be back.

Then he's coming.

She washed her face and put on fresh make-up, took another bath and splashed herself with a lily-of-the-valley fragrance, and this time she got fully dressed. It was seven by the time she finished and then, as she stood winding her watch, she realized that she had been fooled by her own need to see him. Of course he wasn't coming. That was what he had told her and that was what he meant. She looked down at her black dress and sheer stockings and the toes of her shoes and was almost surprised to find herself wearing them. The realization that she had gone ahead, getting herself ready, just as if he were coming, made her despise herself even more.

The evening went by and she did not order dinner. At nine she started to undress but then decided she might as well wait a little longer, having waited this long, and put her shoes back on and stood at the window. She watched the lights come on and the city seemed oppressively close, as though something dangerous and unknown hovered at the back of her neck. The crowds moved up Seventh Avenue like a slowly grazing herd of cattle.

At a quarter of ten the telephone rang.

But now it was so unexpected that she turned and looked at it a moment, warning herself not to be fooled. It's a wrong number, she thought, as she went to pick it up.

"Hello." Her voice was cautious.

"Hi. You still there?" There was a sound of amusement in his voice, and to her surprise she became instantly aware of another world—the one he had been in all day long, gay and active; completely unrelated to hers.

"Johnny?"

"Who else?"

She sat down on the bed. "Where are you?" she asked him, her voice very light and weak.

"Downstairs. In the lobby."

"You mean you've come, after all?"

"It looks that way. What's your room number?"

Chapter 10

She opened the door and he was standing there smiling, looking at her as if this were the first time they had seen each other since the night they met.

"Hi." He walked in, his cap in one hand. "Had dinner?"

She stood with her hands behind her back and watched him. "No. I haven't. I—wasn't so very hungry."

"Well? And what did your publisher have to say?"

"I didn't go. I just stayed here—and hoped you'd come."

He shook his head. "Come on, get your coat. It's time you had something to eat."

She looked at him incredulously. "What?"

"Come on."

He opened the door again and stood waiting for her. She got her coat and slipped it on, picked up her bag and gloves and walked toward him. She stopped, to ask him why he was doing this—but then kept quiet and went on out.

He had borrowed his sister's car and they started up Broadway. She was no longer even aware of being in New York. They could have been anywhere—it was no special city, and no particular time. They seemed to exist together in a vacuum. And as they began to talk, pleasantly and casually, she was surprised to remember that all this had begun from their merely liking each other.

If we only could have met some other time, she thought—not with a war going on. The war changes everything. You can't wait, you don't dare wait, and you go too fast. But without the war I never would have met him at all. She could not imagine knowing Johnny Keegan during peacetime, or what it would be like for either of them. It almost seemed they wouldn't be the same people.

"What do you look like in civilian clothes, Johnny?"

"Like any other guy, I guess. I don't know. Why?"

"I was just trying to picture you in something beside a uniform—and it's funny, I can't do it. But I'd love you in anything. No matter what ever happens to either one of us, I'll love you all the rest of my life."

He was quiet a moment but did not answer her, and then he changed the subject and began talking about how the city had looked before the lights were turned out. Finally he told her they were on the Merritt Parkway.

"Too bad it isn't daylight. This is pretty beautiful along here—I wish you could see it."

"I'll see it sometime. When I come back here to live. If I do," she added quickly, to placate her evil spirits, for *when I come back* had sounded optimistic and might offend them.

Did you hear that? one of them would say to the others. *She's actually got an idea she's going to sell that book and have the kind of life she wants. Never mind,* the others would reply. *We're on to her. We'll take care of that all right.*

She slid down and leaned her head against the seat, watching the black country sweep by them. After awhile the moon rose suddenly, like a balloon jerked up by a string. All her desperation during the day now appeared incredible. Of course he had been going to come. And now she was not tired any longer, but filled with a deep flowing languor, as if she had given herself over to him completely, letting herself drift in the stream of his being and life, with no struggle at all to go in her own direction.

She had no idea how far they had driven when he stopped the car beside a lighted restaurant and they went in. There was only one other couple in the place and they sat down, opposite each other, at a little white-clothed table beside the windows.

He began to look at the menu while Shireen sat, holding hers in her hands, watching him. After a few moments he glanced across at her.

"I know what it is about you now," she said.

"How's that again?"

"It's charm—just plain and simple charm. Only you have more of it than anyone else."

"Whatever the hell *charm* is."

"*I* know," she said proudly.

"What is it?" he asked, as if he knew she would be disappointed if he did not let her tell him whatever it was she had figured out.

"Charm," she said, carefully and clearly, "is the ability to make someone else think that both of you are pretty wonderful."

Johnny smiled. "That's very nice. Now—what are you going to eat?"

"I'm not hungry."

"You can't live on love. It's never been done yet."

"You order for me, then. I want to eat the same thing you do."

But when the food came she could not eat much. She dabbled and took a few bites while Johnny ate everything on his plate, quickly and efficiently, as if food were only a means to an end and not worth much consideration or notice. Then he leaned back and looked at her, smiling as she tried to force herself to get some of it down. But there

66

was no hardness in his face, no triumphant masculinity, only a warm extending tenderness.

Finally she put her fork on the plate. "I can't, Johnny."

"All right, then. Let's get out."

He was always in a hurry, apparently, to get on to the next thing. But though she usually was, too, she felt none of that impatience while they were together; she wanted every moment prolonged, and could not understand why it was not the same for him. Now she was afraid that he would take her back to the hotel and leave her.

They got into the car. Shireen waited, apprehensively.

"We're not far from Litchfield," he said. "Would you like to drive up? I haven't been there in two years and this'll be my last chance."

She looked at him in surprise. "Oh, I'd love to, Johnny. I'd like to see where you've lived."

He must have been intending this all along. And though she wished he had told her earlier, so that she would have had it to look forward to, she was willing to accept this part of him that seemed to demand suspense and a continuing current of things not resolved until he resolved them. It didn't really matter what he did, or why, if she could just be with him.

It was a big white house that stood on a hilltop and when the car stopped in the driveway that curved round the front, Shireen got out and stood silently a few moments, looking at it. Then Johnny unlocked the door, switched the lights on in the entrance hall, and stood aside. She stepped in softly and tentatively, as if she were going into a museum or a library.

"It's beautiful," she murmured. She did not quite know how impressed she should seem and was a little ashamed to have him realize she was not accustomed to such surroundings.

He stopped to turn up the thermostat, and they went on to the living room. It was bright and gay, with soft painted blue walls and a dark red carpet and flowered patterns in the chairs and draperies. And though it looked expensive it also seemed comfortable and unassuming. Shireen felt instantly that she knew his mother, and was a little afraid of her.

He tossed his cap onto a table and she took her coat off and laid it over a chair. He began walking around, stopping now and again to look at a painting or framed picture on a table. Shireen watched him with wistful yearning.

"You must have been very happy here," she said finally, and felt a little jealous of his childhood, which had obviously been so different from hers.

"I was, I guess. I was never here much, though—after I was about fifteen."

She was standing with her hands in the slit pockets of her dress, her feet spread apart and her head tipped slightly to one side. "So that's the way you've got things figured out, is it, Johnny? Never spend too much time in one place, or with one person—is that it?"

"Maybe, I don't know. Let's not dissect me right now. I want to have a look around. Come along?" He reached out his hand and she took it; they started through the house together.

He showed her the shelves in the study where he had his books, among them a large number on airplanes and flying and almost as many on draftsmanship and architecture. He took out a few at random, ruffled through them and put them back again.

"It must be a lot of satisfaction," he said, "to plan a building and see it go up. For awhile I thought I'd be an architect."

"Why didn't you?"

"It takes too long. You have to sit still too much. Flying's faster." He gave a soft laugh, as if he knew he'd made the best choice.

He turned to glance at her. Their eyes met and suddenly they both seemed caught, staring deep into each other. Shireen tried to escape from him, look away, and found that she could not. His hand reached around to her back and drew her toward him. She resisted only a moment and then they were in each other's arms.

"Oh, Johnny—what if you hadn't come?"

"I almost didn't," he said gently.

"You almost didn't—after I'd come so far?"

"You shouldn't have come at all. I tried to forget you were here and convince myself you'd gone back, like I told you to. But I couldn't do it, after all."

"And now aren't you glad?"

"Glad. What a question." He said: "Come on, let's go upstairs. We may as well be comfortable."

They went into his room and took off their clothes, smiling at each other and without self-consciousness. Johnny was undressed first and he lay down on the bed, his hands behind his head, watching her. Shireen turned, stepped out of her petticoat and faced him. Her eyes had turned dark and her face lapsed into sudden serious intensity, as if she wondered how he would find her; but also as if she had lost Shireen Delaney and came toward him only as a woman, a part of time and every woman who ever lived. She sat beside him on the bed, leaning forward, one hand lifting and moving to touch his hair. He reached out and took hold of her and all at once he grinned.

"Chocolate cake with peppermint frosting—that's you." His hands touched her breasts lightly. "You're all the favors wrapped up in one package."

68

Shireen gave a sudden triumphant ringing laugh and he pulled her down against him.

He walked into the hotel room with her and she closed the door. The time had come finally and there was no longer any way to put it off. She had promised him that she would pack and leave immediately, and though she had begged him and pleaded, he would not stay until she got a plane or a train. He said he had a lot of things to do and this was where they must say good-by.

He was smiling as they stood now and looked at each other, but her face had an expression of somber tragedy.

"Come on," he said, coaxing. "It's not as bad as all that."

"It is for me, Johnny."

She could not imagine what it would be like without him. She had told him that she did not want to go back to Miami. She wanted to stay here and he could come to see her whenever he found the time until he was ordered out. But he refused to let her take any further chance of missing Ed. She knew he meant it and that if she did stay he would not come and would probably refuse to talk to her.

Ed had become so vague in her mind and feelings, she could scarcely remember there was any such person; that she was married to him and had been for many years seemed not to be possible.

"You'll make it back all right," he said, talking to her again as if she were a comparative stranger. "And I've got to shove off now." He glanced at his watch. "I was supposed to meet some people for lunch and I'm half an hour late already."

"Call them from here," she suggested, grabbing any pretext that might keep him even a minute longer.

He shook his head. "They'll wait. They're probably getting very happily drunk. Well—"

"Yes, Johnny?"

"Good-by, then—"

"Not good-by, Johnny! Don't say that!"

He raised his eyebrows. "Hey, there—take it easy. It's been pretty nice, you know. Let's not spoil it now."

Shireen looked away, down at the floor. Why did she always have to behave like such a fool, when everyone else was able to be sensible and calm and accept what could not be altered? But she had a terrifying conviction that when he walked out the door she would cease to exist, as if she had given him her whole life and he would take it with him when he went.

"All right," she whispered. "I won't. But write to me soon, won't you?"

Again he looked vaguely surprised. "No, Shireen—there won't be

69

any letters. I'm not going to write, and I'm never going to see you again."

"But you told me last night in the restaurant that you'd write when you got overseas! You told me you *wanted* to write to me!"

"Things have changed a little since then—remember?"

She narrowed her eyes. "Would you mind telling me just what your game is?"

"No game at all, Shireen. But this is the end of the line—this is where I get off. We don't go any farther. That's all."

Something inside her crashed suddenly and fell apart.

She felt as if he had taken everything which was most essentially and deeply herself, looked at it and held it for a moment, and then slammed it back at her contemptuously.

"But you've got to write to me, Johnny! You've got to! I can't lose you! Promise you'll write to me. Promise—*please!*"

"I can't do it, Shireen."

He was looking at her as if she had become a stranger to him. What had he expected she would do—shrug her shoulders and say something polite and sophisticated? Did he think this was only a minor episode, pleasant and exciting, but something she would forget in a day or two, wanting nothing more of it than a mild tender nostalgia?

"I've never made a bigger mistake in my life," she said slowly, through her teeth.

He watched her a long moment before he answered.

"Don't you understand, Shireen, that if we knew each other another twenty years, we'd never have any more of each other than we've had now? We've had the best of each other, already. I want to remember you the way you are—something that can never be spoiled or changed by anything that happens to either of us. Can't you understand that?"

"I cannot! You talk like a goddamned poetic adolescent! Where did you ever get the idea you knew anything about love? You can't go through life like this, Johnny Keegan!" She saw that he was smiling again—that smile he hid behind, through which no thoughts or feelings could be seen. "I don't know what kind of women you've had before, but if you've been getting away with this then they must have been satisfied with damned little! But I'm not! You can't do this to me! I won't let you!"

"Shireen, for God's sake, slow down a minute, will you? We can't see each other any more and you know it. This whole thing has been crazy from the beginning. We got into something neither one of us had any business letting get out of hand the way it did. But you can't expect it to go on this way."

"I don't care what—"

"Wait a minute! Anyway, I'm not the guy for you whether you're married to Ed or not. I never light any place—I can't. I've got to keep moving. I've loved you—God knows I've loved you, and in a way I'll always love you. You're part of my memories now and something I can never lose. And I'm grateful to you for that. I'm glad I'll have you to think about when I need you. But believe me, Shireen, I know myself. I'm not a guy for a long-term contract. You wouldn't want it if I could give it to you—and I can't."

They stood a moment longer looking at each other, Johnny's eyes soft and tender, pleading with her; while Shireen stared at him with hatred and rage and had to fight herself to keep from slapping him across the face. She felt a savage need to hurt him physically, humiliate him in some way she could see. But she did not do it; she cared too much about what he would think if she ever lost her self-control.

He walked to the door and stood a moment with his back to her and one hand on the knob. Then, all at once he opened it and turned around. She followed him, walking slowly, and stood staring up at him. He was smiling again.

"Well!" she snapped.

"Just memorizing you," he said softly. "I don't want to forget anything."

She continued watching him as if he were a dangerous enemy, and her face had a hard mask of contempt and scorn. After a moment he said: "May I kiss you good-by?"

"What for?"

He looked as if she had, actually, slapped him then, and she felt a swell of power and cruelty.

"Well——" he said finally, and made a bewildered helpless gesture— "Good-by, Shireen. And God bless you."

"Good-by."

She closed the door and locked it and turned around.

I'll never think about him again as long as I live. I was wrong in everything I thought he was, and I deserved what I got.

She walked over and sat down on the bed, picked up the telephone book and began to look for the airport number. Then she would call Peggy and see if there had been any word from Ed.

Chapter 11

Shireen pushed open the back screen door and stood there a moment, stretching. Peggy was out in the hammock talking to another Navy wife, a rather pretty girl named Dolly. She could see the back of the swing move and hear the murmur of their voices, low and confidential. Then all at once Peggy laughed.

Shireen walked out to where they were, Peggy lying in the hammock in her bathing suit, Dolly sitting on the grass with her knees drawn up. They were smoking and drinking cokes and they greeted Shireen, who bent over to take a cigarette from a box and then straightened up, lighting it. All three were tanned, with shiny skins, their hair brushed back from their faces and caught with bows or flowers.

"You're finished earlier than usual, aren't you, Shireen?"

She sank down slowly and sat cross-legged on the grass. "Yes. That's that," she said. And added: "Finally."

"Good," said Peggy. "Want a coke?"

"No, thanks. I just had one."

She was on friendly terms with Peggy again—though Peggy had not known there had been any time when she was not—since she had come back from New York nearly two weeks ago. And Johnny Keegan almost never entered her mind at all. She had him locked away so securely that she could scarcely hear a sound from behind the door where she had put him.

Shireen sat and listened to the two girls as they went on talking and she was thinking, how far away we are from each other and how difficult it is to come close enough to convey anything at all of ourselves. Maybe you could only do it in a book. But even that was some vague approximation, since how were you to know if people read what you had meant to write, or only what they thought you had meant to write?

All Peggy had said was "Good," and they had gone on with their own conversation.

Well, probably there was no way to explain to anyone else on earth how it felt when you finished a book you had been writing for more than four years. Or even what the writing had meant. She couldn't be sure she knew herself.

What had she learned?

That writing is a process of self-knowing where day by day, little by little, painfully and patiently you find out what you have thought and felt and what has happened inside you during the time you've been alive. You bring it up and out and slowly come to know what was only dimly conscious or not conscious at all before. That didn't seem like much to have got from those four years and she felt a kind of deadness and despair.

Dolly spoke to her. "I saw the doctor again this morning."

"What did he say? Are you pregnant?" She pretended to be interested.

"He's pretty sure I am."

"Wonderful," said Shireen politely. "You must be very happy."

"Oh, I am. I hope he's right. I want a baby so much—and we haven't much more time."

"That's what's worrying me," said Peggy.

Shireen listened but all she heard were words. She could only think that these two women were essentially lazy and would rather function as females than do something that made greater demands of them.

"If anything should happen to Bert, I want to at least have his child."

"I'd rather have another husband," said Shireen—and was astonished to hear herself. She had not intended to say that or anything else and the two girls were obviously shocked. They both looked quickly away, across the garden, while Shireen wondered frantically if there wasn't some way to take it back and assure them she had not really meant it.

But she had.

Then she told herself that neither of these girls would ever be subjected to any such temptation as Johnny Keegan and so they could afford to be virtuous. But though it seemed a perfectly reasonable explanation, it was no cure for her own vast guilt. The rest of her life would not be long enough to make up to Ed for what she had done.

The two girls began talking again and finally Shireen's remark seemed to have been lost. The men had not been in since the night she had met Johnny, and that was what they all discussed incessantly.

"One thing about the Navy," said Peggy, "they don't want the guys even to remember they're married."

"That's what's so terrible," Dolly agreed. "They think they can go into the service and lose every other emotion they ever had. But Bill never will, I know that. And I'm not worried about him meeting other women, either. We've been too happy."

"It won't happen to Bert, either. Not if he's away five years."

"Ed would never do that to me."

But as Shireen said it she felt her face burn. It's true, she thought. He never would. If there's one thing I know in the world, it's that. And what does that make me? I'm just as bad as I ever thought

73

I was. But she had never wondered if she would have hated herself so much or felt so guilty, if Johnny had not behaved as he did.

The three girls were quiet a moment, and then Shireen reached for another cigarette.

"When do you suppose you'll ever finish that book you're working on, Shireen?"

Shireen had struck one of the kitchen matches and it made a pale flare in the sunlight; she held it between her thumb and forefinger and looked at Dolly with quick surprise.

"I finished it this afternoon. I told you when I first came out."

Peggy sat up suddenly in the hammock. "What? You *finished* it!"

Shireen lit her cigarette and tossed away the match. "Why, yes. I told you that. Don't you remember?"

Peggy and Dolly looked at each other. "But, Shireen—all you said was that you were through. I thought you meant you were through for the day. Wasn't that what you thought, Peggy?"

"Of course. But my God—how can you be so calm about it? Why don't you—I don't know, but shouldn't you *do* something? You worked on it such a long time."

"Yes, I know. It was pretty long."

"If I'd done all that work I'd at least take a drink, or something."

"I suppose," said Shireen. It puzzled her a little, that she had almost no feeling at all. Even the relief had not come suddenly or unexpectedly. She had simply written the last word of the last chapter of the final draft; that was all there seemed to be to it. "But after all, it isn't sold yet. And maybe it never will be."

Peggy got up. "That's got nothing to do with how you should feel right now. I've watched you peck away on that damned thing for three months and I've wondered and wondered how you could do it. Locking yourself up like that every single day. And that's only three months out of four years. I'm going to mix *all* of us a drink!"

She went into the house. Shireen suddenly felt a small exhilaration, having this fuss made over her, as if what she had done was of some importance. And now she was touched to find that it could mean anything at all to them, for she had never told Peggy what the book was about.

Dolly looked at her curiously. "Whatever made you write a book, Shireen?"

It obviously seemed to Dolly, and to Peggy, too, the strangest possible way for a girl to spend her time. Shireen felt that she knew them well, having known so many girls like them—but she was no part of their experience and would never be able to explain herself to them.

"I just wanted to," she said. "I've always liked to write."

Peggy came back with three highballs on a tray and they each took

74

one. Peggy lifted her glass. "Here's to your good luck and success. And send me a copy when it's published."

"Me, too," said Dolly.

They began to drink. Shireen looked like a kid who has been given a prize in school and doesn't know how to accept it.

"Am I supposed to drink, too?" she asked them.

"Of course!"

She took a little sip.

"You will send us both copies, won't you, Shireen?"

"Oh, please don't talk about that. There may never be any copies."

"Of course there will! No one could work that long and not get something for it. What do you do next? What about that publisher in New York? The one you saw when you were up there."

"Oh. That one."

She had forgotten she had told Peggy she had seen a publisher. "Maybe I'll send it to him. He said he might read it."

She knew, in fact, exactly what she was going to do, but had a superstition about ever discussing her plans. People who talked, she believed, never acted. Simply talked their lives away, persuading themselves that talking was somehow the same as accomplishment. She would never have told Peggy she was writing a book if there had been any way to live in the same house with her and keep her from knowing it.

After awhile Peggy and Dolly decided to go for a drive, but Shireen said she thought she'd stay home and write a letter. She waved good-by to them and went back into the house, sat down at her desk and began to type, referring occasionally to a sheet of note-paper beside her.

Dear Miss Marsh:

I read an article about you three years ago in a magazine and since the article said you can sell anything, I'm writing to ask if you will try to sell something of mine. I have just finished a novel and I'd be very grateful if you could find a publisher for me. It is the story of a woman, primarily, but also of an historical period—Jamaica, between the years 1690-1703. I read 392 books, wrote eight complete drafts, or a total of 12,638 pages, and spent altogether 6,202 hours on the entire project. The novel is now 1,539 pages long. This took me four years and four months. If you would be willing to consider handling it for me, will you please let me know so I can send the manuscript to you? I do hope you will at least look at it—or, if you are not interested, perhaps you can suggest what I might do with it, as I have no idea at all how one gets a book published. If you will wire me your decision, I will pay the cost of the wire. Thank you so very much.

Sincerely—

She picked up a pen and signed her name, addressed the envelope and stuck on an airmail stamp. Then she lit a cigarette and walked out and down to the corner to drop it in the mailbox.

It seemed to her that no one could possibly take an interest in a book written by the person who would compose such a dull statistical letter. Why didn't she have some kind of light and color to her personality?

Well—

She lifted the mailbox top and pushed the letter in, bending a little to see what time it would be collected. The next pickup was 5:27. She glanced at her watch. Just a little less than an hour. It might, if things went right, reach Georgia Marsh's office by tomorrow afternoon.

She turned around and walked slowly back toward the house, thinking: There's nothing more I can do. I've done all I can. If it's accepted, my whole life will change. There *can* be something wonderful ahead of me. Or there may be—and I know it—nothing.

She began to hum softly, without noticing what the song was. She strolled toward the back yard, looking at the flowers as she went; a soft half-welcome sadness came into her quietly. The little garden and small house, the hot heavy beat of the afternoon had the feeling of Southern California and all the early years of her childhood. And back where it was more private the hum changed to a song and she heard the words that had been going through her mind:

> I'm waiting for ships that never come in.
> Watching and waiting in vain . . .

And all at once she heard her mother's voice. "Shireen, please don't sing that song! You mustn't sing it!"

Then she saw herself, tall and thin and about eleven years old, turning around to face her mother, surprised at the sound of desperation there had been in her voice. "Why not? Why shouldn't I sing it? I think it's pretty."

"No, darling. It isn't pretty. It's very sad—it's a song for middle-aged people. I hope you'll never know what it means—"

Shireen stood there now in the hot late afternoon and closed her eyes and put her hands over her face, wishing she had not remembered it, wishing she could escape from everything she remembered, or at least from what she felt about the things she remembered. Nothing ever turned out the way they expected it to—I can't remember one single thing. With her eyes still closed she could picture the house they had lived in during the first several years of her life . . .

Chapter 12

... a six-room bungalow, gray stucco on the top part, round gray stones on the bottom, with a screened-in porch half smothered by the grasp of a purple bougainvillea. It was in Marron, a little town flung out from Los Angeles toward the valley and settled there in the heat and dust amid pungent black-green orange groves.

Inside it was cool on the hottest days, and always seemed dark when you first came in from the brilliant sun. She could see and feel it very clearly still: the mauve-gray mohair Chesterfield and chairs, the Oriental rug her mother had brought from "back East," the chair her father always sat in next to the radio, which she had to get out of when he came home at night and wanted to read the paper. Her own bedroom in back off the kitchen with its white painted wooden furniture, the kitchen table covered with oil cloth in a yellow and white geometric design where she would sit painting or writing or talking to her mother while she cooked.

She remembered the cut-glass dishes filled with olives and celery, her mother's "good" china that came out of the cupboard only on Sunday or when there was company and which seemed almost too valuable and precious to eat from. It was part of another life her father and mother had once had—a time when they had been young and happy and full of hope, when her mother had worn pretty dresses and gone to parties and given parties, and had someone to help her around the house so that she was not always working so hard.

That happy time had ended and, though she could not remember when, it seemed she was herself in some obscure guilty way responsible.

"I'm waiting for ships that never come in.
Watching and waiting in vain—

"Shireen, please don't sing that song! You mustn't sing it!"

"Why not? Why shouldn't I sing it? I think it's pretty."

"No, darling. It isn't pretty. It's very sad—it's a song for middle-aged people. I hope you'll never know what it means—"

As Shireen looked at her mother now, everything she had ever felt about her mother's life and all the things she had been learning without knowing she was learning them, came slowly into focus and

77

she saw it clearly: Nothing has turned out the way she expected it to.

She looked at her mother with infinite love and pity, feeling that she was stronger and abler herself than this quiet gentle helpless-seeming little woman who had almost died at her birth. Suddenly she longed to burst into wild tears of rage and anguish, overwhelmed by her unexpected knowledge that all her mother's life had gone astray and that in her mother's own mind it was already too late to repair the damage.

"Someday," she said, with a sudden passionate longing to be able to give her mother the whole world, "I'll get rich and then you'll have everything you've ever wanted."

Her mother smiled tenderly. "My darling child. When you're nice there's never been anyone sweeter who's ever lived—"

"And when I'm bad," said Shireen hastily, completing a sentence she had heard so many times, "I'm the meanest brat who ever lived."

Mrs. Delaney stroked her daughter's head, smiling. "That's right," she said. "You are. But maybe it's a good thing. *You'll* never give your life up to other people. You'll be something yourself and no one will be able to take away from you what you really are."

"*No* one will!" cried Shireen, and all at once her pity for her mother had turned in and centered upon herself and become fierce defiance. "I'll never be like you!"

"I hope you never are. I want you to have more from life than I've had."

By the time she was eight, Shireen had had her ambitions clearly in mind.

"When I grow up," she bragged to her friends, "I'm going to be a slinky-eyed vamp and lie on a tigerskin rug and have all the men kneeling at my feet." And she would practice looking like a vamp, going around with her eyes half shut until one day her mother asked if her eyes were bothering her.

"Maybe Shireen needs glasses," her father said.

"Oh, Dad, for heaven's sake!" cried Shireen angrily. "You don't understand *anything!*" And she ran off to her room to work on the novel she was writing.

She had written several already: *The Far North, A Girl's Right, The Heart of a Thief,* and one which she chose to call *Blah.* This new one was titled *Spanish Love:*

It was a buitiful moonlight night in old Spain. From behind a curtain the shadow of a young senor and a young senorita dressed in old fash-ioned Spanish clothes could be seen kissing each other. Lissen La Clavel I'll go an make a hit with Carmencita. Fine and bring the *fool* to me I'll get all the information out of her and then do away with her. Carmencita was a young spanish beauty with a lot of money. La Clavel was a spanish spy and vamp. La Clavel beat Carmencita by her way's a mile and that way had won the heart of Ricordo. He had once been Carmencita's love'r but La Clavel had won his heart when Carmencita wasn't wise to it. Now they were planing a wicked kidnaping for Carmencita. Ricordo dearest she said, have you any cigerrete's for the one you are holding in your arms? Ricordo carried her over to a bench and lighted her cig for her. I'll go over now and serenade her. Fine tell her to come to your house and I'll be ready with your men. Ricordo called one of his men come with me I'm goin' over an' serenad carmencita go get a ladder. When he got over there he began playing and singing a love song. Soon carmencita came out on the balcony. Ricordo had often serenaded her before and soon he asked for the ladder and got up on the balcony. Oh bueatiful Carmecita wont you come over to my place. Oh Ricordo you look so handsome tonight I certenly will. Ricordo helped her down and picked her up in his arm's and kissed her then he took her to his house. They went behind a curtain and out jumped La Clavel and Ricordo's men all with gun's in there hand's well now we have carmencita in our hand's said La Clavel laughing. Tomorrow we'll get the information an' then do away with her. They kissed each other and drank to carmencita's wealth witch would soon be there's. The next morning La Clavel got the information and killed Carmencita. Now we have all of her money said Ricordo. Well lets blow it tonight. The End.

Shireen read over what she had written with considerable satisfaction. She read almost nothing but what she wrote herself and vigorously resisted all efforts by her parents to get her to take an interest in books. She smiled as she finished the story.

So they thought she was so innocent, did they? Just a kid. Well, she could probably tell them a thing or two.

That was the way she lived two lives.

In one, someone else was always telling her what to do or not to do; in the other, she had complete freedom. She could be anyone she wanted to be, do whatever she wanted to do, and no one on earth could criticize or tell her it was selfish or bad or unladylike. On paper she had what she wanted most: perfect independence.

But in real life she lived like a prisoner surrounded by blank walls impossible to break down, too high to climb over. The walls were plastered with signs: DO NOT COME IN HERE. YOU CANNOT DO THAT. YOU ARE FORBIDDEN TO DO THIS. YOU HAVE HURT MY FEELINGS. YOU WILL BE PUNISHED. YOU ARE BAD. BE CAREFUL. LOOK OUT. THAT IS DANGEROUS. DON'T DO THAT YOU MIGHT GET HURT. There were hundreds and thousands of rules to be obeyed, and they all seemed to be negative or—just as bad—positive in regard to something she hated or did not want to do.

Even during vacation time she could not be free.

Her family always wanted to go some place—up into the Sierras, to Yosemite or Lake Tahoe or the Grand Canyon. Some place. They never could just stay home and not bother her. And they kept insisting that she go along and she could never seem to make them understand one simple fact: that she wanted to live her own life, not theirs, and that she was not interested in them. There was apparently no way at all of getting that through their heads.

"Mother," she would say in a wheedling voice. "Why can't I stay with the Terrences? Mrs. Terrence says she'd *like* to have me stay with them."

Shireen and her mother were on the little sun porch that Mrs. Delaney used for her sewing and she was basting the hem of a new dress for Shireen which Shireen had designed herself out of bright plaid taffeta. While her mother sewed Shireen sat folding into fan shape an extra piece of the material, trying to seem casual about this suggestion, for she had some notion she might be able to take her mother by surprise this time. Insinuate the idea so subtly that Mrs. Delaney would have agreed before she knew what she was doing. And then, of course, she would never go back on her word. That was the one solid concrete fact on which Shireen could always count. Her mother had never once lied to her, or broken a promise.

Mrs. Delaney gave a snip with the scissors and began to thread another needle, holding it to the light and squinting a little. "You can't do that, Shireen. Mrs. Terrence has all she can handle as it is. You'd be too much trouble for her."

"But I wouldn't, Mother! I know I wouldn't! I wouldn't be any trouble at all! I'm there all the time anyway."

"But Shireen, we *want* you to go with us. It's much nicer for the whole family to take a vacation together."

"It is not! I don't want to go, I tell you. I hate driving around in a car and seeing a lot of places I'm not even interested in!"

"Shireen, you're going and that's all there is to it. Your father wouldn't think of letting you stay here. You know that as well as I do. We'd all be worried out of our minds and wouldn't be able to enjoy the trip."

"But why, for the lova mike? What pleasure am I on a trip as long as I don't want to go? I should think you'd be glad enough to get rid of me for a couple of weeks!" If she was as bad as they said, why should they want her along anyway?

Her mother was stitching the hem now, making neat little x's that did not show on the outside of the skirt. "Shireen, darling, we don't want to get rid of you at all. Now, please, let's not argue about this any more. We can't leave you here and there's no more to be said."

"Yes, there is too. I don't want to go and that's that! I've got a lot of things I want to do! And I don't want to waste time going off on a—"

80

"Shireen, look here, I'm sick of arguing with you about things like this. It happens every single time we want to go somewhere, even if it's only for a Sunday drive. Now, I don't want to hear another word. Your father's been working very hard and he's tired and needs a vacation. There are lots of girls who would be delighted to see the Grand Canyon. It's something you can write about someday—why don't you look at it that way?"

"Who wants to write about the Grand Canyon for pete's sake?"

"Never mind. Don't write about it, then. But you may as well go with a good grace and enjoy it. Life would be much easier for you if you could only learn that."

"But I won't enjoy it! I'll hate it—I'll hate every minute of it! You'll wish you'd left me at home!"

"Shireen, will you please start the iron? I have to press this down."

Shireen got up and plugged in the iron. Then she turned to her mother, glowering, her hands on her hips. "Did you hear what I said?" she demanded.

"Oh, Shireen, stop talking like that. Someday you'll grow up and be able to manage your own affairs, but in the meantime you're living here with us. So try to make it as nice as you can for everyone. Isn't that better, when you think about it? Look at Granny—she goes everywhere she can and sees everything she can. And she's always happy."

"That may be all right for Granny. She hasn't got anything important to do any more. But I have. Oh, Mother, please don't make me go. I don't want to go. I really don't want to go! I won't see any of the kids for two or three weeks!"

"Well, they'll be here when you get back. No, Shireen. You may as well be quiet because I'm not going to change my mind. Now, go practice the piano and stop bothering me." She got up and went to the ironing board, slipped the skirt over it and began carefully pressing the hem.

"I won't bother you any more if you'll just tell me—"

"Shireen!"

Her mother turned and looked at her as sternly as she could for a little woman who had never managed to be very stern about anything. When Mrs. Delaney spanked them, Shireen and Douglas laughed as if they were all playing a game. But Shireen realized nevertheless that her mother was angry and she did not want her to be because then she might not finish her dress and she needed it in time for Marian's party Saturday.

She stared a moment at her mother and then turned around, sulkily. She started to walk out.

But she had not gone far when a sudden unexpected rage burst inside her: I can't stand this life any longer! I'm sick of being bossed

81

around. I won't go! I won't go! I won't go! They *can't* make me do something I don't want to do!

"I won't go!" she shouted. "You can kill me, but you can't make me go!"

Shireen's mother looked at her with sudden surprise and dismay, and then quickly she slapped her across the face, not very hard. Shireen recoiled with horrified amazement. Of all the unfair advantages! Just because I'm their kid they think they own me and can do anything they want with me.

"I don't want to hear you talk that way again, Shireen," said her mother quietly. "Sometimes you're a very naughty girl. Why can't you be as nice as your brother is? Douglas never causes us any trouble at all. And you seem to delight in being as ornery as you can."

"Douglas!" said Shireen bitterly.

For all her life, for hundreds of years, since the beginning of time, this had been the story. *Douglas* is nice and sweet. *Douglas* never causes us any trouble. *Douglas* gets good grades in school.

Why can't *you* be like Douglas?

Since the very first night they had brought him home from the hospital. What a sap *she* had been! Looking forward to having a baby brother. Thinking it was going to be fun! And she had even held him on her lap and thought he was wonderful, but then her mother said: "Give the baby back, Shireen. You might drop him." So he was valuable then, was he? Too valuable to be trusted to her? It would be something terrible if she dropped him—worse than when she threw the kitten down the cellar stairs.

It was too bad she hadn't dropped him. She had tried to get her mother to give him away, but her mother refused. And he had been causing her trouble ever since.

He was so beautiful. Her mother kept saying he was the most beautiful baby anyone had ever seen and everyone else thought so, too. But the worst of it was that he was always so *good*. He never got mad. He was generous and gentle and considerate. All he had to do was smile and everyone loved him. It seemed as if no one could help loving him.

They loved him better than they did her and always had and she knew it. She knew better than to believe them when they said they loved them both equally. They couldn't fool her with that. And most of the time she didn't care because they weren't important to her anyway. She had her own life: all the different lives she wrote about and the life she lived away from home, at school, or when she played with other kids.

Let them have Douglas then! It made no difference to her.

But every once in awhile she got suddenly fed up with hearing about how good he was and why couldn't she be like him. She didn't want to be like him! She wouldn't be like him for anything in the world! They could never make her be like him.

"What do I care about Douglas!" she muttered now. "He can go to hell."

"What's that, Shireen?" asked her mother quickly. "What did you say?"

"Nothing. I was talking to myself."

Shireen started out of the room, feeling a sense of panic because she knew she had committed at least two sins all in one breath.

"Shireen! Turn around and look at me."

Shireen paused. Then slowly she turned and faced her mother. She did not really want her mother to be angry or unhappy, because even if her mother did love Douglas best she was always very good to her. She kept her father from punishing her sometimes when he said she deserved it. And she always saw that Shireen got the things she wanted, if there was any possible way it could be managed, going without herself—or making Douglas go without. Shireen, she would explain to Douglas, must have pretty clothes because she was a girl and he should not mind if he sometimes had fewer things than his sister did. She really loved her mother very much.

But she could not understand how this terrible system of parents and children, authority and submission, had ever come about and knew she would never in her whole life be able to accept it. There was something wrong somewhere, something cockeyed with a world that allowed such things to go on—even though she couldn't quite figure out what it was.

"I said," drawled Shireen, "that he can go to hell."

Her mother shook her head sadly. "Oh, Shireen. Sometimes I wonder what's going to become of you. We've tried so hard to make you behave like a young lady and you simply refuse to be one. I've told you again and again that you must not swear—I will *not* have a daughter of mine swearing. So beginning tonight you are to do the dishes alone for one week."

"One week?" cried Shireen, completely aghast that one injustice was being heaped on another. When would these people ever let her alone? "And you mean Douglas can just go out and play after dinner and *I* have to work?"

"Something must be done to make you learn to live in a family with some consideration for the other members."

I'll be damned! thought Shireen. But she didn't say it out loud. No use having to do dishes for two weeks.

She walked out of the room and through the house.

Once her mother gave a punishment she never changed it and Shireen knew it would be completely useless to try to cajole her out of it. So Douglas could go out and ride his bike and play with the kids every night for a week while she would be inside doing the dishes! And what was more she had to go to the Grand Canyon with them anyway. By God, if this was the way life was going to be she might as well give up right now. Here she was, twelve years old, and she might just as well be two for all the rights she had in this world.

She slammed the screen door, as loud as she dared, and ran across the lawn shouting at the top of her lungs for Marian to come out.

If it wasn't one thing, then it was another. She never had had any peace and quiet. Someone or something was always pulling at her, demanding what she could not or would not give. It seemed to have been that way all her life and she was getting good and tired of it.

But what could she do?

No matter which way she turned, they had her blocked off, helpless, at their mercy.

It seemed as if all she could do was just wait until she got old enough to escape from them—and when she did, she'd see to it that never again for the rest of her life would anyone have the ability to grant or deny, give or take back, ask or refuse. She would have her own life and have it exactly the way she wanted and never let herself be helpless again for as long as she lived.

Chapter 13

"Why don't you divorce Dad?" she asked her mother one day. She was convinced that if she had only her mother to deal with she could handle her all right. It was her father who was the final authority, the one real threat to her independence. "I don't see what you want with him," she continued guilelessly, not quite looking her mother in the face. "You could marry someone with more money and not have to work so hard and we'd all be better off."

Mrs. Delaney merely smiled, as if she did not even take the idea very seriously. "But I love your father, dear."

"Love him! How can you?"

"I couldn't get along without him."

"Habit," said Shireen. "That's all it is. Just habit. I've got love all figured out and there's nothing to it but habit."

Mrs. Delaney shook her head. "I don't know where you get these strange ideas, Shireen."

"I'm old enough to know plenty," Shireen wisely assured her mother. "It's a lot of bunk about kids being so innocent. That's all crap."

"Shireen! Where do you hear such language? You mustn't talk like that."

"Why not?" Holy smoke, something else! "All the kids do. So why shouldn't I? And another thing—what's all this I hear about birth control?"

"What?"

"What's all this I hear about birth control?"

Her mother had told her four years ago, when she was eight, that she was to ask about anything she wanted to know. So far she had answered every question.

"Why," she said now, "I don't think I know what you mean."

"Then you'd better find out. I don't want any more kids around here!"

If she ever had a sister, Shireen had often thought, that would be just too much. A brother was bad enough, but a sister—prettier than she was and smarter—she'd never be able to stand *that*.

She had plenty of problems as it was. But the worst of them were her teachers. She had never had one teacher she did not hate.

She seemed to have been eternally plagued by old and ugly women with strident voices, scowling, dressed in black like crows; hideous

85

dried sapless old women who scolded her, made fun of her, criticized her, hounded her, pestered her.

Teachers.

What did kids need with teachers, anyway? Those watchdogs of the grown-up world with tight distended bellies and a peculiar disgusting smell that Shireen was sure came from something that had died inside them. They were the embodiment of everything female which could be cruel, ugly, threatening, restraining. They marched through her life like a procession of harpies in a nightmare; and their sole purpose on earth seemed to be the coercion and tormenting of Shireen Delaney.

They made her stay after school.

They made her write hundreds of lines on the blackboard at recess and during the noon-hour for whatever mysterious crimes she had committed, infractions of the "rules."

They gave her intelligence tests when they did not give them to any of the other kids and then sent for her mother to say there must be some mistake, that Shireen had such a high I.Q. and such low grades, how would you explain it?

They decided, periodically, that she should be skipped a grade or two, and then she misbehaved again and to punish her they kept her where she was.

They even accused her first, when something went wrong.

Like the day there was a terrible smell in the geography class and Miss Murdock sent for Miss Lawson to confer on the calamity. The two of them stood there in front of the class, their arms folded across their heavy jutting bosoms which seemed to be one thick mass of flesh, undivided like the breasts of ordinary women. And all the kids sat there, delighted that there had been an interruption, trying to suppress their giggles.

"It's dreadful," said Miss Murdock solemnly. "In all my years at Whitman School I've never had such a thing happen."

Miss Lawson shook her head. "It's perfectly terrible. What can it be?"

"I'm afraid," said Miss Murdock, and drew her thin lips tighter together, "that someone has been throwing stink-beans."

"But who would do such a thing as that?"

"Well—I think I have an idea."

And Miss Murdock looked straight at Shireen who was sitting drawing a picture she considered to be her final criticism of modern art. She intended calling it *A Frog's Soul*.

Shireen glanced up from her paper, feeling the eyes of her thirty classmates on her, and looked straight at Miss Murdock, lifting her chin as if she dared her to say what was on her mind.

"Shireen, did you throw those stink-beans?" And the classroom burst into laughter.

Shireen's face got red with sudden shame and confusion but, even worse, the terrible injustice of Miss Murdock. Here she was, innocent for a change, and being accused just the same. But the worst humiliation was that Miss Murdock should accuse *her* of throwing stink-beans before she accused one of the boys.

"Heck, no!" said Shireen, suddenly so angry that she became reckless. "Why should *I* throw stink-beans?"

She glared back at Miss Murdock, determined not to be cowed or beaten in front of her classmates no matter what happened to her later. She could feel the awe spreading through the room, and the envy, too. The crisis turned into a splendid moment of triumph. She wasn't afraid of them no matter what they did to her, and they knew it.

Miss Murdock looked at Miss Lawson and shook her head. "Now," she said sorrowfully, "what can you do with a girl like that?"

The question was too deep for Miss Lawson. She shook her head too. "I don't know. I just don't know. She's a bolshevik."

Shireen, very bored now, slumped down in her seat and went on with her drawing. The kids were looking at her, full of admiration. She had done something for all of them. But that night she asked her father: "Dad, what's a bolshevik?"

Mr. Delaney put down his paper and looked at her. "A bolshevik is someone with no regard for law and order. He's a revolutionary. Why?"

"That's what Miss Lawson says I am."

Her father smiled. "Miss Lawson's more or less right, I'm afraid. Have you done your lessons?"

Shireen scowled. "I'm just going to now."

She ran into her room and closed the door, took out her history book, opened it to the lesson and put her own notebook inside. She picked up a pencil and began to write another chapter of her new novel: *The Carnival Kid*. And while she wrote she listened for their footsteps, in case they should come to see if she was studying.

About that time a pretty young woman who lived a few houses from the Delaneys was going to have a baby. Shireen liked and admired her and used to talk to her sometimes in the afternoons when she came home from school. Her name was Margy and she had light fluffy hair and a glowing skin and she seemed happier than anyone Shireen had ever known. She was always smiling or laughing and Shireen had never heard her complain once about anything at all.

Very slowly, for what seemed like years to Shireen, her belly swelled out in pregnancy. Until finally it seemed the baby must be bigger than Margy, and Shireen was afraid she might burst, she looked so ripe.

87

"Gosh, Margy, aren't you getting tired?" she asked her one day. "Isn't it heavy?"

Margy was walking past their house with a bagful of groceries. She laughed at Shireen's question. "Oh, I'll be glad when it's over, of course. But I feel wonderful. I've never felt so good in my life. I have so much energy I don't know what to do with it—I think I'll clean out the kitchen cupboards so that everything will be nice when I come home from the hospital."

When I come home—

Shireen felt her stomach give a small nervous clench, but did not know why. She smiled and waved at Margy and went to holler for Marian to come and play. Then she forgot all about Margy, for Margy lived in some mysterious world apart from hers and only existed for Shireen when she saw her.

She came home the next night at nine-thirty, after having dinner with one of her friends who lived a few blocks away, and found her mother in bed reading, her eyes red and a handkerchief in her hand. Mr. Delaney was out, at a Masonic meeting, which was how it happened Shireen had not come home earlier.

"Mother! What's the matter?" She had almost never seen her mother cry.

She stopped in the doorway, struck by sudden horror. "Margy—" she said softly.

Her mother began to cry again. "She's dead, Shireen—she died about an hour ago."

"Oh, *Mother!*" Her voice gave a sliding wail.

She fell to her knees beside the bed and covered her face with her hands, sobbing with uncontrollable violence. "I knew she would! I *knew* she would! I've known it all along!" But then after a moment she looked up with terrified imploring eyes. "Mother, she can't be dead! I was talking to her just yesterday afternoon and she was so happy and she looked so pretty. She *can't* be dead now!" Her sobbing became almost hysterical and she felt a rush of some terrible unfixed hatred.

Her mother's hand reached out to stroke the top of her head. "Please, darling, you mustn't cry like that. You're making yourself sick. I know you thought a great deal of Margy. I did, too. And it's a dreadful thing, but you can't help it by acting this way. I felt so sorry for Frank—he came here to tell me, and he looked terrible, like a sick man—"

"Sorry for *him!*" cried Shireen. "He's alive, isn't he? Margy's the one to feel sorry for! She's dead. And it's his fault—he killed her! I hate him! I hope he dies! I hate all men—I wish I could kill them all—"

At that moment Mr. Delaney came in the front door and Shireen heard his footsteps. She looked around and saw her father standing in the doorway, looking in at them bewilderedly, holding his hat in his hand. Instantly her hatred found its focus.

She sprang to her feet just as he opened his mouth as if to ask them what was wrong, and faced him, her fists clenched. *"You!"* she yelled, and turned and ran out of the room through the other door so that she would not have to pass him and into her own room, where she slammed the door and locked it.

She heard the details of Margy's death around the neighborhood the next day when the kids stood in little groups, discussing it. They always knew everything that went on up and down the length of the street, and seemed to know it the way savages pick up a jungle drum-beat. After the baby was born a hemorrhage had started and the doctor tried to stop it but he couldn't so she just kept bleeding and bleeding until the whole mattress was soaked and the blood was dripping through onto the floor. And Frank had been there all the time and she knew she was dying and begged him to save her, screaming that she wanted to live, she was afraid to die, she didn't want to die. And she kept screaming while the blood was running out of her and fighting against it until the last moment when she was finally still.

Shireen did not go to Margy's funeral but her mother did and told Shireen how nice Margy had looked, how peaceful and lovely, and what a beautiful gown she was wearing. And there had been so many flowers, even a sheaf of white orchids in her hands.

"What a stupid waste!" Shireen said bitterly. "Why couldn't she have had that dress while she was alive, instead of those old cotton dresses she was always wearing. And what good do the flowers do her now? Why did Frank have to wait for her to *die* to give her a bouquet of orchids?"

And now Margy was dead when only a few days ago she had been alive and she would always be dead. She was dead for all the rest of eternity.

Shireen had asked her mother, maybe two or three years ago, what eternity was and her mother had tried to tell her: "Make a picture in your mind of the biggest mountain in the world, and imagine that that mountain is made of solid rock. Now, imagine that once every thousand years a little bird comes and pecks a grain of sand from the top of the mountain. When he has carried away the entire mountain —that is the beginning of the morning of the first day of eternity."

Shireen could hear the words still, and feel the chills of horror that had run over her body, pricking up gooseflesh. She heard them, not as they had been spoken in her mother's soft gentle voice, but like thunder crashing down a narrow canyon, echoing and reverberating from one wall to another:

"That is the beginning of the first morning of the first day of eternity."

Sometime after that, though she never remembered when it happened first, she began to struggle with an incubus that came every night after she had gone to bed. During the day she never thought about it. She was so busy and so active that she forgot it had happened and did not remember it would happen again when she lay down in the dark and tried to sleep. Then it came, like some grotesque monster that had been hiding in outer space beyond the world's rim, waiting.

She would lie there, flat on her back and still, thinking how wonderful it would be if she were to grow up to look like Clara Bow and how Marian had told her that afternoon that when she had a certain expression on her face she really did look like Clara Bow. Miss Murdock had had to go to the hospital, they said with a nervous breakdown, and she might be away for weeks and it was all blamed on Shireen's class, the worst that had ever been in Whitman School. Shireen felt pleased and rather proud about Miss Murdock's breakdown and was convinced she was to a large extent personally responsible for it. Miss Murdock had said that she had never had so much trouble in her life as when Shireen was president of the class. Don had promised to get her that bracelet she wanted the next time his uncle got drunk and gave him five dollars. She smiled a little then, remembering how he had come that afternoon to walk home with her from her piano lesson and she had not even spoken to him and he had begged her to tell him what was wrong and finally she had said that he bored her. He was crazy about her and his tame helplessness gave her a great sense of power and cruelty. But she never let him become too discouraged for the next instant she would turn and smile at him and kiss him and then he looked at her like a dog. He kept buying her things, Milky Ways and movie magazines and ten-cent-store compacts, everything she expressed a wish for, and Shireen decided she knew what she wanted to be in life. She would be a gold-digger, like Clara Bow.

But now the rhythm of her thinking would begin to change, split up and jump off on tangents. Something was trying to break in, but for a few seconds each night she would be able to hold it off and keep herself from recognizing what it was.

She tried desperately now to hang onto her train of thought. She had been thinking about how she would be a gold-digger. Gold-diggers had an easy life, all right. Not like Mother's.

No—what was I thinking about?

Gold-diggers.

They got everything they wanted and made men give it to them

90

and all they had to do was be pretty and pretend they liked them whether they did or not.

No! I won't think about it!

When I grow up I'll marry a rich old man and then he'll die and I'll—

Then he'll die . . .

Almost subtly she would let herself think it, just as she had somehow known all along she would sooner or later have to do. As if she answered some fatal lure compelling her in spite of herself.

You die, she would think slowly. For a moment it would be only words, without real meaning or significance.

Then: *You really die.*

It sprang, leaping like a terrible giant that had been miraculously compressed into some small hidden space, and fastened itself upon her. The words repeated themselves over and over in her mind, thundering and crashing, spreading out into illimitable space, through time that never began and will never end. She lay there, her eyes wide open, staring into the dark.

Yes—you die. You die. You really die. You die and then you're dead forever. There can't be such a thing as forever. But there is. Forever. It can't be! But it is. You die. You disappear. You never live again. You *never* live again! You die. You're dead. You're *really* dead.

No!

She gave a sudden tearing gasp and sat up, longing to scream and bring her mother to comfort her, but something kept her quiet. She turned on the light. There. It wasn't true. Of course it wasn't true. She wouldn't really die. She would live forever, somehow. She wouldn't think about it any more. Tomorrow she would play harder than ever and when she got in bed tomorrow night she would be so tired that she would fall asleep the instant she lay down. Then it couldn't scare her! She reached over and turned the light out. It had happened tonight and wouldn't happen again and now she could go to sleep.

Chapter 14

Ed and Shireen sat together on the hotel terrace.

They had been there for an hour or so and now it was five o'clock but still warm and sunny, with a light wind overhead that made the palm trees clack. Shireen watched a bird taking a bath in the swimming pool, fluttering his wings, then dipping swiftly in and out again, like a catalina flying boat that had miscalculated its range.

Ed had come unexpectedly last night and they had talked until very late. This afternoon they had gone swimming and lain in the sand and then come here to be away from Peggy and Bert.

She had shown him the telegrams she had received from Georgia Marsh:

THANKS FOR WRITING ME WILL GLADLY READ YOUR MAN-
USCRIPT AND GIVE MY OPINION ON ITS SALABILITY PLEASE
EXPRESS TO MY OFFICE SINCERELY
    GEORGIA MARSH.

And the other one she sent after the manuscript reached her, saying that she would give it her immediate attention.

Ed was pleased and optimistic, but she had not been able to sleep for more than a week and was convinced that Miss Marsh was going to tell her there was no hope of ever getting such a book published. And there was nothing Ed could say that could overcome her stubborn melancholy. It was all hopeless. It was all a waste. Nothing good would ever happen to her. Life was a progressive series of failures, dwindling away, and whatever began in hope ended with defeat.

Sitting opposite him now she had a maddening sense of detachment, almost as if her mind floated off somewhere in space, beyond her reach.

Ed was watching her. In a moment, she knew, he would say: "You're so beautiful."

And, just when she had finished thinking it, he did say it. She looked at him and smiled, but felt inexplicably annoyed. She couldn't be *that* beautiful, after all, for him to tell her so often. And she did not want any favors from him now anyway; the look of adoration in his eyes was a terrible reproach. Since the moment he arrived she had had an ominous sense of dread, a conviction that she was going to let slip some word or phrase that would tell him about Johnny.

For she had finally committed the crime she had expected all her life to commit—though she had not known what specific form it would take. It was a kind of relief, for at least she did not have to worry any longer or wait, to discover just how worthless she really was. But now she had a tremendous need to tell him, so that he would stop thinking of her as being better than she was, and would know her for what she was. And hate her as she deserved.

But she could not do it. He was going overseas. And that changed him—and her.

He must have thought that she was worrying about her book for now he said to her very softly and gently, reaching over to take her hand, "I'm sure you're going to sell it and make a lot of money, darling."

She looked at him quickly, hoping to find reassurance. But it was not there. He had always told her that, from the first page she had written, and what did he know about it? No more than she did. Or not as much. He said it the way he said so many other things—to let himself off easy was what she thought it really amounted to. But he was trying to be kind and she made another sorrowful little effort to smile.

"Thank you, darling. But I'm afraid it was a pretty silly thing for me to do. Spending all those years that way. Why didn't I just play bridge and gossip and go shopping, like any normal woman?"

"Because you're not a normal woman, Shireen, and you might as well stop thinking of yourself as one."

She glanced at him with surprise, wondering first how he had found that out—and then wondering if perhaps he was right. But that was nonsense. Of course she was normal. What reason or right had she to think there was anything out of the ordinary about her? Everyone thought that about themselves—especially the most ordinary ones.

Now he was frowning a little. "Shireen—there's something I want to say to you."

"Yes?"

She was suddenly scared. Had Peggy taken him aside and told him about Johnny? But Peggy didn't know. Johnny hadn't been a big enough fool to write to him?

"I'll probably be gone a long time, Shireen. And you're sure to meet other men." He was talking slowly and not looking at her but down at the water stain from his glass. "You may fall in love with one of them and if you do—I want you to know that you're perfectly free. I never have thought you're the kind of woman who should spend all her life with one man. And you've spent a lot of it with me already." He took a deep breath and then looked at her.

Shireen was staring at him in amazement and unbelief and guilty shame. His words instantly became one more proof, and this one conclusive, that he was generous and good and she was selfish and bad.

93

She looked away from him and down into the glass the waiter had set before her: It was frosted on the outside and full of ice flakes, and a circle of water spread on the paper napkin beneath it. "That won't ever happen, Ed," she said, still not looking at him. Then she glanced up and met his eyes directly. "You can take my word for that."

You can take my word—which is not worth a good goddamn.

"I could never love anyone but you, Ed."

"I hope not, because I don't know how I'd live without you. But I want you to be happy—you know that, don't you?"

There were tears in her eyes now and she ached with pity and yearning for him. How had she ever let him come to feel he could not depend on her? She put her hand over his and held it tight.

"You must believe me, darling. I know I've done terrible things to you, but I'll never do them again. I'll never lose my temper and say mean things like I used to. Oh, Ed—I love you—with all my heart I love you!"

While she talked to him, the tears running down her face, he watched her eagerly, with that same look of worshipful adoration that sometimes pleased her, sometimes made her impatient, but mostly made her ashamed of herself. And then he smiled.

"It's funny," he said with soft wonderment. "But I guess I never really knew until now that you loved me."

Shireen took his handkerchief and wiped the tears away but they kept coming and finally she gave a rueful little laugh, glancing around at the people sitting nearby. "I suppose no one's much surprised these days to see a woman crying in public."

But then her remorse grew greater and more painful and her throat ached so that she could scarcely talk. "If only I'd been good to you, Ed! If only I'd made you happy!"

"You've made me happy, darling. No matter what happens—I've had these years with you."

"Ed!" she begged him. But far down, though she did not quite know it, she was enjoying herself. This was very dramatic, the right scene for her and Ed to be playing just before he went away. "You're too good to me, Ed! I've been a terrible wife—I've been mean and selfish and everything bad. You should hate me!"

"I could never hate you, Shireen. No matter what you did."

She looked at him for a long moment and in her eyes was something between affection and antagonism. The tears were drying. She shook her head and now she was half smiling. "Oh, Ed. If *only* you weren't so damned noble."

Shireen got up the next morning at five-thirty when Ed did, packed his bag while he was shaving, and went out to make coffee. She felt calm almost to the point of indifference.

94

He came into the kitchen when he was dressed and she handed him a cup of coffee. They stood beside the sink, looking through the window into the little garden, and there didn't seem to be anything more to say.

"Nice morning," Ed said finally. In the other room they could hear Peggy and Bert moving around. A friend would pick the men up in a few minutes.

"Pretty," Shireen agreed. "It's a lot like Southern California, isn't it?" No, she shouldn't have said that. Everything that belonged to both of them was associated with Southern California. "Not really, though, I guess," she added.

"Not much," he said. "Except that it all looks faked."

"Mmm—"

She was thinking about what she would do when he was gone. She would pack her things and sign over the car papers, since they had arranged already to sell it. Then she would call Miss Marsh; if there was any encouragement at all she wanted to go directly to New York, not back home. Peggy would be bawling, of course, and she'd probably have to do something to calm her down.

God, this war. Was there ever a time when it hadn't been going on?

Peggy and Bert came into the kitchen. Peggy's eyes were red from crying and she was still sniffling but apparently trying hard to control herself. Shireen did not even look at her, simply indicated the coffee, and heard the two men exchange greetings.

Ed seemed perfectly calm, but she knew that he was nervous and as anxious as she was to have this last moment over. It was like living in the same house with someone who is sick and has to die but who takes a long time doing it.

She repeated the charm to herself: Everything matters—but nothing matters very much.

Ed set down his coffee cup and went to get his bag and then they walked outside to wait. They wandered together down the front walk, and stood there by the palm tree. After awhile she looked up and met his eyes. They both smiled.

"I hope to God Peggy doesn't make too big a fool of herself," she muttered, glancing around. "I don't feel like playing nursemaid today."

"If she does, be a little patient. Not everyone has your will power."

Shireen looked at him quickly. Had he hoped that she would cry and cling to him. But what would be gained? They'd been through this so often before. And if she let herself behave that way it would only tear them both to pieces. What good could it do?

But maybe if I really cared more I wouldn't wonder what good it can do? She began to feel uneasy.

"Here they are—" A dark red convertible came down the street

95

toward them and in a moment had stopped at the curb. There were two ensigns in it, men Shireen had met before, and suddenly the quiet morning was full of noise and shouts and laughter. Ed threw his bag into the back seat, Bert and Peggy came out, and Shireen looked up at Ed. He bent down and kissed her on the mouth.

"Good luck—"

"I love you," she said.

He climbed into the back seat and sat there in the far corner, smiling at her; his face looked sad and wistful. And Shireen realized, with a sudden terrible sense of having made the last irrevocable mistake, that he was going away with the conviction that she did not honestly love him. Peggy was sobbing and telling Bert she could not let him go.

Silly fool, thought Shireen contemptuously. Why doesn't she get a grip on herself? That's no way to send a man off to war.

The car drove away and the girls stood and waved. The men leaned out, waving back until it had disappeared from sight. Peggy gave a cry like a hurt animal and Shireen glanced at her uneasily, wondering what you did with someone in hysterics.

But, somehow, it was a relief. No matter what, she thought, the end of anything is a relief. In every relationship, even the most valuable, there are certain unpleasant tensions—and the ending of it snaps those taut inner wires.

Peggy gave a sudden alarming moan and covered her face with her hands. "He's gone! He's gone! Oh—I wish I were dead!"

Shireen's impulse was to go into the house and leave her alone. But she grabbed firm hold on herself, warning herself to be patient and a little kind. She put one arm around Peggy's shoulder and, as she made the gesture of friendliness, a great wash of genuine pity was released.

"Peggy—" she spoke to her softly and consolingly now—"try not to cry. You'll only make yourself sick. You've cried enough—it can't do any good now."

"Oh, but Shireen! I love him so!"

"I know. I love Ed, too. But they'll come back—that's what you've got to think about now. You're only making yourself suffer this way."

They walked back into the house, their arms around each other, and Peggy was trying to control herself but the sobs kept breaking through. They went into the kitchen and Shireen poured her another cup of coffee. She looked at the clock while Peggy sat there at the table in her bathrobe, her head in her hands, whimpering. I'll call Georgia Marsh at ten o'clock. She'll probably be in her office by then. But I'd better put the call in now; there's sure to be a delay.

It was about ten-thirty when the operator got the call through and then a woman's voice asked who was calling Miss Marsh. "Miss Delaney," said Shireen nervously. "Miss Shireen Delaney."

Of course Georgia Marsh would not remember her name. All of a sudden she wanted to hang up. This was a damned fool thing for her to be doing. Why hadn't she waited? Miss Marsh would get in touch with her when she had something to tell her. But here she was—rushing things, as usual, and would only find out sooner that she had failed.

"Hello—is that you, Miss Delaney?" It was a different voice now. "Yes—"

"This is Georgia Marsh. You didn't get my letter already? I only mailed it last night."

"No," said Shireen guiltily. "I didn't get it. I know this is very silly of me and now I'm sorry about it but the reason I called is that my husband just went overseas and I've got to decide whether I should go back home or not. I don't want to go home and—"

"Then why don't you come to New York?"

Shireen could not believe what she had heard. Miss Marsh was not telling her to go home and wait and see how things worked out and be patient and not do anything foolish and not bother her any more until she was ready to let her know?

"That's what I want to do. Only I can't afford it."

"You can afford it, all right. You can afford practically anything. You're going to be rich and famous before very long."

"What?" asked Shireen weakly. Miss Marsh must be trying to cheer her up because she had said that her husband had just left.

Georgia's voice answered briskly. It was a low and penetrating voice, fast-paced, with a Boston accent and a well-bred Eastern drawl that recurred rhythmically, looping in and out to stress occasional words. "I said you're going to be rich and famous. I'm seeing Morgan Thayer in the morning and I'm absolutely positive they'll give you a big advance. I've never been so sure of anything in my life. Say—how old are you, anyway?"

"Twenty-six," said Shireen apologetically.

"What? All that work—at your age? I can't believe it. Incredible! Anyway, let me know when you'll arrive and I'll try to get a place for you. New York is simply impossible now, but I may be able to get something at my hotel. How much do you want to spend?"

"Why—I haven't any money. I mean, I have seven hundred dollars and my husband is an ensign and—"

"Never mind. I'll advance you some money. Let me know when you're ready to come—"

"But I'm ready right now. I'm all packed. I'll go get on a train or something or other. It isn't as hard to travel nowadays as everyone says. You can always get a cancellation or—"

97

"Hey, take it easy." Georgia was laughing. "Let me check on the hotel space and I'll send you a wire. Okay?"

"That's very nice of you. You're being very kind and I do appreciate it a great deal."

She felt humble and indebted to think of this busy important woman taking time and trouble to find her a place to live. That seemed almost more amazing than anything else. For New Yorkers, she was sure, were nothing at all like any other people she had ever known. She went into the living room where Peggy was curled up in a chair, still in her robe, holding a wadded wet handkerchief in her hand, staring into space. Shireen looked at her with surprise. She had all but forgotten her existence.

"I'm going to New York," she said. "I may leave tonight—or tomorrow."

Peggy looked at her listlessly. "That's fine," she said, and she began to cry again.

Shireen stood a moment longer, wondering if she should try some more to comfort her, and then decided to leave her alone. They had no interest in each other. They *never* had. Each had been an expedient for the other and now the emergency had ended. Peggy was like most women in the world, Shireen thought—a victim of her own laziness and lack of initiative. And Shireen had never believed there was time enough in one life to worry about any other woman. She had all she could do to take care of herself.

She turned and went into her own room and began to pack the few things she had left out. Peggy no longer existed for her.

Thank God. That was finally over. Just when the moment came that she could not stand it any longer. Just in time, it ended. I'll never have to see her again or listen to her talk about Bert or look at those goddamned wire curlers she puts on her hair. She really does look like hell in the morning.

What a relief it was to have anything done, finished, over with for good. So you could throw it out of your life and forget it and go on to something new. Some of her happiest moments had been spent cleaning out closets or drawers, throwing things away, knowing that whatever the symbolism they had had for her, she was destroying it. Each time she finished with something or someone and knew that she had finished forever, it gave her in some sense the illusion of having been granted a new beginning to life—as new as anything could be once you had been born and started the implacable process of dying.

But now each time she caught herself beginning to hum a little she would stop—as if she had been discovered at a funeral wearing a red satin dress.

PART II

Chapter 15

Shireen got out of the cab, carrying her suitcase, and paid the driver. He took the money and stared at it scornfully.

"What's the matter?" she asked him, suddenly determined not to let him intimidate her. Not just the moment she got to New York. "Isn't that what the meter reads?"

"That's *just* what the meter reads, lady."

She glared at him and then turned around and walked off, looking at the buildings for the address. What the hell was the matter with him, anyway? What was he mad at her about? Oh, probably his wife's sick or he hates his job or he's got a pain somewhere. I won't worry about it. I'll never see him again.

But she wished it hadn't happened so soon. Almost like a bad omen.

Someone bumped into her and she begged his pardon but whoever it was had gone on. The city seemed to be coming at her swiftly from all sides, like train tracks in a motion picture. She wanted to turn and run, as hard and fast as she could go—escape into some dark limitless place where she would never be found again.

She walked into the building. Georgia Marsh's name was on the directory and as she got in the elevator she began reasoning with herself. After all, Los Angeles is a big city. It isn't as if I'd spent my whole life in Marron. What is there about this that's so different? It just goes up—instead of out. And six times as fast, maybe. But nothing else is any different. Except me. The way I feel about it. I'd better get a grip on myself.

She stepped out of the elevator and walked along the hall, found she was going the wrong direction and went back the other way. Her suitcase kept getting heavier, and she leaned sideways with its weight. She came to a door marked in black lettering: GEORGIA MARSH.

She stopped and stood there a moment and finally drew a deep breath.

I won't be scared. I'll just go ahead, one thing at a time. She can't very well bite me. She sounded nice on the phone—and maybe she is. But somewhere or other Shireen was convinced that successful people were never nice. If you were a success you were conscious of it every moment, had no time to spare, and were contemptuous of those who were not successful.

She opened the door and walked in. A girl sitting at a big desk looked up coolly and, Shireen thought, with hostility.

There was a spread of uncurtained windows behind the receptionist which showed the top of a clipped hedge and beyond that the peaks of skyscrapers. The furniture was polished blond wood upholstered in chartreuse, the walls had a thick coating of dark green paint, and several prints, matted on scarlet, decorated the walls in groups of four.

"May I see Miss Marsh, please?" Shireen heard her voice coming from far away.

"Is she expecting you?"

"I'm not sure. I sent a wire but I don't know if she got it. I'm Miss Delaney—Shireen Delaney."

Suddenly the girl smiled. "Why, Miss Delaney! Miss Marsh has been waiting for you all day! She wanted to meet you at the station. She went out, but she'll be back shortly. How did you get here, anyway?"

Everything seemed warm and friendly now, drawing her in, not pushing her away. "I didn't want to trouble Miss Marsh. I know how busy she is, so I thought I'd come on up."

"Won't you sit down? Can I get you something? Would you like a cup of tea?"

"No, thank you. That's very nice of you, but I'll just wait."

She went and sat down on a low broad couch, crossed her legs, and picked up a magazine. The receptionist answered a phone call and as soon as she finished that one, it rang again. Three or four different people came in. The girl at the desk told each one that Miss Marsh had gone for the day. The longer Shireen sat waiting, the more she felt that as soon as Miss Marsh came she must tell her she would not be any trouble to her, and then go away quickly.

But she felt lonely and lost and frightened. She should have gone back home. There was no place for her in this city. How had she ever thought there could be? You needed qualities she had never had to get along here.

But she couldn't go home.

It seemed as if she had been trying, in one way or another, to get away from her family for as long as she could remember. They had driven her to the station the day she left to meet Ed in Miami, and Shireen had felt with nervous impatience their reluctance to have her go so far away from them. Even after she had married Ed, they had lived only a few miles away and she had seen them once a week or so.

"Good-by, honey," her mother had said tremulously, as Shireen kissed her. "Write to us, won't you? We're going to miss you terribly."

"Don't do that," said Shireen, and sounded more cross than she had intended.

Don't miss me, for the love of God. If you miss me I'll still feel bound, I'll still feel guilty, I'll still feel tied to you. Let me go. Let me be free. Let me stop being a child!

She said: "Of course I'll write."

The porter had already taken her bags and Shireen looked anxiously at her watch, wishing the train would leave, feeling the drag of family ties, of childhood and girlhood and the long long time she had been shaking it off. But she knew that her mother would cry when she had gone and that she was only being brave about it now, so as not to make Shireen angry. She felt some unexplained resentment, old and still rankling, as if she were to blame herself for every unhappiness her mother had ever known. If only her mother had not been so brave about everything! What kind of compensation was forbearance and bravery for a lost lifetime? Oh, God, let me get away . . .

The door opened suddenly and a woman came in. "Hasn't Miss Delaney wired *yet?*"

Shireen glanced up quickly, realizing that this must be Georgia Marsh. The receptionist nodded toward her. "Miss Delaney got here half an hour ago."

Georgia spun around abruptly, smiled at Shireen, and then walked toward her, holding out her hand. Shireen got up uncertainly and extended her own. Her immediate impression was that Georgia Marsh was very good-looking and a little frightening in her sharp assurance, her quick positive energy. And then realized that her appearance was mostly an illusion she had created herself. It was her silver-blonde hair, parted in the center and brushed smoothly into a low roll, her careful make-up, her slim straight figure, the clothes she was wearing.

"I've been expecting a wire from you! I told you I wanted to meet you—or did you forget? And I was getting worried because I was afraid they wouldn't hold your room another day. What happened to you?" She talked rapidly and her voice was a little strident, as if it had soaked up some of the sounds of New York after dark.

"I—I thought it would be better not to trouble you."

Georgia laughed. "Trouble me! Don't you know that's what agents are for? Come on—let's go in my office." She turned and spoke to the receptionist. "I won't take any calls for awhile. Any messages while I was gone?"

"Yes, Miss Marsh. A lot of them. I told everyone you'd gone for the day. Mr. Steed called about—"

"I told him I can't handle the damned thing for him. It stinks. Never mind—I'll talk to you later."

She walked ahead into her own office and Shireen followed her. This room was much smaller and seemed a counterpart of Georgia's own personality: bright, intense, exact, with enough litter of magazines, flower petals fallen around the bouquets, books piled on the floor, to indicate that she did not worry too much about each precise detail.

Georgia hung up both their coats and then, still wearing her hat, lighted a cigarette and sat down behind her desk. It was covered with stacks of paper, two telephones, a huge inkwell, three framed photographs, paper weights, a cup and saucer, a cigarette box and two ashtrays. She looked now the way she had in the picture that accompanied the article Shireen had read.

Shireen sat on a couch and, to her relief, Georgia began talking immediately.

"My God, you look like a child! How old did you say you are— twenty-six? You don't look it. And you're even beautiful!" Georgia was probably about thirty-six and she did look it, for the years showed in her eyes, in shrewdness and the absence of illusion and a kind of tolerant humor.

"Do you really think so?" asked Shireen in surprise.

"Of course you are!" Georgia was very brisk in everything she said and, apparently, in doubt about nothing. Shireen could not imagine there was any way she would ever catch up to all this sophistication and worldly knowledge, and felt ashamed of herself to have lived so long and know so little.

"Now," said Georgia. "About your book. I took it to Morgan Thayer—let me see—" She picked up a pair of glasses with heavy black slanted rims and held them a few inches in front of her eyes like a lorgnette, peering through them at her calendar; and Shireen was almost sorry she did not need glasses herself, since Georgia used them so effectively. She flipped the calendar shut. "Yes—yesterday morning. They get readers' reports first and then after they decide to take a book they have to figure out how much to advance. It takes awhile—"

"Oh," said Shireen quickly, "I know it may take a long time. But you don't have to worry about me. I've got a job already."

"Already? I thought you just got here!"

Shireen smiled, very pleased with herself. "I met a man on the train who offered me a job."

"How's that again?"

"His name is John Evans. He had the lower berth and this morning he started talking to me and he asked me first if I wanted to be a model. When I said I didn't he offered me a job talking to his women clients about their problems—he's a divorce lawyer. He says he'll pay me a lot of money. I'm going to have dinner with him tonight and he'll give me more details then."

Georgia had been watching her with a look of growing incredulity. She shook her head. "Look. I don't know what this guy's got in mind, but one thing you can be sure of—it's got nothing to do with talking to his women clients about their problems. Most likely he wants you to pose for pictures that'll be court evidence of adultery. Or he may be some kind of pimp. Whatever his racket is—it's not legitimate."

"It isn't?"

And then she felt like a fool. Of course. Anyone else would have seen that immediately. How could she possibly have thought a man would look for his employees on a train? She really shouldn't be let out alone.

"Of course not," said Georgia. "I never heard of anything more idiotic. You've got to get another picture of yourself from the one you apparently have now. You've become a valuable property—to yourself and a lot of other people—and you simply must *not* do anything to damage that property's value."

"Really?"

"Certainly. Morgan Thayer will take your book—I'm as sure of that as I've ever been of anything. And what's more, they'll give you a good-sized advance. You're big time now. I tried to tell you that on the phone—didn't it get across? You're going to be rich. You're going to be famous!"

Shireen felt dizzy. "I can't make myself believe it."

"I know. They never can. There's no way on earth to prepare yourself for it in advance. When the American people swat you over the head with success—honey, you'll know you've been hit. But I've got an idea you can take it. You'll reel a little, but I think you'll stay on your feet. You know—" Georgia cocked her head, looking carefully at Shireen and narrowing her eyes a little—"I'd give anything in the world to be in your shoes right now. Young and fresh and just coming to New York—about to be a tremendous success."

Shireen suddenly looked at herself with new eyes: Georgia's. And was surprised by what she saw.

Maybe she really was lucky. In a way, she did have the whole world before her; and that might be better than having a lot of it behind. She had lived all her life in the future. She had let days go by her, hundreds of them, maybe thousands, from which she took only a little of what she might have because there was never everything she wanted in any one of them. She had been waiting for something. Now, if Georgia was right, she was going to get it, and it did not seem likely Georgia could ever be wrong. Georgia apparently looked into the future, saw what was there, and told her about it. Shireen always had wanted to believe that there are more things on earth than we can measure with scales and calipers.

Georgia got up from her desk. "Come on—let's go over to the hotel and see what they've got for you."

"Oh, that's awfully nice of you, but I know you're busy and I can go ahead by myself."

"Wouldn't think of it."

She handed Shireen her coat and glanced at herself in a mirror that stood on a shelf top, in among several sea shells, some framed photographs, a graceful white Chinese figure, and a silver gravy boat full of pink roses. They went out the door and down the hall towards the elevator. Georgia had said she would send someone to get Shireen's suitcase. Everything seemed to work by magic when Georgia was around.

"You know," she said to Shireen, as they waited for the elevator, "a lot of people aren't going to like you."

"What? They aren't going to *like* me?" My gosh, all I want is for them to like me. "Why won't they?"

"The gods were too good to you. You've got everything—youth and talent and looks. Destiny's favorite child."

"Really?" said Shireen, and frowned a little. Georgia laughed and they stepped into the elevator.

"But you don't seem to know anything about it yet." She lit a cigarette. "I predict you're a late-blooming flower."

They took a cab to the Cheshire House, where Georgia had lived for years, over on Park Avenue in the Sixties.

It had a quiet dark foyer through which occasionally passed elegant women in black with mink coats and careful make-up, taking a toy poodle out on his leash; well-dressed middle-aged men who looked rather tired and bored; very old ladies whose heads shook a little as they got into the elevator. There was a brass placard beside the revolving door with CHESHIRE HOUSE inscribed on it, and private chauffeurs waited, talking to the doorman. In the evening the assistant manager wore a dinner jacket.

Shireen, who had always felt luxury to be her natural environment—even though she had by some unlucky circumstance been born outside it—was delighted with her two-room suite.

It looked nothing at all like any hotel room she had ever seen before. There was a long foyer when you came in with Chinese prints strung along it and a chest with a big pewter lamp at one end. The living room had pale green walls, a raspberry colored couch, draperies and some chairs with a big pattern of splashed roses and boldly drawn leaves, a fake fireplace, bookcases on either side of the windows, two armchairs to match the couch, and a desk beside one window that extended sideways into the room. The bedroom was dull pink with the wood furniture painted off-white.

Georgia told her to come up to her apartment for dinner at seven and then went back to her office. Shireen began to unpack.

Before she locked her suitcase to send it down to the storage room, she took Johnny's picture out and stood looking at it. It was an enlarged snapshot made with a fast camera so that the details were

106

clear and exact. He had on his uniform but no cap and he was leaning against a white painted brick wall with his hands in his pockets, smiling. The picture was cut sharply into light and shadow where the sun slanted across.

She did not quite know when it was she had begun to let him back into her thoughts, but it had somehow happened, probably when she realized that whether he loved her or not was of no real importance. Someday he would. For where Shireen had once set her foot she was convinced that no grass could ever grow again. If it did, she had not stepped down hard enough, and must go back and tramp over the spot a few more times until it was stamped out for good.

What she wanted she must have.

She remembered one spring day when she was six: The previous fall her teacher had given her a cocoon and she had brought it home and put it carefully on a shelf in the garage. Winter passed and she forgot it, never expected anything more from it at all, though her mother told her that in time a beautiful butterfly would appear.

That morning, when there was a heavy spring rain, she went out to the garage to climb into the car and wait for her father to drive her to school. She pushed the door open and went in. It was dim and quiet there and had the faint gasoline smell she loved. And, in the half dark, her eyes caught a yellow flash and she stood there amazed to see on the shelf over her head a great yellow and black butterfly perched beside the broken cocoon, teetering slowly. For a long moment she watched it and then she turned and ran out, closing the door softly and securely so that it could not escape, and rushed back to the house.

"Mother! Daddy! The butterfly's hatched! It's out in the garage! Oh, come quick and see it!" And the three of them hurried out in great excitement.

Her father picked it up very very carefully and held it on his open palm and then he half knelt beside her. Shireen stood, her head bowed, looking at it with wonder and delight. Carefully she reached out to stroke its wings and, lightly though she did, the butterfly lurched and almost toppled.

"Oh!" she cried, jerking back her hand. "Did I hurt him?"

"No, darling," her mother said. "You didn't hurt him. But you must be very careful. He's very delicate. But *isn't* he beautiful?"

"Where will he go?" asked Shireen. "I want to keep him. *Can* I keep him?"

"Butterflies don't have very long to live, dear," her mother explained. "We can keep him here in the garage, but he'll only live a few days."

"But he might fly away. He might be gone. And I want him! Oh!" she breathed. "He's so pretty!"

"I'll tell you what we'll do, Shireen," her father said. "I'll take him in the house and put a drop of ether on his head. He won't feel it and it won't hurt him, but he'll go to sleep. And then he'll never change. He'll be as beautiful as he is now and you'll always have him. Do you want to do that?"

"Yes," said Shireen. "Please do, Daddy. I want to keep him always. Just like he is now."

So they took him in the house and Shireen's father poured ether on his head and when he was dead he fixed him to a white piece of cardboard with a pin. And Shireen kept him and each time she wanted to look at her butterfly he was there, unchanged, exactly as he had been the morning she had seen him in the garage. He would be that way forever, and she would have him forever.

Now—why couldn't the rest of life be like that?

She slipped Johnny's picture into a pocket of her purse, thinking: I'll ask Georgia tonight if Johnny is in love with me.

Chapter 16

Georgia opened the door wearing beige wool slacks and an emerald green blouse with the sleeves rolled up. A dozen gold bracelets clanked on her right wrist. She had the look of a woman who has been working hard, not troubling to comb her shawl of blonde hair, letting her lipstick wear off to a bright red rim. She had on her glasses, carried a section of the paper in one hand and her gold cigarette holder in the other. The radio was turned up loud.

"Germans are retreating toward El Agheila," she said. "With the British hot on their tails. New crisis developing in the Solomons. Axis subs are taking a beating in the Mediterranean."

They sat down on a couch, Georgia drawing up her legs and clasping her arms around them, listening to the announcer's voice with the same rapt concentration she apparently gave to everything she did.

Shireen looked around the living room and thought it was the handsomest she had ever seen. The walls were dark green and the upholstered furniture dark red, or striped green and white. She had several eighteenth-century pieces and a big black lacquer Chinese screen painted with gold leaf and set with mother-of-pearl. There were a dozen or so oils, some which Shireen could recognize but most of them by modern painters far too esoteric for her ever to have heard of. Filling odd corners and spaces were piles of books, silver dishes and boxes, Chinese figures, crystal vases, shells used to hold cigarettes and one filled with daisies.

It seemed to have been accumulated, not decorated, and showed Georgia's taste and personality in everything she had selected and kept. It gave some satisfying sense of solidity and permanence, as if Georgia had lived this way all her life and did not doubt she would live like this for the rest of it.

"And now," said the voice, "your sponsor has a word for you. Friends—" Georgia reached over and snapped it off and then turned to Shireen.

"All settled?"

"As much as possible for now."

"And you like it?"

"I love it. I only hope I'll be able to afford it."

"You will. If you need money, I'll advance you some. But you'll have plenty yourself before long."

Shireen shook her head. "I can't even imagine what that would be like."

"Someday," she had told her mother before she left for Miami, "I'd like to be so rich I can spend ten thousand dollars in one afternoon and not give it a thought!"

"Oh, Shireen!" Mrs. Delaney had sounded shocked, as if it was blasphemy. "You'd never do anything like that. Why, it would be almost immoral!"

"Immoral! I'm so sick and tired of balancing budgets to get an extra fifty cents so Ed can have three haircuts a month instead of two! Money—I hate it! I hope I get so much someday I can *throw* it away!"

"Nothing in the world like money," Georgia was saying. "I think everyone should have it—and I jack up prices for my authors to get all the traffic will bear. There's no such thing as living a decent life without money."

"That's what I think. Especially for a woman—you're completely helpless without it. Of course you've never had that problem." She remembered that from the article.

Georgia laughed. "No, I suppose I haven't. My mistakes are my own, at least, and I suppose I'm better satisfied with 'em for that reason."

Nothing sounded very serious when Georgia said it. Or, perhaps, it sounded more in proportion.

"My childhood, of course, was a torment to me. Like everybody's. It's ridiculous to think children have any fun. They don't. Or why would the analysts be doing such a business? Anyway, then I went to Vassar and my family thought I had some talent for painting so they sent me to Europe. I could mess around with a paintbrush without embarrassing anyone, especially if I never got good enough to take it seriously. I got to Paris at the end of the twenties and had a perfectly marvelous time, as everyone did in those days. I can't say I like getting older, but at least it was something to be young then—and we were younger than the kids are now. After a few months I got married to John Fleming—he's a broker, makes piles of money—and we skipped all around Europe and over to England and across to North Africa and after about a year we came home. I divorced John, and since I didn't have anything much else to do I got married again, to Dick Lennox. I got my first job in 1933. Dick was working for an advertising agency and by that time I was pretty sick of the nightclub-theater-bridge routine and decided to go to work in advertising myself. After that I got interested in a lot of things—publicity and radio and magazine editing and newspaper work and publishing. Dick and I were divorced in 1936 and a couple of years later I married Jim Donovan. I divorced him last year. And that's about it. I started the agency in 1935. Of course, my family gave me up long ago. In Boston, it's what you don't do that counts—I've always done too many things."

Shireen felt abashed and somewhat saddened by Georgia's quick brisk account of her life. Where have I been? she wondered. What happened to those twenty-six years I'll never get back at all? Everyone in the world has been alive, but me.

But if Georgia's right—if they take my book—if I get rich—

Then she would do everything she wanted to do. She would have everything she wanted to have; and she would catch up with the world all at once.

The maid announced dinner and they sat down at a small table beside the window, covered with silver and crystal and embroidered linen. They began to talk about Shireen's book, and Georgia asked her why she had written a historical novel.

"Well, I had to, after all. I don't know anything about the twentieth century. So I figured it out like this: People like to read about the past because it has no threats for them—since things happened the way they did, how could they have happened any other way? It's nonsense, of course, but I believe most people feel that way, whether they ever stop to think about it or not. Also, there's the business of reader-identification. Readers can identify themselves more easily with a historical character because they don't first have to jump the mental hurdle of wondering if maybe this is some living person they're reading about, someone they could not possibly be. And the more people who can identify with one or several characters in a book, the more people will read it. That was the theory, anyway. We'll see if it was any good or not."

Georgia shook her head. "All that work at your age, and with your looks. You must be desperate as hell about something."

"Desperate? Well—maybe. But I always have thought the only genius that's worth anything is the genius for hard work. And when you haven't got much talent, like me, you have to work that much harder. Anyway, there are two kinds of people in the world: those who have to please others, and those who have to please themselves. A writer has to be able to wait a long time for his applause, if he ever gets it at all, so the main problem is to satisfy your own demands on yourself. Not that they're ever satisfied, of course; but you have to live with that, too."

"Got any ideas for your next one?"

"Next book?" cried Shireen. "I'll never write another book as long as I live. Even the sight of a typewriter gags me. I'm fed up to here."

111

Georgia smiled. "That's just afterpains. One of these days you'll find yourself with book again."

"Not me. Once is enough. If I make some money—then I've got what I wanted from it."

"There are plenty of ways to make money, if that was really all you wanted."

"But there are only two ways to make a lot while you're young: One is to entertain the public; and the other is to cheat it."

"And you couldn't square cheating it with your conscience."

"No—I couldn't figure out a foolproof way." They both laughed. "Of course, I wouldn't have anyway," added Shireen, just in case Georgia had taken her seriously.

"Of course not. Your puritan ancestors would have kicked up hell."

Shireen gave a brush of her hand. "I'm emancipated."

"Are you? I've been trying several more years than you and believe me, a puritan conscience is one thing that lasts. What kind of people do you come from?"

"I suppose about the middle-middle class. I wouldn't know what else to call it. Poor enough to want more than we ever had—but not poor enough to have all the energy ground out of us."

Georgia nodded. "That's the yeast that keeps this country working. You'll write another book someday. You may enjoy taking it easy for a year or two and spending your dough, but there's an old adage that's a pretty true one: Man cannot live by caviar alone."

"I'd like to try. It seems to me I've done nothing all my life but work. Since I was about sixteen, anyway."

"How long have you been married?"

"Seven years," she said, and the words came out a flat monotone. Georgia raised her eyebrows. "I never stuck out anyone that long."

"Well," said Shireen. "After all, I had to."

Now, what in hell am I saying, she thought. She glanced at Georgia quickly. But Georgia's expression had not changed and something in her had already persuaded Shireen that she could trust her with what she was, not what Georgia would wish that she was.

Georgia lit a cigarette. "Maybe love is like cheese—and you shouldn't try to keep it too long."

Shireen laughed delightedly, thinking: That's the way *I* should be about men. I've always taken them too seriously. Johnny, for instance. She wanted to talk to Georgia about Johnny, but decided to wait a little longer.

"Divorce is like murder," said Georgia. "I'm only surprised there isn't more of it. No one's ever proved yet that the human animal is naturally monogamous. I don't think he is. We're trying to force ourselves into a mold we don't belong in, and having plenty of trouble doing it. Love and hate are much too subtly interwoven, and sooner or later in every relationship one feeling or the other gets control. Usually, I'm afraid, it's hate—even though it disguises itself in many ways. But of course this is no news to you, since it was the theme of your book."

"Was it?" asked Shireen. She was glad someone had told her what the theme was, for she had never been quite sure.

"Of course. What else? You show a man and a woman—all right, let's leave out the historical claptrap which is mainly window dressing anyway, and which you said yourself you put in because people like to think they're improving their minds as well as being entertained. Leave that out and what have you? Two people—Janetta Denair and Morgan Dufay—fighting it out to the death. The Battle of the Sexes in technicolor and fancy dress with a tidal wave and an earthquake and a Negro slave uprising, just to keep things from getting dull. From the first day she steps onto the dock at Port Royal and sees him they not only love each other but hate each other, too— and spend the next thirteen years trying to see which is going to destroy the other. That was a pretty tangled web you wove." Georgia lit a cigarette. "You're a very clever girl, Shireen."

"Really?" Georgia, in fact, had convinced her. That was what she had written, all right, though she had never seen it so clearly before.

"Sure. You've tapped the stuff that everyone's got stored up in his unconscious somewhere or other. You didn't plot it in advance, did you? That book never came off the top of your mind—not the people in it, anyway. It's got everything that ever hurt you or made you mad, before you were old enough to have any valid judgments."

"Well, I suppose." She was not too sure what Georgia was talking about now. "But Janetta's completely imaginary, and so's Morgan Dufay and every other character in it for that matter. I hate women like Janetta—and men like Morgan, too. But I've read a lot of Freud and stuff; you begin to think anything can happen. I never actually believed any of it, of course. But the theories are interesting to use in writing because it's so completely fantastic."

"And so completely true."

"Oh, no," protested Shireen. "I don't really think so." She looked at Georgia with a troubled little frown. "Do you?"

"Sure. So do you. You feel it, anyway, and that's what you write out of, so whether you're willing to think it or not doesn't matter. All writers have split personalities, anyway."

As she listened to Georgia talk it had begun to seem to Shireen that she was considerably more interesting than she had ever imagined herself to be before. Perhaps she could someday take her place among people, after all.

"Do you like the title?" she asked Georgia.

"Sounds good enough. Publishers have all kinds of theories about

113

titles. But it's my opinion titles don't make much difference, because if a book sells, pretty soon everyone begins to think it has a hell of a title. After all, who'd ever have thought the Bible would turn out to be such a good title?"

They left the table and Georgia sat down to pour coffee. Shireen took out her lipstick and stood a moment, wondering if now was the time to mention Johnny. She felt as if she had known Georgia many years, not a few hours, and that they were and always would be friends.

She crossed the room and handed Georgia the photograph, and her heart had begun to beat fast and nervously. After a moment Georgia glanced at her.

"He's a hell of a good-looking guy. No wonder you miss him."

Shireen was suddenly confused and embarrassed. "Oh—that isn't Ed. He's a friend—of Ed's and mine. His name's Johnny Keegan. I met him six weeks ago in Miami—at a party Ed and I went to."

"And you're in love with him."

"How did you know that?"

"Good Lord, Shireen. Go ahead—tell me about him."

"Well, it's a funny thing, because I only met him by accident. No, I don't know why I said that. I guess you meet everyone by accident."

She went on talking, shy and hesitant for awhile, but then she began to talk swiftly and eagerly and when at last she had told the whole story it seemed as if some hard waxen object inside her had begun to melt and pour warmly and soothingly around her heart.

"The only thing I regret," she said, "is what it's done to Ed."

"But what has it done to Ed? Since he doesn't know anything about it."

"That doesn't matter, because *I'll* never be able to feel the same way about him again. Our marriage really ended the night I met Johnny."

"No, Shireen. You weren't in love with Ed anyway. Probably you hadn't been for years, or Johnny Keegan would have been just another nice young guy. I don't believe there's any such thing as alienation of affections."

"But he's not just another nice young guy, Georgia. He's different from any other man I've ever known."

"The way you feel about him is different. But that's you as much as it's Johnny. Whatever it is you need in a man, he seems to you to be. That doesn't mean that's what he is, though. There's no reason for you to feel so guilty."

"But you don't know Ed! He loves me! He depends on me! He needs me!"

"Well? Suppose he does love you as much as you think. He's getting something, or he wouldn't. Surely, Shireen, you're not taken

114

in by the idea that love is unselfish? That you just give it away and don't expect anything in return? It's the most selfish emotion there is. You know that when you write—don't you know it when you live?"

"I don't know. I only know I feel terrible about it. But I can't help myself. I thought I'd forgotten about him but I haven't—and I never will. Do you think Johnny's in love with me?"

"I think he probably is. Why shouldn't he be?"

That struck Shireen as a new but pleasant idea. That's right, she thought. Why shouldn't he be? I've spent my whole life, after all, learning to be everything a man wants.

And yet, she had never really believed in herself.

Ed loved her, but she was not sure any other man would. In fact, she didn't believe Ed would, either, if he had good sense.

"I was the one who wanted to marry Ed," she said. "He thought we were too young."

She had been sure that being married would give her a feeling of being a part of the world and that she needed the experience of trying to adjust her personality to someone else's. But not to any member or members of her own family. After all, that was impossible. They never had understood her.

Yet she was the one, as it turned out, who had been disappointed by their marriage. For even though the first week had seemed almost intolerably happy she suddenly found one day that the ecstasy was gone. She was amazed to find that this was like any other day, even if she was married, and she felt cheated and bewildered and then angry. The horrified thought came that perhaps marriage, too, was one more of those things you wait for and plan on and then are disappointed by.

"I married you to be happy!" she had accused him. "And I'd damn well better *be* happy—or I'll leave!"

And now she'd been married to him seven whole years, which seemed like a lifetime. But she did love him. At least, she loved him more often than she hated him, and nothing could be expected to stay the same all the time. She'd learned that much, anyway.

"I never expected it to last this long," she told Georgia. "I thought two or three years, at the most. But I feel guilty about that, too. Something's the matter with me. You know, sometimes I think I don't even really want to be married at all."

"Why not? Marriage hasn't taken anything away from you, has it?"

"That's right. It hasn't. Because I wouldn't let it. But my God, how much time and energy and thought it takes just to keep your head above water. Men are like quicksand—they grab hold of you and suck you down and the first thing you know you've lost yourself. Men don't want a woman to have her own life or being, they want

115

everything to center around them. To make them love you you have to make them dependent on you, and then the first thing you know they're so goddamned dependent you can't get rid of them!"

Georgia laughed, so convincingly she wasn't quite sure if she'd said something clever or not. "They don't mean any harm by it. They're only looking for another mother. A boy's best friend is his mother, you know." She shrugged. "Poor boy."

"But Johnny isn't like that. Maybe that's why I fell in love with him, whatever love is." She frowned and tipped her head to one side. "What is it, anyway? And how do you know if it's love?"

"That's easy. Would you like to wake up in the morning and find him still there?" She switched on the radio. "Let's get another news broadcast."

Shireen glanced at her watch. "And then I'll leave. I think I'll write to Johnny. Do you think I should?"

"Why not? I'm sure he's expecting you to."

Chapter 17

By the time she had been in New York three weeks Shireen was convinced she had become a New Yorker. She loved the crowds, the sense of violent explosive life, the feeling of complete anonymity, which was to her the equivalent of having been given a new life and new personality.

No one knows you here, the city seemed to say. No one knows who you are or where you came from. No one knows that you're afraid of so many things or that you don't know as much as you think you should. They don't know about your mother and father and Douglas and Marron and Ed and all the things you've wanted and the years you spent alone.

And, if they did know, they wouldn't care.

"This is the real thing at last," she said to Georgia. "I used to think it was San Francisco, but now I know that was only an infatuation."

Like a girl in love with a man she thought nothing else mattered, that here was the answer to everything, that this was what she wanted and had waited for all her life and that now she would be happy.

"You could drop dead in the streets," she told Georgia, "and they'd only walk around you."

Georgia laughed. "Does that bother you?"

"Bother me? I think it's wonderful! For the first time in my life I have a feeling of freedom! No one cares what I do!"

Perhaps that was what she had been trying to escape: the burden of having her smallest activity assume tremendous importance for someone else. So that she was never free to be herself, without the risk of hurting or giving offense.

Now she could forget the years she had spent writing and stop feeling bitter about them. She became engrossed with the new things she was seeing and the people she was meeting. Every new day was a brand new adventure. As if she had walked through a door into a magic room where she would find everything she could ever have dreamed of wanting.

Each afternoon, around four-thirty, she went to see Georgia.

Her office was a kind of crossroads, always full of people coming and going, telephones ringing, afternoon tea and cocktails; and Georgia, running back and forth, talking to everyone, grabbing telephones, dictating letters, kissing people hello and good-by. Shireen felt herself very lucky to have this exciting place she could come to and always be welcome.

Georgia kept her informed of the progress that was being made at Morgan Thayer. They had sent the book out to their first reader and the report was enthusiastic. She was not supposed to know that, but had been told at lunch by one of the editors who had sworn her to secrecy. Other readers' reports began to come in. And they were all enthusiastic.

"I talked to Phil Thayer today," Georgia told her one afternoon, when they had gone into her private office.

Shireen had found that one reason Georgia worked fifteen hours a day was that a great deal of the time she was not doing anything Shireen would have considered to be work at all. She was having lunch for three hours, or cocktails for two, or gossiping over the telephone for half an hour at a time, or sitting at her desk, as she was now, doodling on a telephone pad and just talking.

Or maybe this *was* work.

Shireen began to wonder what kind of damn fool she had been, shutting herself up like some dusty old scholar, poring over hundreds of books, taking notes and indexing them, writing and rewriting her manuscript. A funny way for a girl her age to have spent so many years. It made her despise herself when she contrasted it with Georgia's life: incessantly busy and full of excitement. There was a kind of orderly chaos she seemed to create around herself, full of people and her dealings with them.

Shireen sat there now, one foot tucked under her, drinking a cup of tea and smoking a cigarette, while Georgia told her what Philip Thayer had said:

"What about the Delaney manuscript? I asked him. Have you seen it yet? And he said: Seen it? What in the hell do you think I am? Don't you know I'm a busy man? Of course I haven't seen it! Well, then, what do you hear about it, I asked him. You've certainly heard about it by now. And don't try to kid me because I know everyone including the elevator boys have read it. Yah, yah, he said. I've heard about it. I hear it's pretty good. Come on, now, Phil, I told him. You know you've heard more than that. And it's getting close to Christmas. Make up your mind. Give the kid a contract for Christmas. Don't try to make a soft-hearted old man out of me, Georgia, he says. *You* know I'm the worst bastard in the business."

"Is he?" asked Shireen anxiously.

"He likes to think so—and I humor 'im. Anyway, I'm sure we'll get the word before long."

"I wish we would. This makes me nervous. All those years—I'd like to know what's going to come of them, if anything."

118

She got a letter from Ed, finally, and he was on his way to the Pacific. The code they had worked out told her that. He wrote that he loved and adored her, thought of her all the time, and missed her more than he could have believed possible. So far, he said, he had not received any letters from her—though she had written him one every day.

But that night she could not fall asleep and began to have terrible fears of what might happen to him. A sudden image streaked through her mind, made up of odd remembered bits from motion pictures: his ship being hit, then beginning to sink very quickly and a terrible pandemonium breaking out everywhere—men locked down in the hold, water pouring in, men hurt, and a sudden gigantic view of Ed leaping into water aflame with burning oil, shrieking as he began to burn, struggling madly against the water and flames and a suction beginning as the ship went down.

No!

She gave a swift brush of her hand at the air, to sweep out the picture, and turned over suddenly. I won't think about it. I'll think about all the nice things we did and the times we were happy together. He'll come back to me. He's got to. I need him. I need him much more than I ever knew.

But she was dimly and uncomfortably aware of some craftiness in letting herself feel that the worst punishment the gods could give would be to take Ed from her. Was she trying to bribe them—using Ed as a sacrifice for her crimes, whatever they had been, and they must have been many?

But it couldn't be that. For it was true that losing Ed would be the worst thing that could happen to her. With all the subterranean hatred and jealousy she had of him, a great part of her life and, in some sense, her very self belonged to Ed Farrell. They had lived together so long and shared so much. And, after all, it was the small multiplied moments of a lifetime that counted. The way their personalities had flowed around each other, like melted wax, fitting into a form until now it was difficult to tell where she began and ended, or where he began or ended.

And yet, when Johnny had told her he loved her there had not seemed to be much left of what she had once felt for Ed. She would never have admitted to anyone, even herself, before that night, that there actually was so little left.

I wonder what it was that happened to us? What caused it and where it began?

But it seemed useless to try to discover the day or hour or even the first word or act that had begun to break the image of their marriage that she had once had. He might have it still but she didn't know that, either. She did not actually know much about him at all,

119

after so many years together. And that was strange in itself, wasn't it? Or were all couples like that—locked away from each other? Though certainly she could not be wrong in remembering that at first there had been at least an illusion of togetherness.

But, of course, nothing happens to you all at once and I suppose that's how it can happen at all.

If she had met Johnny in peacetime, it would have been different. They would never have fallen in love so quickly, for one thing, because you take the time you have. And during a war you don't take as long to fall in love, because time is so short.

Again she remembered, with a soft stealing sweetness, what he had said to her that night as they stood on the beach: "You really are a beautiful girl, aren't you? Everything about you. The way you walk, the way you talk—the way you laugh."

No matter what happens to me for the rest of my life, or if nothing ever happens at all, I've had that much at least. A man I loved said those words to me.

A couple of days before Christmas Shireen came into the office at her usual time. She had had lunch with a woman Georgia had introduced her to, the program director of some radio station, had a dress fitted and a manicure and then gone into some of the stores to get the feeling of Christmas. Georgia was going home, to Boston. And she wondered what she would do on Christmas Day.

I'll simply regard it as the twenty-fifth of December, she decided. Just like any other day.

She said hello to the secretary and saw that the office, for once, was empty. Marie picked up the phone. "Miss Marsh has been trying to get you ever since eleven. I think she's talking to Hollywood right now, but she wanted me to let her know the moment you came in."

Shireen had a feeling of sudden panic, got a little sick in her stomach and went over to sit down: She's heard from him and he's not going to take it. I knew this would happen. I knew it was too good to be true.

I'll go away. I can't stand listening to her tell me.

She made half a move to rise and at that moment Georgia threw the door open. "Shireen! I've been trying to get you all day!" She waved a sheaf of papers she held in one hand. "It's here—your contract!"

Shireen felt almost too weak to speak. "Is it?" Her voice sounded high and light and far away.

"Come on in here." Georgia disappeared and Shireen got up and followed her.

"Is it a good one?" Shireen's face was white.

"Of course!" said Georgia briskly. She was standing with her glasses

120

on now, ruffling through the pages and frowning a little. "I'm going to make them change a few things. But I've already talked to Burton and he's willing to. They're offering you a ten thousand dollar advance!"

"Ten thousand?" Shireen frowned. "Is that all?"

Georgia took off her glasses and stared at her in astonishment; all at once she laughed. "Is that *all?* Look, sweetie, that's more than plenty of best-selling authors get. They have to be sure of selling at least forty thousand copies to offer you that much in advance."

"Only forty thousand?"

"Forty thousand, for God's sake, is a hell of a lot of copies. I know they'll sell much more, but that much they've got to be *sure* of." Georgia went and sat behind her desk, held her glasses balanced in her fingers and leaned forward on her elbows, smiling. "You're in. All they've got to do now is highjack some paper. But one reason I picked them is that they used a lot of paper in 1942 and that's what the present quota's based on. And so—how do you feel now?"

"Why—I don't exactly know. I guess I feel relieved."

"Only relieved?" Georgia sounded disappointed. "Aren't you delirious?"

"Not yet," said Shireen evasively. "The contract isn't even signed. They might change their minds. Something might happen. I don't know what."

Georgia shook her head. "If you could only enjoy your good fortune, Shireen."

"I will. When the time comes."

"I hope so. I sure hope so. But I wonder. This is a phenomenal thing, but you don't even seem to know it."

"Oh, I know it, I guess. Georgia, I want you to tell them one thing: I won't stand for a book jacket with a woman in a low-cut dress stepping out of a coach with four men leering at her."

"Okay. I'll put a clause in the contract: no exposed mammaries. Though this is an age that makes a cult of the female breast, you know. Compensation, no doubt, since most women have given up nursing babies. There's damned little satisfaction, I guess, in a bottle with a rubber nipple. Well, what are you doing on Christmas?"

"I don't know. I got a letter today from an old friend of Ed's and mine—Mike Callahan. He saw Ed and Ed told him where I was and he says he might get to New York over the holidays. It'd be funny, seeing Mike. Here in New York."

"Why?"

"I guess because I've never seen him any place but in Los Angeles. I always have the feeling that if anything at all out of the ordinary happens, it's some kind of miracle."

"That's only because you're convinced nothing will ever happen.

It's too bad, Shireen, because you've got everything to make you happy. And you're not. I wonder why?"

"It's only that I know I don't deserve to be."

"But how can you even think that? A nice girl like you. A really nice girl like you."

All at once Shireen laughed. "But I'm not. I'm not nice at all. I don't really care about anything on earth but myself. And the worst of it is—the only reason I'm even sorry about that is because I know someday I'll have to suffer for it."

Chapter 18

Shireen was in the bathtub, singing with the phonograph and enjoying the sound of her voice reverberating from the tiled walls. She rested in the water, closing her eyes, and had a picture of herself standing in front of a band, wearing a white chiffon gown with a sari over her black hair, holding her hands delicately with the palms up, her eyebrows raised slightly in an expression of subtle pain, singing to an entranced audience of dancers who had gathered around and stopped their dancing to listen to her.

Suddenly she laughed.

You goddamned fool, she told herself. Can't even carry a tune. And the hell with daydreams anyway—that's how life gets away from you. A daydream's good for nothing unless you can convert it into cash. And it looks like I have. Well, I always knew I would.

Didn't I?

She got out of the tub, made up her face and put on a new black dress with long sleeves and a deep scalloped neckline. It had cost her three hundred and fifty dollars and was by far the most expensive dress she had ever owned. Mike was going to be amazed when he saw her.

When she was done she struck a pose and looked at herself in the full-length mirror inside the closet door. She smiled. You look beautiful. And you are beautiful. Maybe no one else is as beautiful as you are. Then she turned away—and instantly forgot what she had been telling herself. The only mirror that counts anyway, she thought, is the look in a man's eyes. That expression, something between longing and lust, showing itself unexpectedly, appearing when she had not calculated to evoke it, seemed the most valuable gift she could ever receive.

And what happens when it's not there any more? When you realize someday that maybe you haven't seen it at all in two or three years?

Oh, but that's a long way off. I won't worry about it.

She had some deep-hidden conviction that passing years would not alter her as they did other women, some belief that if she wanted to enough, she could stay young and beautiful and desirable all her life. Or maybe it was best to die young and never know what it was like to lose that. Except that she did not believe she could actually die, either.

About seven-thirty the doorbell rang and Shireen rushed to answer it. Mike was standing there in his Marine Corps uniform, grinning down at her from his six feet four inches, and they flung their arms around each other. He held her hard against him for a moment and then quickly let her go, keeping hold of her hands, and stood back and looked at her.

Still grinning, he shook his head and Shireen knew that he meant she was almost too pretty to look at. She gave him a little pat on the chin and was suddenly convinced that Mike Callahan, of whom she had scarcely thought at all for many years, was the one man in the world she had most wanted to see. She had an intensified feeling of their long friendship and the companionableness there had always been between them. She was convinced, too, that someway or other Mike was in love with her and that that was why he had never married.

"My God, Shireen! What a joint you've got here! You must really be in the chips."

They walked down the foyer arm in arm, and Shireen gave a sweep of her hand as they came into the living room, and a little mock curtsy. "Like it?" she asked him, and stood with her hands clasped behind her, looking up at him.

"Like it? It's beautiful—and so are you. I've never seen you looking so pretty. I mean it. God, but I'm glad to be here! Nobody knows how the hell it happened—we figure the navigator got things fouled up. One thing we know for sure: they didn't do it just to be nice."

Shireen shook her head slowly, smiling at him, but tenderly now. "Oh, Mike. I'm so happy to see you again." And then all at once she remembered her duties as a wife. "Tell me about Ed. You say you saw him in Shreveport?"

Mike sat down, after lighting her cigarette for her, and Shireen sat across from him on the couch.

Now this, she thought, as she watched him and listened to him talk about Ed, is the kind of man I like. Big and blond and good-looking, without a worry in the world. Being with Mike had always made her feel that there was nothing to fret about and no reason to fight. She had never felt anything in him which seemed to threaten her. He had none of Ed's pleading need for love, which demanded so much from her—and none of Johnny's sensitive perceptiveness or delicate balancing which kept her continuously alert.

He was one part, at least, of what she needed and wanted a man to be—and perhaps before she had everything she wanted she would have to take several men and make a collage of them, pasting together bits and pieces as if she were cutting up magazines and forming a pattern.

There was a naïve boyish enthusiasm in the way he expressed himself, the kind of smile he had, the sound of his laughter, even the

124

open admiration in his eyes when he looked at her. And with it went a sort of embarrassment, like a kid who is still a little shy around girls.

He's like a Newfoundland pup, she thought. With sex appeal.

He told her about how he had heard that Ed's ship was in Shreveport and how much trouble he had had finding him. Everything Mike did turned out to be an adventure, or else he made it into one later when he was telling it. He told her how he and Ed and four other men had sat up all night drinking and singing Navy songs, gone rioting through the streets, fought with some dog-faces, and finally got back to the ship at seven in the morning.

"So far," he concluded, "this has been one hell of a good war."

"Oh, Mike! You mustn't talk that way! Think of all the terrible things that are happening to people!"

"They're happening whether I enjoy life or not. The war wouldn't end any quicker if I took to crying in my beer, would it? You civilians take care of the gloom department."

Shireen sighed and felt instantly guilty. Of course Mike should enjoy life—while he could. He knew as well as anyone else that he might be hurt or killed. "Yes," she said. "You're right. Every time I find myself beginning to feel happy I suddenly realize I'm doing something wrong."

Mike laughed, his happy hearty laugh that never needed much encouragement. "You always have been a prohibitionist at heart, Shireen."

"What? Me?"

Shireen was shocked by this description of herself. Was it possible he didn't know the kind of woman she was? Well, of course, how could he? He had only seen her as Ed's adoring sweetheart and devoted wife. Small enough part of her character, and put on from time to time like a particular costume, anyway. But it was the only one he had ever seen her wear. Funny, she thought, how we can know each other for years and never know anything essential at all.

"Never mind," he said, as she stared at him in surprise, her gray-blue eyes wide and pure as a white kitten's. "You're so goddamned pretty it doesn't make any difference."

He got up and crossed the room and touched her cheek. Then he took her hand and held it and Shireen enjoyed the feeling of his firm palm, his big fingers, the warmth and safeness she felt come from him. She sat and looked up at him for a long moment. Then she said:

"I like big men. I feel so much more comfortable with a big man. That must be my megalomania. Big cities, big mountains, big men. If anything's big enough—I like it." There was a touch of bragging in her voice, as if she were telling him something quite fascinating about herself.

"You mean to say you actually *like* this town?"

"New York?" She laughed and the sound seemed to ripple up from the energy inside her, still lively and free. "I love it!" She went to the window. "Just look at it, Mike. Isn't it beautiful? It's so beautiful it's hard to believe it can be real."

He stood beside her looking out for a moment and then he shrugged. "Nope. It's too big."

Shireen threw back her head and laughed again, triumphantly. "It couldn't be too big!"

He looked at her for a moment, standing with his hands in his pockets. Then he seemed to remember something.

"Come on. Let's go somewhere. Some of the guys are meeting at the Commodore. Suppose we look in for awhile."

She ran into the bedroom and came out with a dark mink stole around her shoulders that had a bunch of purple violets pinned to it. Georgia had told her so often to get whatever she wanted that a few days earlier she had bought the stole. But of course she had not really bought whatever she wanted, since that would have cost about a hundred thousand dollars.

The bar at the Commodore was crowded with men and girls, most of the men in Navy uniform, and the whole room had a flickering excitement that lit it like a summer lightning storm. Shireen was introduced to Mike's friends and sat at the table, listening to them talk and smiling, conscious of some sense of fulfillment at being the only girl surrounded by masculinity.

If there were no other women on earth, she thought—then I'd be really happy.

The men had been drinking rapidly, talking about where they would find women for this unexpected leave, telling Mike what a lucky bastard he was and laughing noisily when he assured them that Shireen was his best friend's wife, going through their address books and occasionally excusing themselves to make a call. They were good-naturedly mad at the Marine Corps for pulling this on them without proper notification.

Now and then they talked about the war.

"Well, anyway," one of them said, "I'm going to be nice to *my* boys when we get out there."

"What!"

"What in the hell are you talking about, Bill? You must be out of your bloody mind! My God, where do you get those ideas?"

"That's a'right, that's a'right. It happens now and then just the same. The fighting gets tough and you've got a bullet in your neck and who's ever going to know if a Jap put it there or not?"

"You sound like a goddamn boot!"

"Listen to 'im. For cris'sake."

126

"Hell, Bill, you make me sick talking like a goddamn fool that way."

"All the same, *I'm* going to be nice to my boys."

"You can't bribe your men to like you. Hey—how about that?"

And they all glanced up as a blonde walked by, holding her head haughtily, her breasts high and pointed, weaving her hips. One of the men made a quick movement as if to get up and then her escort passed them, glared at him, and they all laughed.

"Let's go through that book again. What about that Flatbush number you've got there somewhere? This is no time to count cab fare. Lemme see—"

The talk went on, and after they had been there about an hour Mike turned to Shireen. "Let's shove off." They got up and said good-by to the men. "No cracks," Mike warned as they started to walk away. The men grinned instead.

"How about some food? Where would you like to go?"

"Let's find one of those restaurants you hear about with checkered tablecloths and candlelight and soft music."

"I thought they only had them in Charles Boyer pictures. But we can try. Where shall we look?"

"Let's ask a cab driver. They're supposed to know everything. At least that's the superstition. Maybe it's true."

Mike talked to a driver who said he'd take them to some such place and then he climbed in and sat down beside Shireen; she linked her arm through his and he took her gloved hand and held it. They looked at each other, smiling, highly conscious of being healthy and happy and young and more or less in love with each other and living a quick moment in time when they passed and briefly brushed lives.

It wouldn't ever happen again. It never would have happened at all without a war. But it was Christmas Eve in a city strange to them both, they were together and free of whatever ties they had wrapped around themselves, and this was a moment they both knew was not important but which suddenly seemed to be.

The restaurant turned out to be crowded and noisy, the lights glared, and their table was up a flight of stairs and out alone on a curve in the balcony, with a chandelier not three feet away. Mike quickly ordered a daiquiri for Shireen and another double bourbon for himself.

"Like having dinner on the runway of a burlesque," he said.

And that reminded Shireen of the time she and Mike and Ed had gone to a burlesque in Los Angeles and one of the girls wore nothing but a tremendous white gardenia. Shireen gave a little scream of laughter. "And you said: 'Guess someone sent her a corsage and she thought she had to wear it.' Remember?"

They began to exchange memories, and everything they said struck

127

them as hilariously funny, even funnier than when it had happened, as if they had both discovered for the first time that it was true what their parents had said: college was the best time of your life and later on you would appreciate it. Mike had another double bourbon before the waiter began to serve dinner.

"You should have gone into the Navy," Shireen said, as he finished the second one in two gulps. "There your talents would really have been appreciated."

"Shireen, please, I'd like you to keep in mind that the Navy is only nine-tenths of the Marine Corps."

"Oh, I'll keep it in mind, Mike. Don't worry about me."

"Don't ever forget that the Navy is only—or did I say that?"

"Mike, you're drunk."

"Shireen, please. Don't you know you never see a drunk Marine?"

"I know. Y'look the other way." She glanced over her shoulder. Mike gave a delighted slap at his thigh, as if it was the most comical routine he had seen anywhere. "You're without doubt the happiest guy I've ever known."

"You're the prettiest girl I've ever known and I wish to God you were married to anyone but Ed—"

A waiter going down the stairs behind them dropped his tray at that moment and the dishes made a terrible crash. Shireen jumped and Mike leaned over the banister, grinning and shaking his finger.

"Nice quiet place, just like you said. Better have another bourbon."

"But here's the food."

"Food should not interfere with drinking, Shireen. Have another daiquiri. I always have wondered what you'd be like—"

"Oh, no, you don't."

Mike pretended to leer and bare his teeth. They began to eat and went on talking, comfortable together and completely relaxed. What they said was of no consequence. The pleasurable thing was to be together, knowing where they stood with each other, feeling no need to prove themselves. Mike wanted to know everything that had been happening to her and seemed even more pleased about it than she was.

"And when Ed comes back and you've got a million bucks and are a famous woman—that won't make any difference between you, will it?" His eyes narrowed a little.

As she answered she looked at him directly, her face and eyes perfectly clear, like a magician showing the audience he has nothing at all up his sleeves. "Of course not. We've discussed all that. Ed wouldn't be silly enough to let it bother him if I happen to make some money."

"And how about you?"

128

Shireen went on eating. "It certainly won't bother me. Don't worry about it, Mike."

"I want you two to be happy. I've been in on this thing from the beginning. I'm the guy who introduced you—remember?"

"Certainly I remember." Neither of them was laughing now and Shireen felt uneasy. "You know how much I love Ed—"

A waiter rushing out of the kitchen behind Mike collided with one going in, and both trays crashed to the floor. The captain dashed over, picked up a salt shaker and began sprinkling it furiously over both waiters.

"The whole world's crazy, that's obvious," said Shireen, and Mike ordered another double bourbon.

"Just something to quiet my nerves," he explained.

"Really, Mike, I don't care how much you drink."

"Thank God. I hate a reforming woman."

"I won't reform you—I won't have time."

"Would you if you did?" He looked at her with a kind of contemplative glitter.

"It's hard to tell. I like you the way you are—about as well as any man I've ever known." And I actually mean it, she thought, faintly surprised.

Mike watched her a moment longer and then gave a shake of his head, as if he were under a cold shower. "God." He finished his drink quickly.

About ten o'clock they left and crossed over to stroll along Fifth Avenue. Shireen kept stopping to look in the windows, pointing out evening gowns and diamond necklaces and silver mink coats to Mike, who assumed the expression of a bored but patient and condescending male forcing himself to bear with the vagaries of the female. They stopped in front of a drugstore window to laugh at the cigarette ad which showed a girl with her teeth bared and her breasts uncovered and the slogan: Plain or Tipped, just beneath them.

They got into the moiling crowds on Broadway, moving along almost as slowly and imperturbably as a glacier. Shireen hung onto Mike's arm, feeling some deep joy at being one small part of this great noisy city. They stopped and had their pictures taken, leaning their heads together in the tiny booth, laughing at each other in the mirror. Before a shooting gallery Shireen tugged at his sleeve.

"Oh, Mike—shoot at the targets. Please. You must be a wonderful shot."

He started to go on by. "That's all I've been doing for six months."

"Please, Mike. Please do it for me. I want to see how good you are."

And she stood there and smiled proudly and patted him on the shoulder while he hit one bull's-eye after another. She picked out a

129

kewpie doll for the prize and carried it a couple of blocks and then gave it away to a little girl, wishing her a Merry Christmas.

"Shireen, you're wonderful. You're the most wonderful girl in the world. I've never been so happy in my life. God, you even make me like New York."

She smiled up at him with tenderness and affection and sudden great gratitude for his being there and for being exactly what he was, big and healthy and strong and good-natured, uncritical, uncomplex, undemanding. And for not looking into the future, not even two hours into the future.

After awhile she wanted to go to Greenwich Village. They found a cab and drove down and got out at Café Society. A girl was singing when they walked in and they sat side by side against the wall, smoking and listening to her. They were close enough that she could feel the pressure of his leg against hers and his big confident body, and she realized they had begun to want each other. Years ago, maybe, but now they both suddenly knew it.

She remembered a dream she had had about him once.

She glanced sideways at him, very carefully; his mouth was set and his jaw muscles worked nervously. He looked like a small boy trying hard to behave well at someone's birthday party. She wanted to touch his hand and say something soft and reassuring, but had become self-conscious herself and couldn't do it.

The girl was singing in a voice that was deep and mournful and broke at times as if she were stifling a sob:

> "You'd be so nice to come home to.
> You'd be so nice by the fire.
> While the breeze on high—"

A tear ran down Shireen's cheek and splashed into her drink. She flicked off the next one with her finger. And as she did so Mike turned suddenly and looked at her, his face showing alarm and dismay. Quickly he brought out his handkerchief and Shireen took it, smiling.

"What's the matter, darling? Oh, I know—you're worrying about Ed." He looked around, as if for help.

Shireen blotted up the next few tears. She was not crying, only weeping softly, and found it rather pleasant, though she had not intended it to happen. She pressed his hand.

"Mike—it's nothing. Please don't worry. I'll stop in a minute."

"Poor kid."

He looked at her and seemed for a moment about to say something, but then she saw him decide not to. She gave a slight indication with her eyes and they turned back to watch the singer again.

130

"Under stars chilled by the winter,
    Under an August moon burning above
You'd be so nice, you'd be paradise,
    To come home to and love."

They sat there in silence and as they listened the music and words came to embody whatever it was they would ever mean in each other's lives, fixing the night permanently for both of them. It became a synonym for Christmas Eve, 1942, New York, the war, and this sudden guilty recognition that they wanted each other.

She felt him move a little away from her, pretending that he was reaching for a coin he had dropped.

Neither of them had been brought up to consider the possibility of a situation like this one. Decent people did not feel this way. Decent people guarded against their emotions if those emotions came into conflict with the prescribed set of rules. Otherwise, where was civilization? And they were both highly conscious of all this, though it did not make them less conscious of each other.

The way Shireen had been brought up there were a great many things which did not happen. Life, in fact, did not happen to you if you were properly raised. And turned out, according to expectations, to be a lady.

Chapter 19

The floor show ended and an orchestra started to play. Mike asked her if she wanted to dance. "Let's not just now," she said. "It's so crowded." Better not get that close to him, she was thinking.

They began talking idly about the dancers and the people around them. "They look like a bunch of screwballs," said Mike scornfully. "What I'd like to know is, how in hell do these long-hairs make a living?" Mike had just started practicing law in San Francisco when the war began.

Shireen opened her bag and took out a lipstick and touched her lips with it where the color had worn off. "New Yorkers aren't like you and me," she said. "It takes awhile to get used to them. They've got a lot of tassels on their personalities—kind of like Christmas trees with so much decoration you can't tell what the tree looks like. Even if they aren't natives they seem to get like that after awhile."

"It'd drive me nuts. I like to know where I stand with people. Maybe it's fun for you for awhile, and it helps keep your mind off your worries while Ed's away, but I'll bet you'll be glad as hell to get back home."

"Back home?"

"Sure. When the war's over."

"But I'm going to live here—for the rest of my life. I wouldn't think of going back there!"

"What about Ed's business? After all, he's with his father."

"That's Ed's problem," she said, and then hastily amended: "If I make any money he can open his own business here."

"It'd be a lot tougher in New York, Shireen."

"Well—then he can start a new business." She was impatient and faintly angry with Mike for bringing this up. "He never particularly liked selling insurance anyway. It was his father's idea."

"What else can he do?"

"Who knows?" said Shireen, and gave a quick rap of her nails on the table. "He'll find something. I'm sick of planning my life for Ed's parents!"

Mike pretended to duck a blow. "Okay, okay." He laughed.

Instantly she touched his hand. "I didn't mean that the way it sounded, Mike. But I love it here and I'm sure Ed will, too. Anyway—we certainly can't plan things that far in advance. Of course," she added piously, "I'll leave it to Ed when he gets home."

They were quiet again for a few moments, watching the dancers, and then Mike turned and glanced at her. Shireen smiled, feeling a little drowsy and pliable from the daiquiris, and she drew one finger slowly along the edge of his sleeve.

"Isn't it strange," she said dreamily, "that out of all the years two people may know each other, the only part of another person that really exists for you is the part that touches your own life? Later on I suppose we'll look back at tonight and realize all the other years didn't even count—just this one night. Most of the time even good friends are strangers. It's kind of a lonesome feeling, isn't it?"

Mike had watched her, fascinated, as she sat with her eyes cast down so that she was not quite looking at him, her full lower lip parted a little from the upper. Shireen had a satisfying sense of his admiration and it softened her voice, made her eyes moist and languid and seemed to start the flow of some mystical current between them.

Mike hastily shut it off.

"Never knew you were such a philosopher."

Shireen laughed and felt a little self-conscious, as if she had been reprimanded. Someone shook a finger at her and warned: You're a bad girl.

"Neither did I," she said.

They left there a little after one. Mike and another man raced for a cab and got to it at the same time. There was some commotion for a few seconds and a rising hostility between the two men until some chance tone of voice or Mike's laugh broke it.

"Come on," the other man said. "Let's all get in."

The driver objected. "It's not allowed, Mac."

"Of course it's allowed." He ushered his girl in. "We all came together." He gestured for Shireen to get in, he and Mike dickered good-naturedly for a few seconds and then he sat between the two women and Mike took the jump seat. "Calvert's my name," he said. "This is my wife." And Mike introduced Shireen and himself.

"Glad to have you aboard," said Mr. Calvert.

"Come and have a drink," Mrs. Calvert suggested. "We're right over here on Eighth."

"Great," said Mike promptly. "Thanks."

They climbed three flights to the Calverts' apartment and while the men began mixing drinks Shireen and Mrs. Calvert went into the bedroom. Shireen felt somewhat bewildered but nevertheless excited to be visiting people she had never even seen before. She felt that it was an adventure; she might have read about it in a book, and here it was happening to her.

This was real living, and this was the real world, too; furthermore,

133

these were real people. Not like the people she had known all her life, who had never seemed quite real to her, as if something vital was missing from them even though she had not known what it might be.

Shireen went into the bathroom and came out to find Mrs. Calvert at the dressing table, smoothing the blonde hair up off her neck with a lacquer-saturated pad. Mrs. Calvert glanced at her and smiled and went on fixing her hair. Shireen smiled back but could not think of anything to say and was relieved when Mrs. Calvert began chatting amiably and casually. But she kept part of her attention focused on what the two men in the living room were saying.

"Wasn't that pianist simply divine?" Mrs. Calvert asked her. "Bob and I simply adore him. Real old New Orleans jazz—nothing else like it, is there?"

"No," said Shireen. "There isn't." She had no idea what New Orleans jazz was, much less how the old style differed from the new, if there was one.

"Simply divine!" Mrs. Calvert pounded at her nose with a powder puff.

"Yeah—I guess we're going west, all right," Mike was saying in the living room.

"I was in the last one—"

"Isn't it infuriating—my last pair of nylons!" Mrs. Calvert stretched out a slender leg and frowned. "And in the Cub Room, of all places."

"Here's to you, Mike—may you get to New Zealand. I hear down there you have to beat the women off with a stick."

"Sounds like rough duty—"

Thank God I don't have to worry about what kind of a fool Mike makes of himself, thought Shireen.

". . . still manage to get some pretty good stuff. But it's tougher every day. With the government taking all the alcohol God only knows how they expect the civilians to get through the war. Ha, ha! But all kidding aside, Mike, I envy you. War may be hell but it's a great adventure."

"You won't hear any gripes from me—"

"Shall we join the boys?"

Mr. Calvert and Mike stood up as the two women came in and Shireen noticed that Mike was looking at her now with the air of a man surveying his property. It was apparently the smile he had not dared to give her while they were alone but which had become safe in the presence of other people.

They talked and Mrs. Calvert put on some records and after Mike had had three more drinks they left, thanking their host and hostess and promising to come to see them again sometime. They went downstairs and found a cab.

134

"Damndest thing I ever got into," said Mike, as they went rattling up Sixth Avenue. "Who were those people anyway? How did we get up there?"

"They asked us and you accepted."

"Was *that* it? Where'll we go now? I've still got to get you a Christmas present. Hey—" he turned and put one arm around her shoulders—"Merry Christmas!" He kissed the side of her face and gave her a quick little hug.

"Merry Christmas, Mike."

Suddenly he frowned. "I wonder where Ed is right now."

Shireen turned her head away. "Yes. I do, too."

Mike said that he was hungry and the driver let them out in front of Lindy's. It was jammed and noisy and full of crashing light. While they were eating their sandwiches a couple of Marine lieutenants came up and Mike introduced Shireen; they talked awhile and went away grinning, glancing back once more at Shireen and punching Mike on the shoulder.

"Isn't it strange," said Shireen, reflectively biting into her sandwich. "They all seem to take it for granted you're sleeping with me." Mike looked at her quickly and blushed dark red.

"I told 'em I'm not!"

Shireen smiled. "Of course you did, Mike. I know that. It's just that they can't see a Marine with a girl his last night home and imagine anything else."

"Let's get out of here." They stood a moment outside Lindy's, on the edge of the crowd that was as thick as it had been early in the night, flowing past them like a sluggish river. "Wonder if I can get a room at the Commodore?" said Mike. "The scuttlebutt is that you can always get in there when there's nothing else in town."

Shireen caught hold of his arm, as if he had started to run away. "Oh, Mike! You're not going to leave me!"

"Can't stay up all night very well."

"Why not?"

They looked at each other a moment and they both laughed, as if at some sudden discovery. "You're right. Why not?"

"You'll be gone tomorrow."

"Don't I know it? Well—what shall we do?"

They walked to the edge of the Park where the hansom cabs stood in line across from the Plaza and got into one of the little black carriages. The driver tucked a robe around them, climbed up on his perch and they started off. Shireen linked her arm through Mike's and settled back, close beside him.

"Oh, this is so nice! I've always wanted to do this!" She looked at him eagerly and her face had become suddenly mobile and transparent, as if lighted from behind.

"You're so damned beautiful." He sounded now as if her beauty had begun to hurt him.

She pressed his hand, drew a deep breath and made a sighing sound as of gratified fulfillment. And she turned to look out the window.

They rode along, warm and comfortable, listening to the horse's hoofs, and from time to time Shireen leaned forward to look out at the skyline and point to the silhouettes of the buildings. When she settled back once more against him their bodies seemed closer each time, molding into each other with relaxed ease.

I've got nothing to do with this, she thought. I didn't plan it this way. And anyway, why can't something that's pleasant just once in awhile be *right?*

As they rode along she began to talk about herself, the first time she had ever shown him anything of what she really was, wanted, or had thought about. There was a slackness in her mind from tiredness that induced reckless confidence. She was aware that he had given himself up to her completely, become meek and tame and pliable, and the knowledge created some sense of boundless power.

He seemed to have been stung into a kind of immobility, as if waiting to see what she would do with him. Knowing that created a perverse wish to frighten him, make him realize her power and sense the danger in it. But all the while she talked lightly and delicately, and occasionally glanced up at him with her teeth shining as they passed beneath a street lamp that threw shadows and made her face black and white like a blurred photograph shot through fine silk.

She was enjoying herself tremendously, reveling in the great luxury of talking unrestrainedly to a man who listened as if he had never heard a woman talk before. She felt compelled to show herself to him, as she was or imagined herself to be; and as she talked she laughed from time to time, so that he could not be quite sure how seriously she meant what she was saying. But she sounded very confident, as if she knew all the answers now. She was even a little surprised to hear herself; she had never talked this way before to anyone but Ed and, recently, Georgia.

She had refused before to talk about her writing. Now she told him how she had figured it all out, calculated this and that, and then done it. "You can make a lot of money selling the public Love," she said. "Very little retail, but plenty—wholesale." She gave a pealing laugh.

Mike seemed astounded to find this brand-new Shireen. Probably the picture he had kept of her was a girl in a gray skirt and yellow sweater talking to him on the campus one rainy afternoon with tears in her eyes, begging him to persuade Ed to see her just once more.

"Funny," he said. "I guess I've never really known you."

She laughed again, and now the laugh had a glittering edge to it.

136

"Of course you didn't. Because there's one thing I've always known: You can let people suspect anything else about you, but you must *never* let them suspect you of knowing what you're doing."

"Well, you know what you're doing, all right. And you've worked hard for what you want—I hope you get it."

"But I had to work hard, Mike. Twice as hard as anyone else. I've got a penny-ante talent, out of which I try to drum up a living for myself. And what nobody seems to realize is that it's just as difficult to get a bad idea as a good one."

Mike laughed and slapped his thigh. "Shireen, you're wonderful. I can't figure out where you've been all these years."

"In a convent."

"A convent? With Ed?"

"No, I didn't exactly mean that, Mike. I mean I've been so wrapped up in writing and cooking—and Ed, of course."

She turned quickly and looked at him, her whole face melting with tenderness and some promise she seemed to hold out to him. He could see so easily that there was no harm in her, only warmth and sweetness and sympathy, and some great pleasure—if she could ever be persuaded to let him reach it. He looked at her steadily and she saw his eyes cloud with a yearning ache; her mouth moved slightly and her nostrils widened.

"You're lovely," he murmured. His face touched hers and she could feel the warmth of his breath on her ear, rousing a small but poignant titillation. "Your hair smells so good."

Shireen gave a soft little laugh that was partly a sigh. After a moment she turned her face, one of his hands touched her breasts, and then she felt his mouth; her eyes were still opened, looking at the line of his face and its texture, and then she closed them and seemed to sink, as if a rough wave had pushed her down.

At last he let her go and gave a quick shake of his head. "How in hell did that happen?" She looked at him silently, her lips apart, not quite smiling, waiting again. "I'm going to take you home. This is no good."

Shireen brought out a compact and her lipstick and comb and by the time they came to the edge of the Park again she was sitting a little away from him, but now her manner was subdued and almost meek, as if she had turned all responsibility for decision over to him. He climbed down and helped her, paid their driver and hailed a cab. Driving back she continued to sit quietly, no longer showing off to him, feeling herself aloof from whatever happened between them, blameless and submissive.

They stood in the lobby and looked at each other. It was after four and no one else was around—only the night clerk adding a long sheet of figures, and they stood where he could not hear them talk. Mike

137

took off his cap and scratched his head, stretched out his mouth in a comical grimace, and finally shrugged his big shoulders. Shireen tipped her head to one side and smiled at him with a kind of maternal tenderness, assuring him that she understood his predicament. She still waited to see what he would do.

"I've had a wonderful time, Shireen," he said at last, and looked down at his shoes.

"So have I, Mike."

"Well—"

She waited a moment longer and then asked him: "What are you going to do now?"

"I don't know. Go back to the ship maybe."

"Why?" Her eyes had a clear wide-opened purity.

"I think I'd better." He glanced around, as if someone might be spying on them. "Don't you?"

"I don't see why. You've still got a few hours. If you want to come up I'll make you some coffee. We can read the papers—and talk."

He looked at her with sudden suspicion, as if she must know quite well what a ridiculous improbable suggestion that was, but her eyes were so clear and guileless that the next moment he seemed embarrassed and ashamed of himself. He ran one finger inside his collar and stuck out his chin.

"Yes," he said. "I guess we could."

Shireen, smiling faintly, turned around and walked toward the elevator, opening her bag to get out the key. She stepped in and he followed her and as the elevator started up they stood staring at the wall as if not daring to look at each other. Then quickly their eyes met and all at once they laughed.

"Isn't it funny," said Shireen. "There's really nothing much you can be sure of, is there?"

Mike scowled a little. "I don't exactly know what you mean."

The elevator stopped and she got out, making a little gesture over her shoulder. "I suppose we both thought we'd never see each other except where we always had."

Chapter 20

Shireen and Mike stood in the foyer, inside the door, looking at each other. Both their faces were tired but relaxed and their expressions mingled something of conspiracy, bewilderment, sadness. Mike had his overseas cap in his hand; Shireen was wearing her black lace dressing gown and her feet were bare. There was no make-up on her face but her hair had been thoroughly combed.

"God, but I hate to leave you," he said finally.

Shireen smiled faintly, sorrowfully. "I wish you didn't have to go." She sighed.

"I should hate myself. After all the years I've known Ed. I must really be a terrible bastard—because I haven't a regret."

"Neither have I—and I'm the one who should, after all, much more than you." But I've been selfish all my life; I guess it's too late to change now.

He laid the palm of his right hand tenderly against her cheek. "You're a wonderful girl, Shireen. Nothing like that ever happened to me before."

She bent her head against his hand and then touched it with her fingers, turning her head a little to kiss his palm. She smiled at him and closed her eyes.

"I love you," he said.

"I love you, Mike."

He looked at his watch. "Oh, hell, I'm probably late already. I've got to go, Shireen." His hand moved from her cheek around to the back of her head and drew her to him; her body swayed pliably, as if in perfect obedience, and her eyes closed as he kissed her.

"Good-by, darling. I'll write to you. I'll write today. I'll write every day. I love you."

"I love you," she whispered.

He opened the door and started to move reluctantly away. Her hand trailed down the sleeve of his coat, and fell slowly to her side. He kissed her once more, quick and hard, and walked down the hall. He turned once and waved and she was watching him wistfully, smiling. Then she closed the door and walked back into the living room and suddenly realized she was so tired her own weight felt dead and almost immovable. She started toward the window, caught a half glimpse of Ed's picture on the desk and turned her back. She lit a cigarette and then all at once her head dropped, as if her neck were a broken stalk, and she ran one hand through her hair.

He really was wonderful.

But what about me? What's the matter with me?

But I'm in love with him, after all. So there's nothing the matter. No one can help falling in love. What else could we do? That was the only decent or sensible thing there was to do, under the circumstances.

She looked at her watch. Five o'clock. Afternoon. Christmas Day. If I go to sleep now I'll wake up in the middle of the night. Maybe I can read. Christmas Day—and I haven't called home.

I'll do it now.

Georgia came back a few days later and Shireen told her that Mike had been there, that she had fallen in love with him and wanted to marry him.

"Marry him? Are you out of your mind, Shireen? And have you forgotten that you're already married?"

"No, of course I haven't forgotten. I'm not going to marry him, naturally. I just mean that I wish I could."

Georgia turned her head slightly to one side and made a face. "What about Johnny? You said you were in love with him. And Ed."

"I know. I am. Only now I'm beginning to think you can be in love with any number of men at the same time. After all, love is one of the imponderables. You might as well call it Factor X—and personally, I think it rhymes with sex." She laughed, pleased with herself.

Georgia picked up a pen and began to sign some letters the secretary had brought in. "Then just call it sex and let it go at that."

"But the two go together, don't they?"

"Where in the name of God did you ever get any such idea as that?"

"It's true, isn't it?"

"Certainly not. Why don't you admit it? You wanted Mike to fall in love with you, so you pretended to be in love with him. That's a pretty common feminine trick—nothing very scurrilous about it."

"Oh, but that's dishonest, Georgia. Anyway, the only time a woman can never fool a man is when he's making love to her. So you *have* to be convinced yourself." That didn't strike her as any contradiction until after she had said it, and then they both burst into laughter.

"Well, anyway—" she said, and stood up—"Men are like musical instruments. You have to practice on them to be any good."

Georgia smiled and Shireen congratulated herself she had made a pretty clever aphorism. "Tomorrow morning," Georgia said, "I've got an appointment with Burton and I guess the day after we'll get your contract signed."

"That'll be a relief."

140

While they stood on the corner in the cold trying to get a cab Georgia talked most of the time, but Shireen did not pay much attention because she knew it wasn't necessary to answer and she was worried about the meeting.

She pictured Mr. Burton as looking like a Man of Distinction. He could scarcely look otherwise, she felt, being editor in chief of a firm like Morgan Thayer. And anyway, she firmly believed that all successful New York men must be tall, handsome, distinguished, suave, well educated, fascinating.

"Damn this weather!" said Georgia. "New York has the foulest climate in the world—why does anyone live in it at all I ask myself a thousand times a year. You can't get a cab these days for anything. There's one. No, somebody's crouching in a corner. They should pass a law that all passengers have to sit in plain view. Hey! No, he had a fare, too. Oh, this blasted war! Well—*finally!*" A cab stopped and they climbed in, Georgia giving the address as she sat down. "Are you nervous?"

"I guess I am. I'm not sure. I don't feel much of anything."

"Don't worry about it," said Georgia. "Burton's just a nice guy with hypochondria."

"Really?"

That was both a disillusionment and a reassurance; but even so, his hypochondria wouldn't show and his position at Morgan Thayer would.

"Here we are."

Georgia paid the driver and Shireen noticed that she tipped him, too. She turned around and stepped up on to the sidewalk, excusing herself as someone bumped into her. And then suddenly she remembered something:

That's what that guy was mad about the first day I got here! I didn't know I was supposed to tip him. And she felt depressed to realize what he must be thinking of her.

They walked into the building and as they were going up to the twentieth floor where the Morgan Thayer offices began, Shireen said: "How much do you tip them?"

"What?" Georgia looked puzzled. "Oh—the drivers. Why, I never give them less than fifty cents altogether and usually a twenty-cent tip if the fare's between a half-dollar and a dollar. Here we are. For God's sake, is that what's on your mind right now?"

They went to the reception desk and Georgia asked for Mr. Burton and gave her name. Morgan Thayer had moved into new offices just before the war and everything looked recently decorated and very modern, with woven blond leather on the walls and dark-green leather chairs. The girl smiled as she hung up after announcing them to Mr. Burton, and told them to go in. They walked down a long hallway and Shireen followed Georgia, not daring to glance into the glass-walled offices they passed. They turned, opened another door into a hall with more offices, and Georgia walked into one, guiding Shireen beside her. Shireen entered timidly, feeling like the first day her mother had brought her to school.

Georgia was introducing her and now she remembered to smile and hold out her hand as Mr. Burton came forward to greet her. Mr. Burton was, after all, a man shorter than Shireen by two or three inches and looked less like a Calvert ad than her own father did. She felt somewhat relieved. Still, there was no telling yet what he would say or how she would find the words to answer him with.

He seemed very kindly and cordial and they sat there for a few moments making small talk, most of which Shireen was glad to find she could leave to Georgia since she had some feeling herself of being in a vast underground auditorium where her voice could not possibly carry. They were talking about her and her book and how many copies would be sold and how they hoped, if they could get the paper, to publish it this spring. But she did not quite grasp that they were actually talking about her and whenever she joined in it was with a sense that this was someone else they were discussing, someone she did not even know.

She believed, however, that she was very happy being here at this moment with Georgia and Mr. Burton glancing over her contract once more, though it was a little like being at your own tonsillectomy and just partially anesthetized.

Just enough that she felt like two people—one on the operating table, the other standing by and looking on.

She heard her own name spoken several times: *"Miss Delaney, we are all so pleased . . . Miss Delaney, you can't imagine the enthusiasm . . . Miss Delaney, we are so confident of great success . . . Miss Delaney, we hope you will be happy that your agent chose us . . . ."*

She kept on smiling and nodding her head and answering automatically, but she was amazed and almost overwhelmed by his kindness, his compliments, his enthusiasm. She wanted to look around over her shoulder to see who was back there that he might be talking to.

It's funny, she was thinking. After all those years. What was it I wanted? I guess it must have been this. Nothing much but just this. To sit here in Mr. Burton's office and have someone tell me I did a good job.

She saw him smiling at her again and reaching across the desk to hand her a pen, passing it to her carefully, opened, with the blunt end toward her. She took it, saw Georgia's forefinger with its long red nail press down on the contract beside a blank line, and she signed her name, quickly, with nervous sharp forward-slanting strokes. Then she glanced up at Georgia, as if for reassurance and approbation, and Georgia smiled at her, nodding her head. The contract was passed back to Mr. Burton, who was still smiling and now asking her if she would mind meeting the other editors and people in charge of various departments. Shireen kept on smiling too and said that she would like to meet them very much.

This was what she had hoped for: the opportunity to meet new people and make new friends and find out who it was lived in this world.

Various men and women began to come into the office and Shireen stood up and smiled and shook hands with them all. But the faces did not quite register and neither did the names. There were too many of them and she seemed still to be under the anesthetic. She was meeting people, though, and was glad of that. Some of them might later become friends to whom she could talk and with whom she might get to feel at ease and comfortable. But now they were only two-dimensional to her and their individual personalities remained secrets hidden inside them.

She felt like a child thrust suddenly into a world of grown-ups. Only the grown-ups had the idea that she was one of them. She kept her face fixed in a broad smile so they would not see how frightened she was of them.

When they were all gone Shireen sat down again, relieved, like a hostess whose party has lasted too long and left her tired and thankful when the last guest is finally put outside the door.

Vaguely she was aware of something that had happened today. These people did not know her, in fact, any better than she knew them. She was as two-dimensional to them as they were to her. It was hard to keep that in mind. But nevertheless she was beginning to understand that she was not Shireen Delaney any more.

Now, she was SHIREEN DELANEY. Someone quite different.

Georgia and Mr. Burton were talking about going to Mr. Thayer's office, a couple of floors above. Mr. Thayer wanted to meet Miss Delaney. They three walked out and waited for the elevator. Georgia and Mr. Burton were chatting away; Shireen had no idea what the talk was about. She heard several book titles and names of people she did not know and mostly had never heard of.

They got out of the elevator and passed some more offices and then Mr. Burton stepped ceremoniously back and Shireen walked ahead, realizing that this must be the office of Philip Thayer.

Philip Thayer got up from his desk and came forward to shake hands as Mr. Burton introduced them. "I'm delighted to know you, Miss Delaney. I haven't had time to read your book yet but everyone tells me it's terrific. How about it? Do *you* think so?"

Mr. Thayer was tall and thin with hair that had mostly turned gray, and a mustache. He was wearing a dark blue suit, which was what she thought men looked best in, and she liked his appearance. He seemed quick and decisive and talked to her with a kind of hearty humor, so that she could not be sure if he was joking or not. He frightened her.

"I don't know, Mr. Thayer," she answered seriously. "It's the best I could do."

Mr. Thayer laughed, asked her to sit down and offered her a cigarette. Shireen refused because she knew her hand would shake. She looked around to find Georgia and saw her smiling, casual and composed and at her ease, sitting in a chair with her legs crossed and Mr. Burton lighting a cigarette for her. Georgia's relaxed manner was gratifying, and Shireen hoped maybe some electrical impulses would convey a little of it to her.

"You're very modest for someone who's done what you have. And you look like a child. But you're not stubborn, I hope? Some authors are intractable. Some authors, in fact, are more goddamn trouble than they're worth. They think you run a publishing business for them and no one else. But I'm sure you won't be any trouble to us, will you, Miss Delaney?"

"I hope not, Mr. Thayer. I'll do everything I can to help."

"Yes, I'm sure you will. And are you happy here in New York? Are you being well taken care of?"

"Oh, yes, I'm very happy. Everyone's been so nice to me. I love New York."

"Hmm. Isn't that nice? Well—New York, I'm sure, will love you. Or maybe you're too good-looking for an author. Well, we'll see. You'd have no objection, I suppose, to putting on a pair of horn-rimmed glasses and flat-heeled shoes and an old tweed coat if it turns out the public really wants its female authors to look that way?"

Shireen glanced frantically around at Georgia. "Oh, but I don't think they really do."

"No, no. I don't think so, either. Well, Miss Delaney, I'm very happy to have met you." He got up again, indicating that the interview was over, and so did Shireen and Georgia and Mr. Burton. They all shook hands and left the office. In the elevator Georgia said she and Shireen would continue on down and Mr. Burton said he was going to arrange a luncheon so that all the editors could have a chance to talk to Miss Delaney. Shireen smiled and told him she would enjoy that very much.

The elevator doors closed, Shireen and Georgia looked at each other, and Georgia winked.

"There," she said. "It wasn't so bad, was it?"

"No, it really wasn't. In fact, I enjoyed it. Everyone was so nice."

144

"I should hope so," said Georgia. "They'd damn well better be nice to an author who's going to make them a few million bucks."

"But apart from that, they did seem like nice people. I guess there's no reason to be afraid of them, is there?" Maybe there actually wasn't anything for her to be afraid of. The world was apparently composed of nothing but people, after all.

Outside Georgia suggested that they stop somewhere for a drink. "I'd say this is the time for a mild celebration."

"Let's. But Georgia—you don't think Mr. Thayer meant that about the tweed coat, do you? He doesn't *really* want to change me, does he?"

Georgia laughed. "Of course not. Anyway, suppose he does? You don't have to mind him, after all. He can't very well force you to change. Here—let's go in here."

They went into a small dark bar and sat down, shrugging off their coats and lighting cigarettes. Georgia ordered a dry martini and Shireen a glass of sherry.

Then suddenly they began talking excitedly and Shireen came out from under the anesthetic, felt instantly wide-awake and full of energy and confidence. The waiter brought the drinks and they lifted them and touched glasses.

"Your first million copies."

Shireen blinked. But laughed as if she could believe almost anything by now, and took a sip.

"What's the first thing you're going to do?"

"Gosh, I don't know. I guess I'll get some new dresses and hats and a mink coat. Can I afford it?"

"Of course you can. You're in the charmed circle, Shireen. Do you know what this reminds me of—every time I see it happen? It's like a kids' game where the ones who are successful stand in a circle, grabbing money with one hand and passing it on with the other. While everyone else stands around on the outside, watching them anxiously and trying to figure a way to get into the circle so they can play too. Well, now you're in. You may as well start playing."

"And you do think there'll be a movie sale?"

"I know it. And we'll get plenty, believe me."

"About four hundred thousand?"

"What?"

Georgia's tone startled her and she gave a little jump. "Is that too much?"

"Too much? No book ever sold for four hundred thousand, Shireen!" Georgia pretended to mop her brow. "Good God, take it a little easy. My blood pressure."

Shireen felt as if she had committed a serious fault and was abjectly apologetic about it. "I thought I read somewhere," she mumbled in embarrassment, "that that was what they were paying nowadays for best sellers."

Georgia laughed and patted her hand. "No, sweetie. Prices are up, but not that much. Wow—how you do adjust yourself to the higher altitudes."

"I guess it's because I don't actually know what money is. I never had a hundred dollars before just to spend as I liked."

"I know, Shireen. But try to keep some sense of proportion. Otherwise, everything's going to disappoint you. I hope you'll enjoy this success of yours—but you won't, if you start off at this clip. I know it's hard, but try not to forget all about Marron."

"I won't forget, Georgia. I promise."

Chapter 21

Georgia's apartment was crowded with people, most of them standing, each with a glass in one hand and a cigarette in the other. The maid was passing trays of hors d'oeuvres, and a man Georgia had brought in for the afternoon was mixing drinks at a bar-table set against one wall. The talk and laughter were loud and getting louder, though some of the guests had gone by now. It was almost seven o'clock.

Georgia looked bright and exhilarated by all the commotion. She was wearing a black silk jersey dress swathed around her slim hips, with tight twisted sleeves and a glittering sapphire clip caught through her pearls. She had loosened her blonde hair and combed it into a roll low on her neck.

She had a superb efficiency about these gatherings which was scarcely more noticeable than the vibration of a well-regulated motor. She went busily among them, making introductions, reshifting pairs or groups of people who had got together and remained there helplessly through inertia or some conviction that no matter whom they talked to the same things would be said. But she was skillful in her manipulations and the working of them was never obvious. She enjoyed her own parties as much as anyone else, or possibly more.

This one was being given for Shireen because Morgan Thayer had recently set a publication date for *The Falcon* of April nineteenth, three months away.

Many of the people were from Morgan Thayer and even Mr. Thayer himself had stopped in for a half hour or so. There were several others: story editors from the motion-picture studios, a radio agent, a couple of book reviewers, a man who had written three mystery stories, two or three men in uniform—one of them Commander James Harrington, Georgia's fiancé up from Washington—and an executive for one of the insurance companies.

All of them were either interested in *The Falcon* for business reasons or were old friends of Georgia's, so that the feeling was friendly toward Shireen. Shireen sensed this and was sure that her life would be like this from now on, filled with people who liked and admired her and were glad she had done what she had. It felt much like the birthday parties her mother had given when she was a little girl.

More people were leaving now and Shireen was shaking hands with them and smiling modestly when they complimented her, telling her she was a nice girl. As she stood saying good-by to Mr. Burton, the insurance executive came over. He waited, watching her and smiling faintly while Mr. Burton made arrangements for her to come to the office the following Monday and look at sketches for the dust jacket. He was also going to show her the first draft for the jacket blurb.

"It's nice of you to let me see it, Mr. Burton," Shireen was saying. "I'm sure I'll like it."

"I hope you will, Miss Delaney. We want you to be pleased. And I'd like to take you around to meet some of the bookstore people one of these days. They can do a great deal for you if they like you."

"I'll be glad to, Mr. Burton. I want to co-operate in every way I can. You've all been so nice to me."

He left and Shireen turned to the man who had been waiting, trying to remember what his name was and how Georgia had described him to her. He and his wife and two children lived in the hotel, but his wife was visiting her family out West somewhere. He had a good position, at least one which gave him some prestige and a fair amount of money, but Georgia had been vague as to exactly what he did, as she usually was about people not in her business.

Shireen looked at him and smiled tentatively, waiting to see by his expression or tone of voice if he was on her side or not. Or if maybe he thought she'd been overdoing it a little with Mr. Burton.

He answered her by broadening his own smile and it was friendly, but she felt vaguely uneasy all the same. He was some years older than she—perhaps in his middle forties—and she had never been completely comfortable with men that much older than herself.

"You're getting quite a kick out of all this, aren't you?" he asked her.

"I suppose," she told him carefully, wondering if now he was going to make fun of her for it. "Everything's brand-new, after all."

"I'm Jack MacDonald," he said. "In case you've forgotten."

"Oh, no," she assured him quickly. "I hadn't forgotten."

Someone else stopped to say good-by and Shireen turned away eagerly, hoping that while she was busy Jack MacDonald might disappear and she would never see him again. She knew that he was interested in her, he liked her, and she felt obscurely threatened by it. She almost wished he were not on earth at all, for then she would never have been confronted by him. The worst of having Ed away, she sometimes thought, was that now she was exposed to strange men, when all these years he had protected her from them by the mere fact of his existence as her husband.

But he was still there when the other person left. She looked at him again, deciding to sum him up for herself now, put him in what-

148

ever niche he should occupy, and find some way to be comfortable with him if she could not get rid of him:

Typical successful American businessman. Blue eyes and brown hair, getting a little thin on top there, but not bad-looking; probably spends some time under the sun lamp at his club every day. Likes to drink, play golf, poker, swim, ride horseback, fish, putter around the house, talk to "the boys"—though he's probably at a loss when it comes to talking to the girls about anything but sex. Doesn't read many books, mostly magazines and newspapers and never misses the sport page; thinks any man interested in painting or music is eccentric. Good to his wife but has probably forgotten he ever loved her. Good to his kids even though he probably thinks it's his duty to make a noise like a father every so often. Doesn't trouble his head about anything but business, because if it doesn't help earn a living it isn't important. Wants to be comfortable and always has been, and is already beginning to realize he's missed something.

Or else he wouldn't have been looking at her that way—with curiosity and some sad wistfulness.

I know all about him, she thought. No surprises here. The hell with him.

"I'd like to ask you a question," he said now, and he seemed a little shy, which mollified her. "Would you mind?"

Shireen laughed. "I don't think so. What is it?"

Someone else came up at that moment and she turned to speak to him, while he waited again. When they were alone he went on.

"I've been wondering what you think about all this. I can't tell from watching you. But from what Georgia says, your life's changed overnight more than most people's do in twenty years. It must be quite an experience. Would you tell me what you think about it?" He spoke to her kindly, with no brutal curiosity, but a gentle yearning to participate in her adventure. He was only asking politely if he might share a bit of it with her.

Shireen felt herself blush a little and a glow of warmth rose within her and spread toward him. She was a little sorry for him. It was such an old familiar pattern, known to her forever, it seemed, and she felt with poignancy his unrecoverable years and the things he had missed because he had not known how to get them or even quite what they were. Except that he saw them now in her, as if for the first time clearly.

"I guess the main difference," she said, "is that once you're successful, people begin to notice it if you're nice to them. Before, you can break your neck trying to be nice, but nobody really gives a damn. Then all of a sudden it seems as if they're surprised when you are. I don't know what they expect you to do, or why it should surprise them so much, though."

Georgia, standing nearby, turned her head. "Exactly what they'd want to do themselves, if it happened to them. Spit in the world's eye for all the wrongs it's done them."

"There wouldn't be much point to that," said Shireen, and she and Georgia and Jack MacDonald laughed.

Most of the guests had gone by now, and Georgia went over to the door where there was noise and confusion and talk and laughter as the last stragglers were sent on their way. Then she came back, flung herself on the couch, and stretched her arms over her head. "Whew! I'm beat!" She reached for a cigarette and Commander Harrington leaned down to light it for her. Jack offered Shireen a cigarette which she refused, and they all sat down.

Immediately Shireen and Georgia were off on an animated discussion of the cocktail party, who had been there, who had said what to whom, and what the hidden meanings were or might be in any given comment. The two men listened for several minutes, then Jim got up and mixed drinks. When he brought them to the women, both thanked him with a quick smile but didn't interrupt themselves for a moment. The two men, refused admittance to this closed feminine corporation, seemed to take refuge in polite scornful aloofness, as if asking themselves what the hell kind of nonsense these women were talking anyway.

And then Jack inquired of the Commander how things were in the Pentagon, and off they went into their own world.

"Oh!" said Georgia, after a few minutes. "I almost forgot! Tom Blakely called me today and said someone had told him that you told your publisher you had only one ambition left in life now—and that was to sleep with Clark Gable!"

"What!"

Shireen and Georgia burst into wild laughter. Jim and Jack glanced at them, looking puzzled, and went back to their own talk.

"*Did* you say that, Shireen?"

"Of course not. I'd never say that about a man I didn't know!" And they burst into new laughter. Jim frowned a little, and Jack smiled patiently.

"Well, it's starting to happen already. New people, but the same old gags. And speaking of gags, Shireen, just remember one thing when the publicity barrage starts. There's an old press-agents' slogan that's good advice: Don't read your publicity—weigh it."

Shireen looked alarmed. "Oh, I wouldn't read it for anything!"

Jack glanced at her. He had been watching her, looking over from time to time while he talked to Jim. "Why not?"

"I don't believe in reading what's written about you. If you don't know what's said it can't do you any harm."

"It can't do you any harm anyway."

150

"Oh, yes it can!" chimed both women at once.

Georgia shook her finger. "This one's going to be all right. Don't worry about her."

Jack was watching her thoughtfully. "I hope it won't change you."

"I don't see why it should," said Shireen, a little offended.

"We hope it won't," said Jim quietly. "But success is often harder to take than failure——"

And they all went on talking about Shireen.

That was what amazed her more than anything else. All at once everyone was interested in her. How she looked, what she thought, how she reacted to the things that were happening to her, how she wrote, why she wrote, what she thought about when she wrote. Always before she had been so careful in talking about herself, except to Ed.

Who cared? Who would be interested?

And now, as if by magic, everyone cared and everyone was interested. It was like being the only person on horseback.

All you had to do, she thought with some amazement, was to write a book, and you became a little universe. The whole thing seemed so simple: I just thought I'd write a best seller—and I did.

A couple of days later Georgia told her that she had run into Jack MacDonald in the lobby that morning and he had asked about Shireen. "He was very much impressed by you."

Even that was no surprise to her now, though not long ago Jack MacDonald would have seemed to her very successful and important, not a man who could ever be interested in little Shireen Delaney. The truth was, he probably would not have been: no more interested than she was herself in the cocoon she brought home from school.

"That's nice," she said. "I liked him, too. What's the matter with him and his wife? You said they weren't very happy."

Georgia shrugged. "They're just not in love with each other."

"Then why don't they get divorced?"

Georgia smiled. "My God, Shireen. What are you trying to do—overthrow society? If everyone who wasn't in love got divorced—Anyway, they've got kids."

"That's no reason for them to stay married if they don't love each other."

"Well, some people think it's a reason. Anyway, Eva couldn't support herself and Jack doesn't care if she sleeps around and he does the same for himself. So I guess they've got it worked out as well as they can. A nice typical twentieth-century bake—I've been in too many of 'em myself."

"I don't understand it. I don't see how people do those things to themselves. What kind of life is that, anyway? To go on for years and years——" She shuddered.

"Don't worry about it. Now, Shireen, I've called a few people about this guy who's interviewing you tomorrow—"

It was Shireen's first interview and when Morgan Thayer called to arrange it Georgia had said to her: "I'll inquire around. I know some people who know him." No matter who it was, Georgia knew some people who knew him—or else, knew him herself. She always knew where to go and whom to ask.

Shireen went to meet Allen Bradley, happy in her conviction that newspapermen were omnipotent beings endowed with superior knowledge and perception, cynics who knew all but never told without specific permission. She was a little frightened but nevertheless looked forward to the meeting because she was sure he would be very interesting to talk to.

She got to the Algonquin exactly on time and asked for his table. The waiter led her to it. He was sitting there already, a martini in front of him, and he half got up to shake hands. She smiled at him hopefully and then instantly realized that he was taking careful notice of what she had on, how she looked and how she behaved. And all of a sudden she felt as if she had been spread out for a medical examination and began to wonder how she could cover herself, hide from him.

This was part of being a prospective celebrity she hadn't expected or prepared herself for. His attitude toward her was quite obviously not the same as Georgia's or Mr. Burton's or Philip Thayer's or Jack MacDonald's. He was not simply pleased and happy that she had written a book and was willing to co-operate in the selling of it and be pleasant and affable and unobtrusive at all the right times. He was after something else, and those qualities did not impress him favorably at all.

"What'll you drink?" he asked her.

"Nothing, thanks. I don't drink very often."

"Don't drink? Hmm. Why not?"

"I guess I just don't like it."

"Good enough reason. I do like it. Mind?"

"No, of course not."

Shireen glanced nervously around, wishing she could see someone she knew. But that wouldn't do any good. Well, she thought, if I'm very nice and honest and answer his questions and show him that I like him, everything's bound to be all right. I *hope* it'll be all right.

She looked at him a moment, noticing that he had a kind of tenseness around the eyes, as if from peering to see how he could get ahead of the next guy.

"So you've written a book."

"Yes." She began to examine the menu, for she had glanced

anxiously at him as she answered and saw nothing to hearten her in his expression.

"What about it? Is it any good?"

Shireen put the menu down, having found she could not hide from him behind that. "Gee," she said. "I honestly don't know. I hope so." One hand reached up nervously around her neck and gave a toss to her hair. Apparently he did not like her or believe her as she was and she could not think of anything else to be for him; certainly any pose of nonchalance or sophistication on her part would be seen through like a chiffon handkerchief.

"Best you could do, eh? What'll you eat?"

"I think a chicken hash pancake. They're very nice here, don't you think?"

"Don't know. Never tried it. Waiter, the lady'll have the chicken hash pancake. Nothing first?"

"Cherrystones, please."

"And cherrystones. I'll have the mixed grill. Coffee with. For both. How about you?"

"Yes, thank you."

This guy's got a personality like a razor blade, she thought uneasily. She took the cigarette he handed her and bent forward as he flicked a match with his thumbnail and leaned on his elbow to offer it to her.

"Now, about this book of yours. I hear Morgan Thayer expects to sell a hell of a lot of copies. Is that true?"

"I guess it is. They hope so, naturally."

She smiled timidly at him, wishing he would just be nice. He seemed dangerous, for if he got a bad impression of her he would say so in public. And then all kinds of people who didn't even know her and had never heard of her would think she was terrible. But I mustn't think it's personal, she tried to assure herself. He has to do it, after all—picks away at other people's emotions as part of his honest day's work. I'll look at it objectively.

"How about Hollywood? Expect a sale there?"

"I really don't know. My agent hopes so, of course."

"Of course? Why *of course?* Is that what you wrote for—Hollywood?"

"No, of course not, but I mean—she says—well, it's obvious if you sell a book for pictures you make more money from it. Isn't it?" Simple clear point; he couldn't very well argue with that.

"Oh, I see. And is that what you wrote this book for? To make a lot of money?"

"Well, that was one reason certainly. Is there anything wrong with that? My God," she said in sudden exasperation. "Sometimes I think Americans are as self-conscious about money as they are about sex!"

153

But she instantly regretted that, for it had not come out of the envelope full of snips and swatches of personality she meant to give him today.

"What are you so defensive about? Guilty conscience?"

She gave a long haul at the reins and pulled back on the anger that had begun to gallop away inside her. "I don't know what you're talking about, Mr. Bradley," she assured him with childlike patience. "I wrote a book. I did the best job I could. And, incidentally, I hope I'll make money from it. That's one of the reasons for doing any kind of work, isn't it? This is an economic world we live in. The first thing you have to do is eat."

"It may be one, but it shouldn't be the primary reason."

"What should be the primary reason, then?" He was trying to bait her, trick her into making a fool of herself so he would have a good story.

Well, she'd fool him. She hoped.

He went on. "Writing books is getting to be a goddamned circus. And it shouldn't. It's one of the world's most serious professions and ought to be regarded as such. The fact is, you don't look very serious to me. And what's more, I don't think you're capable of doing any serious work."

"Why not, for heaven's sake?"

She was shocked and indignant. What was this idiot talking about? Didn't he know all the years she had worked, the careful research, the meticulous care with which she had gone over every smallest separate detail?

"Don't pretend to be so innocent. You know why not. You've got yourself done up like a Powers model. Serious women don't do that and there's no use trying to tell me they do. What's the idea? What are you trying to get away with?"

"I'm not trying to get away with anything! And I don't know why you should think I am! If I'd come in here wearing an old tweed suit and horn-rimmed glasses and Scotch brogues, would you have thought I was serious then?"

"If you'd left the paint job off your face too, I might. And if you hadn't made that crack about Hollywood. Look, Miss Delaney, you're nothing to me, believe me. I'm just a guy with a job. I can think of a lot of others I'd like much better. But this happens to be the one I have at present. I'm not trying to find out anything but what I need to pad into some kind of yarn, and as it happens I'm a reporter, not a press agent. It isn't my job to create a personality—so you'll have to let me take at least a glance at yours. You're about to be news, and you'll have to get used to this. It'll happen to you often from here on in. Now, get off your high horse and quit looking at me like I'm your footman and maybe we'll get along better."

154

"But I'm not looking at you like you're—"

"Never mind. Never mind. Just tell me a few things, will you?"

"Of course, Mr. Bradley," said Shireen meekly. "Whatever you want to know—"

One of these days, mister, I'm going to put you in a book.

Chapter 22

About four o'clock Shireen was released by Allen Bradley and went directly to Georgia's office, as if to a haven. Georgia signaled her to sit down with a wave of her fingers and went on drawling at whoever it was in her polite careful well-bred New England voice.

"Oh, but of course, darling—why, you know I do—I certainly will—why, my dear, have I ever said such a thing to you in my life?"

Shireen sat, not listening, surprisingly tired after the interview. It's like dragging your soul out for someone to prod and poke at, she thought. And then trying to stuff it back again, bruised and wounded, and a little dirty.

"But that's totally absurd, you mustn't pay any attention to that at all, and I'll take care of it right away—of course, sweetie, don't you worry about a thing—I will, and you do, too—good-by, darling—" As she clicked the phone down with one finger she added: "The son of a bitch." She put the telephone back in its cradle and leaned forward on her elbows, resting her chin on the heels of her hands, looking at the notes she had been scribbling while she talked. "Do you know what that crud was trying to get away with? Well, the hell with it. How'd the interview go?"

Shireen frowned a little. "I don't know, Georgia. I couldn't figure the man out. He didn't seem to like me. And I don't know why, because I tried to be nice to him. I honestly did."

"Probably he didn't like you. You know the old line about every reporter being a frustrated author. It ain't so far wrong. Another thing you may as well know right now so you can get used to it: This is an age of specialization and no one person is expected to do more than one thing well."

"What's that got to do with me?"

"You're good-looking, aren't you? Well, it's going to follow to an awful lot of people that you should be content with that. It's supposed to be a career, for a woman. Good-looking men, that's something else again."

"Men, that's something else again, period," said Shireen sourly.

"Well, you and I may not like it but that's the way it is. And we can't very well change it—we and the few other women we could get to agree with us."

156

"If women would only realize that their own best interests demand some kind of co-operation—"

"If only there were a Santa Claus. Let's get back to the interview. What did Bradley ask you?"

Later in the day they had dinner together and then visited some friends of Georgia's. Going up in the elevator when they came back, they both glanced at the late editions of the papers piled in a corner, raised their eyebrows in mutual question, and Georgia picked one up and gave the man a quarter. "Come on up and we'll take a look at it. You can break your resolution this once."

"I don't think I'd—" began Shireen doubtfully, and then they got out of the elevator and went into Georgia's apartment, switching on the lights.

Georgia handed her the paper. "Read it to me, while I make some coffee."

There was a picture of her beside the article, smiling straight at the reader and showing all her teeth. She had thought it was a pretty nice picture when the photographer showed her the proofs. Shireen began to read:

"Today I had lunch with Shireen Delaney. That name won't mean anything to you now, but just wait awhile. Anyway, he doesn't start out too bad, does he? *She's written a book called* The Falcon *and Morgan Thayer's publishing it and, as you can see, she looks like an ad for Ipana or Pepsi-Cola.* I don't see why he had to say that. *Until I met Miss Delaney it was my impression that authors were serious people. But Miss Delaney quickly squelched all those romantic illusions.* I don't like the sound of that—I think he's getting nasty. *She came in wearing clothes that were obviously expensive, with a face by Elizabeth Arden and a hair-do by same.* I *told* you he didn't like me, Georgia!"

"Go ahead. Read it. You're started."

"She sat down and after saying coyly that she did not drink— publishers are getting real smart—she proceeded to tell me that she hoped her book would sell to Hollywood because she wanted to make a lot of money. I did not say that! God damn him!"

"Go on."

"So I asked Miss Delaney, being an innocent guy who doesn't know about these things much, if the purpose of writing was to sell books to Hollywood. And she explained to me patiently that it's obvious a book makes more money for a writer if Hollywood buys it and after all, writing is a business just like any other business, isn't it? Georgia, he's twisted around everything I said! I won't stand for this—I'm going to call him up right now and tell him what I—"

"No, you're not. Sit down there, now, and finish it."

"Miss Delaney says she planned it all out very carefully, what kind

157

of book the public likes, how thick a book the public will buy most copies of, what frustrations of its own the public likes to see worked out by its fictional heroes and heroines. She seems to be a very clever girl, Miss Delaney, and I for one don't doubt for a minute that she's going to make all this money she's plotted to make. Oh, Georgia! This is terrible! I can never show my face again! Everyone's going to hate me!" She put her hands over her face.

"Now, Shireen, for heaven's sake. It isn't good, but it isn't that bad. Bradley's always been a bastard—since the day he was born. Here, I'll finish it." Georgia picked up the paper and read the rest through rapidly:

"I asked her what she would do with her money. 'I can't tell yet, very well,' she said sweetly, 'since I haven't got it. Everything will of course depend on what my husband wants when he comes back from the war.' Back to cooking and housekeeping? I suggested, just like a big bully. No—Miss Delaney didn't think she'd care for that. She'd worked too hard to get away from all that. Back to California? No. Miss Delaney's the only Southern Californian not registered with the Chamber of Commerce as an undercover agent. She hates it. Perhaps because no one took her very seriously out there? No, she says it wasn't that. It's just that New York's so stimulating and everything. Well, in case there are any among you wondering how to write a book and make a lot of money, now you know. Miss Delaney figured it all out and I've passed the formula along to those of you who may be interested.'

Georgia tossed the paper onto the table and lit a cigarette. Shireen slouched with her feet straight out in front of her, glowering. Georgia leaned down and patted her on the shoulder and then went to pour the coffee. She set a cup in front of Shireen and began to sip her own.

Shireen gave a deep heavy sigh. She shook her head. "He sounds as if he hates me. And I tried to be nice to him and perfectly honest and I answered every question he asked me, I really did, Georgia. *Why* do people do things like that? I didn't do anything to hurt *him*."

"The thing you've got to remember, Shireen, is that he's been hurt before, and often. Don't ask me how or why or who did it. But you know as well as I do that most of the people in this world are unhappy, one way or another. And unhappy people aren't kind. Not when they're brought up against the thing that's troubling them. He saw you—young, good-looking, successful—naturally it griped him. He wished it had happened to him instead. It's going to gripe a lot of people. Why shouldn't it?"

"Why should it? I don't see why it should."

"You mean you don't want to see why it should. But you'll have to face it, Shireen. You can't expect to be envied and loved at the same time. Anyway, most men don't like women much unless they

158

think there's a fair chance they can sleep with them. Bradley obviously didn't think he was ever going to get in the hay with you. You probably treated him like a maiden aunt, and that upset some more of his self-esteem. Anyway, it's all part of the picture—you said you didn't want to miss anything."

"I don't. I've missed too much already. But I didn't expect things like this to happen."

She brooded about Allen Bradley and his column for a day or so, but then she forgot all about him.

Ed's letters came almost every day, to remind her that her part of the War Effort was to be a faithful loving devoted wife. And each night when she wrote she apologized to him for the way she was living: comfortable and safe and occupied with trivialities. She felt intensely guilty that she was not being made to suffer in some way, but consoled herself that any day now she would.

She saw Jack MacDonald a few more times.

He called occasionally late at night, when she was in Georgia's apartment where they met to drink coffee and hash over the day's events. And he would ask if he could come up and talk for awhile. All three of them knew that what he really wanted was to see Shireen.

He would sit there, looking so relaxed he might be ready to fall apart; and most of the time he simply watched the two women while they talked and lit cigarettes and drank coffee, laughing at things which probably did not seem very funny to him and apparently understanding words he could not hear. While Shireen, though she talked mostly to Georgia and did not pay him much attention, nevertheless altered herself under his observation. But the changes were slight and delicate, amounting only to a heightening of the illusion of femininity.

Another part of her was thinking: Nothing has ever really disturbed this man. He's gone through life brushing up against people and letting them brush him, but he's never struck into them, he's never had a real contact with someone else's personality. Nothing's ever smacked him hard enough to shake him all the way down.

But then she would go to her own apartment and lock the door and before she was undressed she would have forgotten his existence. Still, from time to time she would be reminded of him and reminded that here was a man no one had ever tested and so no one, not even he, knew what he was made of.

Then, about three weeks after she had met him, the phone rang one morning about eleven and he was calling her from his office. She could see him smiling and hear the half apologetic tone as he asked if he had called too early.

"Why, hello, Jack." She was a little surprised to hear his voice. She had forgotten him again. "No, it's not too early. I was having some coffee and reading the paper."

He asked her, after some hesitation, if she would have lunch with him. Well—why not? She was tired of having lunch with women, hard as she was trying to convince herself that women really were wonderful people. She told him she would be glad to.

She met him in the lobby at the Pierre and they went downstairs to the grill. Shireen sat down, drawing off her gloves, shrugging out of her coat, tossing back her hair with one hand, quiet soft gestures into which she had fused some sort of beguilement. She glanced at Jack then, smiling faintly as though waiting for his approval and asking if she had it. He was watching her with a look of wistful pleading, and apparently wanted nothing but for her to be kind to him, sit beside him and let him look at her and listen to her talk. It was the kind of admiration under which she felt warm and safe and glowing, protected from whatever cold winds blew through her life.

He ordered a martini for himself and sherry for her and they looked at the menu. Shireen was chattering away about some people she had met yesterday. "They're really very nice," she said. "They own half of England." For God's sake, she thought, as she heard herself. What's happened to my life lately? *Something* has sure changed.

They both ordered the curry and began to talk, first about the war news and then about Ed and how worried she was about him and how much she missed him and how dearly she loved him. Might as well get that settled right now, she thought, in case this guy's got any ideas in his mind. Men, she had decided long ago, have absolutely no sexual discrimination. They're all like the savages who will lay any female that happens to cross their path going through the forest.

Then they talked a little about Georgia, and Shireen said she was convinced that Georgia knew everything worth knowing and that she didn't see how she could have gotten along without her. It must have been some lucky fate that made her pick up that magazine one day while she was standing idly in a drugstore waiting for a prescription to be filled. Otherwise, how would she ever have found her way through this maze of New York?

"She's quite a gal," Jack agreed. "I've known her a long time—from her first husband on down. I've liked them all so far and no doubt will like any she marries in the future. But she's like all women in business—takes what advantage she can of her sex appeal."

Shireen smiled patiently. "That's what men always say, if a woman's more successful than they are. They've got to have some excuse, after all, to reestablish their faith in themselves as the center of the universe. They even created God in their own image." She shook her head. "I wonder why it is men can't take women seriously outside the bedroom or the kitchen?"

"Maybe because that's the only place you *can* take 'em seriously. What else have they ever done? After all, there's never been one

160

genius who was a woman." He was smiling, apparently amused to see her face flush and her eyes begin to sparkle angrily.

"And how many geniuses do you suppose there'd have been if men had spent twelve hours a day the past several thousand years peeling potatoes and changing diapers? And anyway it's men who decide what genius is. And not only that but society *expects* a man to get out and do something—dig a ditch or build a bridge, make a positive move of some kind. But we don't expect that of women, we don't encourage it and, in fact, we do everything we can to discourage it. We tell her she'll get into all kinds of trouble and furthermore be a hopeless neurotic if she wants or needs something more from life than being a good wife and mother. Women have been the victims of their own biology but they don't have to be any more and the whole present setup has become ridiculous because it isn't needed any longer. Society has to be shifted around a good deal, and once it has been there'll be room for everyone who wants some kind of self-expression to have it. And I think everyone wants it; basically that's what they want more than they want anything else in life. When the sense of having somehow expressed yourself is left out, sooner or later there's a realization of complete waste. Nothing will make up for it!"

And that means you, she thought.

Jack shook his head. "That's a strange way for a girl who looks like you to talk."

"Why?" She looked at him over her shoulder, her eyes wide open, her voice cool and crisply challenging.

"Life could be so easy for you. You don't need to do a thing. Just let yourself be taken care of—and you could find ten thousand men right in this town who'd be happy to do it."

"And what would I do in the meantime?"

"What any woman does—go to movies and buy clothes and listen to lectures and boss the servants around, I guess. What else do they do?"

Shireen looked at him carefully, thinking: So that's the way this guy's been treating his wife all these years. She was building a case against Jack MacDonald, for Eva's sake. This unknown woman—who might have been she.

"And is that how your wife spends her time?"

"That's about it, as far as I know. She does whatever she wants to—I never ask her. When she feels like it she takes a trip somewhere."

"And do you *really* think that's all she wants from life?"

"If it isn't she hasn't tried very hard to get anything else. She's got things pretty easy. I give her whatever she asks for, provided she keeps it within reason and I can afford it."

"You sound like a goddamned patriarch."

161

"Well, I'm not. I'm just a guy trying to get along in a world I happened into—and keep up the installments on my insurance policy. Oh, Eva isn't actually happy, I guess. She's always trotting to a doctor with this or that ailment, but I think it's her imagination. She'd be better off if we didn't live in a hotel and she had some responsibilities, but she likes it this way. She says it gives her more 'freedom'—whatever the hell she means by that. So I let her have it."

The curry was being served now by a man in a striped satin turban and coat. They watched him serve it, using a flourish as he sprinkled the grated orange peel and coconut over the dish. When he had gone away Shireen sighed. "Isn't that ridiculous?"

"Isn't what ridiculous?"

"That man—done up in costume that way. What business has anybody got making him get himself up like that, like some kind of trained monkey to perform for the white folks?"

"Well," said Jack, "I hadn't given it much thought. I don't suppose he minds."

"Nobody minds, I suppose," she said bitterly, "being treated as an inferior. They recognize their superiors and they don't mind. Like Eva. She doesn't mind at all. She's sick or thinks she's sick half the time, but she doesn't really mind. Because, after all, you're as good to her as if she were your pet dog."

"Holy smoke, Shireen."

"Have you ever tried loving her?"

"Sure. For awhile. Love doesn't last."

"Did you try to make it last?"

He shook his head, as if she had backed him into a corner and he was vaguely uncomfortable but expected her to see any moment now that she was being unreasonable and leave him alone.

"I don't know," he said. "I suppose so. I haven't time to think about these things. I've got a living to make."

"You've got a living to make, so you haven't time to live. Is that it?"

"That's about it, I'm afraid. But don't mistake me—I'm fond of Eva. She's a very good woman and I think we understand each other. Suppose I ask you a question for a change. Are you in love with your husband?"

"Of course. I wouldn't be married to him if I weren't. I think you're immoral," she added piously.

"Me—immoral? My gosh. What's the matter? Are you mad at me?"

Then suddenly she smiled. She turned a little and opened her face to him, inviting him to see how lovely she was and not be alarmed. His face muscles slackened and a look of helpless longing came into his eyes.

162

"Of course I'm not mad at you, Jack. I like you very much—you know that. We're just talking, getting acquainted, aren't we?"

And he sat, staring back at her, caught and held by her eyes for as long as she wanted to keep him. Finally she let him go and saw that he had been hanging precariously balanced and the moment she let him break free something inside him staggered uncertainly before regaining its balance. She smiled, and turned back to her food.

"Well," he said. "That's a relief. I'd begun to think you didn't like me. But really, Shireen, I'm not immoral. There are a lot of things you don't understand."

"Like what?"

"About Eva and me. It's true we're not in love but we've got two kids and I'm in a business where a wife and family are an asset and a divorce would be a nuisance—I'd only have to get married again, anyway. So we go our ways. We haven't slept together in years. Eva's in love with another guy; at least she thinks she is, though I don't believe women know whether or not they're in love most of the time. Remember, Shireen, we've been married almost twenty years. What more can you expect after all that time?"

"And you're not even jealous of this other man?"

"Why should I be? That part of Eva's life has nothing to do with me. Anyway, it helps keep her happy. Women seem to have some congenital necessity for romance. When they haven't got it they start getting neurotic and God knows what. You take a very high moral tone about all this, but remember, you haven't been married very long. It'll happen to you, too."

"Oh, no it won't! I won't live like that! I'd get a divorce!"

"Then you'll have a lot of divorces. Because it is not humanly possible to stay in love with the same person year after year. People aren't monogamous by nature—at least, men aren't. Monogamy is an invention of women for their own protection. But take a look around you and you'll see that no one's paying much attention to it."

"All excuses," said Shireen.

"Excuses for what?"

"For your own failure. What else?"

And what about *my* failure?

All at once she was sorry she had spoken that way to him. He was looking at her with bewilderment and a kind of pleading, and she touched his hand lightly.

"I'm sorry, Jack. I've been rude. Please forgive me. I have no right to criticize your life, after all."

He shook his head. For several moments he was quiet and then he turned and looked at her again. "Shireen, you're an awfully pretty girl. That's what I wanted to tell you—before we got off onto all this other stuff."

163

Shireen smiled. *And he still thinks "all this other stuff" is so much talk now evaporated and meaningless and the only thing that's really me is the way I look and the way he thinks I'd feel and act if he ever got a chance to find out.*

She thought of what it was Jack MacDonald must represent to the women who knew him: To the girls who worked for him he must seem a little awesome, a man who sometimes smiled or sometimes was abstracted and they must try to act accordingly; to his daughter he would seem dull because he was a parent, but in addition he would be a source of frustration for he had the power to grant or deny her wishes; and to his wife—he must have been the death of Eva's belief in herself. But to Shireen Delaney he was a simple harmless male without very good sense and he was going to get hurt if he wasn't careful.

Chapter 23

"I think it's very nice for you," Georgia said when Shireen began going to some plays and out to dinner with Jack. "You need an escort and he's a respected reliable person so you can't be harmed by being seen with him. And since he lives here in the hotel anyway, it's not going to be noticed that he comes in and out."

"Well, I can't say he fascinates me. I like him, but that's all."

"That's enough, isn't it? You're not after falling in love again, I hope."

"Certainly not with him. But I wish—" She stopped, frowning a little.

"You wish what?"

She shook her head. "I don't know. There's something somewhere that I must be looking for. I wish I knew what it was."

"I know. I'm looking for it myself. And I don't know what it is, either. The only thing I do know that you don't seem to, Shireen, is that the essence of it is in the very fact that it can't be found. We're the uneasy restless ones in this world. People like you and me—and Johnny."

"Yes, Johnny," she said softly. "I wonder where he is. I wonder, if things had been different—"

Georgia shook her head, as if Shireen had missed the point and she wasn't going to discuss it any further.

Before long Jack was calling her once a day from his office, and then he began calling twice every day. He sent her flowers and bought her boxes of candy and got tickets for the shows she wanted to see. Once in awhile on Saturday afternoons he went with her to an art gallery, but his manner then was patient and bored and amused. He was docile and obedient, and though she knew he wanted to sleep with her he did not try to be persuasive because he was obviously afraid she might then refuse to see him.

They fell into a habit of meeting every evening at her apartment and he would have a drink while she changed her clothes or got ready to go out to dinner. She took his presence for granted, liked him and was glad for his companionship. He filled a space in her life that would otherwise have been left empty.

And, since the first day they had lunch, she had not done or said anything to make him criticize or question himself. She treated him

165

with a casual friendliness in which there was nevertheless a delicate and subtle insistence upon her own desirability. He could never look at her or listen to her without being aware of it and she could see his awareness in the yearning helpless wistful way he had of watching her. But she was not sure if his patience came from fear or a belief that someday, if he waited long enough, he would have her. Passivity, though, had always roused her contempt and she did not respect him for waiting, even while she made him wait.

He did not fit her picture of what a man should be.

For somehow she had begun by expecting a great deal of men, thinking they were something more than human, and each time she found a vulnerability, even when she had gone looking for it, she was triumphant and outraged. What in hell are they trying to get away with? she would ask herself. How come they've been going around passing themselves off as demigods?

Why, look at him! Even *I* can get the best of him.

Jack would wait for her downstairs in the bar and Shireen would come rushing in, brisk and full of energy from the cold, gleaming with excitement. He would get up from the bar stool and they would shake hands and each day his eyes reassured her: this was the moment he had been waiting for since he had left her last night.

"Busy day?" he would ask her, as they rode up in the elevator.

"Busy! Why, do you know it's getting so that I can't remember by night what I did in the morning! I had another interview—some paper in Chicago. And I saw that woman about that radio program she wants me to be on with her. *Life* took some pictures. They wanted to take some in bed, of course, but I wouldn't let them. Had lunch with Georgia and one of the editors from a motion-picture studio, I've already forgotten which one, I get them all mixed up. And I had a dress fitted, and bought a couple of hats." She blew a quick breath, stepped out of the elevator and as she walked down the hall and unlocked her door, kept on talking to him. "And people! I've met hundreds of people, every time I turn around I meet new people. It's like looking at a crowd in a newsreel. Well, maybe someday I'll get them sorted out." She took off her hat and turned to him. "Give me your coat—" and she hung it in the closet.

"Shall I mix you a drink?" he asked her, opening the door of the kitchenette.

"No, thanks. I'm going to change my dress—I'll be out in a minute. Oh, I forgot, I was going to order something for you to eat. *Tsk, tsk.* I really must get more domestic. I should at least have some *cheese* in the icebox."

She heard him laugh and there was an affectionate sound in his voice, as if he thought she was cute and childish and irresponsible—and she was glad to realize she could get away with it. This is the way

166

I've always wanted to live, she thought, and felt a swelling sense of great and perfect freedom.

A few minutes later she came back out and found him having his drink and reading the paper. He put it aside the moment she came in and looked at her. She stood still a moment, smiling, and then sat down across from him. His careful concentration on everything she did had begun to make her aware of the mannerisms she had developed over her lifetime, so that she could almost watch herself as she must look to him:

The way she would stand holding the telephone in her right hand, her left across the top of her forehead with the fingers slid through her hair. The delicate gestures of her hands. The slow movement of crossing her legs. The brilliance of her whole face when she laughed. Her intense eager look when she was listening to someone else talk. He gave her a new pleasure in herself.

Now she sighed lightly, gesturing toward the window. It was growing dark and had the soft sad sweetness of a day not quite done. The buildings were beginning to light up and through the misty smoky air they looked almost translucent.

"It's so quiet here, isn't it? I suppose this is what I like about New York—you can have as much of it as you want, but you don't have to take more. It lets you alone, if that's what you want, or sucks you into itself if you're willing."

"It lets you alone? Maybe. Once you get used to it."

"You're not? After all these years?" She sounded polite, but mildly pitying and contemptuous.

"I don't know—I don't think so. Oh, of course there are some things here I like very much. But there's something else—I can't get over the feeling that everything's so damned urgent. Whether it matters or not, it's got to be important in New York."

Shireen shrugged. He had the same fear of it she had had, but she had conquered hers and he had not. So no matter what he said, she found another flaw. And as the weeks went by she realized that she saw him, not because he interested her, but because she interested him.

She let him kiss her one night and he told her afterward that he was in love with her. She smiled and touched his cheek and pushed him gently so she could close the door. When she told Georgia that he was in love with her she felt as if she had captured another enemy prisoner.

But he was not captured completely. He still had part of his freedom, and there was only one way she knew to take it away from him. And anyway, she told herself, it wouldn't hurt me, Ed will never know it so it can't hurt him, and it's not fair to Jack. Because he really is in love with me.

167

It's only natural and honest, after all. It's my fault he's in love with me—I've encouraged him plenty, God knows. And I never have believed in encouraging a man at all unless you're going to sleep with him.

"You know," she said to Georgia a few days later. "I think maybe I'm falling in love with Jack MacDonald."

Georgia laughed. "That means you're sleeping with him."

Shireen looked surprised. "How did you know?"

"I know you, Shireen. You're a complete puritan. To me a roll in the hay is just a roll in the hay. But you always want to make something big and cosmic out of it."

"But it *is* something big and cosmic. What else do we have? There's birth and death and the union of two people—and sex is the only one that happens to us more than once. Maybe that's why we're careless with it, but we shouldn't be. We shouldn't ever permit ourselves to be and every time we are, we lose something by it. It's the closest we can ever come to some kind of understanding of eternity or the universe, and the minute we let ourselves be cynical or halfhearted we've made a basic compromise that will have some effect on every part of us."

Georgia shrugged. "Then you're making that fatal compromise right now, because you're not in love with Jack and you know it."

"But I think I am," she insisted, frowning. "He's a very nice man, after all. There's nothing really wrong with him when you come right down to it. I might as well be in love with him as anyone else. Anyway, I think I'm getting more sensible—because this time I don't expect anything much."

Georgia laughed. "Poor Jack," she said. "He's coming to a sorry end—and soon."

"Why?"

"The day you stop expecting anything much, you'll be dead."

During the next three or four weeks her life went along as it had, only seeming to pick up speed constantly. There were more interviews and photographs and Morgan Thayer was making plans for cocktail parties and an autographing tour they were sending her on. Practically every evening she spent with Jack and she was gay and compliant and docile; almost as if she existed for nothing but his pleasure and benefit.

And then late one afternoon she walked into Georgia's office and sat talking to her for awhile until Georgia remembered something. "Oh—by the way. Jack called awhile ago and said he just got a wire from Eva. She's coming home."

"Well?"

"That's all. She's coming home."

"I can't see that it has much to do with me."

"He wanted you to call him."

"What for?"

"He may not be able to take you to *Oklahoma* tomorrow night."

Shireen lit a cigarette. "Oh, yes he will."

"Well, you'll have to settle it between you. Anyway, you'd better call him."

Shireen got up, slipped into her coat and picked up her bag and gloves. "The hell with him. Let him call me. I'm going home and listen to those new records."

At seven o'clock she was stretched out on the couch with a pile of records on the floor beside her, smoking a cigarette and listening to *Daphnis and Chloé,* turned so loud it seemed to hammer in her blood. The doorbell rang and she took her time about answering it, knowing it would be Jack. She found him standing there as usual, a look of expectancy on his face that changed almost immediately to a smile. He stepped inside and bent his head to kiss her but, quite unexpectedly, she turned her cheek.

This is getting pretty goddamned domestic, she thought in annoyance. Funny, I never noticed it before.

He followed her into the living room. "I guess Georgia must have forgotten to give you my message."

"She told me. I was busy."

He looked faintly puzzled. Usually she was gay and eager when he came and the contrast was painfully noticeable, as she had intended it should be.

"Oh. Well, Eva gets home tomorrow night. I wanted to let you know in time."

"In time for what?"

"So you can make other plans, Shireen. We can see it a few days from now just as well. You don't mind, do you?"

"I certainly do."

He looked surprised and baffled. "But Shireen—I can't very well go off the first night she comes home."

"Why not?" she asked him softly.

"Why not? After all, she is my wife—I can't very well—"

She cut in quickly and then, having interrupted, her voice continued soft and light, like a reasonable patient parent explaining something very simple to a dull child.

"I'm not interested in hearing about your domestic problems, Jack. Solve them yourself. I've told you what I think about it anyway. The whole situation is so ridiculous it's not worth discussing. And I don't give a goddamn about Eva—the fact that she's coming back has nothing at all to do with me."

"Why, Shireen. What's the trouble, darling? Did something go wrong today?" He got up and came toward her.

"Don't step on those, please." She indicated the records.

She felt a wholly self-righteous anger. He had betrayed her. He

169

pretended to love her, he had said that he loved her—more than anything else in the world. She had given him so much, her time and her self, on which she placed extremely high value. And now he was betraying her for a woman he did not love at all; she felt she had been tricked, and she hated him.

He sat down beside her and began to take her into his arms, but then she turned, moving away from him.

"Please, Jack. I should think you'd have better sense than that."

"Than what?" He kept looking at her as if he had got into a room with a strange animal and did not know how dangerous it might be or how he should try to approach it.

She got up quickly and turned her back. "This really is not the time to start making love! That's the trouble with you men!"

"But I can't help it if Eva's coming home. God knows I wish she wouldn't, but she is. There's nothing I can do about it."

She swung around and stood facing him with her hands on her hips. "Look here, Jack—you may think you can have this thing both ways, but you can't. Because I won't let you! Things have gone to your satisfaction for so long you've got the idea you'll always have what you want just because you want it! Maybe you've been able to juggle other women against your wife, but you can't do it with me! There's nothing you can give me, Jack MacDonald, that I can't live without! So you'll play it my way—or not at all!"

She turned and walked to the window, despising him for the way he had been looking at her, as if he cringed inside himself. He was afraid and his face showed it. Because there was something he wanted from her and now she was threatening to take it away. She stood staring down at the weird rooftop excrescences.

"Men," Shireen had said to Georgia a few days before, "are really so simple. If you make a guy think he's terrific in the hay, like nothing that ever lived before, he'll eat out of your hand. The poor bastards must have awful doubts about themselves because they're so foolishly grateful to a woman who seems to appreciate them. Look at Jack."

Yes, she thought now. Look at Jack.

She had suddenly turned her character over and shown him another side of it, a side that existed for her own protection and benefit, when perhaps he had begun to think that she lived to give him the sense of power and achievement, the secret sexual confidence he could take with him wherever he went. She considered that by now she had given him so much he was her rightful property.

"Shireen—please. You know I love you."

"I know you say you love me. And I know words don't cost a damned thing. I mean it, Jack. You'll have to think of something to tell Eva tomorrow night."

"But I had planned to take her and the kids—"

170

"Jack—please don't give me the details of your family life. I don't *care*—I'm not interested. You can't very well expect it to matter to me whether or not Eva gets what *she* wants. Oh, I'm sick of this!" She felt a wave of intense unexplainable despondency, and some terrible realization of destined defeat.

Then Jack's hands took hold of her shoulders. She swung around, as if something unknown had approached her in the dark, her face full of fear that turned instantly to anger.

"Shireen, please. Don't be angry with me. I love you—"

She gave a sudden tired sigh, and let herself slump against him. His arms held her and his hands stroked her back. Finally he took hold of her chin, very gently, and she let him raise her head. She looked at him, and slowly her eyes took on the pure intense interest of a cat watching its prey.

"I love you," he repeated, as if convinced that by saying it over and over he could make her say it back to him.

"One of these days, Jack MacDonald, I'm going to drop you so hard you'll think you fell out of the Empire State Building." Jack laughed, as if he knew she was joking.

"I'll do whatever you say about tomorrow night, Shireen. But I wish you'd try to see it my way, just this once."

She twisted lightly away from him. "Do as you please."

The next morning he called her and said he had been thinking it over and believed it was best, if she would let him, to spend tonight with his family. She told him sweetly that it was quite all right, whatever he had decided, and went out to have another dress fitted.

They saw *Oklahoma* a couple of nights later and Jack sent two white orchids with a note thanking her for having been so understanding and promising that he would make it all up to her in time. But he also asked her to meet him at a hotel bar down the street, so his wife would not happen through the lobby and see them together.

"This won't last much longer," she told Georgia darkly. "He can't play with *me* like a Yo-yo!"

171

Chapter 24

Georgia reached across the desk and Shireen took the book from her and held it in her hands. Shireen Delaney. *The Falcon*. And on the back of the dust jacket: *The Falcon*. Delaney. She opened it and turned to the last page to see how long it was in book form, and then closed it. Georgia sat and watched her, smoking, doodling on her scratch pad.

She felt an unexpected humbleness. This is something I've done, she told herself slowly, that will be here after I'm dead and will last as long as one person wants to read it.

"Well?" Georgia said. "How about it? How does it make you feel?"

"I don't know. Lonesome, I guess." She put it down. "Well, it's not much longer now, is it? I keep thinking something will happen to me first."

"Nothing will happen. Cinderella's going to the ball."

But neither of them had ever mentioned the possibility that Cinderella might not enjoy the ball after all. That it was perhaps too big a jump to make in one night and land on both feet, particularly in glass slippers.

"So you've got a date with Lawrence Christopher tomorrow night?" said Georgia.

"Yes, I thought I might as well. I don't want to miss anything." But she said it a little apologetically, because she knew that the real reason she was going out with Lawrence Christopher was to see what a celebrity was like.

Lawrence Christopher was one of the most successful playwrights in America, and though there was some discussion among intellectuals as to whether or not he had actually "contributed" anything, he had made a great deal of money. Shireen had met him a few days before.

And she had been more flattered than she liked to admit when he said to her: "My dear, it's been so charming meeting you and now, unfortunately, I've got to run. Some actress or other is having a cocktail party. But I do think you're ever so sweet and pretty, my dear, and I'd like very much to take you to dinner some night. Could you come?"

She didn't want to go, because she was sure she would fail in some way, not know how to talk to him or how to act—not be, one way or another, what he expected her to be. Lawrence Christopher and others

172

like him seemed to her always to have been famous and important, simply born that way.

"Why, yes, Mr. Christopher," she had said. "I'd like to."

"How about tomorrow night?"

"That would be very nice." She'd have to break a date with Jack.

"Then suppose I pick you up at your hotel about eight. We'll think of something gay to do. And you'll be looking lovely, won't you? Of course you will. Good-by."

That made it hard for her to decide what to wear. *You'll be looking lovely, won't you? Of course you will.* As she went through her closet she found something wrong with every dress she considered.

Would he like this one?

Would she look "lovely" to him in that one?

How, exactly, was it that he wanted her to look?

And then all at once she was angry. She took out the newest dress she had and put it on. What in hell did he mean, anyway, saying such a thing to her? She always looked nice. What was the matter with him? She'd wear what she damn well pleased.

But when she got out of the elevator to meet him in the lobby she was anxious and troubled again. She walked toward him, holding her breath. He reached out to take her hand. "My dear," he said, "you look simply charming." She smiled and felt a great relief.

"Now," he said. "You must tell me. Where would you like to go? I think the Colony might be nice—or are you tired of it?"

"No, I'm not tired of it at all. I've never been there."   •

Lawrence Christopher gave her a glance of vague alarm, as if he found it difficult to believe there was someone in New York who had never been to the Colony, but he apparently decided it must be some-one else's fault. Bad advisers, no doubt. He offered her his arm and they went out and got into the cab he had waiting.

"Oh, dear," he said, once he had given the driver the address. "I've spent the most frightful day. I'm working on a new play, you know, and I've been at it since noon. I only left the house once—to go to my analyst."

"Really?" said Shireen.

It seemed safest not to say much, not expose or commit herself, and then she could not be the subject of his secret contempt or ridicule.

"Yes—this is something completely new. I think it's going to be quite revolutionary. If it turns out as I expect, it may change the entire form of the drama—I shouldn't be surprised if it does. The American theater, you know, is dying on its feet. Of course it's always dying on its feet but something's got to be done and many people are looking to me to do it."

This guy's the damndest egotist I ever met, she thought, very much surprised to hear him talk so unabashedly about himself to a stranger.

He gave her a quick sharp sideways glance. "But now let's talk about you, my dear."

Inside her something started and took flight. "About me?"

"Of course. Surely you must know it's quite amazing to find someone as young and pretty as you who's written a book that's going to be a terrific hit. From what Georgia tells me, you're about to create a sensation."

"Oh—did she say that?"

"The guy's a stuffed shirt," Georgia had said, speaking of Lawrence Christopher. "He wants to be seen with you while you're brand-new—like the woman who wants the first platinum mink on the market. Go ahead and see for yourself, but keep it in mind so you won't be too much taken in."

"You must be terribly excited," he said now.

"Oh, yes. I am. Of course."

It was not quite true. She felt calm, almost indifferent, now that it was so close. But she would tell him that she was excited, just to be polite.

At the Colony Mr. Christopher was greeted by the headwaiter with the right mixture of hearty good welcome and servility and they were led into the bar where they sat at a table near the door. He asked her what she would drink and she said a daiquiri, hoping it would not make her drunk before dinner.

Lawrence began to fidget nervously.

He looked around the room. He directed Shireen's attention to a man in the far corner who he said was some kind of international financier, worth over a hundred million. Shireen looked at him. Lawrence kept glancing in the man's direction, glancing away, glancing back again. Finally the financier saw him and smiled and nodded his head. Lawrence returned the salute eagerly, and looked around for others he might know.

A few minutes later the man and his beautifully gowned companion got up and, as they came to Lawrence's table, stopped. He introduced them to Shireen, quickly explaining that she had written that great new book of which they had most certainly heard, and he put it so that both of them were forced to acknowledge they had heard of it and the woman was halfway through a sentence of congratulation, telling Shireen how much she had enjoyed it, when Lawrence broke in and informed them it would be published in a few days.

As they sipped their drinks he pointed out other people in the room. There was the distinguished English novelist and his sweetheart, a Hollywood actress. Lawrence managed to attract their attention, too, and exchanged greetings. He looked for someone else.

"Oh, dear," he said finally, in obvious discouragement. "There's no one amusing here tonight."

Shireen glanced at him out of the corners of her eyes and smiled faintly. Apparently Lawrence Chistopher could only be amused by "names." For the first time she felt a slight superiority.

Now Lawrence was engrossed in studying the menu and presently he called the waiter and began to consult with him in French, turning to Shireen now and then to ask in English what her preference was.

He went on talking industriously as soon as the food had been ordered. He told her about how the Duke of Windsor had said this to him, and Lady Mendl had said that. How this had happened in Cairo and that in Paris. He mentioned various well-known people, many expensive hotels, and several faraway places.

Shireen listened carefully and with pretended interest, but she was privately criticizing everything he said. She had read two or three of his plays and this kind of talk was not what she had expected from him. He was not nearly so interesting about his travels as Johnny, and Johnny wasn't even a celebrity. She felt she had been duped somehow. A man like Lawrence Christopher had no business being like that; not when she and everyone else had been led to think a celebrity was some special breed of animal altogether different from the ordinary breed.

"They've been hopelessly in love for years," he said to her, indicating the novelist and actress who sat holding hands and gazing at each other. "His wife, you know. Catholic—or something like that. Isn't she the loveliest wraith?"

"Oh, she certainly is," agreed Shireen. The girl looked like a wraith, all right, but that was not Shireen's idea of beauty.

"I like to think of her," Lawrence went on eagerly, "simply wafting out the window on a moonbeam when she has gone to him at night in love and is stealing back to her own hotel. Don't you find it a charming picture?"

"Oh, yes. Lovely." This guy's out of his mind, she told herself. Where does he get such screwy ideas?

When they had finished dinner Lawrence glanced at his watch. "Not ten yet. Much too early to go anywhere. My apartment's not far from here—why don't we stop up there? I have some paintings I think might amuse you and I'd love to show you a page or so of my play. It's the first draft, but of course you know what that is, and I'd be interested to have your opinion. Some of the dialogue's quite good, I think."

"I'd like to," said Shireen, telling herself she might as well find out how a celebrity lived, what he surrounded himself with, what was his natural habitat.

Lawrence Christopher had a big living room full of books and paintings and phonograph records. The furniture was sharp blond wood and glass with a few pieces of African sculpture and a battered cigar-store wooden Indian in one corner. Celebrities, apparently, lived something like other people, and yet she was aware that this was the home of the playwright Lawrence Christopher, and was more critical of it for that reason. In many ways it looked like a photograph she might have seen in *Life*—though she had not—in which he would have been sitting at his desk holding a cigarette, staring at his typewriter, and drinking a cup of coffee.

"Isn't that amusing?" he said, as she walked over to look at the Indian because she did not know what else to do. "I've been everywhere, I think, and some of my most exotic treasures I've found right here in the United States. It's really a terribly frightening and strange and fascinating country, you know."

"Yes," she said. "I'm sure it must be."

She went wandering about to look at the paintings and he walked beside her, explaining that this one was a Picasso done in 1910 and he had picked it up years ago for nothing at all, and this was a Dufy which was so gay and delightful and this a Mondrian before which he could sit fascinated for hours at a time.

Shireen looked at it and then said, sadly: "I'm afraid I just don't understand things like that. It looks to me like something any student of elementary geometry could do in an hour with a slide rule and some poster paints."

Lawrence gave a barking embarrassed laugh and assumed the air of a man who is regretful at someone else's ignorance but unprepared to correct it for them. He turned away from the paintings and went to the phonograph.

"What would you like to hear, my dear? Some Schönberg?"

Shireen had never heard of Schönberg and now she was thrown into a sudden conviction that she knew nothing at all. Something had been left out of her or not properly developed and she would have to correct it. But she might as well not try to fool him.

"Yes," she said. "I'd like to. I don't know anything about him."

Lawrence Christopher raised his eyebrows at that and tightened his lips a little, whether in regret or reproval she could not quite tell. But he started the phonograph anyway and, after a hasty glance at Shireen, sat down, closed his eyes and covered them with one hand. Shireen looked at him in some surprise, but all the while the music played he continued to sit like that, not moving, while she tried to listen and hear whatever she could. When it was over he sprang up as if in triumph.

"God, wasn't that exciting?"

"Yes," said Shireen unhappily. Every day it seemed she found out about more things she did not know.

He showed her a couple of pages of his play then and for the first time she felt in contact with him, eager to reassure and encourage him, before she had seen a line of it. She read what he told her to and then handed it back. "It's really very good," she said, her voice and eyes warm and floating with sympathy. "It doesn't seem possible that it's only a first draft."

And she watched him as he shuffled among the typewritten pages, putting the two he had shown her back in place, his face happy and absorbed and unguarded, even a little wistful. She realized for the first time that underneath "Lawrence Christopher" there was a person, as full of misgivings as she was and having as hard a time with his work as she had. Before, she would have assumed he must dash it off between parties and while rushing around the world, scarcely giving it a thought, knowing it would always come out right.

"You really think so?" he asked her.

"I'm sure of it. Everything you've ever written has been good."

"Never as good as I've wished," he said. And then he got up quickly. "Come, my dear. Suppose we drop in at the Cub Room?"

At the Stork Club there were people standing meekly behind the chain waiting to be admitted but as Lawrence Christopher came in the man at the door smiled and unhooked one end to let them through.

"Good evening, Mr. Christopher. It's very nice to see you again."

"Nice to see you, Frank. I've been working hard. Is the Cub Room crowded?"

"Not too crowded, Mr. Christopher."

Lawrence stepped to one side and Shireen walked ahead of him, following the headwaiter along the bar where well-dressed men and women sat perched on stools, past the supper room where music was playing and people dancing and on into the sound-proofed Cub Room. They were given a table against the wall and Shireen said she would have a crème de menthe frappé. She was almost afraid to look around, for fear she would find herself now completely surrounded by celebrities.

Lawrence immediately began smiling and nodding and waving and she had a strong immediate conviction that everyone but she had always belonged in this place and that she was here under false pretenses. She fixed a faint smile on her face and sat there smoking and looking delicately bored, wishing she were anywhere else in the world.

Then she tried to reason it out, talk away her overwhelming sense of inferiority.

Isn't it funny, she thought, how we Americans have cooked up such a wonderful system for impressing one another? Even if we think we don't believe that newspaper publicity and magazine pictures and sudden money make you any different than you were before, you feel it just the same.

177

It didn't help. She still felt out of place, convinced that everyone else was happy and confident and perfectly at ease.

Various people began to come over to their table and each time Lawrence explained who she was. They seemed to be all very famous people: an actor, a best-selling author, an heiress who languidly passed her fingers over Lawrence's hand as she went by and slanted Shireen a glance to see how good-looking she was and how chic her clothes were.

"Where've you been?" she drawled at Lawrence, a kind of pouting chastisement on her face.

"Hard at work, darling. Will you be in tomorrow?"

"Try me."

"Sweet child," he said, when she had gone. "And so frightfully lovely for a girl with all that money. Pity she can't seem to stay married."

"Yes," agreed Shireen. She had never heard of the heiress before. The trouble with her, she was beginning to realize, was that she didn't know who half the important people in the United States were.

"Of course Sherman will send you a bottle of perfume or something," said Lawrence. And, after fifteen minutes or so, Sherman did. "Wasn't that sweet of him?" said Lawrence.

A man came toward the table and Lawrence muttered quickly to Shireen: "Here comes Marvin in a new toupee. Why, Marvin! When did you get to town?"

" 'S morning," said Marvin. "Horrible trip." He glanced at Shireen and Lawrence quickly introduced them, explaining that Marvin was Marvin Miller, the great producer, and that Shireen was the author of that great new book. Marvin took the cigar out of his mouth and he and Shireen shook hands.

"Miss Delaney, I want to congratulate you. I read a twenty-two page synopsis of your book and I was *fas*cinated. Couldn't lay it down."

"Thank you, Mr. Miller."

"It's a great story, great story. It'll make a great picture. I hope we buy it."

"I hope you do, Mr. Miller."

A waiter went by with a loaded tray held high in one hand, glanced at Mr. Miller's toupee and nudged him slightly as he edged the tray past his head. "Look out for your hat," he cautioned.

Mr. Miller exchanged a few anecdotes with Lawrence and they both laughed heartily at the end of each one. Shireen sat listening but completely bewildered, with no idea what they were talking about, but pretending to laugh too. Then Mr. Miller took the cigar out of his mouth again, shook hands with Shireen, and went away. Lawrence pointed out some more celebrities.

178

"It's so amusing," he said, "because everyone comes to the Stork Club to see the people who can't be seen because they're all hiding in here."

Shireen was shocked. Why, this guy's such a goddamned snob he doesn't even know when he's being one. Other people wandered up to the table, one of them a movie actor who kissed her hand and stared deeply into her eyes, apparently determined to overwhelm her with his charm. The novelist and his fragile actress wandered in, as though drifting on clouds, and were placed at the table next to them. Lawrence and the novelist began to talk, across Shireen and the actress, who sat side by side. Shireen waited a few moments, but when the girl said nothing at all, decided she must rescue the situation herself.

"You were wonderful in *Morning Song*," she said, and the girl looked at her with a wan appealing smile.

"Did you think so, really?" She was vague, distant, and her voice did not sound as if it came out of her.

"Oh, of course," insisted Shireen. "I thought it was one of the finest performances I'd ever seen."

"Did you, really?"

"Yes, I did. And I understand you've just finished another picture. Are you pleased with it?" She asked the questions anxiously, determined to somehow conquer her fright and be as charming as anyone else or, if possible, more charming than anyone else.

"It's rather nice, I think. But I'm going to do a play this fall—you know how impossible it is for an artist in Hollywood. It's a frightful place, really frightful. Such dreadful people, and they do such awful things to you."

"I'm sure it must be very difficult," said Shireen.

About two o'clock Lawrence suggested they go to the Champagne Room at El Morocco for scrambled eggs and bacon and coffee. And as they went out several people nodded and smiled to Lawrence, including Shireen in the salutation, and she had a quick sense of gratitude that she had not been ignored.

"It's such fun to take you out," said Lawrence, in the cab. "Because everyone's so charming to you."

The Champagne Room was dim and half-deserted and as they ate, a violinist came to their table and began to play. "Isn't it lovely?" Lawrence asked Shireen. "That melody always make me want to weep. I used to hear it in the cafés in Vienna during the thirties." He shook his head, suddenly morose and sentimental. "I can't believe it. I simply can't believe it. Beautiful Europe. Well—" He gave her a bright frankly artificial smile to indicate that he was going to be brave about this thing. "One can't help matters by being miserable oneself, can one?"

About four they left and took a cab and on the way back to her

179

hotel he made a clumsy halfhearted attempt to kiss her. She had assumed that well-known men were polished lovers and was surprised at his awkwardness. Furthermore, she knew he had been married to an actress and had taken it for granted that women accustomed to such embraces as she saw on the screen must be very discriminating in their private lives.

Was this what they had to put up with?

"Please don't," she said.

He kissed her moistly on the cheek and shrugged his shoulders. "Very well. Most women expect it, you know."

"They do? Well, I don't. I'm in love with my husband."

"My dear, I hope you are. That's very charming. Very touching. Though of course I don't quite believe it. It's not true of one person in a hundred. Love exists chiefly in the fancies of poets and advertising men."

"I'm afraid I don't know much about that. I'm sure I haven't been in love as many times as you've been married."

He laughed. "Well—neither have I."

At her hotel he asked the driver to wait while he got out and reached his hand back to help her. Shireen stood on the sidewalk and smiled nervously at him. "Thanks ever so much. I've had a wonderful time."

"My dear, it's been perfectly delightful. You're so fresh and sweet and unspoiled. I have to go away tomorrow—some party or other for the week end. Suppose I call you Monday."

"I'm leaving on an autographing tour."

"My dear! How dreadful for you. Well—then when you get back."

"All right. And thank you again."

He made a slight gesture, climbed into his cab and was gone. Shireen walked into the hotel and stood beside the elevator, leaning against the wall in complete exhaustion. But she was pleased with the evening, now that it was over. She had visited another world and someday it would surely turn out to be useful.

She went to bed and found herself thinking, as she fell asleep: I've got to learn more know more think more see more feel more taste more. . . .

Chapter 25

Shireen got off the plane very tired, for she had not been able to sleep the night before. She walked out into the brilliant assault of the sunlight and cringed a little from it, discovering that she was almost dizzy as she walked down the stairs.

Two people met her—the Morgan Thayer representative in that city, and one of the bookstore buyers. The Morgan Thayer man handed her a box with two bronze orchids in it and she thanked him and pinned them to the lapel of her suit.

"Sleep well?" he asked her.

"Fine."

"Good. You'll need your strength. Thayer called me half an hour ago and says they've ordered another fifty thousand copies and are wondering how they can make fifty more. Three hundred thousand so far." He looked at her in pleased amazement.

"Good heavens," said Shireen. But could not tell if she was surprised or not, since she had no idea what three hundred thousand was anyway.

In the cab he and the book buyer discussed what kind of speech she should make that afternoon. The buyer was casual. "People never care what anyone says. They forget it while you're saying it, or make up something else to suit themselves. They're only interested in seeing what you look like."

"But I'm sure Morgan Thayer would prefer Miss Delaney to make some kind of more or less serious speech—something in keeping with the dignity of the firm."

Shireen glanced at him, a puzzled little frown on her face. Life seemed to get more baffling every day. Now here she had to worry about making a dignified speech in keeping with the firm.

"I'll do the best I can," she promised him.

He took her to the hotel where she unpacked, bathed, ate breakfast, and went downstairs to meet him, five minutes early. She stood around, watching the people in the lobby, smoking a cigarette, believing herself as unconcerned as if she was simply meeting an old friend for lunch. She must take it all in her stride, be very calm and matter-of-fact—for after all, wasn't this only the natural habitat of Shireen Delaney?

And anyway, the whole thing was vague and amorphous, tasteless, soundless, smell-less, like a wad of cotton. Like ploughing through a cloud in a dream where, at least, if goblins were there she would never see them.

The Morgan Thayer man came and drove her through the city and let her out in front of a red brick building. "I've got to make some arrangements for the cocktail party. I'll pick you up at two-thirty," he said. "Good luck."

Shireen smiled and waved at him as he drove off, and walked up the steps. This was part of the "program" Morgan Thayer had made out for her. It was listed somewhere on the mimeographed itinerary: *Monday, April 19,* 1 P.M. That was where it fitted in and here she was. The "program" worked in wondrous ways, its miracles to perform. Shireen understood that at this point it was not hers to wonder why. She walked up the steps and into the building and found it full of women.

All of them were chattering together with some air of being present at a gala occasion, though Shireen did not know what the occasion might be. Republican Women's Club Luncheon, the "program" had said. She stood there a moment, wondering what to do next, and finally one woman stepped up to her, smiling politely and questioningly.

"How do you do?"

Shireen felt like the times when, as a kid, she had gone for a quart of milk to the grocery store a block away, out of her own neighborhood, and known she was in an alien and vaguely hostile place.

"Have you your invitation?" she asked Shireen, still with that careful delicate politeness.

"Yes, I have." She took it out of her bag and handed it to her, hoping it was the right one. She had so many, back at the hotel in her folder.

The woman looked at it and then her face became warmer, welcoming her now. "Oh, Miss Delaney! Of course! I should have recognized you—there were pictures of you in all the papers this morning. I'm Mrs. Stapledon, Chairman for the Day."

"How do you do, Mrs. Stapledon," said Shireen, wondering if she should ask what "Day" it was, but decided it did not make very much difference since it would be over in an hour and a half whether she knew what it was about or not.

"May I show you to your seat?"

Shireen smiled to indicate she would be ever so pleased by this courtesy and followed Mrs. Stapledon up some more stairs and into a big dining room. On the way she was introduced to a few more ladies who spoke to her politely but vaguely and apparently had no better idea why she was there than she did.

Mrs. Stapledon showed her her seat, smiled again, thanked her for coming, and excused herself. Shireen sat alone. She was now at a long

182

narrow table with chairs only on the side that faced into the great empty dining room. She looked at the card beside her plate:

Miss Shireen Delaney.

That's me.

And then she had a sudden sense of horrified shock.

My God! What am *I* doing here?

There must be some mistake. How did these things happen? For four years she had sat alone in her apartment reading books and indexing notes and writing and cooking for Ed and now here she was sitting at a speakers' table!

What could have happened in between to bring her here?

Something must have gone wrong with the machinery. Someone had got her mixed up with someone else. She must get up and get out of here before it was too late. Or they had her trapped. But she was trapped anyway—trapped by her own book, by the date, by her dreams and hopes and wishes that were now going to come true and overwhelm her, push her down, smother and obliterate her.

She drew a quick gasping breath.

For a few seconds the sense of shock and resentment was great. And then she was enveloped again by apathy, protected by a dulled insensibility and once more she stood outside herself, watching, feeling nothing at all.

Now the women began to troop into the room, locating their seats with a good deal of high-pitched well-bred chatter, and others were taking their places along the speakers' table. A plump woman of fifty or so with florid cheeks and an eager fluttering manner sat down at Shireen's right and Shireen glanced at her card. Mrs. Ernest Batson.

What did *she* do to get here? wondered Shireen, giving her a quick covert glance. It was like turning up in Hell one morning, unexpectedly, and looking around at all the people, trying to figure out what crime had brought them there.

She smiled at Mrs. Batson, feeling that the two of them were stranded here on the social equivalent of a raft and something must be done about it. "Hello, Mrs. Batson. I'm Miss Delaney."

"How do you do, Miss Delaney. My, have you ever seen such a crowd?"

"No," said Shireen. "The room's entirely filled."

"Mrs. Stapledon's done such a magnificent job this year, hasn't she?"

"Yes, from everything I've heard, she has." Shireen took a sip of water and wished she could simply turn and open her mouth and yell for help. She was worrying about what she would say when she was called upon to speak, as sooner or later she would be. Her "serious" speech was not for this occasion.

"Just say whatever comes into your mind," the Morgan Thayer man had told her.

But *nothing* comes into my mind when I face an audience, she wanted to tell him, but didn't dare. Morgan Thayer was counting on her to make a speech and she could not fail them. Look how much they were doing for her and how hard they were trying to sell her book and how many copies they had sold already.

She went on talking to Mrs. Batson for a few minutes and was wishing that she could somehow fall asleep, wind herself up, and keep moving and talking automatically. There were only three or four men in the room and now one of them came and took his appointed seat beside Shireen. She glanced at him, saw that he was a middle-aged perspiring anxious man and felt instantly sorry for him. His card read Mr. Frederick Walpole. She had no idea who he might be.

"Hello," she said, escaping for a moment from Mrs. Batson who had turned to the woman on her right. "I'm Miss Delaney. What are you doing here?"

"Oh, how do you do, Miss Delaney. To tell you the truth, I wish I knew. I wrote a book on medieval trade practices and the next thing I knew I found myself in places like this. What are you doing here?"

"I wrote a book about Jamaica. It's being published today. Can you tell me what this lunch is for or about?"

"I really don't quite—"

At that moment Mrs. Batson turned back to Shireen with a cry that sounded both delighted and predatory. "Why, Miss Delaney! You didn't tell me you had written a book! My dear, I think it's perfectly wonderful. How does it *feel* to be famous overnight?"

A hand reached in front of Shireen and set a cup of pink tomato soup down. Shireen looked at it. Then she smiled shyly at Mrs. Batson who was watching her with a curious eager look, almost lustful, seeking, as if determined to suck from Shireen something that she would be able to use.

Shireen backed up inside herself as she saw the expression, and a rebellious stubbornness rose. She would not tell the woman how it felt. She would not give away part of herself to this ravening stranger. But still she must make some kind of deceptively satisfying answer, for it was important that Mrs. Batson—and everyone else she might meet—should like and approve of her. She did not care why they liked her or even if what they liked was her real self, just so they were convinced Shireen Delaney was a "nice girl."

"I'm afraid I can't tell you, Mrs. Batson," she said with soft modesty. "I'm really not famous."

"Oh, my dear, but of *course* you are! Imagine it happening at your age—it's incredible, I can scarcely believe it. Why—"

Mrs. Stapeldon was standing up now, banging with her gavel, and the room began to grow quiet. Shireen felt her heart pound and a sickness gather inside her. After a moment she had shoved that feeling away too, dulling herself further. She began trying to piece together in her mind some kind of speech, but each time she got a sentence completed she would forget it while she was working on the next one.

Oh, the hell with it! she thought. I'll stand up and open my mouth and say *something*. Something's bound to come out. I've never yet heard of anyone standing up to make a speech and not saying anything at all. That's impossible.

Other people were introduced and made their speeches and she did not hear them but clapped when the others began to clap. She spoke a few sentences alternately with Mrs. Batson and Mr. Walpole in between the speeches.

And then she heard Mrs. Stapledon saying: "—present to you, Miss Shireen Delaney, who has written—"

Oh, God, thought Shireen. I kept thinking it would never really come and here it is.

The room burst into polite applause and she stood up, forcing what she hoped was a bright smile onto her face. She could feel herself trembling with a sudden overpowering terror. She looked out over the room and found it full of faces and all of them were looking back at her, waiting for her, eager, expectant, confident she would tell them something. Not one of them seemed to feel she would say nothing at all. That reassured her a little.

She glanced down in the direction of Mrs. Stapledon. "Thank you, Mrs. Stapledon," she said. But what next?

She opened her mouth and from far off somewhere in the distance she heard her own voice talking, but even she could not catch all the words:

". . . so happy to be here with you today . . . have always wanted so much to visit this beautiful city . . . unfortunately I cannot stay as long as I would like . . . shall return as soon as possible . . ."

All at once she leaned forward a little: "I'm no good as a public speaker. I've never done it before and it scares me to death. You've all been very kind, and I want to thank you."

With great uneasy relief she heard applause and friendly laughter roll toward her and she sat down. Mr. Walpole nodded and smiled and Mrs. Batson patted her on the hand. Shireen felt a rush of warmth and gratitude toward all of them. Suddenly she had a flash of feeling that she was actually enjoying herself.

Mr. Walpole spoke next, making a few jokes about the city which all turned out to be in the city's favor, said a few sentences about medieval trade practices, and then talked about gardening. When he sat down Shireen gave him a look which said he had been brave and

185

entertaining and acquitted himself well and then whispered: "That was *very* interesting."

Mr. Walpole cleared his throat and smiled gratefully. "Thanks," he whispered back.

Finally the luncheon was over. Shireen stood up and a couple of ladies approached the table. "Miss Delaney," said one of them. "We want to thank you for coming today and tell you how perfectly charming you are."

"Oh, dear," said Shireen, and blushed. "Thank you. Thank you very much."

She smiled down at them, they smiled up at her and then at each other, nodded good-by and somehow got mixed up in the crowd.

"Miss Delaney—" whispered Mr. Walpole.

"Yes?" Shireen turned.

"I think I've found out what the occasion is supposed to be. It's—"

"Oh, Mr. Walpole, I simply must talk to you about your garden! I love flowers and you—"

Mr. Walpole gave Shireen a quick helpless glance; she smiled sympathetically at him and began to make her way out. She stopped to thank Mrs. Stapledon, who was surrounded by several ladies, for asking her and for the delightful time she had had.

"We've enjoyed having you ever so much, Miss Delaney. Do come back again, won't you?"

"I certainly shall. Good-by."

She nodded and smiled to take in several other ladies and then she got away, worked through the crowd, down the stairs and out the door. She saw the Morgan Thayer car across the street with the district sales manager at the wheel, gave a skip as she started toward it and then broke into a little run.

"How was it?" he asked her. "Horrible?"

"Oh, no. It was fun."

The rooms backstage at the auditorium were crowded and noisy. "There are some people you'll have to meet," the Morgan Thayer man told her.

"All right. Where are they?"

"This dame over here's on one of the papers. She's an old bitch but don't let her throw you. She'll try, though, so look out. Come on."

They walked over, Shireen wondering why anyone should try to throw her, particularly someone who did not even know her. She was surprised and puzzled to hear him say such a thing, and sure it couldn't be true. She still believed that everyone in America was going to be tremendously surprised and admiring to find that little Shireen Delaney from Marron, who didn't know anything at all, had somehow written a big thick book and was going to get rich from it.

186

"Mrs. Wallace, may I present Miss Delaney?"

Mrs. Wallace looked at Shireen and at what Shireen was wearing and coolly asked her how she did. Shireen smiled and waited.

"You've been given quite a build-up," said Mrs. Wallace. "I got an advance copy of your book but haven't had time to read it. It's much too long for any book but a very good one. You know that, don't you? I hear you did your own research—is that true?"

Shireen was surprised and something inside her began to hurt, as if she had been struck for a wrong she had not committed. "Why, yes," she said. "Of course I did. I spent a great deal of time—"

"Apparently you're going to be well paid for your time. I wouldn't feel *too* bad about it if I were you."

"I don't at all. I only meant—"

"Miss Delaney's a very conscientious worker," interrupted the Morgan Thayer man. "She's fanatical about details. I think maybe Mrs. Wallace would like to hear something about how you went about your research—"

"Never mind. I've done a good deal of research myself. I know how you go about it. What does your husband think of all this? He's in the Navy, isn't he?"

"Yes, he is. He's in the Pacific now. And he thinks it's fine."

"What? The Pacific?"

"No, my book. He's glad I sold it."

The Morgan Thayer man spoke up again. "Mrs. Wallace, it's been very nice talking to you. Would you mind excusing us for a moment? Martha is signaling at us—"

"Oh, by all means. Don't let me keep you. Good-by, Miss Delaney."

Shireen smiled sweetly and shyly. "I'm very glad to have met you, Mrs. Wallace." Shireen and the Morgan Thayer man worked through the crowd. "What in hell was the matter with her?"

"Change of life, maybe. Don't ask me. You can't please everyone. Here's Martha."

As Shireen saw her she realized she had met Martha before and after another moment she remembered where. It had been at lunch in New York a few weeks ago with several other people. She had not been sure what it was for or why she was there and it had been one more of those places she found herself in where she met some people and later forgot them. Sometimes they turned up again somewhere or other in her life, as Martha was doing now. And then she would remember that the first meeting had probably been for a purpose, though in the meantime it had got lost in the sea of other lunches and new people, talk and confusion that had recently made up her life.

Martha greeted her enthusiastically, made some more introductions, told the photographer not to take her in profile, stood Shireen on one side of her and another young woman on the other side. The flash bulbs went off two or three times.

"I've never heard of anyone getting as much advance publicity as you've had," said the young woman. "Would you mind telling me who your press agent is?"

"I don't have one," said Shireen, and noticed that the girl had straggly eyebrows and her clothes were wrinkled.

"Oh, now come—"

"Smile, girls," commanded Martha, and they looked at the camera again. "That's all for now."

Shireen turned away, prepared to forget the girl. She did not look important enough to matter in her life one way or another, not with those clothes and that hair-do.

But the girl was persistent and her voice spoke sharply, following Shireen. "Things like that don't just happen. You've had smart management. That damn fool I hired—"

The Morgan Thayer man was there again. "Miss Beach, I'm sorry, but Miss Delaney has to get out on the stage. Will you please excuse us?"

"Don't mind me," said Miss Beach.

"Who in hell is that?"

"A gal who's just written a book called *Passion Is The Gale*. She's supposed to be very hot right now."

"She doesn't look it."

She walked out onto the stage, sat where Martha told her to, faced an auditorium full of people and took her speech out of her handbag. Two hours from now, she told herself, it won't make any difference. Everything matters, but nothing matters very much.

Chapter 26

She had a half hour to rest at the hotel before she had to get dressed for the cocktail party. Then she came out of the bedroom wearing a cerise satin skirt and a sleeveless black blouse embroidered around the armholes with gold thread and cerise-colored crystals. She wore black satin shoes and her nails and mouth matched the skirt; there was a little line of green shadow above her eyelashes.

"Very sharp," said the Morgan Thayer man. "If only more authors knew how to dress. But it seems to be part of the author persona to wear last year's gunny sack. Here—compliments of Morgan Thayer. Nothing's too good for our favorite author."

He handed her a cellophane box with a big white orchid and Shireen pinned it at her waistline. "Thanks very much. You've all been so good to me."

"You've been kinda good to us, don't forget. I figure there'll be about a hundred and fifty-two people here."

All coming to see me? wondered Shireen suddenly.

And of course that was what they were coming for. That was what the invitations had been sent for. She felt as if she were in the middle of a dream where she found herself in a crowded room with no clothes on. Three people appeared in the doorway.

"On your mark," said the Morgan Thayer man. "Here they come."

After that they seemed to pour into the room, as if they had been dammed up somewhere and the sluice gate had been opened. And she soon realized that this was a world where everyone but the guest of honor seemed to be acquainted and at ease, while she might as well have been from another planet for all she knew of what was going on.

"There certainly are a lot of people here, aren't there?" she said to a man who came up and stood looking at her, saying nothing, apparently just waiting to see what she was going to do.

"Don't be flattered," he said. "You're only an income-tax deduction."

She smiled wistfully, trying to bribe him not to be mad at her.

But she had begun to feel irritated by the noise and confusion and the innumerable new names and faces changing in front of her all day long. She was irritated by the ego behind each face, demanding that it be singled out, remembered, given some special consideration. She was irritated by the way they treated her. As if she were a freak they

189

had come to look at; as if she might easily be tricked into doing or saying something ridiculous; as if they resented her, or were in awe of her and resented that.

None of it had anything to do with her but only with someone they thought was her, and she felt as if her identity were slipping away and she was in danger of becoming what they believed her to be.

She decided that the safest procedure was to smile, cover every feeling she had, talk in brief sentences that said nothing, and get away each time as fast as she could. A couple of hours passed this way. But she was painfully aware of being in a different world than she had ever been in before—as if this time she were behind the bars at the zoo, looking out instead of looking in as she had always done before.

The Morgan Thayer man came up to her. "This guy's a big reporter here. He wants to talk to you alone."

"Bring him on."

He led her over to a small squat man who leered, but Shireen decided this was probably his usual expression and had nothing to do with her. She gave him a bright eager smile, for she still had some hope with each new person that things might be different this time. That this one would see behind *Shireen Delaney* and discover her back there, timid and scared and meaning no harm to anyone if only they would just be kind, pat her on the head, tell her she had been a good girl.

"Let's sit down, Miss Delaney. You must be tired of standing. In fact you must be tired, period."

"Oh, no," insisted Shireen, since being tired did not fit her picture of herself, not even when she was ready to drop from exhaustion. "I'm really not tired at all."

The man, whose name Shireen had heard to be Mr. Mortimer or Mr. Morton or Mr. Morrison, took a drink from a tray going by and steered her to a couch.

All couches and chairs were empty, but the two rooms were packed with people and the suite was full of smoke and nervous voices and laughter. The party was being given for her, she had been told, but actually these people were only here to get free drinks and food, to see each other and to satisfy some vague restless curiosity about a new freak in their midst—Shireen Delaney, this time—tossed up by the peculiarities of the world they lived in. Someone who had conformed so well that she had become, for the time being, a symbol of American life—by being so extremely typical she had become unusual enough to attract attention. She was aware of this and sensed that there was no kindliness and no real warmth in the room, nothing of what she had expected success would give her. She felt bewildered and frightened and a little sick inside.

And now here was this damn fool Morton (which was what he said his name was) who was a hired spy and gossip, paid to poke and prod and peer at people. A kind of freak himself because he was so much the typical gossip that he knew each day what it would please other gossips and snoops to read that night.

"Why aren't you drinking?" he asked her.

"I don't care to."

"You mean the powers-that-be told you not to?"

"No, I just don't want to."

"You mean you're cold sober?"

She looked him squarely in the eye. "That's right."

He shook his head, and it was plain he disapproved. "A drink would relax you."

"I am relaxed," said Shireen firmly.

"Like hell you are. How does all this strike you? How does it *feel* to be famous?"

Her first impulse was to tell him to go to hell, get up and walk away. She had been asked that at least seventy-five times since morning. Here she had written a book so that everyone would be so much in awe of her they would leave her alone, and apparently the idiots did not know this. But she must pretend to like him so he would like her. She was still impelled to try to be a "nice girl," obedient and well-behaved. By now, though, she was a long way inside herself and to drag herself out, bring forth something to extend to another person—even a smile and a pleasant tone of voice—was difficult. She had to fight a snarling reluctance.

"I'm not famous, so I'm afraid I can't tell you how it feels."

He made a face and took another swallow of his drink. He sighed.

"I don't know much about writers. This isn't my beat. They aren't usually news, though they're getting to be more so since the movies began paying such damn high prices—the public knows they make a lot of dough these days so they take 'em a little more seriously than they used to. They like to know how they look and what they eat and what bright comments they can make on world events. So you're news for the time being and news is my business. Where'd you get the idea for that book—who gave it to you?"

"No one gave it to me, Mr. Morton. I figured it out for myself, without help from anyone at all."

"Well, now isn't that nice? Figured it all out by yourself, did you? Tell me something—how come you don't look like other writers?"

"Don't I?"

"You know damned well you don't. Who tells you where to buy your clothes?"

"No one tells me. Everyone knows where to buy clothes."

"Why do you wear your hair that way?"

191

"What way? I part it on one side and comb it. It couldn't very well be simpler."

Two months ago no one cared or noticed how she wore her hair or what her clothes were like. Now, all of a sudden, she felt as if she had been put on a witness stand and must justify herself and everything she did. How had it happened? Somewhere along the way control had slipped out of her hands and she was beginning to have a sense of panic. She had expected that success would give her more control over her life, not less. But now she felt that she was being stalked, closed in upon, backed to a corner. Where was all the respect and admiration, the awe and happiness she had expected others to feel at her good fortune? She hadn't been given anything. She had worked for it and taken the same chances of failure everyone else did. Now, why couldn't they recognize her superiority and bow their heads gracefully?

He looked at her with plain skepticism. "Maybe, but I doubt it. Everything about you has that deceptively simple air, as if it took you a hell of a long time to figure it out. What's the need to be glamorous, as well as bright?"

"But I'm not glamorous——"

"You're sure trying like hell, sister. You should have heard some of the cracks I have."

She glanced swiftly around the room and saw—not a hundred or so people, talking and laughing, smoking and drinking—but a cruel savage horde full of hatred and jealousy, and herself the foolish helpless center for their ridicule. She felt scared and lost and forsaken and had an overwhelming wish to get up and run away and hide.

Here she had been shaking hands with everyone, smiling so charmingly, talking so sweetly and modestly, and now he had made her despise herself. All at once she hated him. He should have kept his mouth shut; he had no right and no reason to hurt her. She looked at him sitting there, relaxed back into a corner of the couch, smiling blearily, his eyes popped and vacant.

"I hear there's one very hot scene in your book," he said.

"There's one love scene, if that's what you mean."

"What made you write about sex?"

"I didn't write about sex. I wrote a story about a man and a woman and it's my understanding—correct me if I'm wrong—that one of the factors motivating the human race is sex!"

"Take it easy." He straightened up a little and signaled for a waiter to bring him another drink. "I'm just trying to get a story, remember. I don't give a goddamn if you wrote a book with nothing but sex in it or no sex in it. But you'd better remember that when a good-looking gal puts on paper for everyone to read what she knows about sex——"

"You mean *that* she knows about sex!"

"Yes, Miss Delaney," he agreed with a sly drawl. "You're not married, are you?"

"Oh, yes I am!" snarled Shireen. "I've been married for seven years and my husband's in the Navy—he's in the Pacific now, on a destroyer!" The tone of her voice summed up Mr. Morton as a contemptible draft-dodger who sat here asking helpless women sassy questions while real men were fighting for their country.

He gave a small start and glanced away from her. "Yeah?" he said after a moment. "I've got scar tissue on my lungs." He looked at her again. "I suppose you're very proud of him."

"I certainly am," she said coolly, and waited for her routed enemy to limp away from the field of battle.

A moment later he got up. "I've gotta run along. Hope you enjoy life as a celebrity."

"Thanks," said Shireen, her blue eyes cold and watchful. "I will."

She turned away, wondering if there was any way she could make herself invisible or perhaps die for a few days. Everyone seemed to be drunk and it gave her a feeling of being off in a world of her own. Several people had gone, a few remembering first to say good-by to her, but most of them simply went, having apparently forgotten that the party had been given for someone. One man snatched a handful of flowers out of a vase on the mantel and now carried them dripping across the room, waving them over his head as he went out the door.

"Miss Delaney!"

Shireen heard the sound in her ear as if a blast of trumpets had blown, and looked up to find a middle-aged woman's face suddenly close to hers.

"How charming of you to come to our city!"

She saw the red mouth, fine wrinkles, crooked teeth; and suddenly felt as she had in one of her nightmares where the moon had broken loose from heaven and come hurtling at her, growing bigger and bigger and she screamed and struggled to wake up. Shireen backed off a trifle as if to defend herself. But the woman was exuberant and undeniable.

"I read your book, my dear, and I'm simply amazed that anyone who looks as young and innocent as you do could have written such a naughty book!" She wagged her finger in Shireen's face and Shireen helplessly blinked her eyes.

She tried to smile but felt as if she were suffocating. "Oh," she said weakly, "it really isn't."

The Morgan Thayer man rescued her, maneuvering the woman away, and Shireen got up carefully, as if trying to brace herself inside. She was instantly confronted by another woman who stood before her, rocking slightly back and forth.

"Well! How does it *feel* to be famous?"

"Fine," said Shireen. She looked across the room, hoping the woman would go away.

"*Fine,*" she mimicked. "Really nothing at all, my dear. Happens every day of my life."

Shireen looked at her in surprise, realizing that she had let herself show through and that the woman was angry. Then she smiled down at her and tried to look kindly and maternal.

"That isn't what I mean. I mean I feel fine—it's very nice."

"Of course you don't remember me," said the woman accusingly. "You were in my store this afternoon, autographing books."

"Oh, I remember you very well."

"I've read your book and I'm surprised you had the nerve to write it. Everyone's going to think you're Janetta."

Shireen laughed. "I'm sure they won't. She's a character I made up, after all."

The woman cocked her head to one side, smiling sagely. "That's what *you* say, of course. And Morgan Dufay? You made *him* up too, I suppose?"

"Of course. He's completely imaginary."

The woman turned her head sideways and looked at Shireen from the corners of her eyes. "Well—I suppose a lot of people would envy you. But I want you to know—I don't."

"There's no reason why you should."

"I wouldn't be in your shoes for anything in the world. You'll never be able to live a normal life again as long as you live."

"I think I will."

"Don't kid yourself. You won't even be able to keep your money. Too bad you didn't write it before taxes went up."

"The country needs high taxes," said Shireen piously.

"Well—it's been very interesting talking to you. I like to see what famous people are like. Authors are generally quite peculiar, you know."

"Are they?" said Shireen. "I don't know any."

The woman giggled suddenly, then grabbed a man by the arm as he walked by and went off with him. Shireen turned around, caught the Morgan Thayer representative's eye, and saw him give her a slow wink. Morgan Thayer was pleased, then. She was getting along all right—or at least fooling them into thinking she was.

He came up to her. "Time to go to dinner," he said. "There'll only be about fourteen people and we'll leave early so you'll have plenty of time to pack and catch the train. You're doing great. How do you feel? Worn out?"

"Oh, no. I feel fine. I'm having a wonderful time."

Chapter 27

Shireen sat at a desk wearing a purple orchid pinned to her dress. She took a pen in her hand and smiled up at the man who leaned over her, holding an open book. The flash bulb went off and she blinked.

"Thanks, Miss Delaney."

"You're welcome."

"All right," said the buyer. "Start them moving."

A line of people began filing past her and she signed her name in each one's book, smiling as she handed it back. She had arrived in town—the fourth one she had visited so far—at eight that morning, been interviewed by three reporters while she ate breakfast, talked on two radio stations, visited a bookstore, gone to a luncheon, and now she was here. That evening there was another cocktail party, then dinner, and at midnight she was to catch the train. In each town a Morgan Thayer representative met her at the train, handed her an orchid, kept her supplied with fresh ones while she was there, guided her about, and saw her off when she left.

"Are you having fun?" people kept asking her.

"Oh, I'm having a wonderful time."

"How does it *feel* to be famous?"

"Oh, well—fine, I guess." And she would try to smile placatingly. Don't be mad at me. I didn't do it on purpose. It might just as well be you. It isn't really me anyway. I just happen to be standing here.

She didn't have much trouble with the people who bought books. They mostly asked her questions she could answer and didn't seem to be mad about anything.

"Miss Delaney, I have an aunt whose name is Janetta and it's such an unusual name I was wondering if you'd ever met her. Her name's Janetta Barnes and she lives in Minnesota. Do you know her?"

Shireen pretended to think hard and then smiled regretfully. "No, I'm sorry but I don't believe I do. I've never been in Minnesota."

"Miss Delaney, this is for my boy friend and he's overseas. Would you mind writing: 'To Joe with good luck'?"

Shireen looked at the girl, who was young and a little nervous, and smiled at her, hoping she would see that she knew how she felt and that she felt the same way herself. She wrote the words. "I hope he'll come home soon," she said, handing her the book.

"Thanks, Miss Delaney. And I hope your husband comes back soon."

Shireen blinked her eyes and her throat hurt suddenly. She wished she could go off somewhere and talk to the girl and maybe they would both cry. Another book was set in front of her.

"Miss Delaney, you look so much like a cousin of mine. I wonder if maybe you're related. Is Delaney really your name? My cousin's name is Dora Martin."

"No—Delaney's my real name."

"That's nice handwriting you have. Did you have to learn it for autographing books?"

"No, this is the way I write."

"Miss Delaney, I've been noticing your shoes. Would you mind telling me where you got them?"

"I got them at a place in New York called *Edouard's* on Fifty-third Street."

"Are they very expensive?"

"Fairly, I guess." Shireen thought she should not say they had cost her sixty-five dollars or the woman might resent all the money she was making and maybe not take the book and she'd make forty-five cents less.

"How old are you?"

"Twenty-six."

"I saw your picture in the paper this morning, but you're much prettier."

"Thank you. It's nice of you to say so."

Finally the Morgan Thayer man leaned over. "Time to go. You can stop now."

Shireen put the pen down and stood up. Everyone was smiling and shaking hands and telling her how co-operative she had been. That pleased her for a moment, since it seemed to give some point to what she was doing.

For by now the world was revolving like a kaleidoscope, the patterns changing but remaining essentially the same. She could no longer tell one town from another or one group of people from another. She was tired and did not think success was much fun, after all. Something was wrong with the picture—it was not what she had expected. But she did not know what she had expected.

Happiness, probably.

Happiness that came like a stray dog and attached itself to your side and wouldn't be driven away. But she did not know what it was and she could not have defined it. So it was like looking for a strange face in a crowd.

Happiness, they said, is only to be found inside yourself. But where? In which part? It ran ahead of you through the maze, darting around a corner just as you were about to catch up with it, and lost itself somewhere in the darkness. It did not answer your call but kept still and in hiding; it had a complete independence, no need whatever to be found.

Still, if happiness was anywhere at all, it must be in success. Or she had been tricked.

The Morgan Thayer men told her she was having a triumphal progress. Her pictures were in all the papers; people crowded into stores to have her autograph their books; everyone who was invited showed up for the luncheons and dinners and cocktail parties.

But Shireen kept getting into trouble or felt that she was getting into trouble. In one town a reporter asked her what her recipe was for writing a best seller.

Without thinking she said: "Get the reader into a trap and keep him there. When you decide to let him out—that's the end of the book." Then her eyes opened wide and she looked at him in horror.

Now he knew her secret! Now he knew that she was conceited and self-centered. She had admitted out loud that she knew she had written a best seller!

She got away from him as fast as she could, but kept worrying all the rest of the day about what he must think of her.

The next city she went to, a couple of thousand people crowded into the store auditorium. There was a dais with a desk on it, a huge picture of herself behind the desk, and stacked in a great pyramid were about two thousand copies of *The Falcon* for her to autograph. Seeing it, she suddenly remembered when she had been a kid and had not wanted to eat her bread crusts. "If you don't eat them," her mother would tell her, "the Bread Crust Man will come and get you and take you to his castle and the only way you'll be able to get out will be to eat your way through walls and walls of bread crusts."

As she stepped onto the dais a light came from somewhere and struck full upon her. She moved back a little in surprise, and heard a faint friendly ripple of laughter run over the audience. A man was sitting in the front row eating popcorn out of a bag, his face completely expressionless. Just like a circus, she thought, vaguely pleased for a moment at being a one-woman circus.

She sat down and the buyer announced that if they would form a line on the right and file by, Miss Delaney would autograph their books. At first she smiled at each of them, but before long it had turned into a production line. A hand took the book from the customer's hand and set it before her, opened. She scribbled her name. Another hand from the other side blotted the page and picked up the book as another one was set down. Now and then a flash bulb went off.

Over and over she wrote Shireen Delaney Shireen Delaney Shireen

197

Delaney Shireen Delaney Shireen Delaney Shireen . . . until finally it was no longer her name and not even a name at all.

She was only vaguely aware of the big room crowded with people, the clerks selling books, stock boys moving them. The buyer, Anne Lewis, stayed there beside her, and she felt protected by Anne's presence. If someone wanted a special autograph, Anne explained that Miss Delaney has a great many books to sign as you can see for yourself and will never get done if you add to her work so please be satisfied with the autograph we're all doing the best we can for you.

"I'll bet as soon as we go home she stops signing and someone else finishes," she heard a woman say.

Shireen glanced up, outraged at this cynicism. Here I am getting writer's cramp and she doesn't even want me to have credit for signing all these blasted books! No one ever wants to believe you do anything—they always want to think someone else did it, someone they've never seen and never will see or even know about for sure.

"Oh, yes she will!" snapped Anne, who was becoming a little cross herself with the stubborn public, which sometimes forgot its sales slip even though it had been told explicitly no book would be autographed without a sales slip dated that very day, no other day. Miss Delaney would sign no books bought at rival stores while being given a "party" by this store. And as Shireen scribbled away she would, from time to time, hear Anne beside her chastising someone for trying to sneak into line or for not having the slip ready or for wanting something more written than they were properly entitled to have.

After an hour or so it seemed as if she had been signing books all her life and would probably spend the rest of it signing books.

"You've been a good girl," Anne told her when she finished the two thousand copies. "I'm dead. Don't write another book for awhile, will you?"

"We'd better hurry," the Morgan Thayer man said. "You've only got an hour to get back to the hotel and get dressed for the party."

Party, for God's sake, thought Shireen. People. Questions. Noise. No one I've ever seen before or will ever see again. And I'm so tired. This isn't what it was supposed to have been.

This isn't even any fun.

A few days later she hated herself and everyone in the world and was sorry she was alive. She was worn out and felt exposed and raw, as if she had been hammered and pounded at. She felt as if she were suffering from a terrible and agonizing accumulation of injustices, and could not imagine what she had done to deserve all this. She believed she was making enemies everywhere she went and was perversely pleased that she was. Let everyone hate her, then, since they were determined to anyway. And, furthermore, she knew she deserved it. If they knew how bad she really was they would hate her even worse, as much as she was hating them.

Several times she felt like simply giving up, bursting into tears and running back to the hotel to lock herself in her room, pack her clothes and get away as fast as she could. But since she was unable to decide how she would live the rest of her life once she had done something so unequivocal as that, she stayed where she was and did what she was told with seeming meekness and humility.

She felt persecuted and spied upon and the four reporters sitting around the breakfast table obviously had been put on earth to ridicule and torment her. They had never existed before but now here they were, looking at her curiously and asking her questions that were none of their business.

"You described yourself exactly when you described Janetta, didn't you?"

"That wasn't my intention," said Shireen, and she looked like a sulky child tired of being asked to sing the song it learned. "Janetta has auburn hair and green eyes." What in the hell difference does it make? Why don't you shut up? Why doesn't everyone shut up and go home? Why in the name of God had she ever written that book and got herself into all this trouble?

"Oh, Miss Delaney, that's the most divine suit. I'm a fashion editor and I'd love to have your clothes philosophy."

"Why—" began Shireen.

"Miss Delaney's clothes philosophy," interrupted another reporter, "is to never spend less than three hundred on a dress or seventy-five on a hat."

"Ha, ha," said the Morgan Thayer representative. "Actually, Shireen is an extremely sensible girl about clothes. She was telling me that she believes in buying just a few things and wearing them forever, weren't you, Shireen?"

"Why, yes," said Shireen. "Of course. But really, let's not talk about clothes—"

"Miss Delaney means that she's so terribly worried about her husband out there in the Pacific with that battle going on and that terrible wound—"

"Oh, he hasn't been wounded yet," interrupted Shireen, and then looked apologetically around the table.

"No? I thought he had. But you can imagine how terribly worried she must be."

"Is it true your father did the research for you?"

"No. I did it myself."

"*Someone* helped you though, didn't they?"

"No one helped me. Anyone can do research, if they've got enough patience." Everyone was mad at her. She had something they wanted.

She had a lot of things they wanted. And so they were jealous and envious and it showed in their faces and the sounds of their voices. Everyone wishes they were me and that makes them hate me.

She looked around the table: I wish you were all dead.

But she still had a smile on her face. She had finally reached a state of such intense nervousness that she did not dare stop smiling for fear she would break into several dozen little pieces.

"Just a question, Miss Delaney. Nothing to be mad about."

"Miss Janetta," insisted the woman who had spoken first; she giggled.

Shireen looked at her coldly. She had an image of herself reaching out, grabbing the woman by her hair, and yanking her head off.

"Do you know how lucky you are?"

"It wasn't all—" began Shireen, and then stopped. "Yes. I know how lucky I am."

"How much of it is autobiographical?"

"None at all."

"But all first novels, you know, are—"

"Please—*I* should know, shouldn't I?"

She was horrified to hear herself say it, and now they were all looking at her with disapproval. They would go away and write terrible things about her and Morgan Thayer would be displeased and everything was ruined. If only she could *somehow* get a little rest and peace and time to be by herself.

Presently they all got up and left, thanking her for the interview and how charming she had been. She tried to fix it as well as she could by smiling, but did not care much any more.

The Morgan Thayer man left her in the lobby. "You've got an hour before it's time to go to the store. Try to get a little rest. You must be tired, aren't you?"

"Oh, no. I'm fine."

As she crossed the lobby she noticed a young Army captain with pilot's wings. Their eyes met for a moment and then she got into the elevator and the doors closed; she leaned against the wall, sick with a sudden sad and old familiar longing. He might have reminded her of Johnny, or whatever it was in Johnny she had wanted.

She was crying by the time she got to her room, and everything inside her seemed to quiver. She sat on the bed, sobbing.

Fear came up inside her then and swiftly took possession, growing monstrously, like an artificial fog. Fear of dying, disappearing forever into the eternity that seemed to have a future infinitely longer than its past. Fear . . . of things she couldn't name, didn't recognize. She wanted to get up and run, away from herself, away from her past and her present and her future. But she sat there, tense and groping, almost paralyzed by terror and anxiety.

If I were dead, she thought.

And stopped, surprised, to consider it for a moment: To give up, to quit struggling, to never worry about little things or big ones, to make no more demands upon herself and have none made upon her. To never want so as never to be disappointed in not getting, to never expect and have the expectation fall short. To be at peace.

And then, alarmed by her own easy acceptance, she went to look in the mirror. She stared at herself for a moment, thinking how far away she had got from the twelve-year-old kid who used to lie in bed, terrified by the beating of her own heart and the knowledge that it would stop someday. All the years that had gone by and the changes that had happened without her knowing it.

She thought of the flyer again, standing there with his hands in his pockets, watching her walk by. And it seemed as if she would never again have such things as an afternoon on the beach, a long drive out into the country without thinking about where she was going or why, a man putting his arms around her because she was pretty and they were both young.

I've got to talk to someone!

She walked over and picked up the telephone and called Georgia's number in New York. The call went through without delay and after a moment Georgia's voice came on, brisk and full of cheerful energy.

"Georgia—" she said urgently. "It's Shireen." And she thought what a great relief it is, having someone to turn to when you're worried or unhappy—someone you can trust. It doesn't stop the worrying but it takes away part of the loneliness.

"Why, Shireen! I wasn't expecting a call from you! Are you all right?"

"Yes, I'm all right. I'm just so tired. And I miss Ed. Have any letters come?"

"Four, so far. Is something wrong? You sound unhappy. You're not worrying about the reviews, I hope."

"No, I don't look at them. I've been told about a couple—but I'm not even going to care," she said defiantly. "After all, *money* is something that everyone respects."

"You're right," said Georgia cheerfully. "There's always some damned snake in the garden."

"But Georgia—nothing's like I expected it to be. I'm miserable!"

"It never is. But it'll be over pretty soon. When you come back we'll go out to the farm and no one will bother you."

She gave a grateful little sigh. "Oh, that sounds wonderful." She had an image of cool green leaves and clear quiet water. "You know, Georgia—I've found out something."

"What's that?"

"I think Americans love success—but hate the people who have it."

Chapter 28

Shireen and Georgia sat in the cab, Shireen hanging onto the strap and staring out the window. She was wearing a black dress with a tulle-wreathed hat, and the mink stole over her shoulders. She looked very deliberately sleek and groomed, but her expression was sullen and frightened. She had arrived back in New York the evening before and they were on their way to a cocktail party Philip Thayer was giving for her.

"I'm sure it's nothing to worry about," Georgia said after a moment.

"Nothing to worry about? How can I help worrying about it? He's never written me a letter like *that* before!"

"I'm sure he only wrote it to see what you'd say. Look at it from his point of view. He's way the hell and gone out there and you're here with a brand-new life, meeting dozens of people every day—he knows they can't all be women. You even told him about going out with Jack."

"But did he have to write me about that damned blonde in Australia? Oh, I wish that letter had been lost! I wish I'd never seen it!"

"Look—the poor guy's got a few days' leave. What if he does take a girl out? And what if he does think she's nice?"

"*Nice?* He says she's beautiful! Why, Ed never thought any woman but me was beautiful in his whole life! This is driving me out of my mind, Georgia! I couldn't even sleep last night! What if he falls in love with her?"

"He won't."

"What if he sleeps with her?"

"What if he does?"

Georgia was smiling, but Shireen looked at her with astonished indignation. This did not sound like Georgia, her friend, talking.

"If he does and I ever find out about it, I'll divorce him!"

Georgia burst into laughter.

"I will. I mean it. I won't share Ed with another woman! I can't even stand the thought of it!"

"But what about you? Maybe he wouldn't like to share you with another man. Johnny, for instance, and Mike and Jack."

"That's different. Or if it isn't different—anyway, what I do has nothing to do with what I'm willing for him to do!"

Georgia laughed again. "Shireen, you don't know how funny you sound. How can you possibly be so jealous of Ed, after the things you've done?"

202

"What I've done has nothing to do with it," she insisted.

Georgia was silent a moment, smiling. And then she indicated one of the cab mirrors. "Take a look at yourself, Shireen."

Shireen glanced toward the mirror and then quickly looked away again. "No—I don't want to." They drove on silently awhile.

"Oh, God," muttered Shireen finally. "I'm so sick and tired of everything I could die! I hate New York! I hate orchids! I hate people! I hate myself! I wish I were dead!"

Georgia became instantly sympathetic. "You're just lonesome for Ed."

"I am. I never knew I'd miss him so much! Having him gone spoils everything! And now that girl—that lousy bitch! If I ever see her I'll kill her! Oh, I *wish* he'd come home!"

The taxi driver turned his head. "Here y'are, lady. Stork Club."

Shireen suddenly sat up, looked out the window and then flung herself back in the seat, beginning to cry. "Oh, Georgia, I can't go! Tell them I got run over by a truck or have measles or anything! I can't go in there! I can't!"

"But Shireen, you've got to. The party's for you. You can't do these things to people. Now come on, pull yourself together and we'll go in."

"I can't go in, Georgia, I honestly can't. I'd rather be hung up by my thumbs or dragged around by—"

"Make up your mind, lady," said the driver.

"Shut up," said Georgia sharply. "Can't you see she's sick? Drive around for awhile. Now, Shireen, you must listen to me—"

And after fifteen minutes or so Shireen dried her eyes and powdered her face and they went. It was a little easier than she had expected, and later she wondered why she had been so upset and why, from time to time, she seemed to lose control of herself for no obvious good reason. It didn't take much, apparently, for her to lose hold of whatever life line it was she hung onto. The structure she had built herself to live in was not a very safe one and someday, if she didn't look out, might collapse completely.

A few days later she and Georgia and some other people went to spend the week end at Georgia's Bucks County farm. And out there in the country it was beginning to be spring, the misty tender nostalgic eastern spring that seemed even to her, a Californian, full of mysterious memories out of some imaginary childhood.

With them was a man for whose latest play Georgia was acting as agent, and a song writer who had written a successful musical comedy a few years before. As they approached her property Georgia began pointing out the neighbors' houses, and then they drove along beside her orchard which was in full bloom, the trees looking as if popcorn had been thrown at them. The house was white clapboard with gray stone at the bottom and shutters painted a pure faded blue.

203

"Oh, Georgia!" cried Shireen happily. "It's beautiful!" She felt at home already.

"Hmm—" said the playwright. "All the comforts of Beverly Hills."

The car stopped in front of the house and Georgia jumped out. "Thank God! Now we can relax!" She dashed up the steps, flung open the door and they trouped into the house, were shown their rooms, and while they were changing their clothes Georgia went off to talk to the servants and make a long-distance call.

A few hours later, to Shireen's great indignation, Jack and Eva arrived. At first Shireen went to her room and said she would stay there all week end. But Georgia came up and stood and talked to her.

"He's been begging me ever since you went away to let him come here, Shireen. And you've got to see him sometime, after all."

"I don't *want* to see him."

"It can't do any harm. Eva doesn't know anything about it. Don't behave like this, Shireen, for heaven's sake."

"Why can't he get it through his head that I'm through with him? What's the matter with men, anyway? Why must they make such nuisances of themselves?"

"Because he's in love with you." Georgia sounded patient but bored. "That's why."

And Shireen, feeling a little as if she had been chastised, agreed to go down and behave herself.

Jack was shy and deferential and they exchanged casual greetings, with nothing to indicate that during the past three days he had been calling her constantly and she had refused either to return the call or talk to him if he found her in.

She had never met Eva before and felt a little contemptuous as soon as she saw her. Eva was about forty and still had some of her prettiness left. She dressed well and her figure was slender, she spoke in a soft feminine voice, but her face was vaguely restless and dissatisfied and disturbingly mournful.

Why did she let him get away with it? Shireen wondered.

You don't get what you don't demand out of life.

And Eva looked at Shireen with something between envy and fear, though Shireen knew the look had nothing to do with Jack. It was merely the look of a plain woman at a pretty one, an older woman looking at someone with years to spend she has spent already.

After dinner they gathered in the living room and the song writer sat down at the piano and began to play. Every so often Jack got up to pour himself another drink. Shireen noticed this with scorn and his wife with a disapproving and anxious air, as if her small boy was being naughty but she did not want to correct him in front of company.

Once, as Jack went by Shireen, who sat on the floor in front of the fire with her knees drawn up and her arms around them, he reached down and gave her hair a tug.

"What's the matter with you!" she snapped, before she could catch herself.

Jack grinned at her. But Shireen saw the look of surprise on Eva's face, and was afraid he had given them both away. Georgia, knitting a sweater, looked wryly amused; the playwright smiled knowingly.

Eva spoke. "Jack, really, haven't you had enough to drink?"

"I'm not doing anyone any harm."

"Play something else, darling," said Georgia to the song writer, who was running up and down the keys in a few practice ripples. "Shireen, what would you like to hear?"

"Anything. I don't care."

She reached for a cigarette and was lighting it when he struck several quick powerful chords on the piano and she stopped, holding the match in her fingers, her heart pounding violently. It was the music she had heard the night she and Johnny sat in his car on the beach at Miami. *That does it,* she heard him say again. She blew out the match and tossed it into the fireplace.

Then she closed her eyes and bent her head forward to rest it on her arms, crossed over her drawn-up knees.

I've never loved anyone else in my life, she thought. And I never will again. There isn't another man in the world who could ever mean the same things to me that he does.

He filled her with intense longing for all the things he was that she wanted but could not name. When she was with him everything that was important to her no longer mattered; and when he was gone his memory was vital enough to make reality unreal. They had met somewhere in the lonely wastes that existed in both of them—as if, wandering through a desert, they had happened to cross paths. And stood and talked together for awhile, realizing they had known each other from whenever their two lives had begun. And then she had lost him again, and been more lonely than ever before, knowing now that he existed.

Suddenly the music ended and for a moment they were all quiet. Shireen finally lifted her head and looked at Georgia.

"What was that?"

"Song from a motion picture that came out quite awhile ago. 'The Warsaw Concerto.' "

There was some conversation in the room and underneath it Shireen said: "That's the song I told you about. I've been looking for it everywhere."

"Funny you hadn't heard it before. It's been very popular."

"It's goddamn lousy corn," said Jack.

"Jack, for heaven's sake!" cried Eva.

"What's the matter? Can I help it if Shireen's got stinking taste in music?"

Shireen looked at him for a moment, but said nothing. The others seemed mildly amused and she wondered how he could have so little respect for himself.

"Let's hear some Chopin," suggested the playwright tactfully.

At midnight they began to get up and wander around, preparatory to going to bed. Eva glanced at Jack, who promptly crossed the room to get another drink. Georgia, taking it all in but refusing to be implicated, kept on knitting.

Eva yawned and stretched and then looked at her watch. "Good heavens! Do you know how late it is?"

"No," said Georgia. "Is it?"

"Quarter after twelve. And we all want to be up early tomorrow, don't we? There's no sense losing the daytime in the country."

"Good idea," said the playwright. "Think I'll turn in, too."

He kissed Georgia casually—Georgia's guests always kissed her, when they came and when they left and at night before they went to bed and in the morning when they got up. And Georgia accepted it like a queen having her hand kissed.

"Guess I'd better hit the sack, too. Didn't have much sleep last night," said the song writer. He kissed Georgia and went out and Eva was still standing there, waiting. Now she began to plump up the pillows on the sofa. For more than a minute no one spoke.

Then Georgia, with more curiosity about Shireen and Jack than inclination to save Eva's feelings, said that she was not sleepy yet. Eva sat down again. "Guess I'll have another cigarette. I'm not particularly sleepy, either."

Georgia kept on knitting. Eva kept waiting. Jack sat and sipped his drink. Shireen knew she might as well go to bed but this was the best amusement she had for the present and she refused to give it up. Eva, she thought, should know better than to try to compete with her. After a few minutes she glanced at Jack, who was now poking away at the coals and stirring the fire back to activity.

"Let's play a game of gin."

Jack looked at her with naïve grateful delight. "Fine," he said, and forgot about the fire. "I'll get the cards."

They sat down and began to play, silently, except for whatever words the game required. The new wood on the fire crackled, Georgia's knitting needles ticked, and Eva ruffled impatiently the pages of one magazine and then another. Now and then someone struck a match to light a cigarette. Occasionally Shireen glanced across the table at Jack and found him watching her with beseechment in his eyes. She looked at him, coldly and levelly, refusing him either comfort or encouragement.

"Eighty-three to a hundred and eight," said Jack, adding the score. "I beat you. How about another one?"

"Jack," said Eva. "You're going to be tired tomorrow morning and you know you said you wanted to get up early."

"No, I won't," said Jack, and his eyes flicked past her quickly. "We'll play one more game." While Shireen shuffled the cards he went to mix another drink; by now he was unsteady on his feet and getting quieter and more sullen.

Eva got up with a flounce. "*I'm* going to bed!" Georgia glanced at her calmly but her amusement was scarcely concealed.

"Let's get the one o'clock news," said Georgia, and switched on the small portable radio that stood on the coffee table in front of her. Eva kissed everyone good night and went on. Shireen kept her eyes on her cards. The radio was crackling and Georgia passed a couple of stations and came to a brusque hearty voice announcing that twenty-one Japanese bombers and thirty fighters had raided Port Darwin.

"I finished reading your book," said Jack.

"Really?" She picked up a card and then laid down her hand. "I'm going out with three."

Jack spread the cards, matched a couple on hers and began to add the score. "It's good," he said.

"I'm glad you think so," said Shireen, indicating that nothing could possibly mean less in her life. While she waited for him to shuffle and deal she leaned her chin on her fist and listened to the radio.

The announcer said that no new Japanese patrols had been found on Guadalcanal since the one discovered two days ago. "Thank God," Shireen said to Georgia. "I'd been worried to death they might send Ed there."

"Hah!" snorted Jack, and they both glanced at him with quick indignation.

Shireen snatched up her cards. "I'm sure I don't know what you mean by that."

"You know what I mean all right."

Georgia leaned toward the radio, but she was watching Shireen and Jack. "It is believed there are a few Japs still hiding out in the interior, but our troops are engaged in mopping-up operations which—"

"You must admit," Jack went on, "it did sound kind of funny."

"What sounded kind of funny?" she asked him, a malicious edge of mockery in her voice.

"You—being so damned solicitous about your husband."

Shireen looked at him, shocked and outraged. "You really are a bastard."

"I wouldn't deny it." By now he had no more interest in the card

207

game but was watching carefully for the first sign that he had got through her defenses. "And may I return the compliment? You're the most complete bitch I've ever known. And I've known several."

Georgia switched off the radio. "Jack, I don't know what's the matter with you. You've been nasty to Shireen all day. And now you're behaving like a boor. You've got no business talking to her that way. Shireen's a nice girl—she hasn't done anyone any harm. Why don't you leave her alone?"

Jack laughed. What he had drunk had made him as belligerent as it seemed likely he would dare be in the presence of these women, both of whom obviously scared him.

"Oh, no," he drawled. "She wouldn't harm a fly. Tear off its wings and then let it go—but never do it any harm. Oh, never do it any harm at all. Yes sir, she's a nice girl all right."

"You're behaving like a goddamned fool," said Shireen. "What did you expect anyway?" She was annoyed but sourly amused at the same time. It pleased her to see a man make himself this contemptible because of her.

"Oh, didn't expect anything, I guess. Must have known it would happen all along. But somehow kept on kidding myself. Funny thing how you can kid yourself when you want to. Funny thing—falling in love. 'Scuse me."

He went to pour himself another drink and Georgia and Shireen exchanged glances of amused superiority. Shireen, her chair shoved back from the table, slid down on her spine with her legs sprawled out and lit another cigarette.

Then Georgia spoke to him sharply. "Jack, you've had enough to drink!"

"Don't talk to me like that, Georgia," he said, a slight whine in his voice. "Leave me alone. I'm not hurting anyone—except maybe myself. And surely you can't object to that. Can she, Shireen?" He glanced around over his shoulder at Shireen, smiling at her slyly. And then he came back, unsteadily, to the card table.

"I suppose," said Shireen slowly, "nothing is more revolting to me than a drunk."

"Revolting? Dear, dear, so I'm revolting. Well, isn't that just terrible that Shireen—*Miss* Delaney, if you please—should have to witness such a sordid spectacle as a man drunk. And drunk over her, at that. Did I happen to mention you've broken my heart—or wouldn't that be of interest?"

Shireen gave a slight unpleasant snort. "Broken your heart! You sound like a schoolboy. Men don't have broken hearts, don't you know that? Even women don't any more. So quit dramatizing yourself. This is nothing but a bid for sympathy and you won't get it from me, I may as well tell you that right now."

208

"Oh, you don't need to tell me. You don't care about anything in the world but yourself, Shireen—you never have and you never will. I found that out, reading that book you wrote. You're like Janetta, no difference between you at all. You're a cold calculating bitch and you'll never do any man any good if you can help it. You're poison. I was just a big enough fool to develop a taste for poison, that's all. The whole thing was my fault. My fault—right from the beginning. I should've known better. I did know better. All my life I knew you should never trust a woman and never love a woman. Oh, I knew all about it and I was too damned smart ever to get fooled. But for some reason you fooled me. Or maybe I fooled myself. Because I knew all about you the minute I looked at you. Do you know what you look like? Like a cat. Just as cruel and just as predatory and just as deceptively soft. God, what's come over me? I sound poetic, damned if I don't." He glanced at Georgia, sitting across the room watching him. "Do I sound poetic to you, Georgia?"

"You sound like a weak driveling idiot, and I'm ashamed of you!"

"Ashamed of me? I can't imagine why. Wouldn't you rather have me get drunk than cut my throat?"

"Jack MacDonald!" snapped Georgia. "Stop it! I won't have you talking this way any longer! Haven't you any self-respect at all? Have some for your wife and family if you haven't any for yourself! You've had an affair with Shireen and it hasn't turned out the way you wanted it to, though I'm sure I can't imagine what else you expected. You knew she couldn't marry you. And it couldn't very well go on for the rest of your lives. So why don't you be glad for what you did have instead of whining and drooling like a spoiled boy because you can't have any more cake?"

"Oh, Georgia," said Jack slowly and mournfully. "It's all very well for you to talk this way but you don't know how I *feel*. I've never been in love before. And then I went and fell in love with that bitch and look what she's done to me."

Shireen jumped up, almost knocking her chair over. "Stop that, or I'll slap you! I haven't done anything to you and you know it! You got what you wanted and now you're sorry for yourself because you can't keep on having it! Think about the harm *you've* done other people—Eva, for instance! Now maybe you know something about what you did to her!"

Jack's shoulders slumped a little more and he sat there, besieged by the two women, looking forlorn and helpless. He was staring down into his glass.

"I didn't expect you to understand," he said finally. "Or you, either, Georgia. You two are too much alike. And God help the men who ever love you." He hauled himself up slowly again and started for the bar-table.

209

But Georgia got there before he did and snatched away the bottle. "You've had enough to drink! Now go to bed!"

Jack stood there, weaving back and forth, looking at Georgia. Then he turned his head and looked at Shireen who stood a few feet away, watching him. He grinned foolishly.

"Maybe that's a good idea, after all. Maybe I am drunk enough. Wonderful thing about liquor—dulls the pain. Fine thing, liquor. Man's best friend. Well—guess I'll go to bed now and leave you two harpies to pick at the carcass. You're both poison. And you're no better than she is, Georgia Marsh. I know a few things about you, too."

"I'm sure you do, Jack. I'd never pretend there weren't a few things to know about me. But let's take me up as a topic some other time. You'd be surprised how much good some sleep would do you right now."

"Sure, sure, I know. You're right. May as well sleep. Wonder if I can make it up the stairs?"

"You'd damned well better," Georgia told him. "We're not going to help you. And be quiet about it—don't wake up everyone in the house."

"Oh, I'll be quiet all right. Mustn't wake up Eva or Tom or anyone at all. Mustn't disturb *anyone*."

He started out, moving very slowly, and he came up to Shireen, who stood without moving and stared at him. "Suppose you let me kiss you just once more. Just once more."

"No!"

"Why not?" He swayed a little closer. "Couldn't hurt you a bit—and I want to. You don't know how much I want to."

"I don't care how much you want to! I've told you that's over and I mean it. Stop bothering me!"

Jack stood a moment longer looking at her, and then he smiled a little, swaying closer. Shireen stiffened. His face was only a few inches from hers and he was smiling, his eyes misty and sad as a spaniel's. Suddenly she swung around and walked away. Jack did not turn his head but stood a little longer with his back to them and then he continued on out of the room. Shireen and Georgia watched him. At the door he turned once more.

"You're a bitch. You're no good. You're no good at all. Funny thing about it, though—I'm still in love with you."

Shireen's mouth made a grimace of disgust and then he was gone, only his arm appearing once more in the doorway, waving back at them. Shireen turned and she and Georgia looked at each other; Shireen's right eyebrow went up a little.

"Men," said Shireen.

"Poor devil," said Georgia.

PART III

Chapter 29

Two or three weeks later Georgia sold *The Falcon* to an independent motion-picture producer for two hundred and fifty thousand dollars. Shireen, at the lawyer's office, was handed a check for two hundred and twenty-five thousand, her own share once Georgia's commission had been deducted. She folded the check and put it in her bag.

"What are you going to do with all that money, Miss Delaney?" he asked her.

"Pay most of it out in taxes, I guess," said Shireen, though she did not believe that could actually happen to her. She still thought she would somehow have most of her million left.

"You're a lucky girl," he said. "I hope you'll be sensible."

"Oh, I will," promised Shireen. She did not want to be bothered with his advice and thought that was the best way to avoid hearing it.

Philip Thayer sent a couple of his investment counselors to talk to her and she listened politely and told them she would think it over.

"I'll be damned," she said to Georgia later, "if I'm going to put all my money into an annuity so I can live to the age of ninety-five on two hundred and fifty dollars a month."

"No reason why you should," agreed Georgia.

"Money's to spend," said Shireen.

"That's what I've always done with it."

Before long they were in the dragging heat of a New York summer. The air was heavy and so wet it was like living under a thick blanket wrung out in hot water. Outside the motion-picture theaters were posters with icicles on them. You had to pull your feet off the tar pavements; all the busses and taxis kept their windows open; women pinned their hair on top of their heads and went without stockings or girdles. The city's tempo had slowed to half its wintertime pace, and it seemed as if people stuck to one another as they passed on the sidewalks.

Shireen kept assuming that she must finally be happy, since she now had the life that approximately one hundred and thirty million other Americans thought of as privileged and exciting. It was what she had always wanted and so she had to believe that no matter what she found wrong with it, it must be the best of all possible lives.

Her greatest trials were with reporters, but she saw them anyway, and complained bitterly to Georgia about it. "I don't *like* to have people prying me open with questions, or trying to find out what makes me 'tick,' as they put it. What right have we to be so curious about each other?"

She was scrutinized by Earl Wilson and exposed by *PM*. Winchell said that she was divorcing her husband. Lyons spelled her name Shirley DeLane. *Time* described her as "lynx-like, persistent, almost ripe."

"What in the hell do they mean?" demanded Shireen of Georgia. "And what would I be if I *was* ripe?"

Life photographed her wearing white shorts and a black sweater and sitting on a stone wall with her arms around two of the neighboring children near Georgia's farm. The wind was blowing her hair and her face was shiny and she was smiling madonna-like at a pretty little blonde girl.

In *Vogue* she wore a black lace evening gown and half reclined on a black and white checkerboard floor with a broken white column behind her. Harry Winston loaned them fifty thousand dollars worth of diamonds for the picture. And the caption stated that: "Miss Shireen Delaney has written this season's big book, *The Falcon,* which bookstores report to be going like wind afire. Miss Delaney herself has the immaculateness of bone china, the silky lure of a well-pampered cat. She is photographed here wearing her own black lace ball gown, made for her by Valentina, wistfully nostalgic with its whirling ante-bellum skirt."

"Holy smoke," said Shireen when she read it. "Who's kidding who?"

But she was pleased by this fancy description of herself and by the picture which, she thought, looked very little like her. It gave her the temporary sense that Shireen Delaney—someone who both was and was not she—was glamorous and remote, made of lace and shiny hair and polished fingernails, without blood in her body or pain or any possible anguish of heart. It was what she had vaguely felt when she had seen other pictures of glossy fortunate women: that they were really only two-dimensional, that they had never put their hands in dishwater or suffered from cramps or had to apologize for burning the toast. And it fit her secret image of herself, the one she wanted to live up to.

But mostly she kept the promise she had made not to read her own publicity. Georgia subscribed to a clipping service for her but when the thick envelopes came every week she opened them and dumped the contents into a big dress box and shoved it back under the bed again. When one box was full she tied it up and got another. Maybe someday, when she was too old to be hurt any longer, she would look at them.

She bought dresses and hats, fur coats and stoles, shoes and handbags and lingerie, all the things which had previously existed for her in fashion magazines, store windows, or some vaguely imagined world where such garments were actually worn. She bought dozens of books, but the sight of them on her shelves was a little depressing, for it looked as if she might never be able to read everything that had been written. She bought three paintings and liked owning them, but was not at all sure she understood them or saw what she should when she looked at them.

And she worried all the time, dragging her worries along with her from one activity to another—but could not tell what she was worried about.

Sometimes she could fix on something concrete, and when she could she worried about that and felt a little better. Ed might be in danger; she had not heard from him for awhile. Johnny had written her only one letter, casual and friendly, and must have forgotten her. She might get sick. In fact, it seemed very likely she would get sick because she had been healthy for so long.

But more often the worries never took shape or form and she was left to grope and wrestle with them in the dark. It got so that she could not be alone, and did not dare be alone. But when someone tried to make a date with her and suggested that they have dinner together two weeks from that day, she cried in horror: "Two weeks from today? Ye gods, don't ask me to make a date for two weeks from today! I don't even like to *think* that far ahead! I have no idea what I'll be doing two days from now!"

Anything might happen in that time. She could be run over by a taxi or catch some terrible disease or—and there it was again, this shapeless formless thing that confronted her.

No, two weeks was much too long to look ahead.

She would be lucky enough to get through today.

She went out with several men she met at various parties but dismissed each one automatically before he had entered her emotions at all, because not one fit the minimum pattern she must match before she could give even the first access to herself. She talked to them coldly and skeptically, to insure against their being misled by her looks, and hated them for being so much less than what she wanted them to be.

Something she had been depending upon seemed to have fallen apart.

What happens to everything? she wondered. Where does it go? You think it's there, and then it isn't. It always disappears.

But what is it?

On her birthday she got two dozen red roses from Ed. He had written and asked her mother to telegraph them. She opened the box and took out the card. *With all my love, Ed*. It was in strange handwriting, written by some florist, and she picked the roses up and cradled them against her breast, speaking to them with sorrowful tenderness.

Oh, my poor darling, she whispered. Are you safe? Are you well? Do you know that I love you more than anything in the world? At that moment she loved him again with all the intensity she had when he was everything she wanted on earth or ever expected to want. She began to cry, for everything she had spoiled in her life, for every harm she had done to those who loved her, for the ideals she had lost and the dreams that had betrayed her. When she finally stopped crying she felt relieved. But it still had not been found.

She wandered into Georgia's office one hot August day looking petulant, nervously snipping her fingernails together. Georgia was talking on the phone, very sleek in a green linen Carnegie suit with big gold rings in her ears and her blonde hair rolled decorously into a net.

"What's the matter?" asked Georgia, when she had finished her call.

"I don't know. I feel rather unpleasant. If I were a cat right now I think I'd get a mouse and torture it."

Georgia laughed. "I take it you didn't like your date last night."

"I didn't. The man's a fool—the most complete egotist I've ever met. Talked about nothing but himself and how terrific he is and everything he's done and is going to do. He got very nasty when I wouldn't sleep with him." She made a face. "What's the matter with men, anyway?"

"It's not men, Shireen. It's people. You keep expecting too much of them."

"But there must be one around somewhere—"

"There is. Ed. Remember?"

Shireen sighed and her head dropped. "I know."

They sat silently a few moments. Shireen lit a cigarette and then all at once she leaned forward. "Look, Georgia—there's one thing I'm beginning to wonder about. Just how important *are* men, anyway? Men don't make women so important in their lives—why should women make men mean so much? Even to the point of thinking they're cheating themselves if they don't?"

Georgia gave a little sigh, and some of her bright vitality clouded over for a moment. "I don't know. I never have made any man a matter of life or death to me, and I don't even know if I could. But sometimes I wonder—sometimes I honestly wonder."

Shireen was surprised. She had believed that Georgia was always sure, always confident, always right and knew she was right. And a quick sympathy came up; she forgot her own restless irritability.

"Georgia, you're just tired. Have a cup of tea. There's four times the caffeine in a cup of tea there is in a cup of coffee—I read that somewhere the other day." Anything that might be troubling Georgia, she was sure, could be fixed by a cup of tea.

Georgia laughed. "Okay."

"And maybe you should be getting more sleep," continued Shireen seriously. "I've found that when life begins to seem like a husk ten hours of sleep give me another point of view."

"At your age, I suppose it does."

Shireen thought she might as well go home. But she continued to sit there because her imagination didn't quite make the jump. She couldn't actually see herself at home doing something—or doing anything—so she stayed where she was. And anyway, maybe Georgia could solve it for her, whatever it was. Someday, she was sure, Georgia would pronounce the one magic phrase, and it would all become clear.

"Maybe I'm through falling in love," suggested Shireen listlessly. "I haven't been in love for five months now." Mike had resumed in her feelings the aspect of a friend, and the love letters he still wrote her seemed puzzling. Occasionally she met Jack in the lobby or the elevator and though he continued to look at her with helpless yearning she could no longer imagine that she had ever been in bed with him. It had happened to her every time she had given some man a portion of her faith and perhaps it was doomed to keep on happening for the rest of her life.

Because each time she could find good reasons why it had happened, how they had caused it, what had been wrong in them from the beginning which she had somehow overlooked or not discovered right away. It was almost as if she kept waiting for some reason to give up her illusions. But of course it couldn't be that. She wanted them to last; it was someone else who destroyed them, deprived her of them, by stupidity or weakness or cynicism or any other flaw.

They began sipping the tea the secretary had brought in.

"You keep forgetting you're married, Shireen."

She smiled faintly. "I do seem to, don't I? And when I first knew Ed was going I thought I'd die." But it would never really matter who or what she lost—there would always be something to take its place.

"What are you doing tonight?"

"I'm going out with that character, that editor or whatever he is. I'm sure I won't enjoy it."

"Why go then?"

She laughed. "I guess just because a girl would rather go out with anybody than with nobody."

"I don't think it's that at all. I think you simply want to convince yourself that the guy is as hopeless as you thought he was at first glance. If for some reason they survive the first test—by being good-looking enough or smart enough or happening to have the right personality—you'll find another one for them. The quicker you can eliminate them from all consideration the better you like it. But in time, you'll eliminate them all."

Shireen laughed. Georgia's words made her sound fearsome, awe-inspiring. She must scare hell out of the poor bastards.

"I suppose," she agreed. "Part of me hates men. Part of every woman hates men—you know that as well as I do. There's no use kidding about that battle between the sexes. It's real enough. Only so far it's been conducted mostly along the lines of biological warfare and that's given men the advantage. But they haven't got it any more, now that we've finally got reliable contraceptives. Men have been getting away with murder for thousands of years—running the world as if someone had given it to them. But they're not going to get away with it when I'm concerned!"

"Unless you fall in love someday."

"But I am in love—with Ed and Johnny."

"Sweetie, that's one of the oldest tricks in the world for someone who's afraid to be in love at all. Parceling it out—so much for you, and so much for you. But it ain't love. Why don't you simply take it for what it is and stop putting fancy names to it?"

"What is it, then?"

"Fear."

"Oh, well—*that*. Of course. Fear is the basis of everything. I've known that for years—all my life, I guess."

"Fear, Shireen, is the root of all evil. It's just about as simple as that."

Shireen was quiet for a moment, looking perplexed. "You might be right. But—my God, if we weren't afraid! Anything could happen to us!"

"Like living, maybe."

"No, thanks. I'll keep my fears. They're very convenient in the long run. They keep you out of a lot of trouble."

I'll keep my fears.

That was the story of her life, all right, and no doubt about it. She was afraid to live and afraid of something unknown she might find life to be. It seemed better not to know, to hide, to put off, to wait. But it was a cowardice for which she despised herself and for which she held her parents responsible. Her parents, and Ed—because he had not been able to show her a way out of her tangled jungle of fears and indecision. Even though she had married him expecting that he would. But the jungle only grew thicker, the weeds rotted, and new ones grew up through the old.

218

Someone should be able to show her, though. And she must not give up looking until she found that person, whoever and wherever he was. For it must exist somewhere—someone somewhere sometime must be able to give her the capacity to lose herself. To shed herself. And gain his strength and security and warmth and peace.

She still had hopes that it might be Johnny, if she could only persuade him to do it. But if not Johnny, then someone else. She would know him when she found him.

Chapter 30

Shireen felt, as she often did these days, that she was completely out of her element.

It was a big apartment and furnished handsomely with Directoire chairs and sofas, low modern tables, more than a dozen oils—all by masters of the French Impressionist school—and vases full of red roses. There were long green velvet draperies and thick Aubusson rugs. Two neat black-uniformed maids passed trays of drinks and fancy canapés. All the people seemed to be rich or talented or both, the women looked very shiny and sleek and she wondered where they found the clothes they had on, since what she was wearing now felt shabby and dull. They had the qualities she thought belonged to every New Yorker as a birthright: self-confidence and sophistication.

The funny thing about it was that she was supposed to be the guest of honor and yet she did not feel like one. She did not feel like any kind of guest at all, but like some interloper.

She sat between a gray-haired book reviewer and a woman columnist wearing a tall metallic turban. She had got caught there between them fifteen minutes ago and had been listening helplessly to their conversation, wishing she could join in but completely lost because she had no idea what they were talking about.

That seemed to be what was always happening to her these days. She was like a sleepwalker, never sure of whom she was with or where she was, but going here and there and everywhere she could and meeting this person and that person and anyone at all who chanced to turn up.

"I simply adore him," the woman was saying. "He sings like a French musical-comedy star, with his face going in all directions!" She was quoting Allene Talmey in the latest issue of *Vogue* and Shireen recognized the quote and was a little shocked that the woman did not give her source.

She looked at the two of them talking and at the whole shrill eager gesticulating room and a thought came into her mind which surprised her: We will all die.

Suddenly nervous and embarrassed, as if she had done them some damage, she reached for a cigarette and the book reviewer lighted it for her. She smiled at him shyly. "Thank you."

She began listening to their conversation again.

220

"Most empty-headed female it's been my ill luck to meet in a long time. Thinks about not a goddamn thing but how she looks and what impression she's making. Well, she made an impression on me, all right. I hope she chokes!"

My God, she thought. I wonder if he's talking about me? Oh, but of course he can't be. He wouldn't do that, with me sitting right here. Then she saw her hostess, an ivory-skinned young woman in a black velvet gown, coming toward them with her arm linked through that of a young Navy lieutenant.

"Shireen," she said, "may I present Lieutenant Worth? Shireen Delaney, Paul Worth."

The reviewer and columnist both glanced quickly up, saw that it had nothing to do with them and went on talking. Shireen reached out, smiling, and shook hands, relieved to see a good-looking man her own age.

"Lieutenant Worth's just back from Europe. He was wounded during the invasion of Sicily."

Shireen looked humble. "I'm terribly sorry. I—"

He caught her bewildered expression and said quickly: "It wasn't that bad. No apologies necessary."

Shireen liked his voice for it was deep and a little slow and had the kind of accent she had come to associate with expensive Eastern schools. And he was handsome in the way she liked a man to be, with a lazy smile in his eyes and a slight twist to his mouth when he grinned. He was the kind of man she could go to bed with. Not that she ever would but it was something she knew the instant she looked at a man; yes, or no, and generally it was no.

"Can I get you a drink, Miss Delaney?"

He was watching her steadily and she saw that his eyes had darkened a little. American men, she thought. God, aren't they wonderful!

She slightly raised the glass she held, still almost full, in her left hand. "I have one, thanks." Marylyn, their hostess, had gone away. And now suddenly the columnist glanced at her watch.

"Oh, my God, I've got to rush! I'm horribly late as it is. Good-by, good-by, Miss Delaney, it's been so nice meeting you. By the way, when are you going to write another book?"

The reviewer got up too. "How can she write another book when there are so goddamn many important cocktail parties to go to?" He rocked on his heels, laughing, and then held out his hand to Shireen. "Don't be discouraged, my dear. Someday you'll write a good book. I'd bet on it. Good-by, lieutenant." They both walked away.

"Good-by," said Shireen and Lieutenant Worth together, and then he turned and smiled down at her.

"The son of a bitch," he said softly. "I hope you don't let it bother you?"

Shireen laughed. "No, I don't. Why should I? Won't you sit down?"

"You shouldn't, of course." He took the seat beside her, reached into his pocket and brought out a cigarette package. "Will you have one?"

Shireen took a cigarette and he lit it for her, their eyes met for just a moment, and then he lit his own. He seemed to be vaguely amused by something but since it apparently was not Shireen, she decided it was most likely life in general. And she was inclined to find men who were amused by life attractive. Perhaps because she sensed in the amusement a confidence and detachment she felt lacking in herself.

"I might as well tell you," he said. "I haven't read your book."

Shireen looked at him with quick surprise, and then smiled. "That's all right," she said. "I don't know why people always seem to think they have to apologize to an author. If I hadn't written it, I wouldn't have read it, either."

"I like you," he said. "You're a nice girl. Much nicer than I expected. Rather amazing, too."

Shireen would have liked to know why he thought she was amazing, but felt it would be bad taste to ask. She didn't know him well enough to start talking about herself. And anyway, there was that uniform he was wearing and the row of ribbons. And this was wartime, so obviously the only decent topic of conversation between them was his experiences.

"Tell me," she said. "Have you *just* come back?"

"I've been here about three weeks. I'm on leave."

"You must hate it." She looked at him very seriously.

Shireen was convinced that all servicemen hated the United States for its comforts and security, for its complete lack of understanding about the hardships the men overseas had to endure. In her mind the war went on everywhere and constantly exactly as she saw it in newsreels: tanks rolling, guns firing, planes falling in flame, ships blowing up, towns collapsing under bombing attacks. There was never a moment of relaxation or quiet, no hours of boredom or waiting. She didn't see how they managed to come back with any rag of sanity left. And then, coming back, to hear these damned silly civilians complaining about gas-rationing and standing in line for cigarettes and the meat shortage and conniving to buy what they couldn't get otherwise on the black market.

Lieutenant Worth laughed again, and something in its sound told her he had sensed what she was thinking. "Hate it? No, I'm pretty damned glad to be back. And don't believe any GI who tells you different."

"But a lot of them say they aren't. They get nervous and restless and they resent the civilians—as they well might." She had donated a

222

pint of blood a couple of days before, which she did every six weeks, hoping to feel they would have less reason to resent her.

"Sure," he agreed. "All God's chillun gotta have someone to resent. Life would be pretty tough without its ready-made scapegoats. At least, life the way we live it now. But for every guy who likes the war there are ten or twenty or fifty thousand who hate it."

Shireen listened to him carefully and was impressed. He had thought about some things which she had not, or he had reached conclusions different from hers; she could learn something from him. Therefore she could look up to him. He's very intelligent, she decided. And interesting. If I ever really get a chance to talk to him, he'll have a lot to say.

"Yes," said Shireen. "But look at the world's history. It's told largely in terms of war."

"A guy named Marx had a reason for that, too."

She glanced at him curiously. Anyone who mentioned Marx out loud she believed must be a communist, and there was a titillation in talking to someone with such radical views, as if it proved how far she had come from her Republican family.

But at her glance Paul laughed again. "Don't worry," he said. "I'm not going to give you the grip."

She made a mocking face. "Aw heck." Then glanced around the room. "Do you know these people?"

"Some of 'em. Why?"

"Just wondering. I don't know a soul. It seems to me I'm always these days surrounded by dozens and hundreds of people I don't know. You'd think just once in awhile I'd run into someone I'd seen before."

He was looking at her now with a kind of paternal sympathy, as if she were a little girl he felt sorry for. "You can't be having much fun," he said softly.

"Oh, but I am," protested Shireen. "I really am."

"Don't try to kid Uncle Paul. Where did you come from?"

"Southern California. I lived in a little town called Marron most of my life. No one's ever heard of it," she added apologetically. She was beginning to feel a little ashamed of Marron but still, she felt she must be honest and admit that was where she came from.

"And have you friends in New York?"

"I have now. I didn't know anyone at all when I came. But my agent Georgia Marsh has been awfully kind to me. I'd have been lost without her. Do you know Georgia?"

"I've met her a couple of times—before the war. Smart dame. And is she the only close friend you have here?"

"Well, yes," said Shireen reluctantly. "I guess she is. Though I

223

know a lot of other people now too—some of them are friends, I guess. At least I like *them* very much."

"Poor baby," said Paul.

Shireen looked at him with slight alarm. Was he feeling sorry for her? And why should he, for heaven's sake? Was she pathetic or something?

"I'm all right," she said.

"No doubt about that," he agreed, smiling. "But it can't be much fun for you. Your life probably looks pretty damned glamorous to a lot of people and it's obvious plenty of them are envying you. But sooner or later you've got to go home and shut the door, and then you must wonder sometimes just where the hell everybody went."

Shireen listened, watching him seriously. How did he know that? He must know a great deal more. But now she saw that he was about to leave her, and wished he would not. It felt as if she had finally found a friend.

"Look, Shireen—is it all right if I call you that?—I've got to meet some people for dinner. But I'd like very much to see you again. Would you have dinner with me sometime soon?"

"I'd love to," she said quickly.

"Could we make it tomorrow night, if you're not busy?"

"I'm not." She was watching him eagerly and a little anxiously. He smiled and briefly pressed her hand. Then he got up.

"Fine." He stood a moment longer while they arranged the time he would call for her and they shook hands. "I'd drop you wherever you're going but I suppose the guest of honor has to stick around until the last dog, et cetera—"

"I think I'd better. Good night, Paul." She smiled up at him, a fresh ingenuous grateful little girl's smile. "Thanks for asking me."

Later on, when she and Georgia were having their nightly coffee, she told her about the fascinating man she had met. "His name's Paul Worth. He says he's met you. Do you remember him?"

"Sure. Good-looking boy. Can't get used to being his father's son."

"What do you mean?"

"His father's Jonathan Worth the newspaper tycoon, as we say in the trade. You didn't think Marylyn was just being patriotic, inviting a serviceman to enjoy her hospitality?"

"I didn't think about it. But why should having Jonathan Worth for a father be so tough to take?"

"After all, where do you go from there? The boy doesn't know what to do with himself. He doesn't want to follow in the old man's footsteps and he doesn't know what the hell else to do. Well, I guess there are tougher problems in the world than that one."

"I can think of several," said Shireen, and she was thinking of all the things Paul Worth had grown up to take for granted that she was just beginning to get. The thousand fears she had he could never have even known about; and she was not inclined to think there was much more to fear.

"Just be careful of one thing, will you?" said Georgia.

"What's that?"

"Don't go getting yourself involved with him."

Shireen looked a little shocked. "But I have no intention of it. I'm certainly not going to sleep with him, if that's what you mean."

"That's what I mean."

Shireen frowned a little. Now, why should Georgia get such a notion as that in her head?

"He's the first guy in months," said Georgia, "that you haven't packed in before you'd talked to him half an hour. And I know the signals by now."

"Really, Georgia—"

"Keep Johnny in mind—if you can't keep Ed."

Shireen frowned. "I don't really think I'll ever see Johnny again. He wouldn't write the kind of letters he does if he loved me. *You* know that, Georgia."

"I think that's exactly the kind he'd write, whether he loved you or not." She shook her head. "Where men are concerned, Shireen, you simply have no belief in yourself at all. How you manage this I'll never know, because you've got everything. But you have to be assured and reassured and I'm afraid nothing will ever convince you you're loved as long as you keep on believing that you're unlovable."

"Maybe," said Shireen, and got up to leave. It was one-thirty. "I don't know."

Georgia walked to the door with her. "Remember," she cautioned again. "We're a mighty persnickety nation when it comes to the private morals of our public characters."

Shireen laughed. "I'll remember."

She rang for the bell and waited for the elevator. A nervous restlessness fluttered suddenly inside her: What in the hell am I doing with my life anyway? What do I want out of living? What am I missing? Something's wrong somewhere. But she couldn't imagine what. She was supposed to have everything now. Everything she had ever wanted. Then what *could* be missing?

She got in the elevator and a fragment of poetry came to her mind. *The desire of the moth for the star, of the night for the morrow. The devotion to something afar from the sphere of our sorrow.*

"Quite a rainstorm we had earlier tonight, wasn't it?" said the operator.

"Yes," agreed Shireen quickly, eager to snatch a little companionship between the fifteenth and twelfth floors. "But these late summer storms never last long."

225

"No, that's true. They don't. Cooled the air a little, I think."

"Yes, I don't believe it's quite as humid."

"Here's your floor, Miss Delaney."

"Thanks. Good night."

"Good night, Miss Delaney."

She walked down the hall, searching in the bottom of her bag for the key, and then opened the door. This apartment had so much loneliness in it. It struck her every time she walked in. She couldn't stay there. She was there each day only when she slept and long enough to get dressed or change her clothes in the evening.

She went into the bedroom and took off her bracelets and laid them on the dressing-table top. Anyway, she thought, I'm tired. I'll fall asleep right away. Thank God. It sometimes seemed as if that had become her chief aim in life these days. To get tired enough so that she could fall asleep and not have to lie there thinking or avoiding thinking.

I wonder what it is—

I won't think about it.

She pulled off her dress and hung it in the closet where she kept things for the valet to collect. I won't think and everything'll be all right. As soon as Ed comes home it will be all right.

That must be what's the matter with me.

Chapter 31

Paul called from the lobby at exactly eight o'clock and Shireen was ready. He grinned at her when she stepped out of the elevator and Shireen felt as if she were meeting an old friend.

"Didn't your mother ever tell you the rules of the game?" he asked her. "Always keep a man waiting at least fifteen minutes—or, preferably, an hour. It's supposed to whet the appetite."

Shireen linked her arm through his and they started out. She was smiling so her face seemed to glisten, the first time she had smiled that way at a man in months. "It's not one of my rules. If I like someone well enough to go out with him I figure I'm as eager to see him as he is to see me. So what's the sense of wasting time?"

"God! An honest woman. Now I can hock my flashlight."

His car was waiting at the curb, a light gray convertible with a black top, and he opened the door for Shireen to get in.

She felt pleased by the courtesy, something she had always expected and got from Ed, but not from many men since. Gallantry was important, she believed, as a subtle continuous reminder that there was a vast difference between the sexes which no amount of economic, professional or educational equality was going to do much to alter. Part of a feminine awareness that sex ranges perilously close to the ridiculous and can only, with tact and some pretense, be kept from breaking into complete farce. And part, also, of the knowledge that to be female is a considerably more serious biological responsibility than to be male. Men, the damn fools, she thought, should know all this and govern themselves accordingly; and she judged a man by how much he had sensed of woman's physical predicament and how he behaved in regard to it.

Now, as he got in beside her, she looked at him and smiled, a free shining expression on her face. "This seems like the height of luxury to me. I don't think I've been in a real car for a year. Only cabs. How do you get gas?" Then she was sorry she had said it, and worried that he would be annoyed with her for asking such a question.

"Coupons," he said, and swung out from the curb. "I got some for my leave and Dad had saved some. Now, Shireen, you didn't think I'd buy on the black market and me a serviceman and all?"

"I wasn't thinking. Anyway, it's none of my business."

"Honey, a girl of your convictions should stick to 'em. Don't ever let any cad drive you around on his black-market gas. Where do you want to eat?"

"Wherever you do."

"You're all dressed up. At least I guess you're all dressed up. It's kinda hard for me to tell when a gal's dressed up and when she isn't. But I figure a mink stole and a hat that looks like French pastry is dressed up. Am I right?"

"More or less, I suppose."

"Then that means some place like Morocco."

"Not to me, it doesn't. I've only been to El Morocco once and it gave me a stomach-ache. Not from the food, either."

He laughed. "I like you better and better. Now, if you want to leave it to me I'll take you to a place I know where there's no chi-chi whatsoever but the food's fine. At least it was, before I went away."

"That's what I'd like," said Shireen happily. "I love good food."

He glanced at her. "You're swell," he said. "You're really nice."

"I hope so. I want to be."

She was happier than she had been in a long long while. Probably since the last time she had seen Johnny. It always got back to Johnny, no matter what happened in between. But she was not going to think about him tonight—or ever again. She had wasted time enough on him and meanwhile the days were passing and she was in a hurry to get somewhere.

The restaurant he took her to was in the West Fifties and was a small dimly lighted one, down a few steps from the street, where they served Italian food. The kind of place she and Mike had been looking for. It was crowded and there was a line waiting for tables, but the headwaiter came up to them immediately.

"Why, Lieutenant Worth! I didn't know you were back. You're all well now, not sick any more? I read about you in the papers. They didn't hurt you bad, I hope?"

People were turning their heads and Paul looked rather embarrassed. Johnny would have played it like a second-act curtain, thought Shireen; she preferred Paul's dark blush and the slightly unhappy look he had. Paul, she became more convinced every moment, was a much finer man than Johnny Keegan.

"No, not bad, Joe, thanks." He had lowered his voice almost to a whisper. "Say—got a table?"

The man looked around frantically. "There's been so much business. You can't imagine. So much business. Ah, here's someone leaving. We'll put you there."

Paul stepped aside and Shireen followed the waiter among the closely spaced tables to one toward the back that was set against the wall, still covered with dishes and napkins and wine glasses and cigarette stubs. Shireen looked at the litter admiringly and asked Paul if he didn't think it would make a nice still-life.

"Fine, Joe. Thanks."

Paul put a bill into the man's hand and sat down beside her and the table was pushed back up against them. A waiter came and began to clear things off and while they looked at the menu they began to talk. She was not cautious with him as she usually was with strangers, for she liked him and wanted him to know her and so she was not engrossed with trying to hide or conceal her essential self.

It was such a relief not to have Johnny there with her every moment—his smile and his face and voice and everything about him making whatever she did and whomever she met less than it would have been if she had never known him.

They talked to each other eagerly all through dinner and later when they stopped at the Blue Angel and the Ruban Bleu. And as they talked they were searching through the labyrinths of their world for familiar doors and passageways. Each door had a label on it and each passageway was marked with a word that might have some of the same meanings for both of them. Whenever they found one that did they opened it and looked in or wandered a distance down the hall, exploring.

Shireen had grown up to believe in God, the Republican party, the individual, the dollar bill, success; Paul in a family where his father thought in terms of millions of dollars and finally in terms of power and not money at all. He had been sent to Groton and Harvard, worked for awhile in an advertising agency, and then gone to war. But they had both grown up in America, absorbing it as they grew, taking this in and rejecting that. The choices had been many hundreds of thousands and the possibility of making enough choices in such a way that they could actually understand each other was infinitely small.

But they found that the miracle had been at least partly accomplished and that they responded similarly to a good many different words: fascism, war, liberal, reactionary, prejudice, radio, café society, honesty, hypocrisy, illusion, cynicism, hope, religion, atheism. And through hundreds and thousands of words they groped their way toward each other.

She was not flirting with him. In fact, she was quite carefully not flirting with him by any of the usual obvious devices or even a conscious intent.

But while they talked he watched her, very frankly absorbed in every expression, every gesture, every inflection of her voice. And sensing his fascination she changed subtly and slowly, responding with delicate precision to what she saw in his eyes. Her face began to relax and a play of expression flowed over it; her eyes lightened,

229

she looked directly at him and glanced away; her long slender fingers formed sudden patterns and then dropped briefly into her lap again. There was an expansion in all her personality. The scared little girl disappeared and a woman aware of her allurement took her place. But it happened without her knowing it, in automatic response to his admiration.

Almost as if, while she talked—displaying to him the things she had learned and read and thought about—inside her another Shireen was doing a kind of mating dance, dressed in a feathered skirt with cherry bangles on her wrists, stamping her bare feet, whirling and smiling, making intricate gestures with her hands. While she only sat talking soberly about things they both believed were serious and important, and was aware that he was already part way in love with her.

About two o'clock they went back to her apartment, laughing as they came in at something one of them had said; she went into the bedroom to take off her hat and comb her hair. Johnny's picture was stuck in a corner of the dressing-table mirror and she looked at it with sudden surprise.

What are *you* doing here?

She pulled it out, opened a drawer and dropped it in, then closed the drawer quickly. She picked up a lipstick and touched her mouth, leaning forward to look at herself, gave a toss of her head that flung her hair back, and walked out again.

Paul was standing, his back to her and his hands in his pockets, looking at one of her paintings. She was suddenly aware of all the girls who must have loved or wanted him, and a little shocked to have had this unexpected keen awareness. She must be more careful about what came into her mind.

"What do you think of it?" she asked him, indicating the painting.

He turned and looked at her, smiling as if he were amused again. "I don't know. It's modern so I suppose it means something in terms of the world we live in. I guess the guy has made something or other out of the twentieth century for himself and tried to put it down. But I'm not sure enough about liking this century, much less knowing if I like what anyone has to say about it."

It sounded very wise to Shireen, who didn't know if she liked the picture either or what it was really getting at, but nevertheless had it there on her wall.

"I don't know a damn thing about any of this," she told him, gesturing toward the other pictures. "I've just got them because it seems you're supposed to have paintings nowadays. It shows that even if you're nouveau riche you really had better instincts all along."

Paul laughed outright at that, watching her fondly, and she laughed with him as if they knew a good secret. "Wonderful! God, but you're a delight. It's funny, how grateful you get for honesty." They stood for a moment and looked at each other, and then Shireen turned her eyes away.

"That Ed?" Paul nodded toward the silver frame on the desk.

Shireen looked as if she had been caught. "Yes, it is. I just got a letter from him today," she added quickly. "He's feeling fine and he's not in any danger."

Paul smiled vaguely, and then straightened his face out, but she knew he had wanted her to see the smile first and whatever he had meant by it.

"He looks like a pretty nice guy."

"He is. He's wonderful." She looked at Paul again, a little defiantly now. Then she said: "Would you like a drink?"

"Sure."

She went out to the kitchenette, set a bottle of whisky on a silver tray with a glass, a pitcher of water, and a bowl of ice cubes. She carried it back to the living room and put it down on the coffee table before him.

"You fix it. I don't understand these things too well."

He sat at one end of the couch and Shireen sat carefully at the other. She lit a cigarette, and found she was somewhat nervous. Both of them were quiet for a moment while Paul mixed his drink and took a swallow and finally he turned and looked at her.

"You know, this has been the happiest night I've spent in—I don't know how long."

Shireen frowned slightly. "Yes. It has been nice, hasn't it?" But now she sounded as if he were a vague and troublesome caller who has stayed beyond his half hour.

They were quiet a moment longer. He gave a light sigh and then looked at her. "Things must have been tough for you since your husband's been gone."

She glanced at him, wondering if he had meant to be sarcastic. "Of course it has. What made you say that?"

"The way you looked at me a minute ago. I didn't really say anything—just that it had been a wonderful night. But you looked as if I'd made a pass at you."

"Oh, did I?" She was embarrassed. "I'm sorry—"

"You can relax, Shireen. I'm not going to try to sleep with you, if that's what's troubling you."

"Oh, but Paul, I hadn't even—"

"As a matter of fact, I think I'd rather sleep with you than any woman I've ever known. But I'm not even going to try and if you want to know why, I'll tell you."

"Why?" she asked quickly, and then thought: Now, that was a silly thing for me to say. I shouldn't even care why.

231

"Because I'm afraid you'd say no, and I'm such a self-conscious bastard I don't want to be refused."

Suddenly Shireen threw back her head and laughed. "You're the first man I've ever met who had courage enough to admit that. They've always got a dozen reasons why you refuse and it's always something wrong with you, never with them. Do you know something, Paul? I like you. I think I like you better than almost anyone I know."

"My God! Of course, you shouldn't."

"I do. And why shouldn't I?"

"I'm no good. I mean it. Don't look surprised. I'm just no damn good at all. I've done nothing but cause people trouble all my life."

She looked at him speculatively, her lips turned up in a smile, her eyes seeming to lengthen. "Me, too. Maybe that's why we get along together so well." They both laughed again and went on talking eagerly, feeling like two conspirators against a dull and stupid world.

She was convinced that she had never before been as happy as she was now. Present happiness was the only kind she ever counted anyway, and all the rest had been a delusion. Neither of them looked at the clock. Occasionally Paul poured a little more Scotch into his glass, but he drank slowly and carefully and was seemingly unaffected by it.

"What are you going to do after the war, Paul?" she asked him finally.

And then was instantly sorry, for his face looked as if she had hurt him. At first he had seemed nonchalant and sophisticated—impressive qualities, she thought—but she knew by now it was only protective coloration for the conflicts and some scarce buried self-doubt. In many ways he was like her; they both knew it, and drew steadily closer together.

"I don't know," he said. "All I really like to do is fish and swim. I guess I'm a natural-born bum. Another guy and I talked it over in a bar in Panama once, and decided it might be a good idea to set up a really plush whorehouse down there."

"What!" cried Shireen, horrified.

He laughed. "Oh. Then you are shockable, after all."

"Well, of course," said Shireen primly, and could not be sure if he was making fun of her or not.

"Never mind," he said. "I'm probably too lazy even to bother with that."

"Anyway, I know you don't mean it."

"Of course I mean it. The average house leaves a great deal to be desired, believe me. There's room for improvement in the best of them and Bill and I made out a pretty extensive list of the things we'd change and the things we'd add. Like to hear about it?" He was watching her with malicious amusement.

"I should say not!"

232

He poured another drink, still smiling, looking lazy and amused and pleased with himself. "I want to run a whorehouse—and be a friend to man," he half chanted. "Make kind of a nice little ditty, don't you think? Now Shireen, suppose you put aside your prejudices and we'll look at this thing from an esthetic and social and economic point of view. Unfortunately, respectable women invariably regard prostitutes as unfair competition and hate them for being what they'd secretly like to be themselves. I think you must agree, though—"

"Paul! For heaven's sake!" All her illusions about him were teetering.

He shrugged. "Sorry if I upset you. I guess it'll be a long time yet before women can stop taking sex so goddamn seriously."

"They never will. After all, it is serious—especially for a woman."

"It shouldn't be. It should just be fun."

"Fun. What a point of view. As though it's a toy of some kind. Men sometimes make me sick."

"Only if you keep expecting them to be nice little brothers. Anyway, I'm sorry. To tell the truth, your question bothered me, and I guess that was my way of getting back at you." He took a long swallow. "Sorry."

The illusions rose back into place again. "Oh, Paul, forgive me! I didn't mean to upset you—"

Chapter 32

"Don't apologize. How could you know a guy my age can't figure out what to do with his life?" He looked back at her. "You writing another book?" He asked it almost covertly, as if he was half afraid to hear the answer.

Shireen gave a sudden ringing laugh that seemed to startle him. "I should say not! I think maybe I'll do a radio program. There's someone who thinks they might want to sponsor me—a cosmetic manufacturer. But don't tell anyone. So far it's a secret. I thought it might be fun."

"Don't kid yourself. It's slow death. What would a nice girl like you want with a radio program, anyway?"

"Why—I don't exactly know. Something to do, I guess."

"You've got something to do."

"What?"

"Write, of course. What else would a writer do?"

"But I'm not a writer. At least, I'm not really a writer."

Paul laughed. "I'd say that anyone whose first book sells a million copies in five months is a writer and no mistake about it. What makes you say such a thing as that? You told me you'd been writing since you were eight years old. You're stuck with it, baby. You'll never stop."

"That's what Georgia says, but I think you're both wrong. I wrote for a purpose and now the purpose has been accomplished and as far as I'm concerned, that's that."

"What purpose?"

"Money. Independence. Fame. Success, I guess. I've got all that now and I'm going to do something else. I want to live a lot of different lives, not just one. I wish I could have lived forever, in every age and every country, seen everything and done everything and felt everything. One life is so little to be given in all the time there is. Wouldn't you think God would have arranged things differently?"

Paul smiled affectionately. "You're still such a baby. And you look so damned grown up. It must be the clothes and make-up."

"I guess. I don't know. I don't care. But I do wish I didn't have to go off on that damned silly autographing tour Monday!"

She was going to autograph some more books out in the Middle West and on the Coast and had promised her parents to come home for a couple of weeks. She had mostly forgotten how much she had hated the first autographing tour and, anyway, it would take her to new places where there would be no telling what new people. But now she had no interest in meeting new "people." Paul had another week of his leave before he had to report to Washington.

And suddenly the thought of all the responsibilities she had, all the things she must do because people expected her to do them, seemed intolerable. She felt conscious of herself again as *Shireen Delaney,* an illusion in the public eye, made out of her own work, the way she looked, newspaper clippings, photographs, rumors, the myth of Cinderella, the American fear and respect of flashy success.

"I wonder if there's any way I could get out of going."

She said it half to herself. She would be gone a month and that now seemed an impossibly long time. If she had only *known* she was going to meet Paul Worth. Something was always interfering with her life.

Was she never never never as long as she lived going to get things arranged just as she wanted them?

"One of these days," said Paul, looking at her sulky troubled face, "you'll quit doing things like that, too."

"Like what?"

"You'll quit letting people bully you and lionize you and you'll start living your own life." He shook his head. "This cockeyed world. I was born with the things you've worked to get. And you've got the one thing I want more than anything else."

"What's that?" She could not believe she had anything at all which could be of real value to someone else. Certainly not to Paul Worth.

"The ability to sit down and write."

"You don't mean that, Paul."

"I do mean it. The one thing I've ever honestly wanted to do is write."

"Well," said Shireen, in a crisp practical tone. "Why don't you then?"

He laughed softly. "The same reason so many people don't do what they want to. They're afraid."

"Afraid of what?"

"Afraid of not doing as well as they think they should—not living up to whatever the hell it is they've come to expect of themselves. I could never be satisfied with doing something mediocre. My standards are too high, and I recognize my limitations too clearly."

Shireen looked at him seriously, wishing there was some way she could help, wanting to give him something. He was as lost as she was, maybe even more lost, still looking for the one thing she had managed to find and had found alone and within herself.

235

"Paul," she said, prepared to settle the entire issue for him, once and for all, "it's all very well to recognize your limitations. But you must ignore them." That was exceedingly good advice, she felt, and if he paid attention to it, would straighten him out. Shireen had great faith in her ability to solve other people's problems for them.

But he only shook his head, as if he had suddenly realized that he was tired, and leaned forward to light a cigarette. She sat and watched him, full of real affection for that self-conscious unhappy deprecating picture he had of himself; the counterpart she found in him of her own guilt and misgivings.

They went on talking, and it began to seem as if they had known each other forever. Finally he said:

"You know, Shireen, there's something I want to tell you, and though I know it's not good sense or good form or anything else under the circumstances, I guess I'm just drunk enough to say it anyway."

"What is it, Paul?" Since he had confessed that he had no direction and no ability to do the one thing he most wanted, her feeling toward him had changed. She looked at him now with a soft maternal protecting expression.

But he was watching her carefully and all at once she felt that he had come closer, that he was reaching out, drawing her toward him. It set up in her a vague sense of fear.

"It's going to sound crazy," he said, "because I don't even know you. At least I'm not supposed to know you because we only met— when was it?—yesterday, I guess. Or maybe it's the day before by now. Anyway, I've never been married because I never found a girl who had everything I wanted. Like that business about writing. Everything had to be just right or it wouldn't do at all. Well—you're the girl I'd like to marry." He gave an apologetic little laugh. "And now that I've said it I don't know why I had to say it at all. I hope I haven't made you uncomfortable."

Shireen was staring at him, incredulous and deeply touched. He had said that he would like to marry her! When all these years she had told herself it was lucky she had Ed because no other man would put up with her. A little suspicion sneaked into her mind: Maybe she didn't have to stay married to Ed, after all.

Then she was instantly ashamed and angry with herself.

What was the matter with her, anyway? Thinking such a thing! And Paul didn't mean it. He admitted he was a little drunk and that was why he had said it. Of course he didn't mean it. He wouldn't want her if he really knew her.

He was smiling. "You don't believe me, do you?"

"No," said Shireen, and looked down at where she was folding the edge of her skirt. "I guess I don't."

Now he laughed. "It's true, all the same." He glanced at his watch.

236

"Hey, do you know what time it is? Five-thirty. When do you sleep, by the way?"

"Whenever there's nothing interesting left to do."

"Then how about some breakfast?"

Shireen jumped up. "That's a good idea. I'll get my coat."

She started past him and he reached out and caught her hand. She stopped reluctantly, looking down at him with a kind of wistful pleading. For a minute they watched each other and then he released her.

"All right," he said. "Go on."

Shireen, wearing a blue silk man's bathrobe, sat on one of the white-shrouded chairs and waited for the phone to be answered. Paul was standing beside her dressed in another robe, smiling down at her. Shireen crossed her legs, gave him a gay little smile, and reached out one hand to him. He took it and came closer, bent down and kissed her on the cheek, and his other hand stroked across the top of her head. Around them the furniture was covered with white slips; it was his parents' house in Far Hills and they had closed it a few weeks ago for the winter.

"Hello." That was Georgia's voice.

Shireen, smiling up at Paul, gave a little start, as if she had forgotten someone was going to answer. "Oh. Georgia—this is Shireen."

Paul made her a signal and left the room.

"What in the name of God are you doing up at this hour?" Georgia wanted to know. "Ten o'clock. Nothing's wrong, is it?"

Shireen laughed. "No. Everything's wonderful, in fact. I couldn't be happier. Remember Paul Worth?"

"Natch."

"He's wonderful."

"Oh, Shireen, for the love of mike. I was just drinking my coffee."

"No, Georgia, wait—I'm out in New Jersey with him, at his father's house and—"

"At his father's house? Shireen, are you crazy?"

"No, I'm in love with him. We got here about three hours ago—we started out to have breakfast and kept on driving. No one's here. But listen, Georgia, I don't think I'll be back in time to keep that cocktail date with that radio agent, I forget his name, so will you call him for me and give him some kind of—"

"Shireen, will you please listen to me for a minute? You shouldn't be doing this. I know Paul's a nice guy and all that. But I've told you and told you a hundred thousand times you've got to be careful about what you do nowadays. You can't run around the country with any man who takes your fancy—"

"*Georgia,* Paul *isn't*—"

"Wait a minute. If you keep on doing things like this, Shireen,

237

sooner or later someone's going to find out about it. Anyway, you don't know Paul. How do you know he'll keep his mouth shut? There's no reason why he should. Oh, Shireen, I wish I could pound some sense into your head. What about Johnny?"

"I told you I'm through with Johnny. Or he's through with me. Whatever it is. Anyway, Paul is *much* nicer than Johnny."

"Okay. I give up. Go ahead. I'll think of something to tell Troy. But for God's sake, get back in time for Thayer's dinner tonight. And remember, you've got to pack first, too. If you don't show up for that tour you're dead. I never could explain that one away. And Shireen—"

"Yes, Georgia?"

"Wear some dark glasses, will you?"

Shireen laughed but Georgia's voice came back at her. "I mean it. You don't know how much your face has been spread around. You still think you're back in Marron. And please try to remember: Delaney's a name that looks good in the columns these days. Ed Farrell is technically a war hero, so take it easy with the current illusions, will you?"

"Oh, Georgia, it's really all right. No one will know about it."

"I hope not."

" 'Bye."

"G'bye. I wish you had more sense. Oh, I'm sorry, Shireen. You poor kid, I know you're lonesome."

"I'm not lonesome, Georgia. He really is wonderful!"

"Sure. Sure. I know."

Shireen hung up, smiling to herself, shaking her head.

Just like Georgia. Always worrying about publicity. As if you could stop living because the publicity might be unfavorable.

For this was something really important; maybe the most important thing that had ever happened in her life. Somehow, out of these past months of aimlessness and drifting, feeling lost and helpless and at the mercy of a world she could not understand, she had found Paul and he was everything she needed.

She had not thought about Ed at all these past few hours. And she had thought of Johnny only with defiance, convinced she had finally triumphed over him.

Other people? Let them look out for themselves. She was looking out for Shireen. It was the one lesson you had to learn in life—there's no one on earth who will really take care of you but yourself.

She got up and went out to find Paul.

He was in the kitchen, slicing some oranges; they had stopped along the way and bought eggs and bacon and oranges for breakfast. "Here!" she cried. "Let me do that!"

He turned, saw the brilliant happy light on her face, and kissed her. Finally she drew away and smiled at him. "Sit down over there

238

and talk to me. I'm very efficient in a kitchen—I cooked for a living for six years, you know." She laughed and he shook his head, smiling and looking at her as if in bewilderment. She turned and went to work, thinking: At least I didn't let this go by me. I'll never have to take a look at myself later on and wonder what would have happened if I hadn't been afraid.

I always *did* hate people who go pussyfooting through life.

Georgia was at Philip Thayer's dinner party that night; she came a few minutes later than Shireen and began talking to her. "Shireen, for God's sake. You look like hell."

"I know. I haven't slept in thirty-six hours."

"Well, try to pull yourself together. People will wonder what you've been up to. Here, come in the bathroom with me. I'll give you half a benzedrine."

"No," said Shireen, who had an idea benzedrine was a cross between hashish and cocaine. "I'm all right."

"Come on. It won't hurt you. Just relax you some, that's all. Clear out a few cobwebs. Benzedrine's a quick psychoanalysis."

Shireen went with her and swallowed the tablet and then they stood there a moment and talked while Shireen drank a glass of water, depressed by her own tired face in the mirror. She was thinking of what Paul had said to her when they stopped in front of her hotel and she had to leave him:

"It's a funny thing, but I said good-by when I went overseas to people who should have meant a lot more to me. My family—friends I'd known for years. But I didn't feel the way I do now about seeing you go away for a month—"

"All I hope," said Georgia, interrupting her thoughts, "is that that boy has sense enough not to tell anyone you went out there with him."

"Oh, Georgia," protested Shireen wearily. "He won't. He wouldn't think of it. We're in love with each other, I told you."

"You can't be serious, Shireen. You just can't. Every time you turn around you fall in love again. I don't know how the hell you define love to yourself. It just doesn't happen this easily—or this often."

Shireen smiled. "I told you how I define it. Friendship with sex. How else would you define it?"

"That's an easy answer. Much too easy." Georgia was clearly somewhat annoyed. "You're such a child. If only you'd somehow learned a little about life."

"I'm learning," said Shireen, and put the glass back. "As fast as I can." She turned around, her face growing thoughtful. "It's funny, though. Nothing is ever much different from what I expected. I guess

239

experience is just learning at first hand the things you knew all along anyway."

Georgia reached for the doorknob and Shireen tried once more to reassure her. "Don't worry about Paul, Georgia. He's completely trustworthy. I know he is."

"Well—I guess war makes strangers bedfellows, to paraphrase—" They both laughed and walked out again, down the hall and back into the noisy party.

Chapter 33

In Los Angeles the station was crowded with men in uniform standing around as if they had been there a long while and, for all they knew, might be there the rest of their lives. *Railway stations.* It seemed to Shireen that some of the worst moments of your life are spent in railway stations. She hated to travel. Travel meant loneliness, being lost somewhere in space, like a tiny spider that has spun himself a long thin web and drifts to and fro with every slight breeze until he comes near enough some twig to catch and fasten to it and find home for a time.

Her mother and father were there to meet her.

She kissed them, noticing that they looked a little strange to her, like people she did not know very well. Both of them were beaming.

"We're so proud of you!" her mother said.

She glanced at her father, almost warily, to see what he would say. "I always knew you'd do it," he told her.

Then he took her baggage checks and while he went to find the porter, Shireen and her mother stood talking. "That's a pretty dress," said Shireen. "It's new, isn't it?"

"Yes, I'm glad you like it." Her mother was smiling, looking very happy. "You can't imagine how much it means to have you home—"

"I'll only be here a few days," said Shireen quickly.

"I know. But it's wonderful to have you here for even a short time. Shireen—have you been well? Aren't you a little thinner?"

Shireen began to get uneasy. "I feel fine. I'm rather tired, that's all. I've been autographing books all over the damn country, remember."

"I worry about you—living so far away. If you ever got sick—"

"Oh, Mother, please! I haven't been sick. Anyway, if I did, I'm not completely alone in New York. I have some friends there. You know," she said, and there was suddenly something intense and reproving in her manner, "I've been much too protected all my life. Do you realize that I don't know anything at all about the world or about people?"

"There are a great many things it's better for you not to know."

Shireen frowned a little and sighed. Here it was, all over again: You are our adored and lovely daughter, different from any other girl who ever lived. We want you to have nothing but happiness,

241

nothing but joy. We want you to be protected from everything ugly or crude. We never want you to feel pain or to know sorrow.

We want you never to grow up, to belong to us always as when you were a baby. We don't want you to live.

"I met the most wonderful man just before I left New York," said Shireen casually, and knew as she said it that it came out of defiance. You see, I'm not just a child. I'm not so sweet and innocent. I'm grown up—things happen to me, just like they happen to other people. And you weren't there. You couldn't stop it. She had written them already that Mike had fallen in love with her, and that she was in love with Johnny, and that Jack was in love with her too but she had broken his heart, smashed it completely, beyond all repair.

"His name's Paul Worth. His father's Jonathan Worth." *That* would impress them.

"The newspaper owner?" asked her mother, and Shireen was pleased to see that she really was impressed.

"Yes. And Paul's marvelous. He's handsome and charming and intelligent and everything you can think of. And he's in love with me—he wants to marry me."

"He wants to marry you? Shireen, what on earth are you talking about? How can you even say such a thing—with Ed overseas? And what kind of man can he be to have told you that in the first place?"

"Mother, really! Love and marriage is not just an endurance contest."

"But Ed—"

"I'm not going to marry Paul Worth, for heaven's sake. I'm going to stay married to Ed. I'm only telling you what Paul said."

"I think you should get out of that city. It's not good for you. One of these days you're going to do something you'll regret all your life."

Shireen laughed triumphantly. "But why is it only the things you shouldn't have done that you remember with any pleasure?"

Her father came up to them and they started through the station together. "Say, aren't you thinner than you were a year ago?"

"Maybe I am," agreed Shireen despondently.

The porter stacked her bags in the car, the three of them got into the front seat and they started out, Shireen sitting between her parents. It was mid-October and the day was hot and flourishing. She looked out the windows as they drove along, and a heavy nostalgia took unexpected hold of her. How beautiful Los Angeles seemed, coming into it from across the desert. The palm trees. The hot bright air. The flash and cleanness it had, the glossy washed look. The mountains behind in a haze.

"It's nice to be home," she said, and the three of them smiled.

Her parents began to ask her questions eagerly. She had written them at length about almost everything that happened to her, but now they went over all of it again. She chattered swiftly and confidently, and in some way was more at ease than she had been in a long while. At home she could let her egotism out, like a dog that has been kept in too small a kennel, and allow it to run and play at will.

"I've got to hand it to you," her father said. "You've got a lot of guts. More than I ever had."

Shireen looked at him. That's right, she thought. I have. And I learned from you what happens if you don't. If you let yourself get sidetracked.

"I don't know about that," she said. "But anyway I wanted to write a best seller and I did." Which obviously proved that she was right about everything else, and had been all along.

"If only Ed could be here to share it with you," her mother said. "Then it would be perfect."

"Yes," agreed Shireen vaguely, and thought around for some way to change the subject. "Did I ever tell you what finally made me start writing that book?" She was talking to her father.

"No, I don't think you did. What was it?"

"Every time you saw me or wrote to me you asked if I'd begun it yet and every time I said no, I got more and more embarrassed. Until finally I had to start it just so I could tell you I had."

"Well, I'll be damned." He looked pleased and a little embarrassed. "So the old man did do something for you, after all."

That was a kind of apology because he had never made as much money for his family as he had wanted to—an attempt to bridge across the years when he and his daughter had been hostile and estranged, both of them caught in a trap they did not understand and could not break out of.

"Of course. You did a lot. And that time you told me I'd never be a writer at all if I wasn't willing to work and work and work at it. I was furious with you—but I never forgot it."

Shireen's mother patted her hand to thank her and Shireen felt a sudden sick aching compassion for her parents. You've taken everything, she told herself, and given nothing in return. You've ruined their lives.

"How's Douglas?"

"Still at Pearl Harbor. I'm afraid they may be sending him out soon. I got that feeling from his last letter—though of course they're not allowed to say anything definite."

"Maybe he won't be," said Shireen softly, gently. "And even if he is, a lot of men go out there but never get where there's any real fighting."

"Somehow I can't believe it," her mother said. "It doesn't seem possible that he's really there. If anything should ever happen to him—"

Shireen glanced quickly sideways, saw her mother's face and felt an agonized twist of jealousy. *She always loved him better than she did me and she still does—even after all I've done. I never can do enough to mean what he does to them. They love him most and they always will but I don't care anyway. I have my own life, I never think about them; they're not important to me. Let them have Douglas. I've got other things and I'll get more yet.*

But that made her feel ashamed, for Douglas was overseas and of course they were worried about him. Why should she expect them not to be, and why should she want everything for herself?

"We've had the house painted," her father said.

"I remember you told me in your last letter. I'll bet it's nice."

A few minutes later they were home. Shireen looked at the house cautiously for a moment, aware again of some vague threat. And then she followed her mother out of the car, calling enthusiastically: "Oh! It's very pretty! And you've planted some new roses!"

They walked up the steps and into the house and nothing was very different from the way it had been when she had left to marry Ed eight years ago. The furniture was the same and stood in the same places. There were a few more books and some new slipcovers but that was all. Shireen commented on them and then her father came in, carrying her bags. "I'll take them to your room."

"Thanks, Dad."

"Would you like some coffee, dear?"

"That'd be nice," said Shireen. "I'll help you." She left her hat on the living-room couch and went out to the kitchen with her mother. And then the three of them sat in the breakfast room and drank coffee and talked and Shireen and her father smoked.

As she talked, telling them about her new life and everything that had happened to her, she became dimly aware that she was trying to give them a part of what she now had; since it was she who had achieved for them what they had failed to achieve for themselves.

You see, she was saying in effect, *it hasn't been altogether a waste for you to have had me. I'm paying you back by being the daughter every American wants to have, beautiful and rich and successful. I can't do much more, can I? It isn't the same, I know, as if I had never been born at all and you had had these things yourselves. But since I'm alive it's the next best thing I can do. I hope it's some help. I hope it takes away some of the hurt and some of the disappointment.*

"Well," said her father, when they had been talking for almost three hours, "I always knew you'd do it, once you set your mind to it. You've done just about everything you ever wanted to since the day you were born."

With you telling me not to because it might be bad for me, she thought. But kept quiet and only smiled.

244

When her father left to go to the office Shireen and her mother sat there alone, silent for a moment. Shireen reached over and tapped the ash of her cigarette into a little pewter tray.

"Poor Dad," she said, her voice very soft. She looked at her mother. "Has he been making much money?"

"Some. The war has helped his business in some ways, but in others—" She gave a little sigh.

"You're not still expecting him to get rich, are you?"

"No. I'm not."

"You did for years, you know. You remember that, don't you? We all did. It was funny, how we all kept hanging onto that."

"He could have, Shireen."

"But he didn't."

"No—but it wasn't his fault."

Shireen was quiet a moment. Then she looked at her mother again. "Nothing's turned out the way you wanted, has it?"

"Of course it has, Shireen. We haven't all the money in the world—not as much as we both expected to have, I suppose. And we were never able to do the things for you children that we wanted to. But we've had a great deal of happiness together and we have you and Douglas."

"But you *don't* have us any more, don't you see that? We're both grown up and we've left home and you never had anything else in your life and now you haven't even got that! And what about your career in opera that you used to talk about when I was little? You had a beautiful voice, but you never really studied or trained it. You let that go by, too."

"Maybe it was never as good as I liked to imagine, Shireen. People get what they work for. To be perfectly honest about it, I was lazy. Other things meant more to me."

"Like Dad."

"Yes. And you and Douglas."

"And now where are you! You've given up everything for us—everything you might ever have done and been!"

"But I wanted to, Shireen. I'm happy enough."

"No, you're not. You may be resigned, but you're not happy. My memory's better than that. I remember a lot of things you may have forgotten—or made yourself forget."

"No, Shireen, I haven't forgotten. And I tell you honestly, as I've told you before—I hope your life will be a very different one from mine. I've never told you anything else."

"It is. It will be. I'll never live your life over again. Oh, Mother, if *only* you hadn't given up so much for us. You wanted a bigger house and you wanted to travel and you never should have had to work so hard. You never had anything you wanted!"

"No one gets everything they want."

Shireen made a quick confused gesture. "But I somehow thought they did. Oh, I knew they didn't but I thought everyone should and that something was wrong with the world if they didn't. And—oh, I don't know what it is. It's me, I guess. Somehow I've been a failure—and I never meant to be."

Mrs. Delaney reached over and pressed her daughter's hand. "Don't talk like that, darling. You mustn't talk that way. You have nothing to be troubled about or to regret. You were what I wanted, remember. I hoped my first child would be a girl."

"Yes—and you almost died. I almost killed you!"

"Shireen, don't talk that way! You didn't almost kill me! How can you say such a thing? It had nothing to do with you—it was the doctor."

"I guess so. But what is it *I* did, then?"

"What are you talking about?"

"Oh, I don't know. I honestly don't know. I'm sorry. Let's do the dishes, and I'll go unpack."

"I'll do the dishes, dear. You go ahead and unpack. And when you've finished I'll come and look at your new clothes. I want to see all your pretty things." Her mother was looking at her with a bright and eager smile.

A spasm of pain caught her throat; Shireen stroked her hand tenderly across her mother's head. "You've been so good to me. And I've never deserved it. But I'm going to pay you back for everything."

"I don't want payment, dear. You and Douglas are all the payment I need."

Shireen shook her head quickly. "No, we're not. We're not enough at all." She went out of the room and started up the stairs. I'll give her that string of pearls she always wanted. And I'll give Dad some money for his business. I'll make it up to them someway. I'll pay them off, I'll even the score, as much as I can.

It won't be the same as if they'd never had me. But it'll be the best I can do.

While she was home she was interviewed and photographed and she signed a thousand or so more books. She went to see a few old school friends, but each time wondered why she had. She had nothing in common with them any longer, and had never had very much. Her life had gone off in such a different direction from theirs and now they acted as if they did not understand her and as if she made them vaguely uncomfortable. They were polite about her success but did not seem genuinely interested or enthusiastic. Somewhere, she knew, she had upset a picture they had of life and themselves in it. The things that had happened to Shireen should not happen to anyone

246

they knew—only to vague mythical people who had never known anyone like themselves.

She wrote to Paul and got several special delivery letters from him. One afternoon he called.

"When are you coming back?" he asked her. "You can't imagine how I miss you. I never would have believed it."

She felt embarrassed and constrained, aware of her mother in the next room overhearing what she said. "I'm glad you do," she told him politely. "I won't be here much longer."

He was quiet a moment. "You sound strange. Cold. Has anything happened?"

"No, nothing at all. It's just that—"

"Someone's around?"

"Yes, my mother."

He laughed. "All right, then. Be a good little girl. Anyway—I still love you."

"I do, too." She felt nervous and annoyed and wished her mother were out. She was doing something her mother would not approve of and knew it and it made her uncomfortable.

"Well—I'd better hang up. This is going nowhere. Let me know when you'll be back."

"I will, Paul. And I'm glad you called. I really am."

"You sound like it." His voice had changed and she knew that he was hurt, doubtful of her. "See you soon."

She hung up and was standing there, looking down at the patterned carpet, when her mother came in. She gave a little start.

Her mother shrugged. "I know there's nothing I can do about it, Shireen, and I know you refuse to listen to anything that sounds like criticism—but do you honestly think this is fair to Ed?"

"No."

"Then why do you do it?"

Shireen turned away impatiently. "It has nothing to do with Ed. I love him as much as I ever did."

"You should. You'll never find a better man."

"I know. No one else would put up with me."

She was quoting her mother, the words she had said to her just before she and Ed were married. But her mother apparently did not remember she had said them. Or, if she did, took them so much for granted that now she thought Shireen was only stating a fact.

"There isn't another man on earth," her mother had said, "who would put up with your disposition. Families have to—but husbands don't. You're very lucky to have Ed and I hope you realize it."

Now she looked at her mother sadly.

For she could not be really angry with her mother. Her mother had done too much for her, given up too many things so that she could

247

have them instead—and Shireen knew about each one of them, what it had been and when it had happened. Whenever she thought of her mother she thought of her with something in her hands, a mop, a spoon for beating cake, a dustcloth, a broom, a dress she was sewing for her. She was always doing something for someone else, never for herself.

"I'll make it all up to him when he comes back. Anyway, he'll never know about it."

"Someday, Shireen, you're going to do something you'll regret all the rest of your life."

She looked up swiftly. "Maybe I will. But one thing I know for sure: When I die I'm going to regret the things I did, and not the things I didn't do!"

Her mother sighed and seemed to wince a little. "I don't understand you. I never have."

"I know. I don't understand myself. I just didn't turn out to be a lady, did I?" She smiled, a little cruelly, and then was instantly ashamed of herself. Why was it always and always like this when she came home? How was it that everything she had ever done was a disappointment and she kept on hurting them? But what could she do to change or stop it? Anyway, it was too late now. The damage had all been done. Whatever she was, she was, and there was no use thinking about it.

A few days later her father answered the telephone and then called her. "It's for you, Shireen. Long distance."

"Long distance? It can't be Paul again. Maybe it's Georgia."

She picked up the phone. "Hello?"

"Miss Shireen Delaney?" It was the operator.

"Yes."

"One moment, please. San Francisco calling. Go ahead, sir. Your party's on the line."

"Thanks. Hello—that you, Shireen?"

"Yes."

"Congratulations," he said.

"Thanks. Same to you. Who is this?"

"You mean you don't know?"

"I'm sorry. But I don't. I haven't the vaguest idea." Several people she had never heard of had called since she had been home and she was getting a little annoyed with this damn fool, whoever he was.

"Remember a couple of guys who went overseas about a year ago?"

Shireen's heart began to beat faster. "Yes," she said guardedly, but she was thinking: Of course it can't be—

"Well—this is one of 'em." And now she knew the voice, husky and soft, with laughter running beneath it.

248

"Johnny!" She sat down hard, suddenly weak and dizzy. "It can't be you!"

He laughed, and all at once she could see him as clearly as if he were there in the room.

"Oh," he said lightly, "but it is."

Chapter 34

She felt as if she were about to faint and for a moment could not speak.

"Hey!" he said. "Is something wrong? Have you hung up?"

"No, Johnny—I'm still here. It's been almost exactly a year, hasn't it?" She spoke softly and wonderingly. "It's hard to believe."

"Amazing, isn't it? How real-life is sometimes almost as interesting as a book." His voice had a sound of light mockery, but there was still that same tenderness beneath each word.

All at once she came to life again. "When did you get back? How did you know I was home? Oh, this is so wonderful—it doesn't seem possible I'm actually going to see you again—"

He interrupted. "I called because I ran into some guys who had seen Ed and I wanted to let you know."

"Oh."

"Well? Aren't you interested?" She could hear a smile in his voice.

"Yes, of course I am. How is he?"

"They said he's in fine shape. He talks about you—all the time." He paused then, his voice dropped lower and the undercurrent of laughter went out of it. "That's a great guy you've got there, Shireen."

For an instant she was angry enough to hang up.

He knew exactly how she felt about him; every letter she had written had told him in every way she could find how much she loved him. And yet he indicated now that his only reason for calling was to remind her once more of her obligation to Ed. It seemed cruel and unfair; if that was why, then he should not have called at all. He should have let her alone, since she had been almost reconciled to it.

"I know he is," she said sullenly. "I know all about it."

They were both quiet for a moment and she felt that in some way he was blaming her, making her feel guilty because she loved him. He's letting himself off, she thought—at my expense.

Then she put those thoughts aside. He was back and he had called her and she would not let him escape.

"Johnny, tell me about yourself. You're all right, aren't you? I got a couple of letters from you, I don't know if you wrote any more, but they didn't tell me anything. Are you on leave or did they send you back for good?"

"Just a leave. And I'm okay. Say—you're pretty famous now, I hear."

"When can I see you? I'll get a plane or a train or something tonight—I can be there tomorrow morning—"

Suddenly he laughed. "Hey, take it easy. I called, as I told you, to let you know about Ed. That's all."

"That's *all?*"

"Sure. What else? I've got to report tomorrow and as soon as my papers come through I'm going home. I'll turn up in New York one of these days. I'll give you a ring when I do."

"What's the matter with you, Johnny Keegan? Weren't my letters clear enough? I've got to see you. And I'm *not* going to wait until you get to New York. Tell me where you are and I'll wire you what time I'll get in."

He drew a deep breath and she could imagine him, shaking his head. "Oh, Shireen."

"What's the matter? Don't you want to see me?"

"You haven't changed at all, have you? Just as impetuous as ever." His voice now was soft and paternal and forgiving, as if he knew she could not help being what she was; but he still left himself unimplicated.

"I want to see you. That's all," she repeated stubbornly.

"I've got to report to Santa Ana. I'll be there sometime tomorrow morning."

"I'll meet you in the Officers' Club. What time?"

He hesitated again and then said, "One o'clock."

"It'll be so wonderful to see you again. I feel as if every dream I ever had came true at once."

"Okay," he said, and sounded impatient and in a hurry to get away, as if he had done something wrong and wanted to leave the place where it had happened. "See you tomorrow."

"Yes, Johnny. Good-by."

She hung up and walked into the living room, smiling happily. Her parents watched her come in, both their faces solemn, her father looking up from his paper, her mother from her darning. She stared at them in astonishment. What was the matter with *them?*

"That was Johnny!"

"So I gathered," said Mrs. Delaney, and went on darning. Her father turned to his paper again.

"I think I'll pack most of my clothes and send them back by Railway Express."

She stood looking down at the floor, one finger to her chin, planning aloud. But neither of them answered so she turned and ran upstairs and began taking things out of the closet. She noticed a letter from Paul Worth stuck in one corner of her dressing-table

251

mirror. She looked at it and frowned and looked away again, hoping next time she looked it would be gone. But it was still there and so was Paul, back in New York, waiting for her.

Well—something would have to be done about that.

She finished her packing and rushed excitedly back down the stairs. "I've just thought of a way to get rid of Paul!"

Her father looked up again but said nothing.

"Have you?" asked her mother.

"I'm going to write him a letter right now and tell him I've come to my senses and it was all a mistake and we must never see each other again. He'll be so furious I'm sure he'll never speak to me again!"

It seemed strange, how completely incapable her parents were of entering into her happiness and sharing it with her. They merely sat there, aloof and reproving. Well, they had always lived by rules and regulations and that was most of what was wrong with their lives. Apparently they were genuinely unable to tell the difference between emotional reality and what was only the hard crust of custom.

She felt sorry for them, but a little impatient, too, as if they were trying again to slow down her life.

"May I borrow your typewriter, Dad?"

"Of course."

She sat down and hastily typed off a letter to Paul and concluded by asking him to send back her letters. *Please don't take offense,* she wrote, *but they might be useful someday if I ever decide to write another book.* She added *Very sincerely,* and ripped it out of the typewriter and signed her name.

She folded the letter and put it in an envelope and while she was addressing it said happily: "I'll bet that's the last I hear from him."

"I hope so," said her mother.

"Can I borrow the car tomorrow, Dad?" He looked up at her, hesitating. "Or shall I go out and buy one?"

He gave a little sigh. "You can borrow it."

The next morning they kissed her good-by. She got into the car and sat at the wheel a moment, smiling at them.

"It was nice to have you home," her father said.

"Promise us you won't do anything foolish," said her mother.

"Of course I won't. I'm just going to see him for a few hours and then I'll go on to New York. I know what I'm doing. Just please don't worry about me. That's all I ask."

"We can't very well help it," her mother said. "The way you behave. You know, of course, that if there was any way to stop you from doing this, we would."

Shireen looked her mother straight in the eye and said nothing, but it was clear what she was thinking. There isn't any way

252

you can, and there never will be again for the rest of all our lives.

Then she kissed her hand to them, backed the car into the street, and drove off.

She was early again, as she had been the day she waited for him in the Officers' Club in Miami. And as she sat there, her stomach churning and her hands wet, she wondered what it would be like to see him again after all this time had gone by and all the things that had happened. She was afraid she might have changed for the worse during this past year; now that she was twenty-seven. But she hoped her expensive new clothes would make up for whatever had happened to her looks and that he would not notice too much difference in her.

And then he came through the door and she jumped up to meet him, watching him as he came toward her, her face quivering between anxiety and a smile.

What should she do when he reached her?

He was smiling and he solved it for her; leaned down a little and kissed the side of her face. "Hi," he said softly. They stood a moment and looked at each other.

His smile was the same, and the same expression was in his eyes. The way she felt about him had not changed. There was the same yearning and the same helpless response; whatever it was that had made her love him was just as it had been. And everything since was some trick she had played on herself.

He touched her arm lightly and they walked outside. She noticed that now he had a gold leaf on his shoulder. They turned again to look at each other, as the wind caught her skirt and lifted her hair. And it seemed they were standing on the beach that afternoon in Florida before she had gone with him to Connecticut, before he had told her they would never see each other again. It was that same hot and sunny day, the same white glare, the same strange languorous dreamy feel to their lives. It was real and it wasn't. He was home from the war again and she had become successful. The time slid away, dissolving. The only difference was that, somehow, they seemed to know each other very much better. Almost as if they had been together all this time, not apart.

"You're really here," she said finally. "And only a few weeks ago I began to think I would never see you again."

"I'm here, all right."

Not that he was glad to see her and not that he loved her.

But now that she was with him it didn't matter so much whether he said the words or not. No man had ever looked at her the way Johnny did.

"Have you had anything to eat?"

"No. I was waiting for you."

"Okay. I've checked in so let's go somewhere and have lunch. How'd you get here, by the way?"

"My father's car. It's over there."

He gave her a quick surprised look. "What in the hell did you tell them?"

"That I was going to see you, of course."

"My God. They must think I'm the world's worst bastard."

"Oh, no," said Shireen gaily. "They know me very well, remember."

They had been walking slowly toward where she had parked the car but now he stopped and stood looking at her, his hands in his pockets, his eyes narrow. "They're used to you doing things like this?"

Shireen threw back her head and laughed; she took his arm and started on. "Of course not, Johnny. I've never done anything like this before—you know that. I just mean that if I decide to do something they know by now it's useless to try to stop me."

She glanced at him, smiling. Aren't men strange? Only one set of values and themselves smack in the middle of it. Women, they honestly believe, were put here to make them think well of themselves.

They drove into Santa Ana, talking together softly and happily, and found a little restaurant where they sat down opposite each other in a booth. The juke box was playing "I Get Along Without You Very Well" and Johnny gave her a quick amused glance before he started to read the menu.

Shireen sat and watched him, helplessly caught by the fascination she found in each gesture he made and every expression that crossed his face. She could never look at him without a heartbreaking longing for complete possession, as if she would not be whole herself until she had him as part of her. But the yearning was unappeasable and carried within itself an almost intolerable pain. Because all that could ever be permitted them were brief moments which tricked them into believing they had broken through the barriers that kept each his own prisoner, only to realize once more that it had not happened and would never happen and she would always be Shireen Delaney and he Johnny Keegan.

He gave a brush of his hand toward the menu. "This is what you can't quite believe. All this food. You just ask for it—and get it." He shook his head. "God."

She stared at him a moment, almost shocked to hear him say something so totally unrelated to what she had been thinking. Then she smiled tenderly, realizing the miracle was not in what he said and probably not even in what he did or how he looked. It was somewhere else, hidden deep within him, or in her.

She laughed delightedly when he told the waitress he would have pancakes and sausages, and the girl said there were no sausages; then

254

he would have pancakes and bacon, but there was no bacon. Well, then, just pancakes. The waitress would see if there were any pancakes.

"Anyway," said Johnny, "I guess it won't be powdered eggs."

He leaned back, his hands in his pockets, and looked at her. "Well—you sure came through with flying colors, didn't you?"

For the first time the success she had had took on real and concrete meaning; it became something which might make Johnny find her more interesting.

"I guess so," she said modestly. "I've been very lucky."

"Lucky, hell. All that work wasn't luck and don't let any bastard try to tell you it was. I heard that some of the reviewers tore it apart. What's the matter with those jerks, anyway?"

She felt embarrassed and wished he had not heard about it. "Well, you know how critics are. They always review the book the author didn't write. Anyway," she added, trying to make a joke of it, "I think if it hadn't sold so many copies it would have been considered promising. I sent you one," she said shyly. "Did you get it?"

"No. It may be waiting when I get back out."

"Don't talk about going back, Johnny."

He laughed. "You're just the same. Everything about you."

His eyes were going over her face, down over her breasts, over her manicured hands folded on the table. For a moment she felt warm and luxuriant; but then he must have noticed her wedding ring, for he glanced quickly away, frowning a little, and Shireen hastily put her hands in her lap. The waitress brought the pancakes and Johnny thanked her.

"Are you glad to be home?" Shireen asked him.

"Sure. Of course I am."

She asked him questions about what he had done, where he had been, what missions he had flown. He answered, but in some oblique way that seemed to glance off—just as he had talked before about his experiences, half belittling them. They had simply become part of him, a few more layers on top of the edifice which was Johnny Keegan's personality, but he was not interested in explaining how each brick had been put in place.

He told her his plane had been forced to make a crash landing behind Jap lines. "It looked like we'd had it, all right. I guess none of us expected to get out—the odds were sure against it anyway." There was some look on his face and sound in his voice that was very much like nostalgia and very close to regret.

"They should never send you back again!"

He laughed softly, and seemed surprised by her intensity. "Why not? Once you've made yourself give up the idea of living and really

255

come to terms with it—well, you find out it doesn't matter as much as you'd always thought it would."

Shireen watched him talk, lightly and casually, her eyes shining with horror as she remembered what she had heard about Margy's death. Margy had not been able to make up her mind to die and come to terms with it. Even as she bled to death she had lain screaming for someone to help her live, keep her from dying.

But Johnny's face had an expression of triumph and conviction, and she felt again what she had long ago believed to be true about him: In some sense he wanted to die. He wanted to cheat the years when he would be old, when the vitality would run down and he would lose the Johnny Keegan that existed now. It was just as true of her, but she had never been able to bring herself face to face with it. Her only solution was to believe that some magic would keep her as she was forever. The same magic, perhaps, that had operated to make all her wishes come true so far.

"You're strange, Johnny," she said finally. "In some ways you're not at all like me." They were so much alike beneath their differences, that it was the differences which surprised her.

He raised his eyebrows a little, then apparently understood what she meant, and smiled.

They went on eating silently for a few moments. All at once he said: "You haven't been sleeping with any other guys since I—since Ed went overseas, have you?"

"Why, of course not," She looked at him as if amazed he should ask such a question.

He watched her a moment longer and then turned back to his food. "Okay," he said. "Just wondering."

She felt pleased, though, and happy to know he regarded her as his personal possession. And anyway it was true. None of the others, Mike or Jack or Paul, had mattered—She could not even believe it had happened.

Chapter 35

"Well?" she asked him, when they had talked awhile longer. "What shall we do today?"

"You're going back home." He sounded as if it had been settled long ago and there was no room left for argument.

"What? But I told them I'd send the car back by someone, and that after I'd seen you I was going on to New York. They're not even expecting me."

"Go on to New York then."

Shireen laughed, pretending that she knew he was joking, but she had a feeling of terrible panic, as though she had unexpectedly lost control of some powerful machine. "I wouldn't think of it," she said lightly. "I'm going to stay right here until you leave."

"Look, Shireen—we might as well get something straight right now. I'm going back out there again and I may see Ed. In fact, I want to see him—and if I do I intend to be able to look him in the eye without having anything to be ashamed of."

He had watched her as he said it and her profile was toward him but now she turned and looked him full in the eyes, her face wide open as if she would conceal nothing. "Well? I certainly don't want you to have anything to be ashamed of, Johnny."

His expression was plainly skeptical, but she continued to look at him with direct clear guilelessness. She knew all about him now. He wouldn't catch her this time. Johnny had to think he was making all the decisions. He would give nothing which was demanded, and would never permit anything to be wrung from him.

"Good," he said when her expression refused to change, and pretended that he believed her, but both of them knew it was a pretense and would only do for the time being. "And now that we know where we stand, how about some dessert?"

"Ice cream. Strawberry. Johnny, I don't care. If that's the way you want it, that's the way it is. All I want is to see you and be with you. The rest doesn't matter. And I *can* see you—can't I?"

"Sure. We'll see each other—from time to time. But don't think I'm going to spend every hour I'm awake with you, because I'm not. I can't do it. I'm not made that way. I've lived my life alone and I can't change now. That's the mistake you're making, Shireen. I've tried to tell you the kind of guy I am but you won't believe it. You

257

still think you can change everyone and everything if you just want to. It can't be done."

"No, I don't, Johnny. I don't want to change you. I love you the way you are—I don't want you any different."

"All right. Let's remember that."

"I'll remember, Johnny," said Shireen meekly, and began to sip her coffee. He looked at her across the table and for a moment his face was tender and revealing.

She did not want to quarrel with him and was, in fact, afraid to quarrel with him. He might get angry and turn away from her. We're all of us different people, she thought, to everyone we know. Depending on what we want from them, maybe. And what she wanted from Johnny was his love, any way she could get it. Though this submissiveness seemed to have little to do with what she usually thought of as her essential self.

But what of it, since a woman in love changes subtly in everything she does and thinks and is.

"Let's go someplace," she said, "where we can talk." Now, that was a perfectly harmless suggestion, wasn't it?

He looked at her quickly and all at once he laughed, then shook his head. "You can't go riding around the country with me, don't you know that? Things have changed the last few months. You've had your picture all over the place and people will begin to recognize you. You can't do the things you used to. Why can't you figure that out for yourself, Shireen? It's simple enough, isn't it?"

"Of course it's simple," said Shireen, trying hard to control her impatience. "But I'm not interested in whether it's simple or complicated. The one thing you keep forgetting, Johnny, is that I'm in love with you."

"And the one thing you keep forgetting is that you've got no business being in love with me. What about Ed?"

"What about him?"

Johnny tossed his napkin onto the table, as if he were about to get up. "Just this: He's one hell of a fine guy, he loves you, and what's more he happens to be fighting a war. That may not mean much to you but I've seen enough of how the guys react when their women start two-timing not to want any part of that routine myself."

She looked around swiftly, her hair swinging to the other side of her face, her gray eyes hostile for a moment. "You're a little late, aren't you?" she drawled. "How come you didn't get all this religion a year ago?" And then instantly she was ashamed; and frightened. Her fingers touched his hand. "I'm sorry, Johnny. Please forgive me."

He gave a little sigh, staring off across the room, his eyes slightly narrowed as if he were concerned with something far inside himself. Finally he turned back to her.

They sat and looked at each other, polite concealment and subterfuge gone from their faces. All the violent longing they had sensed in their first meeting was there, intensified by memory and separation. Only in some moments of obsessive death-awareness had Shireen ever been so acutely conscious of her own individual isolation and the terrors it held. A painful yearning toward completeness, a need to escape from the haunting loneliness of self had become stronger than fear or loyalty or any obligation. She believed as she looked at him that Johnny was as helpless as she, and that it was something they experienced together with greater sensitiveness and anguish than either had known before.

And she thought there was nothing more to it than throwing away her scruples and sense of honor, which seemed a small enough sacrifice to make in return for what he could give her.

She drew a slow shallow breath and he was about to speak. Then the waitress came and began to pick up the dishes and both of them looked quickly away, across the room, jerked apart by the interruption almost as if there had been some rude physical break at a moment of great tension and expectation.

He got up. "Come on. Let's go."

She hesitated a moment, still sitting there and looking up at him, frightened that now he would make her leave him. "Go where?" she asked cautiously, as if she could ward it off.

"We'll go back to the base and get my car—I drove down from Frisco. And make some arrangements to send yours back home. Your parents probably want it. I can drive you out to the airport later," he added, as if in warning to the smile that came onto her face.

She got up quickly then, and put her hand confidingly into his. She had a while longer, this afternoon at least. And she would not think beyond that. Anyway, when that was gone she would somehow persuade him to give her a little more. Tonight, and tomorrow.

She was sure that he felt exactly as she did, but for reasons of his own nature would not admit it to her and possibly not to himself. So she must let him work it out however he would, to leave himself as much peace as possible. They had each constructed some kind of life pattern that attempted to solve the unsolvable and she began to see that she must not try to twist or smash his in order to get at what she wanted. For if she did she would lose him altogether. He could part with her much more easily than with himself, and wanted to lose her anyway, since she seemed to threaten something he was guarding.

He gave her, as if he were conveying a great favor and as if he gave it only for her sake—the rest of that afternoon.

At the base he arranged with one of the men who wanted to drive into Los Angeles to return the car to her father. They put the small bag she had with her into his convertible and set out down the coast. The plan he seemed to indicate was that they would drive a little, have dinner, and then he would take her to the airport. Johnny always assumed, as she did, that it was possible to do whatever you wanted and that a cancellation was sure to turn up just the moment he arrived. His smile would somehow produce it.

But Shireen refused to believe he would make her leave him so soon, and they did not discuss it.

They drove along with the top down, talking together gaily and happily, with nothing to argue about now. She was sure there had never been such a beautiful day in the world before and felt aware of herself and Johnny as if they were the only two people on earth, with no past to admonish them, no future to fear.

She forgot the things she had believed all her life about such moments: That they contained the essence of despair, more treacherous and sad for seeming at the moment complete and indestructible. That love is the flimsiest most untrustworthy emotion of all, never existing in reality but only in the hope and need of the one who loves. And that love has close kinship to death, since it carries the potential of destroying in manifold ways whoever gives himself up to it.

She kept pointing things out to him as they drove along, as if she had just discovered them herself. The brown California hills she had seen all her life that now began to have some different meaning for her. The great red-touched castor plants, the eucalyptus and scrub oak and some prolific bush covered with little orange flowers. When they passed a group of willows she clasped her hands in delight.

"Look, Johnny! How lovely they are! Oh, that's the prettiest tree in the world." She laughed. "Wouldn't it be fun to be God and eat a willow tree for salad?"

He smiled, as if she were an amusing little child. "I think you mean it. You'd really like to eat up everything that looks pretty to you."

"I'd like to eat you—except that then I wouldn't have you left over for the next time I wanted to look at you. Johnny—you don't know how beautiful you are. You're the best-looking man I've ever seen."

His face reddened a little. "I can't think of anything that could possibly matter less."

"It matters to me. I look at you."

"You don't, really, or you'd know I look like any ordinary guy."

She gave a sudden pealing happy laugh, as if this conversation was the most delightful game. Being with him gave her the feeling that some miracle had just occurred or suddenly would occur.

"No, Johnny, you have everything. Any girl would fall in love with you. And I'm sure hundreds of them have."

"You're wrong as hell. I'm just a guy—nothing special about me at all. And I wish to God you wouldn't keep thinking there is."

"But why, Johnny?" She spread out her fingers, palms up. "I should think you'd like having someone think you're the most wonderful thing that ever happened."

"Except that I'm not and I know it. It gives me the feeling I've got to live up to something and I know I can't. I'm not even interesting, Shireen. If you spent a few days with me you'd be bored stiff."

She patted his knee. "Johnny, you're so funny."

"I'm not being funny. I'm serious. I'm serious as hell." He glanced at her sideways a moment and she saw that he actually was afraid. With everything he had he didn't believe in himself at all—only in the myth of Johnny Keegan, and he must protect that myth.

She yearned to put her arms around him and comfort him and somehow make him know that he was what she believed him to be. "I'll love you all the rest of my life, Johnny. No matter what ever happens to either one of us. There can't be anything on earth that could change the way I feel about you."

He was quiet a moment and then he said, almost sorrowfully, "You mustn't talk that way, Shireen. You mustn't say such things."

"But it's true." He glanced at her again. "All right, Johnny. I won't."

For the rest of the afternoon she did not know if he intended sending her back that night, and did not dare ask him. She tried to buy a little more time from him, the only way she knew how. She was sweet and soft and pliable, she asked for nothing, she did not touch him except briefly to lay her fingers on his hand or arm; she could only hope he would find enough pleasure in having her there that he would let her stay. He implied though, in small ways, that they would part almost any moment. And she felt scared and resentful that he should treat her this way, but scarcely dared let herself realize the resentment. For she knew she would lose him the moment they began to quarrel. That would furnish the excuse he seemed to be waiting for.

Near Laguna they parked the car and went down to the beach. Shireen took off her shoes and played barefoot in the sand, running into the water and out again, catching long strands of seaweed and trailing them after her, flinging her black hair about in the wind. She picked up the foam of the waves and held her two hands out to him as if presenting a gift, laughing and blowing into the bubbles. He walked along with her, watching her, laughing now and then at something she said or did.

She felt pleased with herself, at rest and contented. The way he looked at her, she knew he wouldn't send her back today. A triumphant voice inside her said: You'll always get what you want.

261

Late in the afternoon they drove into Laguna and he parked the car and asked her to wait. "I've got to call the base, to find out when they want me to report again." She sat nervously, wondering what she would do if he came back out and said that he had to leave immediately. But when he came there was a bellboy following him.

The room he took them to was small and not very well furnished with a dining alcove and kitchen on one side and a bedroom on the other. Shireen walked to the window and looked out while Johnny tipped the bellboy. She heard the door close and then, slowly, she turned around. They stood, she on one side of the room and he on the other. Finally Johnny gave a gesture of one hand.

"Well," he said. "Here we are." Then looked as if he wondered why he had said it and felt a little foolish.

"Yes, I guess we are."

After a moment she lifted her hands and, not actually aware of what she was doing, unfastened the strand of pearls. She stood holding them in one closed hand. She had a feeling of helplessness and something else that was close to regret. As if she had made some long hard journey and not found what she was looking for at the end.

Why hadn't he told her?

Why had he made her think all day that she must leave him?

He walked toward her and Shireen stood where she was, wondering why, with Johnny, it must be always some ballet of advance and retreat, acquiescence and denial, admission and rejection.

"You got your way after all, didn't you?" he said softly, and there was still a faint smile on his face.

She looked up at him but didn't move, wondering what it could be that made him say these things, so patently dishonest. "What about you, Johnny?"

"I know. Me, too." He grinned, and his face flushed a little beneath the olive atabrine color of his skin. "I'm a bastard—I admit it. Shireen—" His hands lifted and reached toward her. "God, but you're so beautiful."

She was watching him and now there were tears in her eyes. "Am I, Johnny?"

And then suddenly his hands reached around her back and drew her to him, his mouth touched hers, and that moment she had what she had waited for and longed for and not been able to find anywhere else, some loss and completion of herself.

Chapter 36

They were standing together on the breakwater, watching the violent crash of the waves beneath them and looking out toward the ocean. Far on the horizon was a line of bright clear green, like a lighted neon tube. It was a brilliant windy day and Shireen held one hand up to keep her hair from blowing across her face. Johnny was leaning on the iron railing staring down at the water as it rushed out and came swarming back, hurling against the rocks as if in rage, giving some sense of eternal angry struggle.

Shireen, in her pink linen dress, stood beside him happily, talking about how beautiful the clouds were, leaning over to kiss him lightly on the cheek.

They had been together now for two days, and during that time had accepted each other without reservation; she had refused to let herself be aware that this was an episode, occurring somewhere in the midst of their lives, which would end as unexpectedly as it had begun.

Once two girls came up to the car where she sat waiting for him and wanted her autograph. "Why mine?" she asked them nervously, hoping Johnny would not walk out and see them there.

"Aren't you Shireen Delaney?"

"Of course not," said Shireen. "I don't even know who she is." They smiled at her skeptically, and as they started to walk away Johnny came toward her.

"What's going on? Did they recognize you?"

"No. They thought I was someone else."

He shook his head. "You're too well known."

"Johnny, really it's all right. They were only guessing. Don't worry about it."

She looked at him now as he leaned with his arms on the railing, bending forward and tilting her head a little to one side. She touched the side of his face, enjoying the texture of his skin with her finger tips, and gave a little sigh. "I've never been so happy in my life. In fact, this is the first time I ever have been happy." He glanced at her and smiled.

She looked back out toward the ocean and after a moment he said softly: "This has been two days I'll always remember."

She heard the words but not the meaning for a moment.

Then she said, hesitantly, "You don't mean I have to go back?"

"Tomorrow. My orders will be coming through any day now."

"Then I'll stay until they do."

"You can't, Shireen."

"Why can't I? We've been happy together—why can't we be happy a little while longer? We won't ever have much of each other anyway." She felt him slipping away from her and began to get frightened again.

"No, Shireen. We've taken a big enough gamble already. Those two girls recognized you yesterday—and other people may have, too. You've worked hard for what you've got and there's no sense throwing it away now. That kind of publicity would be hell on you—with Ed overseas."

"I don't care about—"

"I know you don't, but I do. I don't think any too well of myself as it is, but I'm not such a bastard as to let you get yourself into a mess of trouble. You'd hate me for it, and with damned good reason, if it ever happened."

"Then I won't even go out of the hotel. I'll just stay there and wait for you. I'll do *anything,* Johnny, that you want—if you won't make me leave you." She faced him imploringly, her hands held out.

He smiled at her. "Sometimes you're just a little girl. But don't look so tragic. I'll be in New York before long. We'll see each other there."

"But look what we'll have lost! Johnny, why is it I can never seem to make you see—"

"Maybe because you always want me to see it your way."

"What's yours, then?"

"You count everything in hours and minutes. It isn't the clock that makes the difference. I've tried to tell you that before. In some ways, we've spent a whole lifetime together—don't you see that?" He was watching her face as he talked and now he smiled, shaking his head. "No," he said. "You don't."

"I certainly don't! Life is made up of whatever time we're alive and that's all there is to it! I don't care if it's hours or minutes or any other damned thing it's called! I want to be with you!"

"You make everything so hard for yourself, Shireen."

"I don't either. I want to stay here, that's all. It isn't very much to ask and it won't hurt you—so what difference does it make?"

"It makes a difference to me," he said softly.

"And what about me? I'm here too!"

"Shireen, you don't really know me at all. I've tried to tell you this before and I'll tell you again. I've spent most of my life alone, coming and going as I please. Don't ask me why. I'm not interested in the reasons. It just happens to be the way I live. And it does something to me when I spend much time with any one person. I begin to feel—"

he made a helpless, groping gesture—"strangled, I guess. After awhile the way you've lived begins to have a force of its own—don't you see that?" He talked to her gently and quietly, as if he were trying sincerely to make her understand something about him for which she was not responsible, which had nothing to do with her, and because of which she should not be hurt or disappointed.

She had been staring at him and finally, when he stopped talking, she lowered her eyes. "No. I don't see it. I love you—and I want to be with you. You'll be gone again so soon."

They stood there a few minutes longer. By now the sun had set softly and the air had a wet dreamy haze. "Let's go back," he said. "It's getting cold."

They started along the cement breakwater.

They had gone partway when a wave came smashing up over the side and almost before she had seen it Johnny grabbed her by the arms and swung her around, putting himself between her and the water. Then they walked on. It seemed too small an incident to talk about, but because he had moved so automatically and naturally to her protection she felt an enormous gratitude and reassurance. The incident became, like everything else he had ever said or done, full of meaning and significance.

They drove back, Shireen sulking on her own side of the car, her hands thrust into the wide sleeves of her coat to make a muff. Johnny talked lightly and pleasantly about other things, but she answered only in monosyllables. Once she glanced at him and thought he looked amused and she was suddenly furious, convinced that he enjoyed torturing her.

"Oh!" she cried. "Sometimes I'd love to slap you!"

He answered her quietly. "For both our sakes, I hope you never do."

Shireen felt ashamed. "I never will. You know that."

Back in town they stopped at a drugstore for sodas and while they sat perched on stools examining the stickers plastered around the mirror in front of them to see what they would order, he tried again to make her talk.

"French soda," he read. "Now what the hell do you suppose they mean by that?"

"It means it's either fancy or immoral—or both." He laughed and she did too, pleased for a moment because she had entertained him. And then she lapsed back into silence and sat staring at herself in the mirror, thinking how sad and pathetic she looked and wondering how he could be so heartless as to do this to her. It seemed incredible she should have given her love to someone who valued it so little. She glanced at him then, morosely telling herself he was the most wonderful man she had ever known—and was furiously resentful at him for being so, since she must leave him.

She decided to look at him with curiosity and detachment, regard him as interesting and provocative, with only a clinical significance for her.

Now let's see what this blasted charm of his amounts to. It can't be much, when you take it apart, and that's what I'll do right now and after I have it won't matter whether he lets me stay with him or not: He's handsome, but then so are a lot of other men—so it can't be that. There's a kind of shimmer and glow, as if he were made up of everything that sparkled and gave out warmth. But you can't explain that and it isn't sensible anyway so it must be something else. There's some way he makes me feel, like maybe rainbows would burst out singing any minute. But it can't be that either because that's nonsense and things like that aren't important. They can't be. I won't let them be.

No, it's something else.

Some secret formula he has. It's something I can't explain, goddamn it, and never will be able to explain if I spend the rest of my life trying! I'll go away and think about other things and forget he's on earth.

He glanced at her in the mirror then and smiled and all of a sudden she began to cry. Tears ran down her face and splashed into her soda. He reached over quickly and took her hand.

"Darling—don't do that. Please."

He gave her a handkerchief and she wiped her face and said in an aching little voice: "I don't want to leave you, Johnny."

But it hadn't done any good, as she could see immediately. He shook his head and turned away and they did not speak for another couple of minutes. She stopped crying. And then he turned to her and said softly: "Would you like to spend tomorrow at the Spanish Inn?"

She looked at him with a sudden brilliant smile, as if he had granted her the most precious unbelievable gift on earth. "Oh, Johnny—*can* we?"

"Sure. If you want to."

The next day they drove back up the coast and out through the valley. They stopped and had lunch, and got there late in the afternoon. Up the walk to the Inn the palm leaves clacked softly and hibiscus bushes were in bloom; somewhere nearby a parrot squawked. The air had a feeling of changelessness, soft and hazy with the quality of dreams remembered vaguely from deep sleep, or like pain which has turned to nostalgia.

They walked along holding hands and she said to him happily: "It was so nice of you to bring me here, Johnny. I'm really grateful."

He looked as if she had hurt him. "I brought you here because I

266

wanted to, you know that. Wait here. I'll go see if they've got a room."

She walked over to one of the tables and began glancing through old magazines. Of course he had. That was what she kept forgetting. Johnny had never done anything against his will—against his conscience, maybe, but not against his will. And yet most of the time he let her believe that whatever they both did he did only for her. It was as if he could allow himself to enjoy nothing at all unless he had first made both of them suffer for it.

He would be angry, though, if she ever told him that. "I'm whatever I am, and I've never yet asked anyone to accept it. I've told you often enough that I've got nothing to offer you." He closed every door in her face.

But even when it seemed to her he was being willfully cruel, she refused to take warning or be alarmed. For the tenderness in him was always there, above and beneath and around everything else, like a protective covering of some gossamer yet very strong fabric. And it was that which she trusted and loved.

Their room had a high ceiling, tiled floors, and ancient Spanish furniture. The bed was four-postered with a canopy and while the bellboy was setting down their bags Shireen and Johnny glanced at it and then at each other and grinned. Johnny grimaced. "What a place for a bivouac." Then he turned, his face decorous again, and tipped the bellboy.

They went out, down the stairs and into the patio where people sat around umbrella-shaded tables, sipping cold drinks. The building rose around them, the curve of the balconies, the steps that led mysteriously away, the higher terraces. In the pool water dripped softly. The great gates of the cloister stood open and they walked in. It was cool and soothingly still. They went toward a gold altar at the end of the walk, passing high stained glass windows set with chunks of semiprecious stones, and stood silent for a time, looking at it.

At last she turned to Johnny and found him watching her with pain and longing in his eyes. All the things we can never have, she thought wearily, or ever be to each other. . . .

He leaned over to kiss her and she moved a little. "Not here, Johnny."

"Just on the forehead—like that."

They stood a few moment longer and then went into the Hawaiian Room to have a drink before dinner.

"Johnny," she said to him eagerly, trying to keep herself from remembering they must part in a few hours. "Try something they call a Deep Purple. I had it here once a long time ago. It's got grapejuice and rum in it, I think, and it's the nicest drink in the world."

They sat at one of the little bamboo tables, beside a miniature waterfall. Up a few steps behind them was a narrow hall lined with

267

buddhas, and Shireen went to look at them, coming back to tell him she had always wanted one and wished she could think of a way to steal it. There was an undercurrent of play in her tones and smile and gestures, as if she were a little girl showing off to a grown-up, trying to please and enchant and win approval. Johnny kept watching her and smiling, seeming at once affectionate and detached, as if he too knew it was a game and was willing to be entertained, since she tried so hard.

"I'll send you a buddha," he said, "if I ever get back to China."

The waiter brought the drinks and Shireen watched him set them down. "Why must you always talk about going away? As if you only got here so that you could go someplace else. I suppose that's the way you are in China, too."

Johnny laughed, and abruptly the balance between them had shifted. He was no longer watching her play like an admiring parent, but was extending his own personality in conflict to hers. "I suppose I'm whatever I am, wherever I am." He smiled, and she felt that the smile said: Me against You. And You'll never change Me, not in any way at all.

They drank silently.

We're wasting our time, she thought, but was sorry it had entered her mind and promptly dismissed it.

"You see how different we are," he said.

"I know how different we are. What of it?"

He looked slightly surprised. "Nothing. But it's a good thing for you to remember now and then."

"Why?"

"Just because you tend to forget it, that's all. We don't believe in the same things—we don't want the same kind of life—"

"I could believe in anything you do, Johnny."

"No, Shireen. Maybe once. It's too late now. Remember what I told you about a way of living having its own force? It's true. You can't change the basic things in yourself without hating the person who makes you do it, sooner or later. We're neither one of us pliable—we're both too much what we are to change, except a little on the surface. We'd get in each other's way." He was smiling again. "Anyway," he said, "I suppose there'll always be enough meek people in the world for the ones like you and me to climb on—in order to get what we want."

For a moment she was surprised, and then she smiled too. Of course. It was true. Why should he pretend it wasn't—and why should she pretend to be shocked. Everything in both their lives proved how true it was.

She leaned forward a little. "Do you know what's the one thing I've ever wished for? To be a queen in an age and land where monarchy was absolute." She had never said that to anyone else and was astonished to hear herself saying it to him. To Johnny, of all people. What an idiot I am, she thought, dismayed.

For a moment they looked at each other and then he glanced away. She had a surprised conviction that she had all at once, and quite unexpectedly, won the battle between them. He lit a cigarette and she watched him as he reached for his wallet, the cigarette in his mouth, his head tipped a little to one side and his eyes slightly squinted against the smoke. He put the money on top of the check, concentrating on that for a moment, and then smiled at her, as if she were an appealing but somewhat naughty child. She recognized the smile as a defense, and her feeling of conquest grew.

"So that's what you want," he said softly.

She laughed. "That's what I want." Now it seemed as if all along they had been playing a game, that it never had been as serious as it had seemed to her, and that she had had the power to win it any time, the way she had now. "But don't get me wrong, Johnny—I still love you."

"And I love you, Shireen. You know that."

It was the first time he had said it since the night in Miami, and the sense of triumph disappeared, leaving her passive and helpless. "You do?" she said faintly.

He was smiling again. "Of course I do. Come on—let's have dinner."

The curtains beside the bed were parted slightly and a thin pale moonlight came into the room. Johnny lay flat on his back and Shireen was turned on her right side so that her body fit his; her head lay on his shoulder and her arm across his chest. They were perfectly quiet and self-absorbed, listening to the flow and pulse of some mutual bloodstream; still, as if they had been lost in deep water. She felt aware of a spreading ease, as though inside her a flower had burst open its petals.

After awhile she moved her head against him and his hand caught reassuringly in her hair, closing on the back of her neck.

"Darling?" she whispered.

"Yes?"

"Are you asleep?"

"No. Were you?"

"No. I don't want to sleep. If I go to sleep I'll lose you. I just want to stay awake and know that you're here."

"I'll be here when you wake up."

"But not for long."

"Don't think about that now. Just feel good. You can't find anything to worry about after that." She was looking up at the faint blur of

269

his face and now she saw his lips move apart in a smile. "Can you?"

She shook her head. "No. I'd never worry about anything for the rest of my life—if I could have you. You don't know what you're like, Johnny. Darling—we are happy together when we have a chance, aren't we?"

"Of course we are. God, who wouldn't be happy with you? You're wonderful, Shireen—you really are wonderful."

And then, because there had been something in his voice she had never heard before, she began to cry. The tears fell onto his chest and she wiped them away. His hand closed hard on her shoulder and his other arm came around to hold her closer. "You mustn't cry, darling."

"I can't help it. Oh, Johnny, how did the world get this way? Why does everything you want always have to be taken away from you? Now, all the rest of my life I'll know you're in the world, but that I can't have you. I won't have anything of you at all. And don't tell me I'll have memories because I don't want memories. I want you. I want something of you—" All at once she moved so that she was leaning above him, resting her weight on one elbow. "Johnny—I know this is crazy, you won't understand it at all. You're going to think I'm out of my mind. I wish we could have a baby."

"I know," he said softly. "I wish we could, too."

She was quiet for several moments, and then she said: "We can't even have that. There'll be nothing left at all—of the way we feel about each other." She bent her head and kissed him softly on the temple.

Finally he gave a sigh. "I guess in the long run it won't matter. We've had a lot together. We can't have everything. That's all." He paused a moment and then went on. "You think we'll always be just like we are now, Shireen. But we won't. What you don't seem able to realize is that if we keep on living we'll get old and the things that matter to us now won't then."

"I don't want to think about getting old."

"But when you are, you won't mind it."

"Of course I'll mind it." She lay down again, a little away from him now, not quite touching him. "You wouldn't talk the way you do, if you loved me. But you never have. I've never meant to you what you do to me." She felt almost angry, frightened and disappointed. There must have been a way, if he had wanted to find it. Why must everything have been left to her, all her life? He could have taken her away from Ed, if he had wanted her enough. Ed had been his excuse to have what he wanted of her, but no more. She had a sudden sure conviction of her own valuelessness.

"You'll never be happy, Johnny," she said.

"I always have been."

She reached to the night table for a cigarette and then struck a match and lighted it. She lay down again, one arm behind her head, holding the cigarette. There seemed a greater alienation between them than if they had never been together at all; she felt his presence beside her as something hostile and dangerous.

"I don't think you believe that yourself," she told him. "Do you know—Ed said something about you once—" As she spoke she was surprised to find that she felt closer to Ed than to him, as if Ed had come to help or protect her.

"What's that?" She could hear a vague challenging smile in his voice.

"He said you were going to spend the rest of your life chasing after some damned rainbow or other—and wind up realizing it was never there at all."

He was quiet a moment and then gave a soft muted laugh. "He's probably right."

"Then why do you do it?" she demanded sharply, and tapped her forefinger against the cigarette, knocking the ash off into a tray.

"It just happens to be the way I am, that's all." His voice was light and bantering, pushing her away from him and retreating back into his fortress, closing the walls against her.

"You could change if you wanted to."

"But I don't want to. That's simple enough, isn't it?"

She sat up again and crushed out the cigarette. "You take everything anyone will give you—and you don't give back anything in return!"

"I give back as much as I can, Shireen. Maybe there isn't much there to give. I've tried to tell you that, but you wouldn't believe me."

"It isn't true, Johnny. There's so much you could give, if you only would." Then she reached over tenderly and touched his forehead. "Oh, I guess it's no use. I'll always love you. All the rest of my life. Whatever it is you are—you're what I want." He had turned his head and was looking toward her, but she could feel his eyes more clearly than she could see them. For several moments they remained quiet, staring toward each other, and then his arms reached out and drew her to him.

"Come here, then. And don't talk any more. We never get in trouble when we don't talk."

"But we should be able to——"

"Be still. Don't say it. There——"

271

Chapter 37

Back in New York, Shireen began to wait again for Johnny.

He called her once but the conversation ended where it always did: She was not to wait or plan on anything at all. When he got there she would hear from him and meanwhile she should go on with her life. Paul called her once but she was out and did not call him back. She bought more clothes and books and silver and began to talk about needing a bigger apartment to keep all these things in. She had more pictures taken and gave more interviews, went to more lunches and plays and cocktail parties, and at one of them she met Dallas Cavanaugh.

Dallas had blue eyes and dark brown hair and when he forgot to comb it every so often a stray lock fell over his blunt forehead. He was broad-shouldered and slim in the waist and if he wasn't exactly handsome he had charm and a vigorous Irish sense of humor. He didn't really need anything else. Though he also happened to be moderately famous.

She went with Georgia one afternoon to a cocktail party given by Jack Gilman, publisher of one of the big weekly magazines.

There were about four dozen people in the living room and they stood packed together like the crowds on a subway. The conversation was loud and frenetic and split by the women's excited sharp high laughter. Two waiters maneuvered deftly among them with trayfuls of drinks and elaborate canapés. At the top of the stairs was a balcony overlooking the living room and off that was the bar, with more of the party in there, standing with their feet on the railing or sitting at small tables, smoking and talking. From up there, the room below seemed completely massed with women's hats and men's partly bald heads.

Shireen was standing on the balcony listening to Georgia and a gossip columnist talk about an actress they both knew.

"Why," said the columnist, "I spent a whole afternoon with her once, trying to get her to make one intelligible comment—just one. Finally I had to write the story myself and put words in her mouth." As he talked he kept looking past and around them, as if he was expecting someone but was not sure who. He apparently grew up someplace where you needed eyes in the back of your head, thought Shireen, and the habit's stuck. "It gave people the idea she was a hell of a lot brighter than she is. Not that she deserved it—but I couldn't

272

write a crappy column and jeopardize my own reputation for some stupid bitch. How'd she strike you?"

"Like a cold douche," said Georgia. "She's a fairly frightening dame. Still, I guess nymphomania always photographs well."

He burst into laughter. "Very good! Wonderful! Mind if I quote you—using so-and-so's name?" He mentioned another actress.

"Please do."

He looked at Shireen then and smiled brightly. "Well—*you* certainly had success with a capital Sex, didn't you?"

Shireen and Georgia pretended to laugh, but Shireen could not think of anything to say in reply. Then all at once he patted Georgia reassuringly on the arm and went quickly down the stairs after some people he had just discovered. Georgia and Shireen glanced at each other.

"Sometimes," said Georgia, "I honestly think he doesn't know this from real life."

"Good heavens, I wonder if he talks about me the way he did about her."

"Of course."

But I've been nice to him, thought Shireen. He wouldn't do that. I'm sure he wouldn't.

A young man came up to them. "Hello, Miss Marsh. Oh, Miss Delaney—I want you to come over here and meet Cecile Conrad." Shireen gestured good-by to Georgia and went along. Cecile Conrad was a name she had never heard a few months before, but she knew now that Mrs. Conrad had a radio program with a high Hooper rating.

She was sitting in the bar at a table with three or four other people and, as Shireen noticed, she was fat and middle-aged and obviously drunk. Her hat had got tilted a little too far over one eye and no one had reminded her of it. She looked up at Shireen, when she was introduced, with unmistakable truculence.

"So you're Shireen Delaney. Hmm—I was wondering what you'd look like."

Shireen smiled and tried to look as if it had been a pleasantry. "I'm very glad to know you, Mrs. Conrad. Phyllis Weatherby has told me so much about you."

"Phyllis is an old friend of mine," said Mrs. Conrad firmly, unmollified. "I haven't read your book, of course." Someone had spilled a drink on the table and now Mrs. Conrad, looking up at Shireen, put one elbow in the puddle and leaned her chin on her fist. No one mentioned that to her either. The others sat idly, smiling, watching the two women.

Shireen said with an air of sweet innocence: "That's all right with me, Mrs. Conrad. Some of my best friends haven't read it."

"And what's more," continued Mrs. Conrad, "I don't intend to."

Shireen could not think of anything at all to say to that. She just stood there like a child who knows it has punishment coming and is prepared to take it. But she consoled herself with the thought that Mrs. Conrad, being so sanctimonious, was a pretty ridiculous spectacle, drunk, while *she* was behaving like a perfect lady.

"Of course, it's a free country, but I should think you'd feel like a fool, admitting you wrote a book like that. How will you ever explain it to your children? They'll be ashamed of you. I have four boys—all of them overseas—and I want to tell you right now that I think a woman like you is an affront to decent respectable sober—"

"I beg your pardon, Miss Delaney." It was a man's voice, just behind Shireen, and she turned with great relief, hoping it would be someone who would rescue her. But she had never seen him before.

"I don't know if you remember me. I'm Dallas Cavanaugh and I met you about four months ago at Linda Martin's."

"I'm sorry," began Shireen, and started to say she did not remember having met him, when she saw by his broad grin that he knew it as well as she did. "Yes," she said. "Of course I remember you. It's very nice to see you again."

"I've just heard some news I think will interest you—Would you excuse us, please?" He looked down at Mrs. Conrad and the others, and he already had hold of Shireen's arm. Shireen turned apologetically to Mrs. Conrad.

"Run along, run along," said Mrs. Conrad. "Don't mind me." The fist she had propped her chin on slipped and she lurched slightly.

Dallas Cavanaugh steered her ahead of him, muttering, "Wouldn't you think the old bitch would at least serve some saccharine with her cyanide?" As they came to the balcony they met Jack Gilman, who stopped them to say he was glad they had met and that he knew they would like each other.

"Dallas is the best goddamn foreign correspondent in the business. Like somebody said, he costs me too much dough—but he's worth it."

Both Shireen and Dallas laughed, Jack Gilman went on, and they started working their way down the stairs. Dallas was just behind her, talking in her ear. "You civilians put up with much more from each other than you've got any business doing as self-respecting people. What did you let her talk to you like that for? I happened to be standing near enough to get it and I finally got so goddamned mad I decided that if you weren't going to do anything about it, I was."

Shireen smiled back at him over her shoulder, feeling very pleased that he had rescued her from the female dragon. "Well, it wasn't really so bad, was it? And she has a column or a radio program or something."

"So she has a column or a radio program or something," he drawled. "And that's why you let her talk that way to you?"

"No, not exactly. After all, she did say she has four sons overseas."

They had reached the bottom of the stairs now and a waiter stopped with a trayful of drinks. Dallas took one and Shireen did too, reaching out with her left hand. Dallas glanced at it. "You're married."

"Yes."

"Then why didn't you tell her that? A husband's no easier to part with than a son."

"Well—I don't know. Let's not talk about it. Tell me where you've been." He was wearing an Army uniform with captain's bars on the shoulders, and a shield on his left sleeve.

"CBI," he said.

"You just got back?"

"About a month ago. Look—let's get away from here."

People kept going by, brushing against them and apologizing. They went into the library which opened off the other end of the living room. Only a few guests were in there, sitting around talking rather quietly; a fire was going. They sat down on a couch and he gave her a cigarette and lit it. Then they began to talk, about the war and about politics, with Shireen asking him questions and listening to what he said in absorbed fascination.

She was convinced and had been for years that the twentieth-century version of the knight in shining armor was the foreign correspondent, now become even more exciting in his role as war correspondent. He traveled to far lands, he knew everyone and saw everything, he had the limitless power of the press behind him. He was after the Holy Grail of truth in the service of the American people; he wrote down whatever he knew or thought he knew, so that everyone could be amazed by the extent of his knowledge, about which he was himself both nonchalant and rather scornful. He feared nothing and was awed by no one; he barged in on statesmen, he sat in a bar drinking cognac while empires fell, he flew the Atlantic and Pacific and went through the Balkans on muleback. He was full of secret sorrow for all he had seen and the dreams he knew had gone awry, and life had tired him at an early age.

This was what she saw and felt as she sat watching Dallas Cavanaugh and listening to him talk.

Everything he said impressed her and she didn't want him to think that she was a silly shallow girl, interested only in pretty clothes and night clubs. She wanted him to realize that she was as serious as anyone, that she understood the world's problems and took them very much to heart, and that she was concerned with many many things beside herself. Whenever he began to talk about her, she quickly changed the subject back to something impersonal and important.

He told her he had had dengue fever and malaria and that finally, after three or four months in hospitals, they had sent him home for a rest. There was some weariness about him, as if his vitality had failed and he had to keep dredging deeper and deeper into himself to bring it up.

"You do look tired," she told him with intense sympathy. All the places he had been, all the things he had done, all the people he knew, she found reflected in the lines about his eyes.

"I'm tired, all right," he said, grinning. "In fact, I think if I get much tireder, I'll be dead."

"You mustn't talk like that," said Shireen, with soft maternal reproval. "Are you writing another book?" She knew he had written one, and though she had not read it she intended to do so tomorrow.

"I wish I were."

"You should. Think of all the things you could tell people. And we all of us need to learn—God, how we need to learn."

He shrugged. "I think about it, but I never get any farther than articles these days. You can do one of those and be done with it in two or three or four weeks. With a book you've got to be able to think a long way ahead. I can't do it any more."

"You mustn't let that happen to you. You could change it in one day, if you would."

"Could I? Maybe. Only I'm not so sure I want to. I've got a way of life worked out for myself and though it may not be a very good one, it seems to suit me. I can't say I always like it. In fact, sometimes I hate it, but I don't think I'm prepared to part with it. There are several things about it that are pretty comfortable and it fits me the way I like—not too tight, a little loose around the shoulders, sags in the back, maybe." He spread his hands, grinning. "But anyway it's comfortable."

Shireen shook her head, looking very serious. "And won't you *ever* write another book?"

"Oh, I've made a couple of outlines—something always happens. I go out for a drink or someone comes to town I haven't seen for a long time or I don't feel so good. Practically anything will do for an excuse." He looked at her carefully. "How about you, by the way? Are you working on another one?"

"Oh, me. No. I'm never going to write anything again for the rest of my life."

"You're kidding."

"I should say not. Why should I?"

"What will you do instead, then? Settle down and be the good housewife and raise a flock of kids?"

Shireen laughed, but not with amusement. "Hardly."

He looked puzzled, and curious. "What, then?"

276

"Why—I don't know for sure yet. Whatever I feel like doing. I haven't quite decided."

"What's gone wrong?"

Shireen felt vaguely uncomfortable. She always tried to guess at the rest of the iceberg from what was clearly visible; he was taking soundings and measurements. "Nothing. Why?"

"You mean you're perfectly satisfied, just as you are?"

"Perfectly satisfied? No, of course not. Who ever is? You can't have any imagination at all and ever be perfectly satisfied, do you think?"

"But *you* should be better satisfied than you are."

"I don't know what you mean."

"Yes, you do. You've got practically every reason there is in the world to be very happy. And you're not."

"Why, that's ridiculous. I am happy—honestly I am. Please believe me. I'm happier than I've ever been." She gave a nervous little laugh. "Only I'm afraid to say that, for fear something will happen."

"How's that again?"

"Of course," said Shireen, beginning to sound brisk and confident, convinced she was about to say something which would amuse him, "I've always been sure it's the things you expect to happen—whether they're good or bad—that never happen."

"So you plague yourself with expecting everything bad and never let yourself expect anything good?"

"That's right. And so far it's worked out pretty well."

"So far it's worked out to make you goddamn miserable."

"Oh, no!" she protested, unaccountably alarmed.

He grinned. "Okay—I'll take your word for it."

He told her that he had to leave and asked if she would see him again and she said that she would. She liked him and felt a deep sympathy for him, as if he had been hurt and needed comfort and healing. They shook hands and he left.

Georgia was gone already and Shireen got into a taxi and went off to meet some people for dinner. She sat in one corner of the cab, hanging onto the strap, thinking of what Dallas had said to her. Strange, he should get the idea she was unhappy. He seemed like a pretty intelligent man, too; she wondered how he could have been so mistaken about her.

Oh, well. When he knew her better.

She wiped her mind free and sat there, looking out the window. After awhile she glanced up unexpectedly and saw her face in the cab mirror. She looked at herself in shocked surprise.

What?

Is that me?

What am *I* looking so sad about?

Chapter 38

Shireen and Dallas came out of the theater where they had seen *Angel Street*. They were hurrying, Shireen almost running and Dallas close behind her. It was snowing and the sidewalks were covered with a light powder that had not yet melted or been trampled into slush, though black footprints had tracked across it. Dallas, still pulling on his trench coat, went out in the street to signal for a cab while Shireen stood under the marquee. A cab rode up and Dallas grabbed it; she ran out and jumped in, laughing.

"Where do you want to go?" he asked her.

"How about the Ruban Bleu? Maybe that girl will sing 'September Song.' "

She looked at Dallas as he gave the driver the address and was suddenly very pleased with him, with the light sprinkle of snow on his dark hair and the wavy wisp that had fallen over his forehead. She reached over, unexpectedly for both of them, and brushed her fingers lightly across the top of his head.

"Snow," she said.

He looked at her, grinning fondly.

During the past couple of weeks they had seen each other often and almost immediately had developed a friendship that seemed old and trustworthy. They talked about everything that was of interest to either of them, argued and quarreled sometimes, but always liked each other; and Shireen never hid from him since she had no ambition to make him love her.

A few nights earlier they had gone back to her apartment about midnight, after seeing a movie and stopping at Hicks for a soda. Shireen glanced through her telephone messages while they rode up in the elevator.

"Fix yourself a drink if you want one, Dallas. I have to call Georgia." While he went out to the little pantry she asked for Georgia's room.

"Paul Worth called me today," Georgia told her. "He says he left a message with the operator several nights ago asking you to call back but you didn't."

"Of course I didn't. And I certainly don't intend to now. What's he bothering me for?" She was sitting at the desk, her feet propped on

278

an opened bottom drawer, absently watching Dallas as he came back and poured some bourbon into a glass.

"He says there's been some misunderstanding and he wants to get away this week end and come up here and talk to you."

"But I don't want to see him! I won't see him. Johnny may be back by then. Wouldn't it be a fine thing to have Paul popping in with Johnny here?"

They talked a little longer and she hung up. Dallas, she realized then, was looking at her and smiling.

"It must be tough," he said. "Having to brush the flies away from the honey all the time."

Shireen picked up her cigarette holder and stuck it between her teeth; she tipped her chair back a little. "There aren't that many flies. Paul is a kind of—uh—old friend."

"So I gathered." He was grinning. "And Johnny's another old friend and all hell would pop if they happened to get together."

Shireen looked away from him and closed the drawer. "No, not exactly that."

"And anyway it's none of my business. But it answers something I've been a little curious about."

"What's that?"

"How a girl like you gets along with her husband overseas."

"The same way any other girl does, of course. I happen to be very much in love with my husband."

He smiled but said nothing.

"Well—I am!"

"Okay, okay." He shrugged.

Shireen stared at him and then finally said: "Dallas, if I didn't like you so well I'd be furious with you. I don't know what business you have drawing conclusions about me."

"None, of course, except that I'm very much interested in you. However, I've got no intention of baring my big fangs at you. I'd like to, God knows, but I'm frankly too goddamn tired to be a wolf."

She got up and wandered around, straightening lamps and end tables so they set square; he watched her.

"It's funny," he said. "The effect you've had on me."

"How's that?" she asked, pretending to be indifferent, moving the inkwell to the exact center of the desk.

"Well, there's a girl I'd been seeing. I met her in a bar one night and we began sleeping together. I guess because both of us were lonely. I even liked her pretty well. Then, after I met you, I began to see her less and less and now I don't see her at all and sometimes I can't even remember her name."

Shireen was flattered. "I'm sure I don't know why, Dallas. I haven't

279

the slightest intention of having an affair with you and I certainly don't care how many women you sleep with."

"I know you don't. That's what's funny about it. It seems like I'd rather just be with you—and wonder." He didn't sound pathetic or pleading and he was smiling as he talked, apparently amused to find this in himself.

"Well," said Shireen finally, "I suppose there's something or other I should say. But I don't know just what it is."

"Nothing at all. Anyway, you're sure pretty. That's the prettiest face in the world."

She glanced at him in quick surprise and then smiled, irresistibly pleased. "That's very nice of you, Dallas. I didn't know if you thought I was pretty at all."

"Like I told you, honey—I'm tired."

Sitting in the cab now they talked about the play, what they liked about it and what they did not like, and were glad to find themselves in agreement so they could admire their own opinions. They thought and felt alike about many more things than they disagreed on, and she had realized already that she had much more in common with Dallas than with Johnny.

Except that it was Johnny she loved.

They went upstairs into the dark crowded little room and were led around between the squashed-in tables to a seat against the wall. Dallas ordered crème de menthe for Shireen and bourbon and water for himself and they sat and watched the show. Three men were singing risqué songs and when they finished and stood there bowing, Shireen glanced at Dallas and gave a bored sigh.

"What is this nonsense, anyway? This eighth grade attitude we have toward sex in this country? It must go along with puritanism— Surely you don't find it in Oriental countries, do you?"

Dallas didn't answer. And apparently had not even heard her for he was sitting staring into his glass and Shireen had the feeling that he had suddenly left her, swamped by some tidal wave from deep inside him. It had happened before and each time gave her a feeling of great pity and maternal protectiveness.

She sat quietly, watching him, and after a few moments he glanced at her and then gave a quick sheepish grin, as if he had just realized what had happened.

"I'm sorry. What did you say?"

"Nothing. Dallas, what's the matter? Are you worried about something? Talk to me, if it'll help you any."

He gave her hand a grateful pat but then drew back his own without letting it linger. Shireen was amused by the caution.

"Thanks, honey, but it's nothing I can talk about. At least not in a couple of hours and not to you."

"Why not? I'll listen no matter how many hours it takes. Is it your work, Dallas?"

"Partly. But it isn't the work I do—it's why I don't do more. And it's headaches and pains in my arms and legs and spells of passing out on my feet like that one just now. Oh, hell, I'm making myself sound like a cripple. I'm a beat-up guy, that's all. Funny, too, I don't know how or why it happened. But I guess I'm finding out."

"Oh, Dallas, you poor darling. Do you really have all those things wrong with you? But how are you finding out?"

He sneaked her a quick glance. "I'm going to an analyst."

"What!"

Dallas gave an embarrassed half laugh. "See? I knew it."

"But what in the name of God do *you* need with an analyst, Dallas? Why, you're the nicest guy I know."

"Being nice hasn't got much to do with it unfortunately."

"And you're certainly not—"

She hesitated and he glanced at her again.

"Not nuts?"

"No, you're not!"

"Of course I'm not. Relax, honey. Why should it bother you so much if I get myself analyzed?"

"Why, I don't know. It doesn't bother me, of course. I just think it's silly, that's all. Anyone might have a headache."

"Not every morning for years, they don't. And if they do they'd damn well better find out what's cooking down there in the subterranean passages."

"Well—" Shireen was, for some reason she could not locate, considerably upset to think of Dallas Cavanaugh being psychoanalyzed. "I guess," she said finally, "I always thought it was the last resort before they brought in the strait jacket."

"I suppose it sometimes is, but that's slicing things a little too thin. After all, we're most of us neurotic these days, aren't we?"

"Don't look at me. *I'm* the most normal person there is."

"What? Do you honestly believe that?"

"Well, anyway, I'm as normal as I want to be. At least I know what I'm doing."

"Do you?" He looked at her again for a moment and then ground out his cigarette.

Shireen was watching him and she felt nervous and annoyed. "Of course I do, Dallas! I wanted to write a best seller—and I did!"

Dallas burst into laughter. "Wait'll I tell my analyst that one."

"Do you talk to him about me?" she asked, curious and flattered to think that two men were possibly discussing her, what she was, why she was that. And she wondered what could be said between

281

them in that secret room. Did Dallas maybe tell his doctor that he was in love with her?

Dallas gave her a glance of slightly impatient amusement. "Yes. I talk to my doctor about you."

"And what does he say?"

"It isn't what he says. It's what I say."

"Well, then—what do *you* say?"

"Shireen, do you know I'd sometimes like to spank you?"

"Why—Dallas! Why?"

He shook his head. "Poor Ed. God, how I pity him."

"What?"

She felt that Dallas had suddenly and for no reason at all turned on her and become her enemy. And she could not imagine what she had done to deserve it.

"Don't pity Ed. He loves me and he's very happy with me. I'm his whole life—he couldn't live without me."

"That's not true about anyone, but think it if you need to. And how about you, Shireen? Are you very happy with him?"

"Of course."

"What about this guy Johnny Keegan?"

"What about him? I love Ed but I happen to love Johnny, too. That's simple enough, isn't it?"

Dallas shook his head. "A woman like you—suddenly given all the money she could use and complete independence. It's easy enough to see what would happen."

"Because it isn't in the Book of Rules?" she asked him sarcastically. "It's not written down anywhere that you can love two men at one time? Men don't permit it, since it makes them even a little more insecure than they are to begin with? I'm not interested in rules, Dallas. I'm an individualist."

"And *you're* the individual?"

Her eyes hardened and she looked at him slantwise. "Just what is it that makes you so interested in my—"

"I'm not!" he snapped. "Only take my advice and hie yourself off to the nearest analyst. Quick. You're in trouble."

She was very angry with him but could not think why she should be, so she turned it to scorn. "At least you hope I am. Because it would make you feel a little better about yourself."

The expression on his face changed quickly and he looked away from her down at the table. "I'm sorry," he said after a moment. "Let's go home. I'm tired and I've got to be up early tomorrow morning. I have to finish that article this week and so far all I've done is sit and stare at a lot of blank sheets of paper."

Her face and voice softened all at once, and she touched his hand.

"Oh, but Dallas, wait just a little longer. Maybe she'll sing 'September Song' for the next show. Please, Dallas?"

"I really should—well, okay."

He was at her apartment a little earlier than usual the next night and she opened the door for him with another book on Asia in her hand. He glanced at the dust jacket as he walked by her.

"Still surveying the international situation," he said.

She followed him into the living room. "You know, this is a very fascinating book. Why, I didn't know that the Kuomintang was reorganized in 1924 with Russian advisers. How did they happen to get so far away from Lenin's principles?"

He looked at her and smiled. "That's kind of a long story to begin right now. Daddy'll tell you all about it some other time."

"You think I'm being silly, don't you? You think there's no sense in me trying to learn about these things."

"Honey, I admire your industry. But I wish you were applying it to something else."

"What, for instance?"

"Writing another book, for instance."

"Oh. Do you want a drink?"

"Not right now, thanks. I think I'm loaded already."

"So early in the day? How come?"

"Same old story. I was working on that article this morning when some kids I'd met in China called—back on leave. So I spent the afternoon drinking with them."

"Do they think it'll end soon?"

"How do they know? Every guy back from the Pacific is supposed to come straight from MacArthur or Hirohito. They don't know any more than we do—they only fight the war."

"I'm sorry. That was a pretty stupid question. Sometimes I wonder how we civilians can be so dumb. You guys must get awfully sick of us."

"What do you mean: 'you guys'? I'm a civilian too, remember."

"No, you're not, Dallas. It's different with you. You've been there. You're part of it."

He shook his head. "I've been there, but I'm not part of it." He was sitting with his legs spread and his hands clasped between them, looking down at the floor. "You know, being a war correspondent is a kind of funny business. You're there, you get shot at, you take the same chances. You don't have to, but you do anyway. Partly because you don't have to, I guess. But all the time you know you don't really belong to it, and everyone else knows it, too." He gave a soft self-deprecating laugh. "Those kids this afternoon—all I could do was listen. And feel like a goddamn fool."

283

"But you shouldn't, Dallas. You're doing something that's necessary."

"Yeah? I wish I thought so."

The telephone rang and she got up to answer it, saying: "Must be Georgia. Want to have dinner with her?" She picked up the receiver and said hello.

"Shireen?"

"Yes."

"Johnny. Just got into La Guardia about an hour ago. How are you, girl?"

"Why—I'm fine. How are you?"

"What are you doing? Are you busy? Can you have dinner with me?"

Suddenly the three weeks they had already missed went through her mind, days that Johnny had destroyed for both of them. She wanted to refuse, simply tell him she was sorry but that she had something more important to do.

"Of course I can."

"I'm just around the corner. All right if I come on up?"

"Yes. Oh, Johnny—a friend of mine will have dinner with us. Someone I want you to meet."

"Georgia?"

"No—Dallas Cavanaugh." Across the room Dallas was gesturing and shaking his head and Shireen frowned at him.

There was a momentary silence at Johnny's end. "Who is this guy?" Clearly he had not expected to find Shireen busy with any friend at all.

"He wrote *World We Lost*. He's a wonderful man—you'll like each other."

"No doubt. Anyway—I'll be right up."

She put the phone down and turned to Dallas. "You'll like Johnny, Dallas. Really you will. He's a wonderful man." She thought it would be nice for them to know each other; they might sit down together sometime and have a talk about her.

"He's a wonderful man. I'm a wonderful man. This'll be great—I can see it now."

She went into the bedroom to put on her hat and had just come back when they heard Johnny's sharp staccato knock at the door. She gave a nervous little jump. "I'll let him in," she explained, adding, as she started out of the room: "I'll be right back."

"Oh, take your time."

Chapter 39

When they had given their order for dinner Shireen sat quietly between Dallas and Johnny and listened to them talk about the war: the places they had both been and what they had seen, things they had done, how bad the food was and how stupid the upper echelon. And she noticed again how Johnny slurred off his experiences, touched on them in some sideways manner so that he gave the impression of being a man to whom amazing things happened automatically and naturally.

"Distinguished Flying Cross," said Dallas, glancing at the ribbons on Johnny's chest. Shireen frowned, for she had already told him about Johnny's heroism and modesty and was sure he meant to be unpleasant. "That's not very easy to get. What's it for?"

"They gave 'em out with the rations one day." He changed the subject quickly. "You've spent a lot of time in China? I want to get back there one of these days. Next trip out, if I can make it."

"I spent about three years there. Certainly not long enough to know anything about it."

"It's a hell of a place. Wonderful for Americans."

"It won't be. One of these days the Chinese are going to take over China."

"I don't know about that," said Johnny. "Where in the hell would they be right now without us?"

"Maybe they'd have got this war over a long time ago without us. Chiang Kai-shek would have been out on his ear if we didn't keep propping him up."

"We'd damn well better keep propping him up if we don't want the Reds to take over."

Shireen sighed and wondered how she had ever been so foolish as to bring them together when she knew all along they thought differently about almost everything. What Johnny believed in was either absurd or dangerous to Dallas and what Dallas believed Johnny saw as impractical daydreaming or subversive radicalism.

Dallas lit a cigarette and went on talking. "I've never been in Yenan and I don't know what's going on there. The only thing that makes me at all suspicious is that every report you hear is so glowing. But one thing I do know: Reds or no Reds, the Kuomintang and everything it stands for has got to go before the Chinese people have any chance at all."

Johnny dismissed the entire subject. "We're on opposite sides of the fence." He glanced at Shireen, who was sitting there looking unhappily as if she had invited the wrong people to her party and had no idea what to do about it. "What've you been doing?"

"The queen's been in the countinghouse," said Dallas. "Counting all her chips."

"Why not?" demanded Johnny. "Since she earned 'em."

"Sure. Why not? I still maintain Shireen's one of the few women in history to make a million bucks before she was twenty-eight— without having to take her clothes off to do it."

"Dallas, for heaven's sake!" said Shireen. Dallas grinned at her maliciously.

She wished he had not come with them and was blaming him for being there. She had realized that whatever her relationship with Johnny was, it was so intensely personal and intimate that he became almost a stranger to her when other people were around.

Now the men in the orchestra took their places, the leader turned to face them, raised his baton, and a flood of music crashed into the room; the lights dimmed slowly and everyone seemed to relax, instantly relieved by the semidarkness.

Johnny asked Shireen to dance with him.

"Would you mind, Dallas?"

"Go ahead. I never got past the two-step, myself."

The floor was almost empty at first and they danced without speaking to each other for three or four minutes. Other couples began to appear around them, and Johnny's arm drew her closer.

"Relax," he said. "You're trembling. What's the matter?"

She looked up. He was smiling at her and there was nothing left of the antagonism he had shown Dallas. In his eyes and smile was that same magical nostalgic tenderness that had made her fall in love with him.

"It's you," she said. "I've missed you so much—I thought you'd never come."

"It took a little longer than I expected."

He did not tell her why or what he had been doing and she knew it would be useless to ask. It still had not occurred to her that these evasions and mysteries might be so integrally important to him he could not alter them without feeling himself in danger.

Then, after a few moments, he asked her: "Where did you pick up that character?"

"Dallas?"

"Whatever his name is."

"I met him at a cocktail party."

286

"You get mixed up with the damndest people."

"There's nothing wrong with Dallas. He's a very nice man. Why? Don't you like him?"

"Sure, I like him all right. But he doesn't know what the hell he's talking about. The guy doesn't make much sense, that's all. He sounds like a Red."

Shireen laughed. "Dallas? He's about as Red as I am. He's a newspaperman, and they all talk that way. Anyway, you mustn't blame him if he seemed nervous—he's being analyzed."

"That does it. I can't figure you out, Shireen. What makes you spend your time with people like that? Lawrence Christopher—and now this Cavanaugh. Don't you know any decent people?"

"I don't care what you say about Lawrence Christopher. I think he's an impossible snob. But Dallas is one of the most decent honest men I've ever met. And there's no reason for you to talk that way about him just because he doesn't happen to agree with you—"

"Hold it. Don't get so excited. That's what I've been trying to tell you is the matter with New York. It's full of fouled-up people and if you stick around long enough, you'll get so you can't tell the difference yourself. You'd better start figuring out what you want."

"I've got what I want. Johnny, I don't see why—"

His mouth brushed against her temple. "Shh—listen to the music."

Her eyes closed for a moment, gratefully. It was always so much better when they didn't talk, for the words seemed to cut across what they felt and vitiate its meaning. She was sure that whatever it was they meant to each other was buried far inside each of them where it existed in some perfect state, eternal and inviolable, created from her deepest needs for a man and his for a woman. It had no part in any of the rest of her life, but some importance far greater than everything else.

The music ended and they went back to the table. The three of them managed to keep some kind of conversation going but she was intensely relieved when dinner was finally over and they got up to leave. There was some discussion between Dallas and Johnny as to who would pay the check; Johnny became so insistent, smiling all the while and saying that after all it was he who had called, that Dallas finally shrugged his shoulders. When they were outside waiting for the doorman to get them a cab, Dallas turned to Shireen and said he would have to leave.

"Oh, Dallas." Shireen tried to pretend she was disappointed. "So soon?"

"Still got that article to work on." He looked at Johnny and held out his hand. "Nice to have met you."

Johnny shook hands with him, smiling again, as if he would make one last effort to leave a good impression. "Maybe we can get together

287

pretty soon." And Dallas, with a wave of his hand, walked off. Shireen and Johnny got into a cab.

"Where'll we go?"

"Back to my apartment?"

"Okay, for a little while. I left my bag in the lobby. I haven't even checked into a hotel yet." He smiled at her, as if to say: So you see? I came as fast as I could.

While Shireen went to take off her hat and coat, Johnny wandered around. She came out and found him standing before the desk, his hands in his pockets, looking at Ed's picture. He did not move when she first came in and then, as if he had sensed her there, swung around quickly. His face was red.

"How long will you be here?" she asked him, because she was nervously anxious to take his mind off Ed and it was the first thing that occurred to her.

"I have to report to Washington tomorrow."

"Can I go with you?"

"Of course not."

She started to protest and he made a quick gesture. "I'll save you the trouble of saying it. That part of it's over. If we see each other at all from now on, it'll have to be on a basis of simple friendship, nothing else."

"Why, that's crazy. How can we?"

"We can—if you want to. The truth of it is, you don't."

"Of course I don't. And neither do you. So what are you talking this way for?"

"Shireen, it seems to be pretty damned easy for you to forget that you're married. One of us has got to have some sense of responsibility to Ed, and if you won't, then it'll have to be me. That's all there is to it—there's nothing more to talk about."

"I have as much sense of responsibility to Ed as you have! You make me awfully tired with this noble character pose of yours, Johnny. Stop and think back sometime and remind yourself how all this got started. You've done as much to hurt Ed as I have, because it was you who began it."

"That's not true."

She sighed. "All right. Think whatever you like that'll make you feel good. All I'm interested in is that I love you and I love you very sincerely and honestly. And I'm willing to take the consequences of how I have to feel when I do something that I know is wrong."

Johnny was quiet a moment and then shook his head. "No, Shireen. We shouldn't see each other. I've thought about it and I know I'm right. If we do you know what'll happen. And I've got to prove to myself that I've still got something of myself left. I can't let you do this to me."

Unexpectedly, Shireen stamped her foot. "I haven't done anything to you, Johnny Keegan! If you haven't sense enough to see——" And then suddenly she stopped, her mouth open, for he had crossed the room and picked up his cap. "Johnny! You're not going!"

"We don't do anything but fight when we're together. We can't seem to agree on anything—and it's just not worth it. Life's too short."

She stared at him. "Do you really mean that?"

"I do."

It was worth it to her, no matter how much they disagreed or how often they quarreled; for she believed that love was love, never changed or altered, no matter what you did to it.

"You don't love me," she said.

"Stop talking nonsense."

"You don't! You talk about responsibility to Ed! You haven't any responsibility to anyone on earth and you know it! This is *my* marriage we've both been tampering with—you're not going to lose anything. But if you think Ed's and my life could ever be the same after that night in Miami, you're out of your mind. The whole thing's washed up and has been from the moment you decided, for whatever reasons you may have had, to tell me that you loved me. But you'll go on with your life exactly the way it was before you met me—knowing now that there's one more woman in love with you. And that's all you were after to begin with."

The expression on his face changed completely for an instant, as if somewhere inside him everything had broken apart.

"No, Shireen—that isn't fair. You think I haven't lost anything by all this and that you're the only one who has. But since apparently you won't be satisfied unless you think that knowing you has changed my whole life, I'll tell you this: Whatever you may think, this business of making love to another man's wife is a new one for me. I've always had sense enough to keep out of a mess like this one, whatever other damn fool things I may have done. I never would have believed I could make enough compromises with myself to get into a situation like this. Well, it happened somehow and, I think, without either of us willing it. But I have lost something. I've lost my self-respect. And that was something I'd had a long time and put a pretty high value on."

Shireen watched him as he talked, his voice low and faded, as if he had to make a great effort to get the words out. And then she looked away, ashamed.

Finally he came and took her in his arms and kissed her. After several minutes he released her a little and looked at her, smiling.

"Come on," he said. "Let's hit the sack."

The next morning when he left he refused to tell her when he would see her again. He might be gone two days or two weeks. She

289

stood at the door and pleaded with him and each word sounded useless and empty as she said it.

"You want to wring everything there is out of every emotion," he told her. "Don't you know yet you should always sell out before it gets to the top? Or you lose your shirt." He was smiling.

"You're a complete romantic, Johnny. You're the most unrealistic man I've ever known."

He touched her face. "Less than you think, believe me." And then he went out and a moment later waved back at her from down the hall. She closed the door, went into the living room, and looked around.

She frowned a little and shrugged her shoulders, then picked up the phone and called Dallas's number. His voice sounded sleepy when he answered. It was ten o'clock.

"I'm sorry, Dallas. Did I wake you?"

"What are *you* doing up at this hour?"

"Oh," said Shireen idly, as if she had called him on a whim and not from some desperate necessity to hear a reassuring voice, "I get up early sometimes, you know."

"Where's your fly-fly boy?"

Shireen laughed, a little pleased to hear him make fun of Johnny. "He's gone. Had to go to Washington to get his orders."

"He'll be given some mysterious mission, I suppose. Flying toilet paper to MacArthur."

"Now, Dallas, that isn't very nice. You make Johnny sound—"

"Like the poor man's Byron he is."

"Why, Dallas—I think you're jealous of him."

"Jealous, for God's sake? Of that jerk? Well, maybe you're right," he agreed then, a little lamely.

"Talk to your doctor about it," she suggested, teasing him.

"I did. Last night."

"Really? And what did he say?"

"He said: 'Yes.' "

Both of them laughed and Dallas said he had to get up and have breakfast and go to work. "I know what'll happen. I'll get going on that article two hours before midnight Saturday. That's what always happens to me these days."

"Come over here and work."

"Not a chance. I wouldn't get two sentences done, and you know it. Anyway, since the major's gone, do you want to have dinner with me tonight? Some friends of mine are giving a party."

"I'd love to. But Dallas—I don't want to be alone today. I really don't. If I'm alone I'll have to think, and I don't want to!"

"I can't imagine anything," he said, "that would do you more good. Good-by. See you about six."

"No, Dallas! Please! You don't understand!"

"Good-by." He hung up.

Shireen slammed down the phone and glared at it. She sat for a moment looking at her bare feet and polished red toenails, and then she called Georgia's office. I've got to find something to do. I don't care what it is. Something. I can't sit here all day and read. I can't sit here all by myself. I've got to see someone and talk to someone. Georgia understood her predicament and told her to get dressed and come over and they would go out to lunch. With a great sense of relief Shireen hung up and went into the bathroom.

Thank God.

Later that afternoon, when she got home, she found a florist's box and opened it eagerly. There were two white orchids, with no fern or ribbon, just the flowers, the way she liked them. She took the card out of the envelope.

Must be losing my grip—even spoiling you.
Johnny.

Chapter 40

She made up her mind that she would not talk to Dallas about Johnny, for she was sure that if she did she would hear something she would not like. And she didn't mention him until they got back to her apartment after the party, at almost three. Then she couldn't keep quiet any longer. She felt that Dallas knew something she should know, or knew already, but had never put into words.

"You haven't even mentioned Johnny." She said it almost accusingly.

He grinned at her.

"Well?"

"What?"

"Tell me what you think of him."

"Why, for God's sake?"

"Because I want to know. What did he seem like to you?"

"I've known a hundred of him. Comes a war and all of a sudden they crop up; you never know where they've been before and usually it doesn't matter. But they take to a uniform and the sky and combat as if they'd been waiting for it all their lives. He's a pretty familiar type, Shireen."

"He's not familiar to me. I've never known anyone like him."

"You just never knew very many people at all, macushla."

"Maybe he's naturally adaptable. There's nothing wrong with that, is there?"

"There's something wrong when he can adapt that easily to war. And like it. Your boy Keegan really likes the war. It gives him a better chance to show off than he ever had before or ever dreamed of having. He's not much good, Shireen. I don't know how you can kid yourself."

"You don't know him, Dallas. There's something you don't see in Johnny."

"No argument there, I don't. Oh, I know there's a little jealousy involved, because no matter what I think about these fellas who make such an easy adaptation to war—I'm envious of them too. I'm a goddamn coward myself. I never have been able to feel nonchalant with bombs dropping around me."

Shireen smiled at him tenderly. "You're no coward if you've got courage enough to admit it. It's certainly nothing to be ashamed of if you get scared. But Johnny has something—I'm not sure what it is. In fact, I don't have the vaguest idea what it is and I wish to God I could find out because it's affected me like nothing ever did in my life before. Some kind of charm that's almost uncanny. I've never known anyone who had it to anything like the same degree."

"I know," said Dallas. "And what's more he's got it under thermostat control. Shireen, you're so damn naïve. Didn't you see what went on last night between him and that hat-check girl?"

Her heart began to beat faster. She did not want to hear or know anything about Johnny that she would not be able to explain to herself in such a way that it would seem all right. Certainly nothing that had to do with another woman.

"No," she said, not looking at Dallas. "I didn't."

"It wasn't anything much, but it sure told a lot about the guy. He smiled at the girl when he handed her his cap and looked at her for a couple of seconds and all of a sudden her face went wide open and for a minute she looked completely helpless, like a bitch waiting for the male. And the funny part is, I think it's such a habit by now he didn't even know he was doing it. But there was a kind of cruelty in it that made me sick at my stomach. It isn't healthy for a guy to have that much sex appeal—warps his character."

"Oh, well," said Shireen, and now that she had heard it it didn't seem so bad and anyway she could find excuses. "I know all that. But I don't think he can help it—it just happens every time he so much as smiles at a woman."

Dallas shook his head. "You mean Johnny Keegan's got some special formula? He shoots out invisible sparks or has his own electromagnetic field? You mean he's just plain different from other men? Who are you kidding, Shireen? He may be a little better looking than the average guy, but he's not that different. The truth of it is that he has to keep building himself up in his own estimation. He thinks he's not much—and with good enough reason, as far as I could tell—so he's got to see a flattering reflection of himself in the face of everyone he meets. That goes for men, too, though of course he's got a different gimmick with men. He pulls the 'aw shucks t'ain't nothin'' business on them. He didn't like me and I'd be willing to bet he told you so. But he'd have liked me all right, even if he did think I'm a Red, if I'd fallen for the Keegan brand of hooey. Only he knew he wasn't getting across to me with that fake modesty and that man-of-mystery routine. And Johnny Keegan's a guy who's pretty easily shaken. He can't afford to be around someone who doesn't think he's the most fabulous character they ever met. Why do you think he keeps on the move all the time?"

"Oh, Dallas!" Shireen got up suddenly and walked a few steps

293

away. "Don't tell me any more. It isn't true and I don't like to hear it."

"I'm sorry. You asked me. Anyway, Shireen, whether you'd asked me or not I'd have told you sooner or later. God, I don't see how you can do this to yourself. Because you're the one who's doing it. Not Johnny. I may think he's a jerk, but I know better than to imagine he could get away with this if you didn't let him. There's something you want from the guy and it'd be a good idea if you could figure out what it is so you'd know if it's worth the beating you take for it or not."

She was standing half turned away from him, gazing at the picture she now had of herself: a poor innocent woman, helpless and mistreated, undeserving her fate. "I know, Dallas. I suppose you're right. And I wish I did know. But I don't. And even if I did, I'm afraid it wouldn't make any difference. I'd still feel the same way."

Dallas shrugged. "I can't figure you out and I guess there's not much sense trying. You're a woman and I'm a man; we're two different races of people."

More than a week went by and she did not hear from Johnny. She felt ashamed each time Dallas asked her and finally told him to mind his own business. She spent her time with him and his friends—reporters and foreign correspondents waiting for reassignment or passing through New York—and she found them all fascinating because they knew so much.

She kept reading books on Asia, its history and present politics, in order to correct her ignorance so that she could talk to the people she met at cocktail parties. What else she could do with this knowledge she had no idea, but it seemed a clear necessity to learn everything she didn't know. And every day she became convinced that she knew less, as she continued meeting people who knew things she had never even heard about. So she would dash home from having lunch with someone, grab up the book she was reading and go at it furiously, a notebook beside her and a pen in her hand. She had a frightened feeling of running to catch up with someone or something, stumbling, falling down, getting up and going on again, but whatever it was she was chasing kept getting farther and farther away.

I'll never make it, she would think desperately. And she would look at all the books on her shelves that she hadn't read. There just isn't enough time in the day. And there aren't enough days or months or years.

It was almost six o'clock and the office was quiet. The last of the authors had gone and the telephone did not ring very often. The secretary had left and only one reader was still in a back office, taking notes from a manuscript.

Shireen sat on a flowered couch with her feet under her and Georgia sat at her desk. The lights were on and it looked black outside, though whenever there was a strong gust of wind the snow swirled up against the windows and was caught for a moment in the glare of the lights. Shireen could see her own reflection in the window—some girl she didn't know very well but who looked quite pretty—sitting there in a black suit with an ermine hat on her black hair and an ermine muff lying on the couch beside her. Her face was a little vague in the reflection and sometimes when she moved, a flaw in the glass cut jaggedly across and divided it in two, like the puzzles they used to have in newspapers for matching cut-up parts of different faces.

They had been talking about Johnny.

"I wish he'd make up his mind what he wants."

"You haven't anything to worry about, Shireen. So far he's given in to you every time. You can't want much more from the man, can you?"

"He hasn't given in at all. He keeps saying we've got to stop seeing each other, but he doesn't really want to. So I haven't won anything there. It's still just Johnny, doing as he damn pleases and making himself feel virtuous by torturing himself about it first. He's a puritan who thinks he's got himself done up as Dionysus—but he's not fooling anyone. Unless maybe himself."

"No, there's more to it than that. He needs to convince himself that you're not important to him. That's the pattern of his whole life—no one matters to Johnny Keegan but Johnny Keegan. If that's taken away the whole card house collapses and he's got nothing left. Anyway, Shireen, you've got an unfair advantage because you're married and you tell him you love Ed. But you expect Johnny to give you so much of himself that he won't ever be quite the same again."

"That's right," said Shireen. "I don't want him ever to be the same again. I'm not—why should he be?"

"But you can hardly blame him for wanting to protect himself."

"I *do* blame him. I think he's a coward."

"Oh, now Shireen. That's not quite fair. Really, for a nice girl you sometimes say the most alarming things. But I'm sure you don't mean them."

"I certainly do mean them, Georgia. And I don't see anything very alarming about it. Why should Johnny protect himself against me? If he's worth a damn at all, what can I possibly take away from him or do to harm him? I hate people who go at life that way—pussy-footing along, trying out the quicksand to make sure they won't fall

295

in. God damn them, anyway. They're cheating. I'm not trying to protect myself against anything as far as Johnny—or any other man—is concerned. I'll take my chances on getting hurt. And if I do—well, that's tough. But I'm not going to hold part of myself out, just in case. Just in case *what?* This is the only life we have. We may as well live it, for God's sake. That's what I hold against Johnny Keegan. And that's why I can't respect him."

Georgia made a gesture with one hand. "The truth of it is, Shireen, you don't want to respect any man. You only want to find out that in one way or another you're better than they are—even if you are a woman."

"And so far that's what I've always found out." Shireen laughed. "How do you suppose I ever got to be such a bitch? I certainly wasn't brought up to be one. I couldn't be more different from what my parents wanted if I tried."

"You do try, don't you?"

There was a sound in the other room and Georgia and Shireen waited a moment, to see who it was. "Hey! Where are you two women?" It was Dallas. And a moment later he came in.

"Hi," said Georgia, and waved her hand to indicate that he should sit down. "We were just talking about you."

Dallas glanced at Shireen as she smiled up at him. "What were you saying?" He was grinning as if he either could guess or did not really care.

"We decided we like you better than anyone else," said Georgia. "What will you drink?"

"Bourbon, if you've got some."

Georgia went out of the room and he sat down beside Shireen. He looked at her for a moment and she stared back at him, slightly smiling, still a little defiant. "I wonder what you've been up to?" he said.

"Not a damned thing."

He watched her a moment longer. "You know—it's funny—but I can never look at you without seeing the damndest most uncomfortable image: some kind of beautiful predatory creature, sitting quietly and serenely, with the bones of the men she's devoured strewn all around her."

Shireen gave a sudden laugh, a ringing sound that came from a quick unexpected release of energy. "That's the most ridiculous thing I've ever heard." She was tremendously pleased.

At least they were someone else's bones—not hers.

She felt safe and protected by her own ruthlessness, part of an eternal pattern: Circe, turning men into swine. Kipling's deadly female of the species. Lilith, the dark goddess. *What ailed us, O gods, to desert you for creeds that refuse and restrain? Come down and redeem us from virtue, Our Lady of Pain.* The devouring vixen of history and poets, forever luring men to their doom. From Cleopatra to Becky Sharp to Theda Bara. Beautiful, cruel, fascinating; the symbol of some vast uneasy rift between the sexes.

Dallas shook his head. "You don't think it's ridiculous at all. You're proud of yourself. I wouldn't let myself get mixed up with you for anything in the world."

Shireen took a comb out of her bag, threw her hat on the couch, and went over to a mirror Georgia had perched on a shelf, in among the photographs and sea shells and stacks of books. She began pulling the comb through her hair.

"You're safe enough, Dallas. Because I haven't made up my mind whether or not I want you yet."

She heard him laugh and then Georgia came back, carrying his drink. As Dallas took it he said to Georgia, "This little playmate of yours, here. If you took her seriously it's enough to make your fingernails curl. The modern American woman. God preserve us. The one thing they never think of, apparently, is growing up to be decent mature responsible human beings."

Shireen turned around quickly and her eyes were bright and angry. "Don't talk like such an idiot, Dallas. You know what happens to women like that."

"Sure," said Dallas. "I know. My mother's one of them. My sister's another. They turn out to be pretty nice people."

"But they never get anywhere."

"They get to be wives and mothers and sometimes they're even pretty happy."

Shireen gave him a look of disgust and put her comb back in her bag, then took her hat and went to the mirror again. "That's no idea of happiness that appeals to me. I've seen it and I know where it leads and I can tell you one thing: It's a mirage, and sooner or later it goes where all mirages go. I don't want any part of it." She snipped her thumb and forefinger together, exploding that mirage in midair.

"Honey," said Dallas, "all I hope is you don't grow up too late."

"Don't worry about me. I'll get along."

"Shireen's bark is worse than her bite," said Georgia then. "I think I know her better than almost anyone, and she's one of the sweetest people I've ever met. Why, just look at her, Dallas. She's young and beautiful and intelligent and talented and rich—and in spite of all that she isn't conceited. In fact, if anything, she's too modest."

"Well," said Dallas, and he was grinning again, "I should hope so. That's about the first thing any successful person in this country learns, if he's either got good sense himself or an agent who has. Those high income reports go down the public throat a little easier with a chaser of humility."

"That's right," agreed Georgia. "But no one ever had to tell Shireen that. She's just naturally humble—she even makes fun of herself."

"Smart dame," said Dallas. "That's always been a good dodge for placating envy. One thing you can say about Shireen, she's not dumb. In fact, I'll even agree with you, Georgia: Shireen's a wonderful girl—in spite of herself."

Shireen was standing in front of Dallas now, looking down at him, with her hands resting lightly on her hips. "What's the matter with you, Dallas? You talk as if you don't like me today. I think you must be falling in love with me."

Dallas stared back at her, still grinning. "Not me, honey. I'm not in this poker game. You can deal me out. This is one time I'd rather kibitz."

Shireen and Georgia glanced at each other, as if to say: You see? The poor bastard. He thinks he's going to save himself some trouble. And he doesn't even know he's in it up to here.

Georgia laughed. "You're not fooling anyone, Dallas. If Shireen wanted to she could twist you around her finger so fast it'd make your head spin."

"Oh, now—Georgia," protested Shireen.

She wished Georgia had not said that and wondered why she had. Why should she warn him? What was this? Georgia going over to the enemy?

Oh, well, she must think he was a pretty nice guy and probably didn't want to see him get hurt. Dallas was not a man she would ever fall in love with and, if he loved her, sooner or later he would be made unhappy by it. Still, she felt a vague resentment for, one way or another, Dallas belonged to her to do whatever she wanted with him, and Georgia had no business interfering.

I'm no good, she thought. No one should ever love me. When they do—look what I do to them. If they knew what I am, they'd never love me. No one would.

She looked at Dallas and Georgia, discussing the war news now. "Let's go," she said. "Let's go out somewhere."

Chapter 41

Shireen and Georgia and Dallas sat in the Barberry Room one afternoon about four-thirty talking to a radio agent named Ernest Troy. Georgia had known him for several years and during the past few months they had been dickering over the possibility of a radio show for Shireen. Shireen listened and now and then she glanced resentfully at Dallas, who sat there with a complacent half grin on his face. She could not imagine why she had brought him along, except that they had had lunch together and then gone to the Museum of Modern Art and when it came time to meet Georgia and Troy she had invited him to join them.

"Why don't you come out from behind that smuggery?" she asked Dallas in an undertone, while Georgia and the agent were both talking at once.

Shireen did not like Ernest Troy very much herself.

He was a middle-sized man with blue eyes and dun-colored hair, dressed in an unobtrusive well-tailored brown suit, correct white handkerchief, correct white carnation. His appearance was almost conspicuously ordinary and he clearly wanted to keep it so, for he deviated at no point from the Brooks Brothers businessman. Nothing about him had to do with Broadway or Hollywood except, perhaps, the careful suavity of his manner, over which he kept as close watch as a cook with cake in the oven.

Shireen did not feel that the conversation actually had much to do with her. Though of course, in a way, it would be fun to have a radio program and dash around like Rosalind Russell playing a career woman.

She had a quick montage image of herself standing at a microphone, smiling and holding a script, watched by two hundred dazed faces in the studio audience, an assistant producer's finger pointing at her through the plate glass, the studio clock moving round, an announcer's booming voice presenting: *Miss Shireen Delaney!*

That's not me, she thought then. That's someone else.

Or maybe it is me. Why not? I can do anything I want to. I've proved that—and Georgia says I can. I might as well do everything there's time for.

"I think you could be terrific, Shireen," Ernest Troy was saying. "Of course we'll have to make a few changes in you."

Shireen became quickly alert. "What kind of changes?"

"Oh, your hair, maybe. Your eyebrows, maybe. Your clothes."

That turned her instantly against Ernest Troy. Georgia, who always picked up any hint of trouble like a receiving station, broke in: "That's nothing for us to be concerned with now. When shall we make the tests?"

"I think we can set it up in four or five days. Okay?"

Georgia looked at Shireen. "All right with you?"

"Yes, I guess so." But it was not all right with her any longer, not if he thought he was going to change her.

Troy signed the check and they went out. Georgia took a cab to her next cocktail party. Troy shook hands with Dallas and Shireen and went off. They turned the corner and started up Park Avenue. There had been a heavy snowfall and the snow had begun to melt, leaving the trees coated with ice. Shireen pointed at them, remarking how beautiful they were under the street lamps, like trees made of crystal.

"They look as if they're reaching for something, don't they? You know, that's one of the things I like best about living in the East. The change of seasons gives you the feeling that you have more time."

"Not enough to squander it the way you do."

She knew he was talking about Ernest Troy and the radio program, for he had already told her his opinion of that. "I know that stuff is nonsense," she said. "But it's part of the business I'm in."

"What business? The business of writing books—or the business of being Shireen Delaney? I think writing was never anything but a means to an end with you."

"As it so happens, you're right," she said coldly. "And what's all this hooey about writing, anyway? What makes it a sacred art? Because once upon a time it was part of the mumbo-jumbo the high priests kept to themselves? It isn't any more; we all learn it in the first grade and from then on it's a tool for anyone to use to get whatever he wants from life." She glanced sideways at him. "What are you sore about? Because I happen to know what I want?"

They came to the corner and stopped for a red light. Shireen stepped back from the curb a little to avoid getting spattered with slush, and Dallas turned around and stood facing her. She had violets pinned to the dark mink of her coat and the scent of her perfume seemed sharper in the cold air. She felt aware of herself as being beautiful to him, and had some sense that that was part of what had made him angry.

"If you knew, it wouldn't be so bad. But you're floundering, throwing yourself away. You don't even know what's going on around you. The whole world's burning down and you're going on some

300

crappy radio show, selling man-trap perfume or some other goddamn thing."

Shireen looked at him for a moment, her mouth tightening and her nostrils flaring out, as if the look could scare him. And then she stepped down off the curb and into a puddle that instantly soaked through her thin soled shoes. But she kept going, and Dallas walked beside her.

"Please remember that my husband is at war."

He snorted. "And you think that gives you some idea of what it's about? Over here in America where everything is so safe and sure? Where no bombs will ever fall and maybe blow off one of your legs or smother you in a pile of debris, just before the rescuers get to you? I don't think you know much about it. You don't even want to know about it—just enough to make you sound smart and knowing and 'serious' at cocktail parties."

She was furious with him because she knew that with all the guilt she carted around wherever she went, nevertheless he was right. The guilt was only a bribe, to keep the gods from suspecting she was lucky enough to bother.

"And how much does Jack Gilman let you say that you want to?" she demanded.

"Unfortunately, you're exactly right. He lets me say damned little; or, rather, he leaves in damned little of what I do say."

"Well, then," she asked triumphantly, "how much better are you than I?"

Dallas laughed. "Oh, God—that wasn't even the point. Look, baby, I'm not trying to prove that I'm good and you're bad or that anyone's good or bad. That's something I don't believe in and you know it. All I was saying was that it's too bad for a girl like you to be so willingly deceived. Look at the life you're living, and the people you know."

"Well—?"

"Well, none of it's worth much, that's all. You spend too much time with people who can't give you anything you don't already have, and not enough with yourself."

"I spent six thousand hours of my life alone writing." Her voice sounded bitter every time she spoke of it.

"Yes, and if you hadn't, you wouldn't be worth a damn—to yourself or anyone else. Not because what you've written so far is worth much, but someday it may be. I think it will. I think you've got something you don't know anything about yet; don't ask me what."

"Dallas, I wish you'd leave me alone!" Her voice had become excited and there was a sound of fear in it. "Everyone wants to change me! I wish people would let me be what I am! I'm not hurting anyone!"

He spoke to her gently. "But why should change be such a terrible thing? What are you afraid will happen if you change?"

"Nothing. I don't know. I want to be let alone, that's all." She stopped and looked at him, her whole face and body tense. "Can't you understand that?" she cried.

He winced a little, almost as if she had slapped him. "Yes. I do." He turned and started to walk away. "G'bye. I'll call you tomorrow."

She watched him take a few steps and for a moment was glad to be rid of him; then she ran after him and caught his arm. "Dallas! I didn't mean I wanted you to go! Don't leave me. Just—just be nice to me, Dallas. That's really all I want. I never meant to hurt anyone, I really didn't, I—"

He shook his head and his eyes closed for a moment. "Darling, don't—" He took her arm. "Where do you want to go?"

"Let's go home and have dinner sent up and play the phonograph—and not fight about anything. Can we? Sometimes I feel awfully tired, Dallas, I don't know why."

"I know. Me too. Come on."

The evening began to be very pleasant. They talked without animosity or disagreement. Dallas had a couple of drinks and she had a glass of sherry and then they ordered dinner. Shireen had put on one of her hostess gowns and she drifted around the room in a swirl of pale green chiffon, soothingly conscious of his admiration. When dinner was over they listened to some music without talking. In the midst of the *Pathétique* the phone rang and she went into the bedroom to answer it, closing the door behind her so as not to disturb him by turning it low.

It was Johnny.

"I'm downstairs," he said. "Can I see you?"

"What?"

"I'm—"

"Why, of course, Johnny. Come right up."

She dashed frantically into the living room. "Dallas! It's Johnny! He's downstairs—he'll be here in two seconds—you've got to get out!"

"Good God. Only Keegan? I thought the joint was on fire."

"Hurry—oh, please, Dallas, don't be so *slow!* If he finds you here he'll say I was busy and should have told him—and he'll go away—" She was following him down the hall, pushing him a little. "Don't take the elevator—he might be getting out. Walk down a couple of flights. Don't be mad—I'll call you tomorrow—" She ran back without waiting for his answer to pick up the empty glasses, dumping some of the cigarettes into them so the trays would not be too full, and ran to put them away, opening a cupboard and setting them on a high shelf in case he went there for a drink.

This time, she told herself, it'll be his way. I'll do whatever he wants and not suggest anything at all myself. The bell rang.

"I didn't expect to find you in." He looked her over. "That's a snow-job for sure."

"You just got back from Washington?"

He nodded. "I was home for awhile first. Have a nice Christmas?" He looked happy, and amused by his own secret, which she still had not discovered.

"Yes, very nice, thanks." She turned and walked along the hall toward the living room and he followed her. "Did you get your orders?"

He nodded, and she began to feel annoyed that he kept on smiling.

"Were they what you wanted?"

"Sure."

They looked at each other a moment. "How did you do it?" She wished he would once tell her that the magic had failed to work.

"I asked. If you ask for something you usually get it, don't you? For some reason, that's what it never occurs to most people to do."

She lit a cigarette impatiently. All at once it seemed incredible that she should love him, and she began to suspect that she did not. "You're leaving soon?"

"In a few days. I'm driving up to Connecticut tonight."

She stood and looked at him and now it was difficult to keep the hostility out of her eyes. I don't know what kind of a game you thought you had cooked up or what you're trying to do, but one thing I damn well do know—and that is that you and I are finished, washed up. I haven't got the time it takes to figure you out any more. And so, my friend, farewell—

"You're driving up there tonight?" she repeated. "And you didn't think I'd be in and if I hadn't been you'd have gone back overseas without seeing me again. Is that it?"

"I'd have seen you."

She turned away. "I don't know how. Oh, Johnny—" She gave a sigh. After a few moments she glanced at him again and found him watching her, with that faint appraising smile that told her plainly how much he knew she belonged to him. Well, she had given him every reason to believe that she did.

But there was one thing he did not know about.

The secret charm *she* had kept and hidden away: all the other things she could do and be interested in, so that it would not really matter when he was no longer there. That was the little island within her he could not know existed. And that was why, in the long run, she gave nothing real of herself to Johnny Keegan. She told him she loved him and needed him and though it was true in a sense, she

303

was lying, too, cheating him in the same way she had complained to Georgia that he was cheating her.

She was thinking of that as she looked at him and then he said: "You're everything any man could ever want, Shireen."

The expression on her face and all her feelings changed.

"I love you so much, Johnny." She had never once told him that without some response on his part that seemed composed of bafflement and despair, and something else she suspected of being smug vanity.

"I know," he said now.

She was quiet a moment. "Is that why you came back?"

"Partly, but not only that, and you know it. For myself, too."

"You really wanted to see me again?"

"Of course I wanted to. I'm no philanthropist, Shireen. A hell of a long way from it. You know damned well what you mean to me."

"You never tell me, Johnny."

"In words. Words have no meaning. No, Shireen, there's no use kidding about this. I'm a selfish bastard, and though I'd have had more respect for myself if I'd been able to keep away from you, I finally decided that after all I'm going back overseas, too. And I'm as likely to get knocked off as the next guy. And I want you. What could be simpler than that?" He was smiling again.

"That's all I ever tried to tell you, Johnny."

But she felt an intense disillusionment. It had taken them so long to reach this point, what should have been the simple beginning of their relationship. And it was he who had done it, lost them so much of the little time they could have had, and made them waste most of what they had had together.

He shrugged again, still smiling. "Well, that goes to show how much smarter you are than I am, doesn't it?"

"No," she said. "It goes to show how much of a puritan you are. I'm sorry, Johnny," she said quickly then. "I shouldn't have said that. Can I drive up with you?"

"That's what I came to ask you."

But what if I hadn't been here?

I wouldn't have been, if Dallas and I hadn't got into that fight. We'd have had dinner and gone to a show and Johnny would have come and gone—

Why could he never plan anything in advance?

She turned and went into the bedroom to change her clothes. There wasn't time to argue or change him. She'd have to accept whatever he gave her and not spoil the present by trying to make him into something different from what he was.

PART IV

Chapter 42

Whatever you wanted, theater tickets or plane reservations or an apartment, Georgia knew someone to call. Georgia was incessantly doing favors and asking favors and she had a network spread out all over the city of people she could call on who had once called on her or who might someday call on her. A week or so after Johnny had left, Shireen bought a co-operative apartment in the Sixties, overlooking the Park.

Anything she wanted—just like magic.

It made no difference that the place had been found through Georgia and that the belief in her destiny was Georgia's—for Georgia was her agent, an extension of herself, operating in her behalf.

Georgia knew a decorator, too, a Mr. Hastings, who was very expensive but so chic he was worth it. Anyway, Georgia could talk him into giving Shireen some cut prices because she had sent so many clients to him and he was grateful to her and also he was interested in writing a book about people whose homes he had decorated and Georgia said she would have a conference with him and tell him how to go about it. Almost everyone Georgia met she promised to confer with so that she could tell them how to write that book and frequently she did and sometimes the book was written.

Shireen did not want to be bothered with the details of the decorating and told Mr. Hastings so. She would make a gesture or two, speak a few words, and her will would be done. Everything was so ridiculously easy, once you had money. Especially if you did not quite realize its market value.

"I'll give you the general idea," she said, "and will you go ahead and draw up some plans so I can look at them?" Georgia had told her to ask for plans.

"Certainly, Miss Delaney." This was a big commission and Mr. Hastings was very eager and respectful.

"I want it to be dramatic," she told him, "but not flamboyant. I like green—emerald green—and ivory and dark red and bright yellow and pale gray and black and white. Definite colors, but not garish ones. I want simplicity, but a feeling of elegance. And put in a little humor, somewhere, but don't let it get whimsical. I like modern furniture, but I don't like it severe and I detest this functional stuff. But it must be comfortable. Do everything on a fairly large scale—I can't stand little chairs and tables and couches. Do I make myself clear at all?"

"Oh, quite clear, Miss Delaney. I think I know exactly what you want. I'm sure you'll be delighted."

"And—uh—" said Shireen hesitantly, for she hated to talk about money and wished that she had all the money in the world and need never think about it—"don't be too extravagant, will you? Do you think we can do it for twenty-five or thirty thousand?" The apartment had five rooms and a terrace and foyer.

"I think so, Miss Delaney. I'll try."

"Please do," said Shireen, and shook hands with him and he left.

She walked back into the living room. That's that, she thought. And wondered what the hell she could do next.

She kept herself very busy spending money.

She bought all the things she had once been afraid she might never have: silver soup tureens, pure satin quilts, English bone china, thick crystal vases, embroidered linen sheets, stacks of soft-piled towels. All the luxuries the magazines called "appointments" for fine living. Obviously enough, if the appointments were right, the life would be right, and satisfying. All she needed to do was to get into her own home, have Ed back, and everything would be wonderful. The constant fretting that went on somewhere inside her would stop automatically and she would be like a girl in an ad, smiling up from the depths of a contented soul. Or wherever it was those radiant girls smiled from.

For years Shireen had read the magazines and looked at the pictures and filled scrapbooks with photographs of the things she admired and wanted and longed to have. Often she would show them to Ed.

"Look, darling, isn't this beautiful?" she would ask him wistfully, showing him a picture of some lavish living room, or a table setting so lovely it seemed a shame to think of spoiling it by sitting down and eating. He would look at her, an intense mournful guilt on his face and say, with shame in his voice: "Maybe someday you can have it."

While she would be thinking: But I never will if I wait for you. Whatever I'm going to have in life I've got to get for myself.

For it had very early become clear to Shireen that you could not live any kind of life that was worth being lived, without these things. Mink coats, diamond earrings, strings of pearls, brocade evening gowns, lace negligees. Closets full of dresses and drawers full of gloves, shelves full of shoes, tree racks covered with hats like a fruit tree in full bloom. Then—trips to Bermuda by boat in the kind of staterooms the steamship lines advertised, flights around South America, Europe for three months if you happened to feel like it, whenever you happened to feel like it. The knowledge that these things existed in the world and were not only pictures in magazines and

308

ads, but were possessed and used by some people, made her dissatisfied and unhappy and convinced that her entire life would be a failure if she did not someday have them, too.

And in addition to all this there was fame and success. Your name in the paper if you got married or divorced or had a baby or went to a night club. The incalculable bliss of being admired and envied.

Destiny's favorite child.

Well—she was that now, all right. And almost the only one who didn't seem to think so, was Dallas Cavanaugh.

When Mr. Hastings sent her the plans for her apartment and samples of the fabric, she showed them eagerly to Dallas. "Won't it be beautiful?" she asked him.

"I guess so," he said.

Shireen was hurt. "You don't seem to like it."

"What do you need it for?"

"What do I need it for?" She laughed scornfully. "I don't actually need it, Dallas. What's *that* got to do with it?"

"It's just something to show you off, isn't it?"

"It is not!" She looked away. "What if it is?"

"It isn't a place to live in, you know."

"Of course it is! Oh, Dallas! Why must you spoil everything?"

"What do you mean? It spoils the view if you can see it clearly, but it looks great if you've only got a blurred image?"

"I never do anything you approve of!"

"What does it matter if I approve or not? The truth is—you don't much approve of it yourself. It isn't you, Shireen."

"It is, too, me! I don't want to talk about it any more." She quickly gathered up the sketches, taking them away from him. "I wish I'd never let you see them." He was smiling at her and the smile made her angry.

For a moment neither of them spoke and then he asked her slowly, "Has money always been important to you?"

"I was brought up in the United States," she snapped. "I suppose it has."

But in spite of their arguments and occasional quarrels, their friendship continued and improved and Shireen knew that in many ways Dallas Cavanaugh meant more to her than anyone she had ever known. Still, she did not fall in love with him nor, so far as she knew, did he fall in love with her.

When Johnny had been gone about a month she got a letter from him; she sat at the breakfast table in her living room and read it and began to cry. It was the first time she had been genuinely aware of him since he had gone, and now it felt as if she had been fighting off the tears all that time.

309

I want you to know, Shireen, that if you hadn't been married I'd have asked you to be my wife. I'm sure you know why it was impossible to tell you that while I was still in the States. Anyway, that part of it's over. We may see each other again sometime, I hope we will, but as I've tried to tell you, I don't believe you should ever go back to something once it's finished. And there's no kind of happiness you can get at some-one else's expense—we both must know that by now. But I hope you'll write to me—I find you're the one person in the world I want most to hear from. I can't tell you where I am or where I'm going, but I think you'll be able to figure it out. If I should never see you again—thanks.

Johnny.

Well, then—here it was. She could have had him, after all.

Johnny Keegan, who waited for no one, who would never settle down or take a wife, who was his own law and complete in his own being. As she read it, some of the plaster began to peel off the image she had of Johnny Keegan.

He should have told me this before, she thought, or not at all. It's still the same pattern. Nothing's any different. We've come as close as we ever can, and it wasn't close enough.

We were never honest with each other. We thought we were, of course, but we weren't. We were each of us watching our own in-terests and that defeated us. But why couldn't we see it? It's so easy to see. Well, we did see it. We simply didn't want to change, any more than someone going to an analyst wants to change. He wants to get rid of his troubles, all right, but he doesn't want to give up any essential part of his carefully constructed personality, all the defenses he's built against his fears. And neither did we.

Georgia smiled when Shireen showed her the letter. "You always get them to put it in writing, don't you? And you finally got what you wanted."

"No, I didn't. How do I know what he means by that or even if he means it? I'm beginning to think I was never in love with him, after all."

"Anyway, Shireen, write to him, since he asks you to. It must be pretty lonely, knowing you may be dead in a few weeks."

"So may I."

"You've got better odds."

"I'll write to him—one of these days."

"Be sure you do. And soon."

But she put the letter away and kept forgetting to write. There were so many things she had to do and the weeks went by fast. She was at her apartment every day to watch it taking form. When it had been painted and papered the rugs were put down, the draperies got hung in one room and then another, and Mr. Hastings began to move the furniture in. Each time a chair or couch or lamp or table was de-

310

livered, Shireen met Mr. Hastings there, and they watched it being put in place.

"It's so beautiful!" she told him gratefully, over and over again. "I've never seen anything so beautiful in my whole life."

"It's going to be a fine setting for you, Miss Delaney."

Shireen smiled at him, but tactfully did not acknowledge the compliment, since that would indicate she considered herself beautiful enough to suit such beautiful surroundings.

One day, when it was almost completed, a terrible thought occurred to her: What if someone someday should spoil this? Drop an ash on the rug, or move a chair out of place, or break something? That would be awful! She wouldn't let it happen. Nothing must ever mar any part of it. It must stay exactly as it was.

She ran one hand delicately over the raw silk of the couch, caressing it. I'll be so careful, she told herself. And everyone else will have to be careful too.

This apartment was the one thing she had ever felt belonged to her and only to her. Furniture, lamps, rugs, paintings, ashtrays. They could never change their minds or go away or disappoint you in any sense at all. They could not contradict you or demand anything from you. They could not keep you in suspense or make you feel ashamed. And you didn't have to be afraid or shy of them for they could never know anything about you that you didn't want known.

Dallas came in, late one afternoon, just as the men were leaving for the day. A few more pieces would still be delivered but it looked pretty much the way it was going to when it was finished. Shireen and Mr. Hastings were standing in the foyer and he was saying: "The nurseryman will come tomorrow to put in the plants around the buddha."

"Be sure he understands that the light will strike it from the left side only. . . . Hello, Dallas."

She noticed that he was smoking and wished he had left the cigarette in the hall, because the ashtrays had not been put around yet. But she introduced him to Mr. Hastings and then mentioned, casually, that there were no ashtrays. Dallas, smiling faintly, stepped back out in the hall and pushed his cigarette into the jar of sand that stood beside the elevator. Mr. Hastings, bowing slightly and smiling and then shaking hands with Dallas, went out.

Shireen turned to Dallas, who was looking around him.

The foyer was a fairly large semicircular room. The floor was lacquered black with cream-colored scrolls inlaid around the edges. In the center was a round marble-topped table on a blackamoor pedestal, and four benches stood against the walls, upholstered with crimson-and-cream-striped satin cushions.

"Well—" said Dallas. "As foyers go, it doesn't exactly haul you in, put a drink in your hand, and tell you to make yourself at home, does it?"

He walked into the living room and she followed him anxiously. "Do you like it *now*?"

He was quiet a moment. "It's overdecorated," he said. "In very good taste."

Shireen pretended to laugh. "But do you like it?" she insisted.

"Oh, sure. I like it. As long as I don't have to live in it."

"You men," said Shireen.

"How about Ed? Will he be comfortable in a setup like this?"

"Of course he will. Ed's not like most men—he has wonderful taste. He likes everything I do."

"Oh."

She led him around and showed him everything, explaining, pointing things out so that he would miss nothing. Finally they came back to the living room. He stood with his hands in his pockets and smiled at her.

"Alice in Wonderland."

She had been moving a lamp she had just noticed was some small fraction off center, and now she turned to look at him. But his smile was affectionate, so she laughed a little at herself and apologized for always setting things exactly at right angles.

"So now you're going to play house for awhile."

"No," she said, a little sharply. He did not admire her house and it made her feel personally negated. "I'm not going to play house. I'm going to *live* here."

"With every lamp exactly in line? Oh, honey—I'm sorry. I just came out of my analyst's office and I guess I must have forgotten to put some of the blocks back in place. Incidentally, what's going to happen if you and Ed have kids? There doesn't seem to be any place to put them."

Now, what was he talking about that for when the furniture had just been moved in? Couldn't he see for himself that children did not belong in a place like this? They would be completely out of keeping with the entire décor; it was a ridiculous notion.

"I'm not going to have any. I've told you that before."

"Shireen, this place will be like a goddamned mausoleum in five years. Just you and Ed—rattling around. Life has to keep repeating itself, or it begins to die. Don't you know that?"

"Will you please not lecture me about anything today?"

"What made you decide you didn't want to be a woman?"

"But I do want to be a woman. I can't imagine anything more convenient. I think it's fine."

"Children are certainly part of any woman's life."

"Nonsense. It's a matter of choice these days."

312

"Look, if you would learn one simple thing, you wouldn't need to know much else: You can't tamper with biology."

"According to the gospel of St. Freud?" she asked him with polite scorn.

"According to the gospel of old lady nature."

"Nature!" cried Shireen, and stamped her foot. "Don't talk such nonsense, Dallas! Nature makes no mistakes! You can't fool old mother nature! That's so ridiculous I won't even discuss it. Nature has made plenty of mistakes—thousands or millions of mistakes. Just because it happens doesn't make it *right,* does it? That's about as sensible as thinking that history was inevitable or for some fatalistic reason had to happen the way it did!"

Dallas shrugged. "Honey, you've got all this thought out much too patly. You're afraid of something and you're running like hell and hiding to keep yourself from knowing what it is. You could get over this dislike you have of children, you know."

"I could not!"

"Go to an analyst—find out where it comes from."

"Go to an analyst? Do you think I'm out of my mind?" And then she was instantly sorry, and put her hand over her mouth. "Forgive me, Dallas. I didn't mean that the way it sounded. Anyway, I don't want to get over disliking children. Because if I got over it I might want to have some—and I don't want to!"

Dallas burst into laughter and Shireen laughed too, a little sheepishly. He flung one arm around her and hugged her. They walked across the living room and into the foyer and, as Dallas opened the door, Shireen turned around and looked back. Her face was wistful.

"Gee," she said. "I hate to go away and leave it. But I guess nothing will happen."

"What *could* happen?"

"I don't know. Anyway, I won't worry about it. I'm sure nothing will." She looked up at him with quick questioning. "Will it, Dallas?"

"No, of course not. It'll be just like this when you come back tomorrow. And the day after. And every other tomorrow that's coming up." He rang for the elevator, watching her.

"I hope so," she said. "If anything happened to it, I'd die."

Chapter 43

Dallas went home to Santa Fe to spend a few weeks. "As soon as you get back," Shireen told him, "we'll have a big party."

They often talked, without either of them noticing it, of how "they" would do this or that—even how, when the war ended, they would do certain things the war prevented them from doing now. And then he was gone and she was busy with all the last details of moving into her apartment.

He called her several days later.

"How is it out there?" she asked him. "Are you enjoying it?"

"It's great. I've done a lot of horseback riding—and haven't written a line. Best way to avoid writing I've found so far. The first week you *can't* sit down. Look, I'll tell you why I called. I've been telling Mother about you and she thinks you sound like such a sweet girl and she's sure you must be lonesome in that great big city with your husband overseas, so she wants to know if you'd like to come out and spend a couple of weeks in the desert. She thinks it'll do you good to get out of that sooty place and have some home-cooked food." She could hear the grin in his voice.

"That's very nice of your mother," said Shireen, a little coldly, to show him she did not like the way he pretended to be able to see everything that was supposed to be kept hidden. "I'll come as soon as I can get a ticket. I'll wire you. And please thank your mother for me, won't you?" Four days later she was there and he met her at the station in Lamy, still with a grin, as if he hadn't wiped it off his face since their telephone conversation.

He looked quite different from what he had in New York. There he had always worn his uniform. Now he had on a pair of faded blue jeans with cowboy boots, a white open-collared shirt, a brown tweed sport jacket, and sun glasses. It struck Shireen as an extraordinarily becoming way for a man to dress, and that, with the tan he had acquired, made him look handsomer to her than she had ever thought him to be.

"Hi." He gave her a light kiss on the forehead and stood there a moment looking at her, breathing her perfume, smiling. "So you came."

"Of course. Tell me something—are the reporters friendly?" She waited for him to laugh and, when he did, explained: "I've been

314

saving that since I thought of it in Des Moines." She looked around.

The railway station was small, made of rough plaster painted beige-yellow with a bright orange roof and now, as the train pulled out, she could see the low rolling hills covered with dry grass and green scrub pine. The air was blue and clear with a sparkle in it and the sky floated with flat-bottomed clouds. The shadows were sharp and jagged and uncompromising, striking cleanly on the walks, the buildings, the faces.

She felt something inside her expand and respond to the vastness, as if she had been waiting for it and needing it. "Oh, Dallas, I'm so glad you asked me to come. I love New York, but it had begun to feel as though the buildings were leaning over and every time I went to a restaurant it was like trying to eat inside a kettledrum with a symphony going on."

She looked back and found him watching her seriously, but then he turned his eyes away. Shireen was sure at that moment that he loved her and to believe it gave her comfort and reassurance. If not Ed, then Johnny. If not Johnny, then Dallas. It was always a good idea to have something in reserve.

He put her bags in the car and Shireen took off her hat and tossed it onto the back seat. They drove around a curve in the road with a little church set in it, and started off toward Santa Fe, through the soft yellow hills. Shireen began chattering away about all the things she had been doing, laughing and making fun of herself—until all at once she got the feeling that what she was talking about was not real but only something she had imagined. She decided it must have been Dallas's silence which had caused it. She should have asked him what he had been doing, except that it had been implicit in her mind that out here with her not around he couldn't have been doing anything much at all.

Then she asked him, trying to make a joke of it because she was embarrassed. "You must tell me all about yourself, Mr. Cavanaugh—your neuroses, your psychoses, your traumata."

He glanced at her, smiling sourly to show his disapproval, and looked back at the road. They had come out onto a plain with mountains at the end of it, fading away in deepening layers of blue-violet. Shireen stretched her arms and legs, flexing and expanding her muscles with a kind of feline grace, and she could feel from him a nervousness and vague hostility at her sensuousness. She shook her hair and laughed.

"You know what you should do?" he asked her.

Now he was going to advise her again. "I have no idea."

"Come out here and spend a year all by yourself. Pick out a nice high mountaintop and sit there until you figure out what you are and what you're doing and what the hell it is you want from life."

315

"But Dallas," she said sweetly, "I already know."

"What!"

"More of everything!"

"Oh, gag—gad, I mean."

"Well, what's the matter with that? What I've got isn't so bad, so why shouldn't I want more of it? Are *you* so damned sure of what you want?"

"I'm sure of a lot of things I don't want. And you haven't got that much figured out yet."

"What is this? Some kind of contest? I've got this figured and you've got that and my score is higher than yours, so there?"

Dallas sighed. "I'm sorry, Shireen. You do funny things to me. I wish I didn't like you so much."

She smiled and looked at him from the corners of her eyes, and her voice lightened. "Like me, Dallas? You love me, but you're afraid to admit it. Why don't you relax—and let yourself be in love with me?"

"That crazy I'm not."

"You're afraid."

"Maybe. Anyway, I'm not afraid of being afraid."

"Well, Dallas—I love you."

He glanced at her sharply. "Don't talk that way, Shireen! What's the matter with you? You've got no business saying such a thing and you know it!"

"But why not, Dallas?" she asked him innocently. She was enjoying teasing him, seeing him uneasy and disturbed. "I do love you, so I may as well say it. There's no harm in that, is there?"

"Of course there's harm in it. You shouldn't even think it! We have no right to love each other."

"Oh," said Shireen. "My husband again. Well, it's not taking anything away from Ed if I love you. What's love? Strong friendship, that's all."

"Don't be silly. You sound like a damned little fool. The thing I guess I haven't made clear is that I'm really a hell of a Victorian guy. In my book another man's wife is strictly out of bounds."

She was quiet a moment, and then said softly: "Isn't it funny? Men are so much more romantic than women."

"If by women, you mean Shireen Delaney, put it that way. Don't talk about women and men when you mean you and me."

Suddenly she was exasperated. "Dallas, for the love of God, shut up. What did you ask me out here for, anyway?"

He looked at her and then he grinned again. He took a corner sharply and Shireen slid against the door with a slight jolt. "For my own amusement, if you want to know. I was wondering how a high-octane radar-controlled celebrity would get along out here in the

316

boondocks. No one's going to know whether you paid twenty bucks for that suit or four hundred, and Leonard Lyons almost never drops into the New Mexican Room."

Shireen laughed. Poor Dallas, he was trying so hard not to fall in love with her. He was looking for every reason he could find not even to like her.

"Those things aren't important to me, Dallas, and you know they're not."

"We'll see."

They passed the armory and drove along a pink dirt road bounded by vacant lots and a scattering of houses built like small pueblos with low adobe walls around them. In among them were some midwestern bungalows with lawns that looked as if they must put up a fierce struggle for life. He turned onto a paved street lined with poplars and stopped in front of a white wooden house with green shutters and a border of flowers. The lawn was neat and more flourishing than those on either side and there were petunias in the window box.

Shireen looked at it and suddenly it was as if she had gone back fifteen years in her life.

"Here we are," said Dallas and got out. Shireen followed him.

She stood there, frightened again, unsure, saddened, resentful. For an instant she wanted to turn and run away. She was flooded with nostalgia that carried on its surface a flotsam of memories: Her mother—washing dishes, cooking, sewing, mopping the floor. The kids she had played with, running and shouting, climbing trees, getting into fights, riding bicycles, standing in knots talking. Her father, coming home tired and out of sorts. The smells of the house, steamy on a wet Sunday with the smell of chicken frying; her father's cigar smoke filling the room while he listened to the football game; laundry soap with the clothes being washed; chocolate cake in the oven.

She felt sick and unexplainably scared, as if she were being dragged backward in time, as if she had never gone away at all. And then Mrs. Cavanaugh appeared on the porch and came forward to meet her, smiling. Shireen looked at her and the emotion brought up by memories showed in her face, wiping out the sophisticated illusion of careful make-up and smart clothes.

She went toward her, holding out her hand and smiling.

"I'm Shireen Delaney, Mrs. Cavanaugh, and I want to thank you for inviting me. It was very kind of you."

Mrs. Cavanaugh, who looked a little like Dallas but mostly like anyone's mother in a house dress and apron, shook her hand warmly. "I'm so glad you could come. Dallas has told me a great deal about you—and I'm sure you must be lonely. I hope you'll be comfortable and happy here with us."

Dallas came up to them, carrying one of Shireen's bags in either hand. He kissed his mother lightly on the cheek, looked at each of them for a moment, and they went into the house.

It was like coming home. Antimacassars on the overstuffed furniture, the smell of lemon pie, fresh flowers in all the vases, Dallas's picture on the upright piano, Mr. Cavanaugh's on the mantle, his sister's and her children's pictures on small end tables. Mrs. Cavanaugh showed Shireen her room which was small and immaculately clean with maplewood twin beds covered with white candlewick spreads, a little dressing table with some more family pictures on it, a desk, two lamps held up by colonial ladies in pink skirts, freshly laundered white dotted curtains at the window. The closet had been emptied and there were a couple of dozen wooden hangers stamped with the cleaner's name and address, and in the bathroom were several dainty white guest towels.

"Do you think it's pretty?" Mrs. Cavanaugh asked her eagerly, when Shireen exclaimed over everything. "I hope you'll find the bed comfortable."

"I'm sure I will."

"Now, if there's anything at all you want, you'll be sure to let me know, won't you? I want you to feel right at home."

"I do already," Shireen assured her, smiling.

Mrs. Cavanaugh went out to finish getting lunch and Shireen unpacked her clothes, hung the dresses and slacks in the closet and put everything else away in drawers, out of sight. When she was done no one would have known she was there at all. That was her idea of being a good guest.

Then she went to find Dallas and his mother. They were in the kitchen and Dallas was drying some dishes. Shireen came in smiling, walked over and took the dish towel out of his hand. "Here," she said. "Let me do this."

Dallas went to sit on a low kitchen ladder that was back against the wall, lighting a cigarette and sitting there watching her with a vague speculative smile on his face.

Shireen, who had come with a conscientious determination to spread light and good cheer in all directions, began talking to Mrs. Cavanaugh about her garden and the Parker House rolls she had rising under a dishcloth and whether the best pie crust was made with ice water. Or was maybe boiling water better?

Mrs. Cavanaugh kept calling her Miss Delaney until finally Dallas said, "Mother, for God's sake, her name's Shireen." Mrs. Cavanaugh laughed at that, a little nervously as if she didn't like to have her son use such language in front of a guest, and she and Shireen exchanged knowing looks on how men are: Once they go away and get out in the world they're never the same again, are they, and there's nothing you can do about it.

318

Shireen glanced at Dallas and he was watching her as if he found this whole scene very amusing. What's the matter with you? thought Shireen irritably. I know my way around in this world as well as you do.

Did he think she was *only* a dress designed by Hattie Carnegie, a face by Elizabeth Arden, a photograph in *Vogue,* a line in Earl Wilson's column, a book that had sold a million copies, a fancy apartment in New York? He was acting as if finding her here had some element of humor in it. And yet he knew that this was where she had spent her life. Maybe it was only that he knew how much she had hated it but had never understood why—partly because she did not know well enough herself to be able to tell him.

They had lunch—chicken pie with green peas in it and a crumbly crust, salad made of a pear and cottage cheese with a stem of watercress and a blush put on with artificial coloring, peppermint ice cream and chocolate cake. "I save all my points for Dallas," said Mrs. Cavanaugh when Shireen told her how wonderful the food was. "He likes to eat and he hasn't had much good food in China, I'm afraid."

"I haven't had any like this, Mother."

Shireen looked at him, looked at herself, too, and thought how different we are to our families, how different we are when we're with our families. Dallas in Paris, Dallas in Shanghai or Calcutta or New York was certainly not Dallas in Santa Fe. Good God, she thought, and felt a little tired—how far we fall short of what they expect of us. How we disappoint them. We never fit exactly the picture they have of us, and they're always hurt by it. Why couldn't we have just turned out the way they wanted, the way that would have made it worthwhile for them to have had us? But she hadn't. Probably Dallas hadn't, either, though it might seem so to his mother now when he was home after so many years away. But it wouldn't seem that way if he were there long. And Dallas must know it as well as she, for he did not come often and he never stayed very long.

Dallas had not mentioned it but Mrs. Cavanaugh told Shireen he was writing a couple of magazine articles. "If he'd only work harder. Dallas has a great deal of talent, but I'm afraid he's lazy."

"That's right," agreed Dallas. "That's why I wanted you to come out, Shireen—so I'd have an excuse to knock off work."

"Oh, now, Dallas!" protested his mother. "I don't know why you say things like that. It isn't true, Shireen. He wanted you to come—we both did—because you're such a nice girl. Why can't you be nice, Dallas?" She shook her head, as if she had tried hard to bring him up with good manners but sometimes it seemed almost useless.

They finished lunch and sat drinking coffee and Shireen wasn't sure whether or not she should smoke until Dallas offered her a cigarette and grinned at her hesitation. "It's all right, Shireen—Mother

319

resigned from the League for Protecting Our Daughters Against the Evils of Nicotine, didn't you, Mother?"

"Why, Dallas, I never even——" Mrs. Cavanaugh began to protest and then she laughed and reached over to clasp his hand. "Don't pay any attention to him, Shireen, please——"

Just like home, thought Shireen, and wondered which of them felt more out of place, she——or Dallas.

And then Mrs. Cavanaugh smiled at her son, a quick radiant proud smile. "It's so nice you're here, Dallas." She turned to Shireen. "I wish *you'd* talk to him. It's time he stopped this wandering all over the world and settled down. He should marry some nice girl like Rosemarie——she's such a sweet girl, and she'd make a wonderful wife and mother."

Shireen looked at him quickly. She had never heard him mention Rosemarie and she felt a sickness of jealousy. For Dallas, in her mind, belonged to her and to no other woman, whether she ever had him or not. How could he possibly be interested in this Rosemarie——now that he knew her?

She smiled at his mother. "I'll talk to him."

Shireen tried to insist on helping with the dishes, but Mrs. Cavanaugh was more insistent that she go for a drive with Dallas so that he could show her the town, and they went out the door hand in hand. "That was my dutiful-daughter persona," she told him gaily. "Bet you didn't know I had that one up my sleeve."

She waited until they were in the car and then she asked him, very casually: "Who's Rosemarie?"

"Didn't you hear Mother? She's a very sweet girl who'd make a wonderful wife and mother."

"And are you going to marry her?"

"I don't know. I may."

"Are you in love with her?"

"Enough."

"Enough for what?"

"Enough for marriage."

"Don't try to impress me, Dallas. You're the most sentimental guy in the world. Look how seriously you take *my* marriage."

Dallas isn't naïve, she told herself. He knows that fidelity has its limitations and that it's more important to live than to follow rules. He's afraid of me for some reason. He's afraid of me and of this Rosemarie too, and of any other woman he can't leave the next morning and forget before he's finished his coffee. And if that's it, then he's afraid of himself.

"I'm sentimental enough, all right, but as far as getting married is concerned I'm afraid I'm a little too old to be starry-eyed about that. By the time you're thirty if you've lived the way I have you've lost a lot along the way. I'm not trying to sound like a hardened old cynic but I think I'm past falling madly in love—with anyone. I don't even believe in that kind of love any more. In my opinion it's one more romantic illusion of the Western world and belongs in the attic along with Santa Claus and some of our other relics."

"Gee," said Shireen sarcastically. "Travel sure is broadening, isn't it?" She gave him a glance of disapproval and resentment, for he had just informed her that she was a failure. "I suppose Rosemarie knows all about this and won't mind in the least if you give her what's left over from your Balinese princesses and Chinese whores?"

Dallas had told her about having been very much in love with a Balinese girl, and Shireen had never been able to see why he could have fallen in love with that girl but was so cautious about giving himself up to her. She'd have seen clearly enough, though, if it was someone else he had failed to fall in love with, that time had something to do with it. Time and too many experiences and the pessimism of exhaustion.

"When I marry Rosemarie—or whoever it may be—she'll damn well know what she's getting. I've got no intention of marrying any woman until she does. If I do get married I want a wife who will be a friend and companion, one who thinks marriage is for two people and their children. And I expect to give her the best of whatever I have, certainly understanding and sympathy and fidelity. If she feels cheated with that—well, I think you might admit yourself that's not such an outlandish notion of marriage."

Shireen scowled. "The whole subject bores me. Let's talk about something else. Tell me about Santa Fe—"

Chapter 44

The next day a couple of reporters came out and Shireen talked to them with her pose of innocent surprise and self-belittling modesty. She sat perched forward on her chair, bending toward them as if with eagerness, her ankles crossed and her hands clasped in her lap except when she formed a quick descriptive pattern and then dropped them again. Dallas watched her, smiling and smoking a cigarette.

She told them she was so happy to be in Santa Fe. The people were so charming and everyone was so nice to her. No, she wasn't writing another book just now—she glanced at Dallas and saw him grin. Well, it was very nice of them to say they had enjoyed reading her book. Yes, she certainly had done an awful lot of research. Yes, her husband was overseas and she was terribly worried about him and it really wasn't possible to do much work when you were as worried as that. No, she wasn't in Santa Fe to get background material, just to visit Mrs. Cavanaugh and Dallas—they were such old friends. Oh—this dress. No, she didn't quite remember where she had bought it. No, she didn't care who they put in the movie—that was their business, not hers. Yes, it certainly had been a big surprise when her book sold so many copies. Oh, don't mention it. She was only too glad to have had them come and talk to her; it was very nice of them, really.

When they left, Shireen went to the door as if she were the hostess, since Mrs. Cavanaugh was out somewhere, and Dallas strolled over and stood behind her.

She closed the door and turned around, smiling sweetly, and looked at him. "They were nice, weren't they?" she said, still somewhat under her own spell for she felt that she had been very sweet and that they had liked her.

"I'm sure you charmed them, macushla," he said, but there was sarcasm in his voice. Shireen never knew quite when to expect it, but every so often it was there, as if she had somehow disappointed him, not lived up to some picture he had of her. "But why tell them you're going to write another book—when you aren't?"

"But Dallas—I am."

"You've always said you wouldn't. You've said it to me and I've heard you say it to a dozen other people."

Shireen walked across the room and picked up a cigarette and

322

Dallas followed her to light it. "Oh——" She shrugged and gestured, wishing he had not brought the subject up. "I was sick of it for awhile. Someday I will." She was going to suggest that they take a walk and look at the cathedral with the Cimabue over the altar.

But he stood before her with his hands in his pockets looking at her steadily, and Shireen glanced at him and then away, feeling uncomfortable, as if she were being pursued and trapped. She turned away to tap off her cigarette, and then sat down and stared back at him defiantly.

"Not at the rate you're going, you won't," he said. "Any more than I have. That's what I kept thinking, too: one of these days. But the days go by. And you don't do it." She sighed and told herself she had heard all this before somewhere sometime and didn't need him to tell her again. "Especially if the first one's been a bigger success than you had any reason to expect. That makes it tougher, you know."

"I know."

"You *have* been thinking about that then?"

"A little. Lately. But it's not really important. That won't bother me—not when I decide to do it."

Dallas laughed impolitely. "Other people, maybe. But not Shireen Delaney. Shireen Delaney isn't really human, is she?"

"Now, Dallas," she said in a childlike voice, still hoping to placate him. "That's not nice."

"I know it isn't. But it's something you'd better watch, all the same. It's not that easy, Shireen. Believe me, I know what I'm talking about. I went through something like what's happened to you, myself. I wrote *World We Lost* because I really wanted to—to say the things I didn't get a chance to say in my press dispatches. And I never expected much from it. And then it was published and all of a sudden I found myself being lionized, just the way you have been, with cocktail parties and people thinking I was an oracle and ladies' clubs wanting me to lecture them and all the rest of that crap. And I thought someday I'd do it again. But you know what? I don't—because I'm scared. What if it isn't as good as the last time? What if it doesn't sell as many copies? Oh, hell, you don't really put it that way to yourself. I was never that honest until I started lying on a couch listening to myself talk and some funny things began to come out. No, I kept telling myself the same thing you do—I was busy, there was so much to do, I was still young, I had a lot of time. And it's so damned much easier to listen to yourself talking at cocktail parties or to bend someone's ear in a bar and see on their faces right then and there that they think you're a hell of a smart fella."

Shireen sat, letting the ash burn long on her cigarette, watching Dallas and listening to him, and then she was no longer afraid of him. He had started to attack her and ended by exposing himself, and she

323

wished she could take him into her arms and comfort him. At that moment she loved him the way she loved Ed—because he seemed to need help. Because she was sorry for him and for every human being on earth and for herself as well. Her eyes watched him with brooding tenderness as he sat on the arm of the overstuffed chair, his shoulders slumped a little, his feet spread, staring away at something she couldn't see.

"I've lived most of my life alone," he said quietly. "In hotels and boardinghouses and other places that make you sick of yourself. And that gets to be an excuse, too. I'd sit around, feeling sorry as hell for myself, wishing I was somewhere else, or that I could just forget all about everything and become a hermit. Then I'd go out and maybe meet someone in a bar and talk for hours and it'd seem at the time as if the conversation was making good sense and maybe getting somewhere and I'd get some weird feeling of elation and be sure I could do anything on earth I wanted to. Including writing one more book or a hundred more books. And then I'd pay the bill and go out and each time I'd be surprised to find that nothing was any different than it had been. And still no book was even started. But all it really amounts to is that I'm scared. I might not know what words to put down. A blank sheet of paper in a typewriter has scared hell out of a lot of people. Now—I don't know. Maybe I'll just quit kidding myself."

Shireen walked over to Dallas and caught him by the shoulders. He looked up swiftly and her face was close to his.

"Dallas! If you feel this way you've got to stop this nonsense and get to work! You've only got one life—I know that's a goddamn cliché but it's something we've got to remember every single day of our lives. Because the minute we begin to forget it, we're dead! Believe me, I know what I'm talking about. I *do* know, Dallas!"

He smiled at her. "Relax. Hell, I didn't mean to upset you. I started out to talk about you. Not me. I can live without it."

"Without what?"

"That kind of success."

"No, you can't, Dallas. It's the most important there is in the world. All this talk about love—that's all nonsense. The only thing that matters is to be successful, in whatever way you think of success for yourself. Oh, Dallas, that's something I do know about!"

"Your father, you mean, wasn't a success with a capital dollar sign."

"That's right, he wasn't. And it ruined his life. It made me realize that to be successful is the only thing that makes your life worthwhile at all. Nothing is any good if you don't have that."

Dallas shook his head and got up and walked away from her. "Good God, Shireen."

324

"What's the matter, Dallas?"

She had meant what she said so sincerely, so intensely, and she meant so much to help him, to do him good. Maybe even to inspire him, so that the first thing tomorrow morning he would take himself in hand and sit down and write that second book and never worry about it any more or be frightened any more because she, Shireen Delaney, had shown him how to go about it. He might even dedicate it to her.

"You know," he said, "I don't think I can take it any more. I don't know if it was the malaria or too much liquor or too many women or the war or what the hell it is—but I haven't got enough energy left."

"For what?"

"For America. I want out of here—quick." He made a swift hard contemptuous gesture.

Shireen smiled at him pityingly and then said in a wise voice: "You can't run away from disillusionment, Dallas. It happens to you once, and you've had it. There's no way you can escape from that."

"Who in hell's escaping? That's all you hear in this country. If you take a bath you're escaping back to prenatal life. If you take a drink you're escaping into oblivion. If you stay here you're escaping and if you go back overseas you're escaping! Why do we have to keep scourging ourselves with this bloody fiction of escape! Escape where? Escape from life? There's only one way to do that that I know of, but while you stay alive there isn't much chance for escape. So why can't we at least keep the right to make a few choices without having to feel guilty if we pick the one that makes it a little easier?" He gave his head a quick shake, as if surprised to hear himself, and sheepishly tried to joke. "Hey—who wound me up?" He laughed.

Shireen was shocked. "How can you reject your own country? You're an American, no matter where you go or what you do. Everything this country is, is part of you."

"Part of you, Shireen. Did you hear what you said a minute ago? That to be successful is the only thing that makes life worthwhile?" He squinted his eyes a little, as if it hurt him to repeat the words.

"Of course."

Poor Dallas, she thought. He looked so tired. Even his voice sounded tired. Maybe some vitamin pills—she would suggest to him that he take—But he was going on talking.

"Do you realize what this means? It means that there are one hundred and forty million Americans with the idea that they must be successful. It's around them everywhere, from the time they're born. Their parents tell them about it, they get it in school and in books and magazines and newspapers and movies and over the radio and in the ads. They breathe it in and soak it through their pores. Be Successful. That's the thing to do. No matter how you do it—it doesn't even matter how you do it just so you stay out of jail. One way or another and no matter what it costs you—Be Successful."

"Well," said Shireen, thinking that Dallas was unnecessarily excited about all this. "A lot of them are."

"But not a hundred and forty million. Not even one million."

"Of course not."

"Of course not, she says. But for God's sake, Shireen—look what that does to the ones who aren't! You're one of the lucky ones—All right," he said quickly, as she opened her mouth to protest, "I know you worked hard. But you were lucky, too. And look what it's done to you. You're convinced now that you couldn't be wrong about anything at all. When Ed gets back and the poor bastard tries living with you again he's going to wonder what in the hell became of his wife. You may not know it—I didn't know you before—but you can't be much the same person you were when he went away."

"I'm no worse now than I ever was!"

He laughed. "But the difference is, now you can be as difficult as you always wanted to be. It's my guess there'll be no living with you, for any man, no matter how much patience and guts he's got."

"Dallas, that's ridiculous! You most likely got this idea from that analyst of yours, and please remember, I met *him*. The fact is, I love Ed and I'm going to be so nice to him and my money isn't going to make any difference at all between us and—"

"Oh, Shireen. Who are you kidding? It can't help but make a difference. You've changed. Of course you've changed. You couldn't help it. No one could in a country that puts the emphasis on money and success that we do."

"Well, then—what if I have? Why should success be the one thing that doesn't change you?"

"That's all I was saying, honey. But you see what it's done to you on the positive side—this notion of success we have. And it does exactly the same thing, negatively, to the ones who never get it. We keep telling ourselves there's always room at the top. That's a lot of crap. There's so much and no more. A hundred and forty million people can't very well stand on the top rung of the ladder. So where does it wind up? With most of us feeling cheated, wanting more than we can ever have, apologizing all our lives to ourselves and our friends and our families for failures that would never be counted as failures at all if we had a less cockeyed standard to begin with. Why should you have felt that your father was a failure? Why should your mother have thought so? Why would you have hated yourself and thought you were worth nothing at all if you didn't make a million bucks? It ain't healthy, honey, that's all. It just ain't healthy."

Shireen thought that Dallas was excusing himself for his own

326

failure to sit down and write another book, and also for the fact that she had made more money than he had. But she liked him too well to say so, and she was sorry for him, too. He had been hurt enough by whatever had happened to him. She smiled at him tenderly.

"Maybe you're right, Dallas. I suppose you are. But all the same, I'm glad that I'm one of the ones who's successful."

He spread his hands. "Come on, little girl. Let's go for a walk. Just one thing more—Do you realize, by any chance, that you don't know what the reasons are for what you've done with your life?"

"That's not true. I know the reasons for everything. I always have."

"No, you don't. You've forgotten. But you'd find out again—if you'd be analyzed. That's the real thing you learn in analysis: how well you've been remembering what you forgot."

"But I don't *want* to remember what I forgot, Dallas. That's why I forgot it!"

Chapter 45

They walked around the narrow little streets of Santa Fe together and Shireen conscientiously wanted to see everything and know about everything. Dallas talked to her about the town's history, told her the name of this plant and that tree. They visited the Cathedral of St. Francis, the museum, the Palace of Governors. When he was writing she read books about Santa Fe's history, its archeology and Indians, and then she talked to him about what she had read, eagerly trying to please him and win his approval. He went shopping with her and stood around smiling and bored while she bought several hundred dollars worth of silver bracelets, a broad silver Navajo belt, suede moccasins, and a painting of a misty landscape with three pink-cloaked figures going toward a church.

They went horseback riding several times in Hyde Park and one day Shireen's horse started up a steep slope, racking his way through the pine and cedar while she clung to him desperately and fought off the branches as they smashed into her face. Finally she hauled him to a stop and jumped down and the next instant he was gone, tearing the reins out of her hand, and she heard him crashing away through the trees, leaving her there stranded and helpless.

She peered down and could see Dallas looking up at her and grinning, still astride his horse. She was convinced that she would never get down and suddenly hated him for being down there safe while she was up here on top of the world.

It was all his fault anyway. He was the one who had suggested going for this ride.

"You told me you knew how to ride!" he shouted at her.

"I do!" she yelled. "It's that damned horse! *Why* did he do that? He had no reason to dash away like that!"

She looked around, hoping he would come back and somehow get her down, but he was no longer in sight and she could hear him off in the distance, blundering through the low pine branches.

"Do you want me to come and get you?"

"I can get down by myself!" she shouted furiously.

She started to pick her way carefully along the slope, moving sideways. Her hands were wet and she wanted to cry with terror and rage. If she fell she would be killed and she could see herself losing her footing, rolling over and over and finally lying at the bottom, bloody

328

and bruised, dead or unconscious, and Dallas bending over her in horror and regret.

Then he'd be sorry!

When she got a few feet from the bottom he swung down off his horse and came forward with his arms held out. She jumped and he caught her, but she instantly pushed herself back from his chest and looked up at him, her face dirty and scratched, her hair tangled with pine needles, her expression outraged and accusing.

"Are you all right, honey?"

"Yes! I'm all right!"

"Hey, what's the matter? What are you mad about?"

She stamped her foot. "I hate the wide open spaces! I detest nature! I'm never going to have anything to do with it again! Every single time I ever have something like this—" And then she stopped, for Dallas was laughing until he almost doubled over. "What's so funny?"

"You are. Oh, God, Shireen, you're the funniest little character in the world."

Instantly her anger was gone and she felt pleased with herself. These were the times when he liked her best, loved her in whatever way he did. When she suddenly betrayed herself as a child. Not when she was being a siren dangerous to men, not as a calculatedly successful and independent woman, not even when she became very serious and talked to him philosophically. Just when she returned for a moment to her own childhood and he knew that he was older and wiser than she and had nothing to be afraid of.

"Well—" she said, consciously playing the part a little longer, because it had pleased him. "Maybe I am funny. I can't help it. But what about that horse? Where's *he* gone now?"

He put one arm around her and hugged her briefly to him. "I'm afraid you don't identify very well with horses. Come on, hop up here behind me and we'll see if we can find him."

Dallas's house was close to the edge of the town and they would go out walking toward the Museum of Navajo Ceremonial Art, past it and along the roads that wound and wove behind the town. Shireen loved the subtle colors of the desert, the silver-gray camisa and rust-red earth, the blue distant hills and dark-green piñon. She liked the small cornfields and the cottonwood trees that glimmered along little straggling streams. She had a passionately romantic conviction that some vital part of her belonged to this kind of earth and air and sky.

"Maybe I love it because it's so big," she told Dallas as they walked toward home one day. It was late afternoon and there was bright yellow sun on the land, sharp long shadows and violet clouds. "If anything at all is big enough," she confided, "I like it. There's great

329

excitement just in the mere fact of bigness." They were holding hands and she looked up at him. "Don't you think so, Dallas?"

"No," he said. "I don't think so."

Shireen shrugged.

"I'm an extremist," she told him. She kicked at a little rock.

"I know. But you're getting old enough to get over it."

"Get over what? What's that got to do with age?"

"Children are never moderate about anything."

Shireen laughed at him. "You're always lecturing me and advising me. Do you really expect me to pay any attention to you? I don't have to pay attention to anyone, Dallas. Never again—for the rest of my life. That's one thing money *will* buy. Complete and absolute independence." She felt in communion with the great space around and above her, equal to it, excited by it, buoyed up out of herself. And it wrought an exhilarating defiance. She had a sudden conviction that she could destroy him completely, incorporate him into herself and annihilate him, and this seemed a right and justifiable end. She cast him a sideways speculative look, as if wondering where to begin. He looked helpless and she felt a keen surge of contempt.

But the next thing he said surprised her, as if the mouse had played a trick. "One of these days you're going to meet your own Morgan Dufay."

She scowled, and pretended not to understand him. But she had an uncomfortable sense that he knew what she had been thinking and feeling: Dallas was sometimes like a water-witcher, discovering by his senses the buried flow of sorrow and anxiety.

"I'd hate a man like Morgan Dufay," she said lightly. "I've never known anyone like him and I never would. Because if I ever met such a man I'd have nothing at all to do with him." Her face and voice became imperious, dismissing this dangerous varlet from her presence.

"He's what you're looking for, whether you know it or not. You need him, in fact, for your conscience's sake. A man you can hate without having to feel guilty about it. One of these days you'll find one you can convince yourself deserves to be hated—and then all hell's going to pop."

Shireen laughed, but she felt angry and outraged. "You talk the damndest nonsense, Dallas Cavanaugh. I'm in complete command of my own life—though I realize that's the one thing people can't forgive you for."

They had reached the crest of a low hill. Shireen walked a little ahead of him and now she stopped, standing with her feet apart and her hands on her hips, her breasts lifting high under the silk blouse as she breathed. She glanced around and saw that he was smiling, as if he had caught her playing, like a kitten, at being fierce and strong. Her eyes darkened threateningly and she looked away, back toward the sunset, refusing to acknowledge him or change the pose she had struck. All at once she wanted to be finished with him and go on. If he was not going to submit she was done with him anyway: his fear had left the victory to her.

And then she forgot about herself and became absorbed in the sunset while Dallas stood quietly beside her. Neither of them spoke for several minutes. She felt some flow of sympathy and understanding begin again between them, through their mutual response to the sunset. As if they had both become a little ashamed of their pettishness. The sun was gone and had left a mark like a streak of blood drawn by a wet finger; slowly the clouds turned gray and poured across like smoke. There were pale green bands in the sky and a fire-red line along the edge of the mesa. And they could catch the wet green smell of twilight.

She turned and looked at him and there was pleading in her eyes. Let's not fight each other, Dallas. Let's be kind. We're so lonely, each separate one of us dropped down here in the midst of eternity. We need so much help from each other and so much comfort and warmth.

But who begins? Which one of us is not afraid to begin?

She swayed a little toward him, and then saw that he instantly rejected her.

"If you'd lived in some other time," he said, "you could have ruled empires through the men who'd have loved you. You're the kind of woman who always has."

She turned away, hurt and dismayed. They started back down the hill, toward home again. "That's not what I want or ever wanted. I'll do the ruling myself." But she was instantly sorry she had said it. You're always spoiling everything, she told herself. If you were halfway smart, you'd keep these things to yourself.

Dallas changed the subject and began talking about how, when he was a kid, he used to poke around hunting for Indian relics. He talked about the Indians and their civilization which had interested him and made him want to be an archeologist until he found out that he was more interested in what was going on in his own confused world. Shireen listened and asked him questions and they got into a discussion about whether the Plains Indians had been more advanced than the Pueblos and what constituted an advanced civilization anyway. When they talked abstractly they never quarreled.

As they reached his house he stopped and turned to her. "Thanks for coming out here, Shireen. There was no way I could explain it but I needed you like hell. I don't know what it is but I'm so damned tired inside sometimes I think I won't make it."

She looked at him a long moment. "I know, Dallas." She pressed his hand. "And I'll help you if I can."

She knew that he meant a great deal to her, friendship and companionship of a kind she had never had before. They felt together so many of the same things. No matter what he told her about herself, no matter how angry she got with him, she always knew there was no cruelty in him and no need to hurt her. Only that he tried to find in her certain solutions for himself and expected her to be less of what she was and more of what he needed.

But both of them knew she could never actually help him, being in such great need of help herself. And they did not seriously blame each other for having proved inadequate, each for the other's needs. If she had been different, from the beginning of her life—and if he had been different. Then there might have been a chance. But as it was there never had been and they seemed to have known it all along. Shireen was beginning to suspect that all her relationships were doomed before they began and to accept belief in their ultimate dissolution with passive fatality.

Perhaps this was to be her punishment.

They went into the house and found it full of his mother's afternoon activity: smells of chicken frying and rolls baking, fresh flowers in Shireen's room, stacks of ironed sheets and towels still just a little damp on the kitchen table.

A few days later they set out early in the morning to drive to Taos. Shireen asked Dallas to stop at the post office so she could mail a letter.

"How often do you write Ed?"

"Every other day. But this letter is for Johnny." She laughed. "It's the first one I've written him since he went away—five months ago." There was bragging in her voice.

"What's the matter? Get into a fight before he left?" Shireen had not talked about Johnny much since he had gone.

She shrugged. "No. No fight at all. He wrote and asked me to write him, in fact. He said he wanted to hear from me more than anyone he knew."

"Then why didn't you write? I thought he was supposed to be your one true love."

She laughed again. "Is there any such thing?"

"Don't try to be cynical, Shireen. It doesn't become you. What did you tell him you're doing in Santa Fe—visiting your sick grandmother?"

"I should say not. I told him I'm visiting you and having the most wonderful time of my life and that I think you're wonderful and all the things we do—"

"What a little bitch you are."

"Me? Why—Dallas. After all, he said he wanted me to just be friendly with him and stop being in love with him and remember all my duties and obligations. I'm only doing what he told me to." She reached up one hand and flipped out her hair.

"Anyway, now I'll know what to expect."

"Oh, but I'll write to you, Dallas. You know how much I like you."

"Sure. When you don't hate me, you like me fine."

"You don't know what he did to me," she said. And as she spoke she could see herself and Johnny facing each other in the hotel the day he told her he would never see her or write to her, and she could feel again the shock and sickness. "Let's not talk about him any more."

They had lunch in Taos and then wandered around the town.

Everywhere they went Dallas stopped to talk to people, and she partly admired his easy friendliness which never seemed motivated, as hers was, by a desire to learn and know and add to himself. And partly she felt offended and jealous that he should share her time with strangers. She listened impatiently, wanting to get him away and back to herself again. She would feel happier as soon as they walked on, talking their own private conversation, pointing things out to each other, discovering and sharing. But the next moment he would stop again, to speak to a child or an old Indian, giving himself away to them.

She thought resentfully that that was the real cause of their failure together. He had squandered himself, all his life, on things that didn't matter, and now he was too much depleted. It wasn't she, after all; it was he.

At night they stood on a street corner in a crowd of people and watched some Indian dancers around a bonfire. It had turned cold and the sky was black; showers of stars fell close to the horizon. Shireen was excited by the brilliant colors, the sweep of feathers, the pounding of the drums, the stamping and swirling and the slow hard decisive movements of the dancers. The crowd pressed around them, straining and noisy, and Dallas kept his arm about her, as if to keep her from getting lost or stolen. Occasionally she turned her head and looked back at him, smiling eagerly and confidingly, to see if this had the same meaning for him it had for her.

He was standing directly behind her and as the crowd pushed around them he was pressed closer until she could feel the heavy swift beat of his heart against her back. Everything else began to blur and fade out and she could be aware of nothing but their two bodies, closer than they had ever been before. And the need to be closer still.

Suddenly she turned her head and looked at him.

He had been staring straight toward the dancers, but with a dark glazed look in his eyes as if he were not seeing anything. Then he looked down at her. Shireen's mouth was opened a little, as if she

333

were about to ask him a question, and for a few moments they stared at each other. Then he gave a quick impatient jerk of his head to indicate that she should turn around and keep her mind on the dancers. She hesitated a moment, but then obeyed him and turned back.

When it was almost time for her to leave she made a suggestion. "Why don't we drive back to New York together, Dallas?"

It was early evening and they were sitting in his car on a hillside over the town. The radio was playing some soft insinuating melody that had worked its way into both of them almost without their hearing it. Across the faint gray mass of houses smoke drifted west with a soft wind as the piñon fires were lighted and there was a smell of recent rain on the desert, like wet incense.

They had been sitting there for several minutes without talking, Dallas on one side of the car with his arm along the seat back, Shireen leaning against the door and looking out. She felt strangely peaceful and happy and yet she wanted to cry.

Dallas did not look at her, but after a moment he answered softly. "We can't do that."

"It would be a nice trip, Dallas. It may be the last thing we'll ever have."

"I know. But it wouldn't be a good idea. Someone might recognize you. Gossip would get around." He smiled. "Didn't I tell you about the nightmare I had the other night—that we were being chased by Walter Winchell?"

They both laughed.

But she refused to accept it. "We could stop in auto courts and if we were careful no one would ever know it."

"No. I know what would happen. It's better for both of us if we keep it like this."

"Why is it better?"

He tangled his fingers in the ends of her hair. "Look, honey—I've had enough affairs. I am not interested in proving to myself that I can still do it. If I need a lay I go find some bimbo who'll accommodate me, for cash or because she wants it herself."

Shireen jerked away from him. "Dallas, really. Sometimes you're disgusting."

He laughed. Then he began to mimic her. "Oh—sex. Of course. Common biological phenomenon. No use being sentimental or romantic about it. Husbands, and all that rot. Simply a matter of men being male and women being female and let's all look it in the eye without wincing. We've very cool and scientific about it, aren't we? Until some raw spot is touched. And then: *Dallas,* you're being disgusting. You still prefer to think that sex and love are synonymous. Well, I suppose you can't help it. All women do. It's their stock in
334

trade—the stock of the respectable ones, anyway. Otherwise, there are a hell of a lot of lazy useless females who would have to quit trading on being wives and mothers and sitting on their fat cans squawking for that electric dishwasher and mink coat, and give a little something to their men. Three-fourths of them even contrive to be frigid."

"Not me, Dallas," said Shireen, and smiled at him maliciously. "I've been told I'm a good lay."

"I don't doubt it. You probably are. You're so goddamned egotistical you'd most likely cut your throat if any man ever got out of bed with you without being convinced it was the greatest thing that ever happened to him." He looked at her a moment longer, smiling. "You're really a whore at heart, Shireen."

"Well. That's a nice thing to say to me." But she was, nevertheless, mysteriously pleased. "Anyway," she said, "you know what I think of women."

"What you think of them? And what are you, in that case? Some superior separate species? The Shireen Delaney species?"

She laughed. "I suppose. At least I've always thought that men were superior to women—except me."

"Why don't you write a book about yourself in the twentieth century—like you wrote one about yourself in the eighteenth?"

"I told you that book had nothing to do with me. Most people haven't got enough imagination even to imagine that anyone else has any."

"Still, it was *your* imagination, wasn't it? You wrote down all your own daydreams and it turned out they're also the daydreams of several million other women who are goddamned mad and resentful because it's a man's world and there's nothing much they can do about it. Why don't you relax, Shireen?"

"Relax!" she cried. *"Everyone* says that to me—*all* the time. And why, I'd like to know? You can't relax, it's impossible. This is no century to relax in. I'm sick of the word!"

"Well," drawled Dallas, "don't relax then. You won't anyway. You've got yourself wound up tight and one of these days you're going to snap. I'd hate to be around when that happens."

She glared at him. "You won't be. Don't expect to change me, Dallas Cavanaugh. Why should I change—for you or anyone else? Everyone else in my life comes and goes, but *I* stay right here with me."

She turned away from him and stared off into the distance. It had grown dark. And almost immediately she was sorry she had spoken that way to him. He was going away soon and she would miss him— for all the rest of her life.

"Dallas," she said, and reached out her hand to touch him. "I'm

335

sorry. Let's not quarrel. There's nothing for us to quarrel about. Let's just be nice to each other. Can we, please?"

And Dallas, without answering, put one arm around her shoulders and drew her to him. She curled her legs up and lay her head on his chest, clasping the lapel of his coat with one hand. They did not speak at all for several minutes, though from time to time she moved her head against him, like an animal seeking comfort.

"It's funny," she said, feeling her way along in her thoughts as she tried to put them into words. "But I guess I must have expected that if I got my book published and made a lot of money, everything would be solved. And nothing is, after all. I'm still no happier than I was before—maybe not even as happy as when I was working, because then I at least had a lot of illusions that I don't have now."

"Poor baby," he said, and his hand was stroking her hair absent-mindedly, as if he was not aware of doing it. "Of course it couldn't do any good. Because it has nothing to do with whatever is really eating at you."

She was quiet a moment. "I guess maybe the people who are most successful are only the ones who are the most scared."

She looked up at him then and, after a moment, he looked down, but somewhat reluctantly, as if she had compelled him. The thought occurred that he was sorry for her and that he pitied her as any grown-up pities a child, for its helplessness and dependence; and so he was not afraid of her.

He kissed her, quickly and violently, the first real kiss he had ever given her, with his tongue searching in her mouth. Her arms went around him, holding him with a determination that this time he should not escape. She would capture him and he would never escape from her again—he would need her the rest of his life. Suddenly he broke away, moved back and turned the key in the ignition.

His movement was a rude shock and automatically her hand reached out to cover his.

"Dallas! Don't do that! Don't go!"

He flung her hand off. "If that happens, I'm not sure I'd ever want to leave you and—oh, the hell with it! You're *married,* aren't you?" He gave her a quick angry glance, backed the car out swiftly, swung it around and started off up the highway.

Shireen smiled to herself.

"Dallas," she said softly. "You forgot to turn on the lights." He reached out and gave the switch a jerk and the road ahead of them flared in sudden brilliance. A rabbit skittered across and disappeared into the darkness again.

Chapter 46

Shireen sat curled up on a chair in the living room, trying to keep her mind on the book she was reading—another history of New Mexico. Dallas was in his room working and she could hear the faint efficient click of his typewriter. Mrs. Cavanaugh had gone to some woman's luncheon and would not be back for two or three hours and Shireen kept waiting for Dallas to come out.

She was leaving the next day and she felt angry with him.

Why should he keep on with his damned work when she would be gone so soon? Why was he willing to give up two or three hours with her? And why was she always having to wait for men, wait for them to finish something more important or even less important, before they could give their attention to her?

At last he came out, looking very pleased because he had completed the article, and gave her the last few pages to read. "I'll finish something in here," he said, and went back.

Shireen was impressed each time she read something of his, though it never quite seemed to have been written by him. He wrote so well, so much better than she could, and so differently from what she would have written. It was clear enough that their lives were set in opposite directions, and the degree of difference made her feel inferior. She should have his interests, be more like him and less like herself; for she felt that he was essentially better than she was.

When she had read it she got up and walked into his bedroom. His back was to her and he was going over some pages, making corrections. "This is very good, Dallas. You've got a wonderful political sense."

"Thank you." He said it gratefully. Then he got up and turned to face her, his hands in his pockets. "Now, if I only had a little horse sense."

They stood looking at each other, and the small room seemed to have an insistent almost oppressive intimacy. Shireen leaned back with her hands braced against his desk, watching him and smiling.

"Dallas—" she said after a few moments. "What are you afraid of?"

He turned and lit a cigarette. "You. And you damned well know it."

"But why?" Her eyes were wide open and innocent.

337

"Don't stand there and look at me like that. Because I'll tell you right now I'm not going to——" He stopped and ground the cigarette out, angrily.

"You're not going to what, Dallas?" Her voice was soft and the words came out faintly, with her breathing.

"I'm not going to sleep with you!"

"Well? I haven't asked you to." She was still smiling.

"Oh, yes you have. Everything you do and say and every way you look asks for it."

She made a clucking sound. "You men. Always so suspicious."

"And isn't it a pity we are? Because if we weren't you could take us home, one at a time, and gobble us up at your leisure——without the nuisance of ever having one of us try to escape and save his hide."

Shireen laughed. "Dallas, you're wonderful. You're the funniest man in the world."

"Yeah. I knock myself out. I'm a scream all right."

"But you're wrong, Dallas. I'd never hurt you. I love you."

"You do not. Look, Shireen, I like you better than any woman I've ever known. There are some things about you that are very fine ——but there are some others that scare the hell out of me."

"I don't want to scare you, Dallas. I think too much of you. In some ways, I think you mean more to me than anyone else in the world."

"I know. And if you weren't married I might be a big enough fool to ask you to marry me. But I'm damned glad you are because it keeps me from making the biggest mistake of my life."

"You keep talking this way, Dallas. As if there were something sinister about me. Why should I want to harm you? And how could I, after all——if you've got any command of yourself?"

"I don't think you want to, at least you probably don't know you want to. But that wouldn't keep you from doing it. I don't believe you can help yourself. Because you're essentially destructive. You can't have any deep-going relationship that doesn't have to end with you in complete possession of the other person's mind and body and everything he thinks and is. Wait a minute——I want to say this, we may as well understand each other. And once you've done that it's over for you and you can go on. But what about me, or whoever the poor bastard may happen to be? I've thought about this a lot, Shireen, and for awhile I was afraid I wouldn't be able to help myself. If I slept with you I'm still not sure I could. Now——are we straight?"

Shireen was watching him sadly, almost as if she were being punished. It is true, she thought. It's all true. But how did he find out? And do other people know it? Does Johnny know it? And then she was defiant again.

"It's too late now, Dallas. Because no matter what happens, for the rest of your life you will have known me."

She saw the yearning in his eyes and thought contemptuously: he doesn't even know what's happened to him. There's always something missing. I don't think I ever really want it to last anyway.

I'll give them up, she thought—as if men had become a bad habit she must break—and go on with my life.

But the next morning when they sat under the hot sun in his car at Lamy, waiting for the train, she felt mournful and lost. She did not want to leave him; she wanted to cling longer. Where would she go next? What would she do? Who would she find?

"I can't imagine how I'm going to get along without you," she said.

"You'll get along okay. That's one thing I'd never worry about." He sounded lazy and amused. Maybe he was trying not to feel anything that would hurt him, while she wanted to feel this moment to its deepest essence, everything there was in it.

"Remember all the things we've done together?" she went on. "Going to the Russian Easter services and the newsreels and all the plays and walking around the city and talking and driving in Central Park until five in the morning. What will I do without you? Oh, Dallas—it's going to be terrible." It seemed at that moment that Dallas Cavanaugh was the one person she could not get along without, and that the things they had done together were the only significant ones in her life.

"Honey," he said, "this will be as nothing at all in a high wind, five years from now."

"But I'm not interested in five years from now. I'm interested in today, right this minute—and right this minute I'm miserable at the thought of not seeing you any more—not for a long long time, and maybe not ever!"

"You're making too much out of it. Take it easy. You're only making it harder for yourself."

"But, Dallas—I don't want to make it easy for myself. I like you and you're going away and I don't *want* to feel nothing. I want to feel terrible—and I do!"

He was grinning. "One thing about you, Shireen, you'll never die of boredom."

"No," she agreed. "But I may die of hypertension. Oh! Here comes the train!"

He got out and she followed him, watching with dismay as the train came plunging down the track, straight at them; then she turned away, shutting her eyes hard and putting her hands over her ears.

The train stopped. A porter got off and Dallas went to give him her bags. She began to feel a sense of panic. In five more minutes she would be on—she would be gone.

He turned to her and she looked at him pathetically. "I hate trains," she said. "I always have. They always mean you're losing something."

"Good-by, darling. I'm glad you came." There were tears in her eyes now; all at once he seemed to make up his mind. "I want to tell you something before you go. You're everything any man could ever want."

"I am?" she asked him, staring in wonder. "Then why is it no one wants me, do you suppose?"

She had spoken in clear honesty and bewilderment, and his face winced a little. He bent hastily and kissed her on the mouth. "Go on. Get aboard."

"Oh, Dallas—"

"All aboard!" the conductor shouted.

He took her arm and steered her to the train and then lifted her by the elbow. She went, like an automaton, and stood at the top of the steps looking wistfully down at him, as if from a prison. The train began to move and she glanced frantically around, as though she had not believed until this moment that it would go and carry her away from him. She dashed off the tears with the back of her hand. He was walking along beside her, still grinning, but now it looked as if the grin was to keep any other emotion from showing.

The train moved faster and faster. He ran beside it for a few yards until it got going too fast for him to keep up. He broke off and stood there and she leaned out, waving at him, crying. She stayed until she could no longer see him. And then she turned around and went to locate her bedroom, frowning and keeping her eyes away from everyone she passed.

He's gone, she thought. That's over.

She made a great many resolutions while she was on the train, and told Georgia about them when she got to New York.

"I've got to get myself in hand again. This drifting has gone on long enough. I've wasted two years of my life lately."

Georgia smiled. "Wasted how?"

"By not writing, I guess. I begin to get the feeling that it's the only thing in my life I really count. Everything else—" She made a quick exploding gesture with one hand and blew a puff of air. She laughed. "It doesn't even matter that I'm not very good at it. I do the best I can and though it's never what I want, it satisfies something. I suppose you have to have some sort of excuse for living the way I do. And maybe that's all anyone who writes or paints or sculpts is doing anyway—excusing themselves for refusing to live like other people or be like them."

"I'll say one thing for you, Shireen. No matter what you do, you could never be a real bitch—because you're so completely honest."

They both laughed. "So now that all your men are gone and there are no new ones that interest you, you'll write again. The captains and the kings depart."

"Something like that. I never have been able to mix men and writing, I know that. Something goes wrong with the formula. By the time I started writing *The Falcon* I'd known Ed for so long that nothing new was happening between us. And when I met Johnny I was almost finished."

"And what if Ed comes back?"

"That doesn't matter. Nothing very new could happen to us. I know all about him and he knows all about me."

"You don't know him the way he is now—and he won't know you. A war's happened to him, and success has happened to you. There'll be more difference than you think."

"Well—we'll see." She did not believe that Georgia was right this time, and could see no reason to give it much thought now in any case.

Two weeks later she got a telegram from Dallas:

SHOVING OFF SOONER THAN EXPECTED WONT GET BACK TO
NEW YORK WILL TRY TO CALL YOU FROM FRISCO LOVE
DALLAS

She read it and sat for awhile, quietly, feeling a soft tender sadness. But she had accustomed herself to the idea when she left him in Santa Fe. She wished that things could have been different between her and Dallas, between her and Johnny, between her and everyone she had ever known. Somehow, somewhere, they had all failed each other. I wonder if it was my fault, she thought, and then stopped herself. It wasn't anyone's fault. It just was. We couldn't do any better. We didn't know how.

Next time I'll look for the signs.

She began to stroll around the living room, carefully examining it again.

No matter what happened, no matter who she lost or how lonely she became, she had this apartment and everything in it. And each morning, when she first got up, she went through every room, admiring each piece of furniture, each painting and lamp and vase, smiling and happy and reassured. For she could never quite believe everything would still be there the way she had left it the night before. And throughout the day she would make several tours of inspection, before she went out and when she came home; or she would stop whatever she happened to be doing and go through the entire place again, to convince herself.

She alternated between wonder and unbelief that this should

341

actually be hers, everything in it paid for and owned for the rest of her life—and a kind of arrogant assumption that of course it was hers and had always been hers, by right, if not in fact. *This* was the kind of place she belonged in and would have had, but for some unlucky fate that had given her the wrong set of parents, or else had not permitted them to have what they should have had.

The living room was large and instantly impressive.

It was cool and clear, not cluttered with too much furniture or too many knicknacks, purposeful and definite. The walls were pearl gray, the carpet pearl gray, and the thin gray curtains across the windows —looking onto Fifth Avenue and the Park on one side and uptown on the other—seemed to lend enchantment to the city as a veil does to a woman's face.

There was a tremendous dark-red raw-silk couch against one wall and opposite that stood a black marble fireplace, with green and gray striped love seats on either side, facing each other. Between them was a low black lacquered table, shaped like an artist's palette, with plants growing from a bottom shelf to fill the cut-out curve. Two couches, dark-red, made a half circle facing the fireplace.

A grand piano stood in one corner and there were several other chairs—white with sputtering short green fringe, white chintz with a chartreuse and green and dark-red pattern, another one covered with a rough green fabric. Some of the end tables were lacquered black and some were made of grayed rubbed wood. The lamps were straight crystal columns or rococo plaster painted white and there were several big vases full of dark-red roses and polished magnolia leaves. Against one wall stood a scarred stone buddha about five feet tall, surrounded with plants and caught hold of by vines, as if it had been picked up just as it was in some demolished shrine, already half reclaimed by the jungle.

The whole thing gave her a sense of safety, as if she had become a fortress.

And, looking at it, she forgot about Dallas. He had not been very important, anyway. She had done with him what she had done with every other man she had known—magnified his importance to her and given him a significance he had never had. She had done it with Ed and Johnny, even Jack, for awhile. And what she had suspected long ago she had now proved to be true: the need for any one person was always an illusion. For the world was full of people, and if one of them disappeared, there would soon be another to take his place.

"I get along without you very well," she hummed, and walked into the library.

All of you, she said to herself.

She stood and looked at her desk, admiring it. It was the biggest desk she had ever seen, with a silky polished surface of dark-green

342

Hours	Monday	Tuesday	Wednesday	Thursday	Friday	Saturday	Sunday
9:00 9:45	Dress.	Dress.	Dress.	Dress.	Dress.	Dress.	
9:45 10:00	Breakfast.	Breakfast.	Breakfast.	Breakfast.	Breakfast.	Breakfast.	
10:00 10:30	Secretary.	Secretary.	Secretary.	Secretary.	Secretary.	Secretary.	
10:30 11:00	Study French.	Study French.	Study French.	Study French.	Study French.	Study French.	
11:00 12:00	Piano lesson.	Practice piano.	Practice piano.	Practice piano.	Practice piano.	Practice piano.	
12:00 12:30	Newspapers.	Newspapers.	Newspapers.	Newspapers.	Newspapers.	Newspapers.	
12:30 1:00	Lunch.	Lunch.	Lunch.	Lunch.	Lunch.	Lunch.	
1:00 5:00	Shop. Galleries.	Write.	Write.	Write.	Write.	Write.	
5:00 5:30	Change clothes.	Change clothes.	Change clothes.	Change clothes.	Change clothes.	Change clothes.	
5:30 7:30	Give cocktail party.	Read.	Read.	Read.	Read.	Read.	
7:30 8:30	Dinner.	Go out.	Dinner.	Go out.	Give dinner.	Dinner.	
8:30 12:30	Optional.		Theater. (Movie)			Concert. (Opera)	
12:30	Undress.	Undress.	Undress.	Undress.	Undress.	Undress.	
1:00	Sleep.	Sleep.	Sleep.	Sleep.	Sleep.	Sleep.	

lacquer and on it there was nothing but what the decorator had intended: a big crystal inkwell, a bowl of white and yellow daisies, some silver-framed photographs, a telephone, and half a dozen letters stuck into a silver English toast rack. This room was smaller, and though it had been decorated just as carefully it had considerably more warmth and less elegance. Two of the walls had bookshelves reaching from floor to ceiling, the carpet was beige and there was a small coral couch and big square chairs in light yellow-green.

It's all mine, was underneath everything she thought and felt.

She sat down at the desk now and took out a pen and ruler and some yellow paper, leaned forward with the fingers of her left hand run through her hair, and began to work out her schedule. She had been thinking about it, juggling hours and days in her mind, and now that she had it about the way she wanted she was going to write it down and see how it looked. She smiled a little as she worked, feeling a great satisfaction as the neat symmetrical graph took shape. The pattern was strict and meticulous and gave her more to do than she could comfortably get done so that she would have no free time for idle thinking—worrying, was what she meant. It accounted for every minute.

I'll be so busy, she thought. And so useful. I won't lose a minute. Every single one will count for something, give me something I need, add something to me. It was like building a cage around herself—a cage that was infinitely protecting but not confining, because she could break out of its walls as easily as if they were made of toothpicks. She was building it herself and putting herself in it—so it could not frighten her.

She worked for an hour or so, drawing the graph, and at last she sat back and looked at it, her head tilted to one side, smiling with a look that was almost affectionate.

Why, it even looks pretty, she thought, gazing at it in awe-struck delight. *This* is what I should have done long ago.

Chapter 47

She took her schedule and stood up to go across the hall and give it to her secretary.

When she got back from Santa Fe, Shireen had decided that she was so busy she would need a secretary and she had hired one, a woman of about forty-three who talked fast when she came to be interviewed so that Shireen was a little frightened by her and decided she must be very efficient. Her name was Mary Carlisle and she came every morning at nine-thirty. It was her duty to make out checks, hire and oversee the two servants, keep the house in perfect order, arrange the flowers, take telephone messages, answer letters, run errands, and index the notes Shireen took from whatever books she read.

By the time Shireen had reached the door, however, it occurred to her that it was unsuitable for an employer to go running to an employee, so she picked up the telephone, switched on the interhouse system, and pushed the buzzer. She asked Mary to come into her study and then leaned back in her chair again, lighting a cigarette.

Mary came promptly and Shireen looked up at her, smiling. She was eager to have Mary like her but could not be sure that she did.

"This is my schedule," she said pleasantly, extending it toward her. "Will you please make up three copies, and keep one for yourself? I'll start on it next Tuesday."

Mary took it and stood for a moment looking it over, and then Shireen saw her smile and slowly lift one eyebrow. "Afraid you'll forget to undress before you go to bed unless you remind yourself?" Mary asked her.

Shireen felt a little nervous, but pretended to laugh. "Oh, I've always been like that. I love schedules. They seem so efficient or something, don't you think?"

But a surprising thought had come into her mind. This woman doesn't like me. These cracks she's been making from time to time— she meant something by them after all. But why, for heaven's sake? What have I done to her?

"What happens if your husband gets back?"

"Why, he'll be working, too, of course. We've never interfered with each other." She had answered before it occurred to her that it was none of Mary's goddamned business.

Why is it, she thought now, looking at her, that flat-chested women always wear flat-heeled shoes? And then realized that she was only getting back at Mary by thinking something unkind because Mary's scorn had hurt.

Take it easy, she warned herself.

"Anything else?" Mary asked her.

"No, that's all. By the way—did you tell Delia that that silver tray is tarnished?"

"I did," said Mary. "And she was terribly sorry. She polished it this afternoon. I watched her."

Shireen glanced away, unaccountably embarrassed. "Thanks. I'm going out as soon as I change my clothes. I'll see you tomorrow."

Mary smiled at her and left.

Shireen sat and frowned at the closed door. That woman, she thought, has a face like a pudding thrown at a wall. But then she changed her clothes and went to a cocktail party and forgot all about her.

Shireen woke up happy and purposeful on Tuesday morning. She felt that some long trance had come to an end, that she had rescued herself from inertia, and that now she was going to begin to live the most satisfying life of all. She was as convinced of this as she had been a few months ago that the only way she could tolerate living was to be completely purposeless and try everything that came along, like a trout snapping at flies.

Delia woke her at nine, having been advised by Mary Carlisle of Miss Delaney's new schedule and its extreme importance, and while Shireen took a bath and got dressed she listened to a news broadcast. From time to time she glanced at her watch, to be sure that everything was on time.

She had breakfast and then went into her study and called Mary. Mary came, wearing her same gray tailored suit, with a notebook in her hand. Shireen dictated answers to half a dozen fan letters.

When she had finished that she said: "You'll have to call the agency and get another couple. I don't like Delia's cooking. It gets worse every day."

"They told me at the agency, Miss Delaney, that the woman was a very good cook."

"Well," said Shireen, and wished that Mary would not argue with her, "she isn't. And she's sloppy in the kitchen."

"It looked pretty clean to me when I was out there this morning. They're trying hard to please you."

"They've got to do more than try. The mirrors in my bedroom have had some smudges on them for the last two days. I won't have anything less than perfection."

Mary whistled impolitely.

Shireen wished she could think of something to say to win her over to her side. She had tried to be very nice to her and believed that Mary Carlisle should be a devoted and interested secretary. But somehow she wasn't.

"I've got too much to do," Shireen went on, "to bother myself with household routine. I want it to run like a clock and I don't want to have to wind it."

"It's not easy to get good servants nowadays, you know. The days when they were glad to get any kind of job at all are over. The agencies don't even have many names on their lists. And they simply won't work the way they used to. I know, because I've been hiring servants for years. Unfortunately, you're getting your first experience with them at a time when it's very difficult."

I'll be damned, thought Shireen. Now she's telling me I'm nouveau riche and don't understand these things.

It was too bad the newspapers reported every detail of the life of anyone who became successful. But what Mary said was true, after all, and she knew it. She wanted servants to take care of the things she needed but she was uneasy with them and with the whole idea of some people existing to serve other people. It made her feel intensely guilty and she did not want to see them any more than necessary or even talk to them if she could avoid it. She preferred to use someone else as her intermediary; but Mary seemed to line herself up with them.

"Well," said Mary, "I'll see what I can do. But we've had two couples at this house in the last four weeks."

"I don't care how many we have," insisted Shireen. "I'll keep changing them until I find someone who will do things exactly the way I want them done."

Mary shook her head. "I guess you can't help it. I suppose getting a lot of money all at once would give anyone a sense of power."

"This has nothing to do with a sense of power, Mary, really it hasn't," said Shireen, trying again to be placating. "It's just that I've worked hard for what I have and I want things to be right. I've always been a perfectionist." And that's the difference between us, she added in her mind.

"I guess that must be it. Because I've sometimes thought it would be nice to have the things that you and other people like you have. I'd never actually envy you, because I don't think there's much difference in people so far as talent or ability is concerned. I've talked to you and I know I'm as smart as you are. My brain is just as good as yours. But I want to enjoy life a little more. Everything seems pretty grim with you."

Good God! thought Shireen. This damn fool woman! Why don't I fire her?

347

But she didn't because she was afraid that, since Mary disliked her, all she would have to do would be to tell her she was fired—and the cap would be off the steam valve. She was convinced that that would be the opportunity Mary had been waiting for to let loose with exactly what she thought about Shireen Delaney, and Shireen was afraid to hear it. So she must keep trying to make Mary like her and turn her into a friend instead of a thinly disguised enemy. Otherwise she would have failed, because Mary must like some people, and so she must like her, too.

"Oh, it's not so grim," apologized Shireen. "I've been taking things pretty easy for a long time now. Anyway—" and she prepared to get rid of her, for Mary made her feel nervous and uneasy and full of self-doubts—"after lunch today I'm going to start working on a new book. And I don't want any interruptions of any kind—unless the house catches on fire. Don't call me for anything less."

"Okay. Genius mustn't be disturbed. I've heard about that." Mary got up and started slowly out of the room, as if she was thinking about something but had not quite made up her mind to say it. Then she turned around. "So you're starting the new book today, huh?"

"Yes." She stared levelly at Mary, wondering what she was getting at now.

"Tell me one thing. Aren't you nervous?"

Shireen's face remained expressionless. "No," she said quickly. "Why should I be nervous? You just sit down and begin writing, that's all."

"But after the big success you had with the other one. Doesn't it make the second one tougher? There are plenty of people who'd love to see you fall flat on your face."

Shireen blinked her eyes. Were there? That was a surprise. She had some secret notion, if she ever stopped to think about it, which she never had, that everyone was rooting for her. Little Shireen would do it again.

Well—it was obvious Mary must be hoping she'd fall flat on her face.

"I suppose there are," said Shireen. "But I'm afraid I can't bring myself to worry much about that."

"Maybe someone's sticking pins in your image," said Mary, and she went out and closed the door.

Shireen sat there and felt how hard her heart was beating. She detested the knowledge of her own heart pounding away inside her and it made her furious with Mary for having upset her and caused it. I'll be sensible about this, she thought. The poor woman—nothing to look forward to but going home to a lousy little flat and that drunken bum she's married to. While I've got everything she wants in the world. That's why she hates me. She can't help herself. Anyway, I'm not going to think about that now. I'm not going to think about anything. I'll study my French lesson and practice the piano and have lunch and then I'll begin writing. But when her mind came to the idea of writing it closed up and refused to go any further.

Shireen had lunch in her study on a tray, and while she ate she read a few pages of Toynbee, Volume One. She would peck away at Toynbee page by page and in a couple of years or so she would have digested the whole thing, and added that much more to herself. She rang and the butler came and took away her tray. She looked at him and smiled and thanked him, wondering if Mary had told them that they were fired. She couldn't tell, by his face.

Damn servants anyway! Why didn't they simply do their jobs as well as she expected them to? Why should they be so much trouble? Well, she wouldn't think about that, either. She glanced at her watch: three minutes of one.

She walked quickly into the living room, crossed it and went out onto the terrace where she stood at the railing, looking down at the people dragging themselves along in the summer heat or sprawling around on the park benches and in the grass. Some of them were lying with newspapers over their faces; nurses sat gossiping and watching the children play; an old man was throwing crumbs from a paper bag to a circle of pigeons that had gathered round. It looked to her as if everyone in the world was being lazy and enjoying life, waiting for what would happen to them next and out there, ready, so that it could happen.

She raised her head to watch some birds in silver flight up Fifth Avenue, looking at them in wondering admiration for their beauty and freedom.

For the first time in a year and a half she was once more emotionally aware of what it had meant to her to write that first book. How much she had missed. How she had disciplined herself and shut herself away from the world almost as if she were in a convent. How she had never let herself get away with anything at all: not with being tired or not in the mood, not with diversions she might have preferred, not even with being sick.

That's what people don't know about, she thought resentfully, looking at them down there in the park and on the streets. You hand anyone who's got three dollars to spend a part of your life. Four years and a half she had handed them. Four years in which she had not moved or changed or done anything else at all. Four years that she had given up completely.

And all at once those years, which she had tried to forget—had tried to make up for in as many ways as she could find, solacing herself with Johnny and a mink coat, Mike Callahan and her expensive apartment, cocktail parties and a pair of diamond earrings, Dallas

349

Cavanaugh and servants, custom-made clothes and Paul Worth, paintings and silver and hours of talk with dozens and hundreds of people—all at once those four and a half years were back again.

And she wondered if it had been worth it for what she had got.

Her mind went back to Marron and her friends in school who had gone along, getting married to nice young men like Ed who sold cars or insurance, were lawyers or doctors, and had had babies and played bridge and bought a little house and furnished it and hoped someday for a bigger house and waited for their husbands to get a raise, and by now the oldest child was maybe four or five—

Holy God! she thought, with sudden shock.

Of course it was worth it! I could never live that life.

I'd have gone crazy if I'd had to live that life. There's something in me that makes it impossible. Maybe I've missed part of the world, but they've missed much more than I have. They don't even know about the kind of life I have now—and I know all about theirs.

She looked around her: What if it isn't everything I want?

I guess it isn't anything at all I thought it would be when I first wanted it, but it's better than *that*. And anyway, now I'm in it and I've got to stay in it. It would be a hell of a long way down to fall. I'd rather have problems with the income tax and Mary Carlisle's jealousy, than not have to pay an income tax and not have anything for anyone else to envy.

She looked at her watch again. It was one o'clock, exactly.

And she turned away and left the terrace without a backward glance, crossed through the living room again—for the first time without seeing it—and went into the library and closed the door. She sat down and took out her portable typewriter and put it on the desk, opened it and set the top on the floor beside her. She noticed that her hands were a little damp and wiped them off against each other. She opened a drawer and took out a stack of yellow paper and laid it there beside the typewriter. Then she looked at it for a moment.

All that paper was blank now, and it was just a ream. Only five hundred pages. It looked like quite a bit, but she knew better. It was nothing at all. As the days and weeks and months went by she would cover those pages with words, and she would finish one draft and read it and realize how terrible it was and go back and do the whole thing over again, trying to make it some better, and then she would do it again and again. Suddenly she looked at the stack of paper as if she had come face to face with an enemy in the dark.

And she was appalled by that other Shireen Delaney, the one who had already done this. The one who was back there in the past somewhere, but who seemed another person altogether from the one who sat here at the desk today.

How did I ever do it?

How did I ever write all those pages?

Because now I haven't the slightest idea even how to begin. What will I write about? What can I say when I don't know anything? Whatever made me think about doing this again? I was right when I made up my mind I never would.

But she knew part, at least, of what was making her do it again.

She needed more money. The income tax had shocked her, in spite of all the warnings she had been given, for she had somehow not been able to believe the government would actually take that much money away from her. And now, though she had paid for the apartment and the furniture and everything in it, she had only about fifty thousand dollars left; and the way she was living, that wouldn't last more than two or three years.

What do you write for, Shireen? she asked herself. Love—or money? Money, I guess, when you come right down to it.

Money, and one thing more. To be *Shireen Delaney*. Not just Shireen Delaney or, worse than that, Mrs. Edward Farrell. There was no such person in the world as Mrs. Edward Farrell.

She picked up a sheet of paper and rolled it into the typewriter with a quick jerky motion. And then she sat and looked at it, remembering what Dallas had said: "Not at the rate you're going, you won't . . . Especially if the first one's been a bigger success than you had any reason to expect . . . I thought someday I'd do it again . . . But you know what? I don't, because I'm scared . . . What if it isn't as good as the last time? What if it doesn't sell as many copies? . . ."

And she had listened to him and felt sorry for him. Actually, she knew, she had been feeling smug about herself. Poor Dallas. His problems were not hers. "When I make up my mind," she had told him, "it won't bother me."

Well—and it wasn't going to bother her, either. She wouldn't let it.

And then the fear came at her again, swooping down like some great fierce attacking bird, and she closed her eyes, trying to hide.

I'll fail, she thought, with overwhelming conviction. I'll never be able to do it again. And if I do, it won't be any good. I know it won't. Why should I even try? Why do I make myself do this? It would be so much easier to relax, let go, give up, sink back into obscurity. And be comfortable again.

But I couldn't be comfortable *again*. Because I was never comfortable at all. I felt trapped. I had to get out. And now I'm out of that one but somehow I'm in another one. And maybe this is even worse.

Stop thinking! she told herself furiously. Stop thinking and write. Write a word, some word, any word. You can change it later. Just get started!

She poised her hands above the typewriter. And then she looked up across the room and over at the closed door, as if someone had opened it and spoken or beckoned to her. She stared at it a moment, challengingly. Then suddenly she got up, crossed to it swiftly, and with a quick decisive gesture turned the key in the lock. There, she thought, with some sense of satisfaction, and she walked back to the desk and sat down.

She began to type rapidly.

Chapter 48

For two months and a half there was no interruption to Shireen's schedule. She forgot, in fact, that it was a schedule she had made up and imposed upon herself and it became an inevitable way of life. If anything were to interfere, she had some premonition that vague but dreadful things would follow.

One afternoon in the middle of September, Mary knocked at the door.

Shireen had been sitting there, restless and unhappy, for two hours, but had not written a word. Now she looked at the door with a glare. What was she being bothered for?

"Come in!"

"It's Miss Marsh. She says she must speak to you. It's very important. It's about your husband. I'm sorry."

Shireen's face turned white and she felt a shock of pure terror. If anything had happened to Ed! She reached for the telephone and she was trembling all over.

"Georgia! What is it? What's happened?"

"Shireen—he's all right. Don't be frightened—"

"He's *all right*? Then something's happened to him? He's been hurt. Oh, nothing can have happened to Ed!" She had no idea what she was saying and had never felt so scared or lonely or angry in her life. If anything had happened to Ed, she would hold the entire universe responsible.

"Shireen, don't go to pieces like that. Give me a chance to tell you. Jim called me from Washington because he wanted me to let you know. He's had another malaria attack—a worse one, this time— and he's in the hospital."

"Georgia, he might die! Oh, my God! What if he dies!" Before she'd had a chance to atone!

"Shireen, he's not going to die. He's had it before, only this time he'll probably get a leave home."

"But why didn't he tell me? His letters only said he was in a rest camp. Why didn't he tell me he was sick?"

"I suppose he didn't want to worry you. It's actually something to be almost grateful for. Now, you're not going to be upset, are you?"

"No, I won't—no more than I can help. I'm glad you called." They talked a little longer and she hung up. She noticed for the first time then that Mary was still in the room, standing near the door, watching her.

"I'm sorry," Mary said. "Apparently it's nothing very bad."

Shireen felt herself looking a little more pathetic than she needed to. Perhaps Mary would like her better now, to see how unhappy she was and how much she loved Ed.

"Miss Marsh says it's not too serious. He'll be all right in a few weeks. And then he may get a leave home." She shook her head. "I haven't seen him for two years."

"Two years? It must have been tough, having him away so long. Because apparently there's nothing else in your life but that one man. I feel sorry for you," she said, with no trace of pity. "You haven't much to be happy about at all. Except maybe this apartment, and you worry so much about that I guess even it doesn't make you happy. Well, I've always heard about the poor rich."

Shireen had a quick vision of herself clawing her nails down Mary's face, and then felt a sick frightened shock at the intensity of the image.

My God, she thought. I'd better look out. What's the matter with me lately? She forced herself to laugh.

"Yes," she said. "The poor rich. It's the oldest story in the world—have everything on earth but still aren't happy. Well, I've never been able to waste many tears over that one, myself. I'd much rather have everything and not be happy, than have nothing at all and still not be happy. Just a question of whether you'll take your misery in a silver goblet or drink it out of an old bean can."

"Uh-huh," said Mary. "Is there anything else?"

"Nothing I can think of. Did you finish indexing those notes from Jung?"

"I finished them yesterday afternoon," said Mary, who had always finished everything before Shireen asked her about it. "But I'll be damned if I can imagine what you're going to do with all that stuff: Jung, Freud, Horney, Chinese politics, abstract art, anthropology, history of the Middle Ages. What are you trying to do, anyway? Become a walking encyclopedia?"

If you don't get out of here, thought Shireen, I'm going to kill you. I'm really going to kill you. Her heart was pounding and her hands were wet and she had a terrible feeling that in a moment something inside her would explode.

"Oh," she said, and looked down at the desk, away from Mary's face, "my memory isn't very good. I have to keep notes or I forget everything. Well—I'll see you tomorrow morning."

"Okay. Good luck on your opus."

"Thanks."

"Don't mention it."

The door closed and suddenly Shireen grabbed hold of her hair and pulled. She wanted to scream, jump out the window, destroy something or someone, or herself. I can't imagine what's happened to me. I've never hated anyone like this before, have I? She tried to remember. Or maybe I have. Maybe I've hated the whole world for a long time. Or myself. Oh, I don't know! And why should I think about it! I won't think about it! I'll write instead. That keeps me from thinking.

She looked down at her typewriter and the blank sheet of yellow paper in it.

And then she glanced across the desk and saw the photograph of Ed smiling at her trustingly. She stared at it for several moments: Oh, darling, if you'd only come home. Everything that's ever gone wrong has been because you're away. I need you—I don't know how to get along without you. I've depended on you all my life and when you're away from me I do crazy things, I don't mean to but I do.

A rush of memories went by, not separating into scenes or images, but sweeping through like a motion picture run at triple speed: the leftover feelings, strained through her own wishes, of the early months, the first two or three years she and Ed had known each other. But now they seemed like the memories of things she had wished for which had never happened and she could no longer separate what she remembered from what she wished was there to be remembered.

It did seem, though, as if they had been very happy. As if each had trusted the other to be the one person he most needed. The future must have appeared then to be a promise, not a threat, as it did now. All their energy for living and all their hopes must have been high, their illusions intact. It seemed like a happy age of great innocence.

And perhaps it had been. But she couldn't be sure.

She sat, quiet now and very tired, and thought about Ed and how she wished she could go backward in life. The future rose menacingly before her. She could surround herself with defenses to block it out—her apartment, her clothes, her careful schedule which succeeded well enough in leaving her no time to think, whatever ostensible practical purposes it might serve—but it was coming on, remorselessly.

She had a wild nightmare image of giants advancing toward her, slowly, inexorably, and herself cringing and trembling in a corner from which there was no possible escape. Her eyes widened with terror as she stared at the picture in her mind, and then she shut them quickly and put her hands over her face.

Three hours later she stood on the terrace talking to Georgia.

She had had a bath and put on fresh make-up and she wore a misty gray chiffon gown, gathered tight to her waist with a drifting skirt and some drapery that crossed over her bare shoulders and floated down the back. A dozen or so people stood around the living room drinking cocktails and solving all national and international

355

problems, and someone had begun to play the piano. She and Georgia had walked out there so that Georgia could give her a verbatim report of Jim's call from Washington.

"Maybe this is the shock I've needed to bring me to my senses," Shireen said, when Georgia had finished. "There's no use fooling myself any longer—Ed's the only man I've ever loved. And when he comes back we're going to be as happy as we always should have been. I'll make up to him for everything—I'll spend all the rest of my life making it up to him."

Georgia gave her a look of surprise which turned to the kind of amusement you might show at hearing a friend recite his New Year's resolutions.

"And you think Johnny and the rest of them won't have made any difference?"

Shireen stared out across the terrace railing. It was pale early evening and the lights were beginning to come on, giving the city a kind of serene unreality. Thin white clouds streaked across the sky and pink puffs floated here and there. The air was warm and seemed quiet; the roar of the city sounded as from a distance and the laughter and talk behind them had a pleasant muted sound.

"I was in love with Johnny," she said softly. "I wouldn't change anything and I have no regrets. I don't know any other way it could have happened, once we had met each other. The world's too full of hypocrites feeling smug because they've never done a thing in their lives but resist temptation. That's no virtue."

"No, Shireen. I don't think it is, either. It's one of the basic facts of our western civilization, though. Hypocrisy is the glue that holds it together. And it affects all of us, whether we accept it or not. You have more regrets than you think, I'm afraid."

"Maybe. I don't know." All at once she laughed. "Of all sad words of tongue or pen, the saddest are these: What a jerk I've been!" They turned around, both of them laughing, and walked back inside. Shireen went over and began talking to Philip Thayer.

Six weeks later Ed arrived in New York and Shireen drove out to La Guardia to meet him.

He had called her from San Francisco twenty-four hours before, and that had been the end of her schedule. She had dashed around frantically ever since, called people on the telephone, ordered flowers, talked to the servants about food—not afraid of them for once—spent the afternoon at Elizabeth Arden's, given instructions to Mary. And all the while she was in a state of such tense excitement she felt as if the strings that held her together might snap any moment.

She was excited by the fact of Ed's coming, but the actual existence of Ed she could not conjure up. She was half persuaded that

356

he did not exist and had not ever existed, and that she was in some
dream state from which she would wake to realize he was not coming
because there never had been any such man as Ed Farrell except in
her mind.

He had seemed real to her for a few minutes, while she was talking
to him over the phone. But now she sat on a bench in the crowded
terminal and waited for this man who was not coming.

She had decided before she left home that, quite objectively, she
was prettier than she had been when he had seen her last. She should
be, for heaven's sake. She had taken good care of herself, had plenty
of sleep, expert people kept her in condition, and she wore the most
becoming clothes that could be bought. She was bound to be prettier
than the Shireen Delaney he had last seen who washed her own hair,
manicured her own toes and fingers, and had her clothes made by a
dressmaker in Marron. Or the girl he had first known, dressed in a
gray skirt and yellow sweater, white socks and white crepe-soled
shoes with no jewelry but a fraternity pin, her nails only cleaned and
buffed, her face undecorated except for the bright pink lipstick.

That poor kid, thought Shireen.

This Shireen Delaney was something altogether different.

This one was glossy and finished and looked as much like a magazine ad as like a woman. She smelled of expensive perfume. She wore
gold bracelets and a thin strand of pearls around her neck. Her hair
was fresh and gleaming as black lacquer. Her dress was black silk
and impressively simple, cut to show her figure without being obvious
about it. Her tanned legs shone like bronze and she wore ankle-
strapped shoes. Her face was smooth and serene, her blue eyes shiny
with excitement. And the men turned around and looked back as they
went by, while she pretended not to be so much as aware of them.

The announcer's voice came over the speaker system: "Passengers
from Flight 385 unloading at Gate Number 9. Passengers from
Flight—"

Shireen jumped to her feet and ran. People got in her way and she
dodged around them, following the signs to Gate 9. Out on the field
the plane was standing in a flood of light and people were coming
down the steps. Some of them had reached the gate. But she could
not find Ed. What if she had missed him?

And then she saw him.

He stepped out of the doorway, turned back to speak to someone
inside, and started down the stairs. Shireen raised her arm and waved
and as she did he saw her and his face broke into a broad grin. He
began to run. She watched him coming toward her: Oh, I'll be so
good to you, darling, she thought. I'll make it all up to you—

And the next moment he was there and had his arms around her
and she felt the solidity of his body. Her hands held his face and

357

she bent back to look at him, smiling, tears in her eyes. He caught her up quickly with a triumphant laugh and kissed her. Everything she loved about him was bright and new again and no other part of her life seemed in any way significant. To have him there made her realize, as she had not while he was away, the subtle insistent power of the years.

He would be everything in the world to her from now on. For the rest of their lives.

She linked her arm in his and they began walking, and there was in it a feeling of all the times they had walked that way, around the campus, along the streets of Marron and Los Angeles and Miami.

She asked him if he was all right. If he had had any more malaria attacks. He looked thinner than when he had gone, and tired.

He shrugged, as if it was something he didn't want to talk about. "I'm okay. I may get an attack now and then, but it's nothing to worry about. Hell, it was the luckiest thing that ever happened to me. Look! I'm back here with you." They smiled at each other as if they had succeeded in a secret conspiracy against the world.

When they got to the car Shireen handed him the key and, in her mind, it was a symbol. Ed was back. Now she wouldn't have to make every decision alone. Now there would be someone to help her and advise her—someone she could depend upon. Thank God.

He opened the door and she got in, smiling happily at him, touching his hand. He walked around, tossed his bag onto the back seat, and got in beside her. He was still smiling, as if something pleased him so much he could not get over it. He looked at the dash board.

"Pretty fancy job you've got here."

"Do you like it, Ed?" she asked him eagerly. "But wait until you see the house! You're going to love it! It's the most beautiful thing you've ever seen!"

"I'm sure it is, Shireen. If you like it."

Good Lord, she thought, in amazed wonder. What have I been doing with all these other damn fools? Ed's the only man I've ever known who appreciates me. She felt an intense gratitude. She wanted to pour all her affection over him at once, make him realize how glad she was to have him back and how much she loved him and how hard she would work to make him happy.

"Oh, darling, I've missed you so much!" she said. "You can't imagine how I've missed you."

"Have you?" There was no irony in the question, only wondering thankfulness, and a wistful need to believe her.

They looked at each other and after a moment he put his arms around her and kissed her. The kiss was so familiar. The feel and taste of his mouth. She knew it so well. This was nothing new, no experimenting, no wondering how it would turn out. She had forgotten how wonderful it was just to know someone thoroughly.

At last he released her and turned back, looking at the dashboard again with a faint quizzical expression. "It's been a long time since I've been in one of these things. I hope I can remember how they work."

"Of course you can, darling."

Ed was home. This was the happy ending. The things she had worked for, the money she had made, the success she had had, now all fell into place. This was what it had been for.

Chapter 49

He began to drive and they talked: Shireen, as she always did with him, babbling away excitedly about everything that popped into her mind; Ed answering her with his lazy comfortable voice that was like a balm ministered to the rough raw wounded edges of her ego. Was it possible he had been at war? He wasn't as different as she had expected. Maybe this talk about how the men would come back changed beyond recognition was all nonsense.

Quite likely she had changed far more than he.

She watched the road ahead, the white line unraveling before them and then being eaten up as the car overtook it. And she sat very close to him, her arm resting on his leg, as she always used to sit when they were driving. It began to seem as if he had never been away.

"You know," she said, "I suppose I might never have realized how much you mean to me—if you hadn't been gone so long."

"You mean that, Shireen?"

"Of course I mean it, darling. Otherwise I might have taken you for granted, the way people do when they've been married a long time. But I've met a lot of men since you left, of one kind or another, and not one of them could be compared to you."

"It's good to hear you say that. I may as well tell you the truth—it's something I've done a lot of worrying about."

"You were worried, darling?" And now she had talked herself so thoroughly into what she had said that she was astonished he could have been worrying. "I kept telling you over and over in my letters how much I love you and missed you."

"I know. But so much has happened to you—you've met so many new people. A lot of them must have been much more interesting than I am. I'm a pretty simple guy, after all. I was afraid you'd have outgrown me."

"Oh, darling! How could you even think such a thing?" She leaned closer and kissed the side of his face, her fingers touching him lightly. "I could never love anyone but you."

Ed sighed a little. "I hope not. I don't know what I'd do if you ever did. You're the only thing that matters to me. It's crazy, I know, but the way I feel about you is more than love—it's adoration, I guess. You're my whole life, Shireen." He said it simply, not begging for reassurance, but stating a fact.

As he talked Shireen watched him with tears in her eyes and her throat aching painfully. A tremendous flood of pity and affection, shame and repentance and renewed devotion, rose and spilled over in tears. "Oh, Ed, my darling! Could you really have doubted me so much?"

He glanced at her with faint surprise. "Here, here," he said, and his voice had a rough softness, like a father speaking to his hurt child. "What's going on here? Don't cry, Shireen. You mustn't cry, darling. I don't want you to be *unhappy* with me back. Come on, now—no more tears. Be a big girl."

That was something else she had forgotten. How patient he had always been. No matter how childishly she behaved, he was ready to coax her out of it, make her feel wanted and loved. It was no wonder she loved him. The only thing strange was that she could ever have forgotten that she did. But that, of course, was because of the kind of person she was. No goddamned good.

"I've never kidded myself about you, Shireen. I think you're much too good for me and I always have. I've never been able to understand how I was ever lucky enough to marry you."

"Oh, Ed!"

She was really crying now, her head on his shoulder and one hand holding onto his arm. She cried hard. For his goodness and her unworthiness. For the whole mixed-up world. And for her own vows for the future. I'll never let him down again. I'll never say another unkind word. I'll never lose my temper. I'll never look at another man. I'll never hurt him in any way at all. I'll pay him back all the rest of my life for everything he's given me and no matter how long I live or how I try I'll never be able to make up for how bad I've been. The sleeve of his uniform was getting wet and she sniffled and brushed if off.

Shireen led him through the apartment room by room, showing him everything with great pride, like a little girl displaying the presents she has been given for Christmas. Ed followed her, enthusiastic, but looking somewhat dazed.

When they got to the bedroom, which she brought him to last, she pointed through the French doors. "On a clear day," she said, "you can see the Empire State Building." And they both laughed. But then, almost immediately, found that they were self-conscious about being alone in a bedroom.

"Look at this vase, Ed," she said quickly. "Isn't it pretty? It's Orrefors crystal—it's very hard to get nowadays, you know."

"Yes." He looked at it and frowned a little with the concentration. "It certainly is pretty."

"The decorator did an awfully good job, don't you think?"

"Yes. It looks as if you'd done it yourself."

"It looks the way I'd have done it if I'd known how."

"Yeah, the guy's good all right. No doubt about that."

"It was expensive, but I think it's worth it."

"I'm sure it must've been. They say prices have gone up a lot in the last couple of years."

"Oh, they have! It's terrible. I don't know how people who don't have much money are managing to get along."

"I guess they must be having a tough time."

And there the conversation gave out.

Both of them had become aware that it was pretty strange for them to be standing there talking like that. Two people who had once lived on ninety dollars a month. When the crystal vase had cost one hundred and thirty-five dollars. Which meant that to pay for that vase, three hundred people had bought a copy of *The Falcon*. Hundreds of thousands of people were represented in this apartment. Work they had done, in factories and on farms, working as dishwashers, clerks, accountants, dressmakers, selling insurance and hosiery and breakfast food. Earning money and then spending part of it on a book they expected would make them forget for a time the lives they had. And she had written it to forget her own life and find the means of buying a new one.

Now she and Ed stood in this elaborate apartment and looked at each other with a sudden forlorn knowledge that they were much farther away from the past than it had seemed in the first few excited minutes of being together.

Ed shook his head. "Gee," he said, and forced himself to grin. "It's kind of strange, isn't it?"

"What is, darling?"

"You—me. Us being together again. And here." He made a helpless gesture. "So far away."

"So far away from what?"

"I don't know. I feel as if I've been gone such a long time." He glanced uneasily around the room, all creamy white and green and filled with bowls of flowers, shining silver, crystal, satin, and raw rough silk.

Shireen came up close to him, moving with sureness and self-belief, soaked and surrounded with the manifestations of her invincibility. She was smiling. "Don't worry about it, darling. Don't think about anything. Just kiss me."

He looked at her with a momentary expression of alarm, as if he had come face to face in the dark with a stranger. And then he put his arms around her—and the violent emotion which had brought them together first and never worn itself out over all the years of living together sprang up again, like an animal that had been crouched, waiting for someone to beckon.

362

Next day, in the middle of the afternoon, Shireen took Ed to meet Georgia. She was eager for them to know each other and become fast friends, and was pleased and happy that they seemed to like each other instantly. They sat and talked for awhile and Georgia kissed him when they started to leave.

"You're a sweet boy—you're everything Shireen said you were. She's a very lucky girl."

Ed blushed. "I'm the one who's lucky."

Shireen took his hand. "Isn't he wonderful?"

The three of them stood there a moment in a glow of friendship and love and mutual admiration that was almost intoxicating, and then Shireen and Ed went out. Georgia had offered to let them spend his leave at her farm, but they were not going until tomorrow.

Shireen wanted to have dinner at home the first night so he could see her new dishes and silver and how nicely everything was served. She had found a couple that satisfied her. It was a warm Indian summer night and they ate on the terrace, looking at each other over candles and a mass of late summer flowers, Ed in his uniform and Shireen wearing a gown of white chiffon that left one shoulder naked, with a sari over her black hair. Ed had looked at her as if he could not believe his eyes when she had walked in, for she had insisted that he stay out of the bedroom until she was dressed so she could surprise him.

And when he had exclaimed over her until he had all but run out of adjectives, Shireen laughed and glanced flirtatiously aside for an instant. "I'm glad you like it, darling. I've got lots of beautiful clothes now. And when you're out of the Navy we can dress for dinner every night. Won't that be fun?" She had been bubbling all day with plans about what they would do, and Ed had not demurred at anything.

"We will if you want to," he said, and she kissed him.

"Oh, Ed! You'll never know how I've missed you. You're such a darling—you're a perfect angel."

He glanced up, pretending to look for his halo, and they walked out arm in arm, laughing, to the terrace. "Isn't New York beautiful!" Shireen clasped her hands. "This is the most wonderful city in the world. And do you know why?" She looked up at Ed, waiting for him to take his cue.

"No," he said. "Why?"

"Because it belongs to anyone who loves it enough!"

He looked toward the skyline, the great black multishaped blocks of buildings across the Park, like cardboard stage props that had had holes cut in them here and there for orange light to show through. And as he looked his eyes narrowed a little. Shireen watched him, puzzled, and then, for some reason she did not know, came a slight pluck of alarm. "Ed—what are you thinking about?"

363

Ed snapped abruptly to, as if he had been called to attention, though he did not move but only turned his head and looked down at her. He was smiling again, but this time it looked a little forced.

"It's big, isn't it?"

"Of course. That's what's so wonderful about it."

She laughed, for she didn't want him to be moody. Moodiness was not Ed's role in life. He had never been moody before, so why should he start now, when she wasn't planning on it? Anyway, she wanted him to be happy, delighted with everything she was giving him and showing him.

"You know me and my megalomania," she said teasingly, but bragging at the same time, for in her opinion megalomania was an interesting and enviable symptom. Everyone should have it. If they ever expected to amount to anything in life.

But he had spread the first little stain of doubt.

What did he mean: It's big, isn't it? And in that tone of voice. Was he afraid? Was he worried about his own abilities to compete in a city of seven million people? But no, it couldn't be that. For while he was gone she had had some picture in her mind of Ed with a tremendous office, employing hundreds or maybe it was thousands of men, giving orders, making millions of dollars, tremendously powerful and important. It might take him a few years, of course, but she never doubted he could do it.

She hadn't asked him yet if he had any plans for what he would do when he got out of the Navy, and now the impulse came but she quickly checked it. It was too early to talk about that. Let him rest. He'll think of something. And if he doesn't, I will.

They sat down to dinner and Shireen was animated and excited, talking, talking, talking, as if she could not stop if she tried. She told him anecdote after anecdote, all of them about herself. How this had happened to her and that had happened; what this person had said and what that one had said and what she had said in reply; how this person had complimented and praised her, and how that one had criticized or damned her. She was completely fascinated by her own conversation and herself as the subject. Nothing she had ever heard had seemed half so interesting.

Ed listened with admiration, sympathy, awe, or—if the story called for it—a display of contempt or anger at whoever had mistreated his wife. He seemed as much impressed by her as she was. They were both amazed to find themselves sitting where they were sitting, eating the kind of food they were eating, being served by a maid in a pretty black and white uniform, with hundreds of books in the library, paintings on the wall, dozens of bottles of liquor in the pantry, and the fact that they need only decide what they wanted and Shireen would write her name on a slip of paper—and they had it. The name *Shireen Delaney* had acquired magic. A magic that astounded them.

"Gee," Ed said. "I'm the luckiest guy in the world."

"You're lucky, all right," agreed Shireen. "Darling, would you like to have coffee in the living room?"

"Fine." Ed came around and drew back Shireen's chair. She got up gracefully, trailing her white chiffon gown, ran the tips of her fingers along his cheek, and walked ahead of him. The maid brought the coffee in on a silver tray and set it where Shireen indicated on the coffee table.

"Would you like a liqueur, darling?" she asked him as she poured the coffee. "There's any kind you want on the bar-table. Honey, I've forgotten—do you take sugar or not?"

"One lump," said Ed. "I never used to drink coffee at all. Neither did you. Don't you remember?"

Shireen laughed. "My God, you're right. And cigarettes, too. I didn't smoke until you went into the Navy. And cocktails—but I only drink one occasionally, even now. Boy—I sure have gotten sophisticated, haven't I?" She smiled up at him as he took the cup from her. "Sometimes I don't know myself. I mean it, Ed. Sometimes I don't."

"Sometimes," said Ed, "I'm not sure I know you, either."

Her gray eyes sharpened. "You don't mean I've changed for the worse?"

"You're much more beautiful."

"Oh."

She crossed her legs and sat far back on the dark-red sofa, sipping her coffee from the tiny cup and looking around over the rim of it at her house. She looked at it carefully, caressingly, every piece of furniture, each picture on the wall, the stone buddha in his private jungle of ferns, the tremendous lamps, the gray chiffon curtains floating ever so gently as a breeze stirred through them.

It was all hers, everything there, every . . . single . . . thing. She had worked for it and made the money and bought it and paid for it. And it belonged to her.

"It's a wonderful feeling," she said, "to own something as beautiful as this and know you got it by your own efforts, with no help from anyone on earth."

Ed had been sitting in a nearby chair, watching her as she looked at her possessions, and his face had helplessly exposed an ache of yearning and the beginning of a new and painful doubt. Now, as she glanced at him, he smiled and the look was gone.

"Yes," he said. "It must be. You should be very proud of yourself."

At that, though, Shireen's superstitions sprang out of hiding and cocked an eye on her. "No," she said quickly, "I don't exactly mean that. It's much too good to be true. I don't deserve it. Oh, Ed!" she

365

cried with sudden intensity. "Sometimes I'm scared to death! I don't deserve to have all this—you know I don't! What if something happens? What if I lose it?"

He got up swiftly and came over to her. "Darling, don't talk like that. You shouldn't even think of such things. What could possibly happen? How could you lose it?"

Shireen put her cup down, and she was staring away across the room. "But I might. I might get sick or I might get killed or—I might never be able to make any more money." And at the last she turned to him in despair.

"Darling, darling—none of that will happen. Why, you've always been the healthiest—"

She gave a flash of her hand. "No! Don't say that! Something will be sure to happen then!"

And he burst into laughter, as if he knew her again and she had come back to him in some form he could recognize. "You haven't changed so much, after all. You're as superstitious as ever. I've always said, Shireen, you're like a medieval witch."

Shireen laughed. "I know. But all the same, let's not take any chances. And Ed—it's not really a joke. I am scared. What if I can't write another book?" She looked at him hopelessly, for something he could not give—because she had not faith enough in him to take it.

He had always tried, though. "But you are writing it, darling. And it'll be good, you know it will. Everything you ever do will be good. I'm sure of that."

"You are?"

"Of course I am."

"You haven't even seen it yet," she said, her voice and eyes accusing.

"But I know you. And I believe in you."

She dropped her head onto his shoulder and he put his arms around her and held her close against him, but carefully, so as not to muss her. "You do believe in me, Ed, don't you?"

Chapter 50

At Georgia's farm they were very happy. No one else was around and they spent every minute together suspended from the world, which they both seemed under tacit agreement to ignore while he was on leave.

He did not often talk about the war or what he had seen or done and, when he did, spoke calmly and with detachment, as if he had never permitted it to touch him. He seemed more embarrassed than pleased by the medal he had been given, and told her any other man on his ship had as much reason to be wearing it as he.

"And a lot of 'em much more—because plenty of those guys were really scared."

"But you weren't scared, Ed?" she asked him, like Elaine speaking to Lancelot, her voice light and respectful and quite humble before this example of masculine bravery.

"I don't think so. If I was I never admitted it—even to myself."

That was the thing she had sensed in him when they had first met. And she had somehow felt then that if she married him, if she were close enough to him, she could absorb that fearlessness—like the savage convinced he can gain courage by eating the flesh of his brave enemy, or of the lion or tiger. And yet, after all these years, Ed was still courageous—and she was afraid of more things than ever.

But her money helped now. Money was a wonderful antidote to fear.

Time drifted by them, soft and ceaseless. Shireen did not think about writing or her schedule, and they did not talk of what Ed would do when he got out of the Navy. Georgia had some horses and they went riding every day. It was too cool to swim, but they walked and played tennis. Sometimes they read, taking turns reading aloud, or listened to the phonograph. Shireen talked a great deal, but increasingly less about what she had done and intended to do. It was as if she had a temporary amnesia. She felt happy and content and inclined to believe that she could go on this way indefinitely.

"It's only knowing what other people expect of us that gets us into trouble," she said to him once, when they were walking through the woods.

The forest was emptying, with a continuous sifting of leaves toward the ground. It had rained earlier in the day and the wetness gave a

367

translucent quality, clear and etched, to the subtle colors around them; yellow, pale green, copper, sherry.

Ed glanced uneasily at her as she walked beside him switching a flexible stick she had picked up, concentrating her attention on the smells and feel of the air and how everything around them looked. "Is that it, Shireen? Or is it what we expect of ourselves?"

She wanted to ask him exactly what it was he expected of himself, but again decided not to. She was a little afraid to find out, anyway. For there never had been a time when Ed had had her ambitions or needs, though she had always believed she could make him have them and continued now to think that since she had achieved her own he would, necessarily, have to emulate her.

"I don't know," she said. "Let's not think about anything unpleasant right now." Ed laughed, but she did not see why.

When they had been there four weeks Georgia called and asked if they would mind if she and Jim spent the week end with them and Shireen was delighted. Ed seemed to be, too. And all at once she felt as if she had lost herself in him, in something she was doing for him which was entirely contrary to her own nature. It made her resentful, but she was alarmed by the resentment and tried to conceal it by being extraordinarily pleasant and considerate. She began to wish his leave would end so that she could go on with her life.

The morning after Georgia and Jim arrived, the two men went out to ride and Shireen and Georgia sat at the breakfast table, smoking and drinking more coffee. They had talked excitedly about what had been going on in New York, about people Ed did not know, and Shireen had wanted him to leave because he did not know them and it made her uncomfortable to realize how much her interests had diverged from his. They would have to begin all over again, with her new life, but it wasn't time yet and he seemed to be in the way.

When he kissed her good-by she looked at him and saw a stranger. Who is he? she thought. Where did he come from and how did he get mixed up in my life? She sat silent, waiting to hear the door close behind them. And she avoided looking at Georgia, for she felt Georgia knew what was in her mind.

"He's a sweet guy, Shireen," she said after a moment. "And he adores you."

Shireen lit a cigarette. "I know it. And I know I don't deserve him. He'd never do the things to me I've done to him. He's too good for me." Her face had turned moody and sullen.

"Isn't that for Ed to decide? You're something he's pretty proud of having, you know."

"He should be, after all."

She looked at Georgia in dismay.

"You see?" she said. "That's what I mean. I open my mouth and

368

out comes something like that. But where can it possibly come *from?*"

"From what you feel, I'm afraid."

She frowned. "Well—whether I feel that way or don't, I've got to quit talking like that. Before, it didn't matter so much. But now it would be terrible."

"It certainly would. Ed is enough aware as it is that you have money and he hasn't—"

"Oh, but he has. All the money's in a joint account. It belongs to him as much as it does to me. That's what we always agreed—and that's what I've done."

"But money, unfortunately, is something it's very easy to be sensible about when you don't have any, and practically impossible when you do. Can you honestly say, Shireen, that way down deep you think that money is Ed's as much as yours?"

Shireen thought hard. "No—I don't. I worked for it and I got it and it's mine. That's what I think. But Ed doesn't know that," she added hastily. "He thinks I mean what I say."

"Don't kid yourself. He knows it all right."

Shireen looked at the flower pattern on the dishes. This was something she did not want to talk to anyone about, even Georgia.

For she was beginning to have a terrible sense that she had lost the battle already. But where? On which field? She didn't know. She couldn't remember.

These past two years she had learned so many ways to keep herself from thinking about it. She had run, stopping sometimes to look back, found that she was still pursued and then, with her hands over her eyes, run blindly on again. But it seemed she ran through a maze—between blank walls that showed her no way out—that turned and twisted back upon itself and reached so high above her head she could scarcely see any longer if there was still daylight up there. As she ran the walls seemed to grow, getting slowly taller, and the maze became more complicated and tortuous; new alleys opened out of it, until at last there was a hopeless realization that she was trapped for the rest of her life. She would never escape.

But from what? Who had built the maze? What was it that pursued her?

It was no use thinking about these things. She must not stop or look back but keep on running. She might still find a way. Ed would help her. Unless, as Georgia seemed to have been suggesting, he was lost now too.

That couldn't be—it mustn't be.

She would somehow keep him from knowing what she actually thought and felt. Even though she was half aware that you could never hide from others the things you felt, whether you said them or

369

not. Those were the things they knew most clearly and they were what dictated the course of a relationship, if it was to be clear and straight and honest, or warped and twisted by the lies that were never put into words. For though they were buried deeply they sent up flowers, rank ugly troublesome blossoms she was sometimes shocked to find growing in what she had imagined was the neat and carefully cultivated garden of her mind. And, not liking the looks or smell of them, she would snap off the bloom and believe she had killed the root. Until another came out on the same stalk, or a little way off, on a different stalk but from the same root.

"I wonder—" Shireen said slowly and softly—"if Ed minds my success very much?"

"I don't think he 'minds,' Shireen, in the way you probably mean. He's very sincerely proud of you. But sooner or later you're going to find out that the poor boy is afraid."

Shireen looked up sharply. "Afraid? Ed's not afraid of anything. He told me he was never once afraid in the war, not even when his ship was hit."

"Maybe he wasn't. Ed isn't the kind of man who would let himself know it if he was afraid. Physical courage is his prop in life. But there are worse things waiting, as someone put it."

"I don't know what could be worse than going to war. After that everything else should be simple and easy."

"The fears society foists on you are worse. In a war, at least the issues are clear. You do or you don't. You live or you die. You're mangled or you come out whole. But he gets back here and all of a sudden he's boxing shadows. He may be sent out again, though Jim doesn't think that's likely, or he may even be discharged. And if he is that brings you up against it a lot sooner. Both of you."

"Up against what? He can start a business, right in New York. That's something I've been wanting to talk to you about anyway. You know a lot of people, Georgia. Don't you think between us we could—"

Georgia smiled and shook her head. "That's what I mean. Don't you see how cockeyed that is, right at the beginning? What man wants to have his life fixed up for him by a couple of women? How about letting Ed figure it out someway?"

"But I'm afraid he doesn't know how!"

And then she gave a hopeless shrug of her shoulders. She was aware of self-disgust and some obtuse disappointment, a sense that she had been cheated or had cheated someone. A quick defiance flared up.

"And maybe he doesn't know how, Georgia. And why shouldn't he be helped by a woman? What kind of a crazy world is this where men are brought up to think they have such natural God-given superiority that if a woman makes more money than they do or is smarter or more successful, they're so outraged they simply go to pieces? As if the world had double-crossed them and collapsed right under their feet?"

"Sure. You'll never hear me say this is a nice sensible world we live in. Men do resent women like you and me. But who are you going to blame it on? Their mothers, for making it impossible for them to grow up? Or the paucity of most women's lives and the lousy relationships they have with their husbands so that they substitute their sons for their husbands? That brings it back to men again, anyway—and I suppose makes it more comfortable for us. Take my word for it, Shireen. Leave him alone, as much as you can. If you don't you'll be making a serious mistake. You'll have to watch the guy fall apart, and it won't be a pretty sight. And don't ever forget there's an equation in the masculine mind between money and virility. God knows why, but it's there and it makes a situation like yours that much more complicated. Anyway," she added, "you and Ed need each other. Or, at least, you need the *idea* of each other."

Shireen sighed. "I'll leave him alone—I'll wait and see what happens."

But she had never in her life been able to wait to see what would happen. She had always been forced, by something inside herself, to try to make something happen. Good or bad. Helpful or destructive. Wise or foolish. But make something happen. Never wait. Never leave anything alone to see what would come of it. Don't let the dough stand overnight so the yeast can work, but throw it in the oven and get some kind of result, any kind, but at least a result.

However, she did resolve.

Two weeks later Ed's leave ended and they said good-by at the airport. Shireen was not going with him, though neither of them quite knew how the decision had been reached.

"You should go on with your work, Shireen," he told her. "You had it started and it would be hard for you to travel around and keep working—and God knows where I'll be or where you could find a place to stay. Anyway, you've already taken out six weeks to be with me."

Shireen blushed, for she did not want to know that he considered it magnanimous of her to have given him that much time. "Oh, but darling—everything comes second to you, you know that."

"I know," he said.

And they both knew he was lying. They had known each other too long and lived too close during the years when Shireen was dependent upon him, not to understand each other now. And she sometimes wondered how much he knew about her that he had never mentioned and would never mention. In the relationships between people it

371

seemed wiser to be ignorant. If you knew—No, better leave the apple on the tree. You could only be sadder by picking it off and taking a bite.

She went back immediately to her schedule.

She had made up her mind about the rest of her life. I'll love Ed, she had decided, and work. And that's enough. I'll work and work and work. You don't need anything else. Ed will always be there, so I'll never be lonely. It was the only solution she had been able to find. She had groped helplessly, grabbing for one thing and then another, thinking that if she could catch it long enough to examine it closely she might find that it was this unnamed unknown thing she was looking for. It must be somewhere. She had simply mislaid it and sooner or later she would find it again, but she would only find it by looking.

Well—

It had not been in any of the places she had looked, and she couldn't spend the rest of her life searching for something she could not identify. She hadn't enough clues to go on, and not enough years to chase every random chance. The restlessness behind this constant search she convinced herself could be driven away if she worked hard enough. The solution would be found in writing—her own private and reliable world.

She considered Georgia.

Georgia worked almost every hour of the day. And Georgia was happy, wasn't she? Anyway, what the hell was being happy? That was no clearer than love or success or any of the other abstracts she had been trying to pin down. So the answer was to be incessantly busy. Too busy to think. And, in the end, too busy to feel or to be aware of the absence of feeling.

Chapter 51

When Ed had been gone about three weeks one of the columns carried an item to the effect that Lt. Edward Farrell had come home on leave and then left by himself for the Coast and that he and Shireen Delaney had agreed on a divorce. Shireen was furious, but Georgia advised her not to let it trouble her.

A few days later she had lunch with Philip Thayer in the Barberry Room and he asked her what was going on.

"Oh," said Shireen. "You mean that nonsense about Ed and me getting divorced. Why, I don't know what it is. Someone's paid to make those things up, you know that, Phil."

"I know that. But I also know they sometimes don't make it up. Now, look here, Shireen, you know I never stick my nose into my authors' private lives, but I like you, you're a nice girl, and I just want to give you a piece of advice for your own good. It doesn't mean a goddamn thing to me what you do, one way or another. But your present reputation is a valuable asset. It's something all of us have worked hard to build up. The public thinks of you as a typical American girl, born in a small town, going to college, getting married to a nice young guy, being faithful to him while he was at war, and now helping him to get rehabilitated. And that's important, Shireen. The public loves Cinderellas because, as far as they know, it may happen to any of them. You're average; it happened to you; hence it may happen just as easily to any other average girl. The fact that you've also gotta work like hell to make it happen and then be goddamn lucky into the bargain—they don't think so much about that. They don't want to. You know this country as well as I do. Do you follow me?"

"Yes, Phil, I follow you."

"Then keep listening. Now, this averageness of yours is an asset—to you, to me, to all of us who are interested in you. If you divorce Ed Farrell you lose contact with the people in Podunk. They don't do it themselves—they stick it out, if it kills 'em. And it'll be better for you and all of us if you stick it out. Sure, I know there may be a temptation to try something new, now that you can afford it. But think it over, Shireen. You want your next book to sell in Podunk, don't you?"

"Of course I do, Phil. But honestly, there's nothing to worry about. Ed and I are very happy."

He looked at her carefully for a moment. "Are you? Well, then, that's fine. But stick that advice in your hat somewhere. You may need it one of these days. I've seen a lot of women get suddenly rich and famous. They don't keep their heads."

"They don't?" asked Shireen, in wondering innocence. "Why not, I wonder?"

"How do I know why not? The fact is, they usually don't. First they buy a mink coat—one of 'em got chinchilla—then they buy a new house, and next they get a new husband. It makes the damn publishing business look like Hollywood. You were a good example to other women while Ed was overseas and you keep on like that. Everyone else in the country will be getting divorced. I tell you, life's getting too complicated. Business is getting too complicated. If the goddamn government would only leave us alone. Say, did you take my tip on that stock?"

"Yes, I bought two thousand shares."

"Well, sell it."

"But it's still going up."

"That doesn't matter. Sell it. The times are precarious, girl, haven't I told you that before? We've got to keep our eyes open. Don't let yourself get caught napping, Shireen."

"Yes, Phil. All right."

Every few days she talked to Ed. He had been sent to a Navy hospital because he had had another malaria attack, and when she heard about that she was frantic.

"I'll come out there right away, darling!"

"No, Shireen. It isn't necessary. It really isn't necessary. I wish you wouldn't."

"You don't want me?"

"Of course I do, but there's no reason for you to come. I'll be out of here pretty soon. I don't want you to interrupt your work."

"It isn't important, Ed—"

"Yes, it is. It's very important. Please don't come."

"But I should. I feel guilty back here. I feel as though—"

"Don't worry about it. I'll be back there pretty soon. It looks like a discharge, after all."

"Oh, Ed! How wonderful!" And of course it would be wonderful. It was what they both wanted more than anything. Except that, hearing it, she felt a little sick for a moment. It created so many new problems. Well—they had to be faced sometime.

"Oh, darling, I hope so," she said, after an instant's pause. "Then we'll be really happy."

"I know we will, Shireen."

But when she hung up she sat there a moment, bewildered and helpless. *Something's wrong. I don't know what it is, but something's wrong. What is it that's happened to us? But* nothing *has. Everything's all right. As soon as he gets back and gets to work and we get settled again—it'll be all right then.*

Ed was discharged in January and once more she met him at the airport, full of many very good resolutions. They kissed each other and walked arm in arm to the car and he got behind the wheel and started driving.

Ed loved her. Ed needed her. That was the thing to keep in mind. "How do you feel, darling?"

"Fine. I feel great. I don't even know why they discharged me."

"We can do whatever you want to. We can go to Florida for a few weeks and you can lie around in the sun—"

"Oh, but I don't think that's such a good idea. Do you?"

"Not if you don't, darling. I'll do whatever you want, you know that."

Holy smoke, she thought, *what a good wife I am. Hardly any women would be as nice as this to their husbands—especially if they had everything I have. They're mostly only nice to them because that's the way they earn their living.* She decided that she wasn't so bad after all. She had just had more temptations and more opportunity.

And she would not make any decisions for Ed. She would let him do exactly as he liked. *Georgia was right. No one wanted to be treated like a helpless irresponsible infant. Not even if that was what they were. But she mustn't even think that! How had she got it into her mind that Ed was helpless and irresponsible? That was absurd. No, she wouldn't think it.*

"Isn't it a shame," she said, trying to get off onto something where she could not make any mistakes, "that now you can't wear your uniform any more? You look so handsome in it."

Ed laughed softly. "I'm afraid I can't feel very bad about that. I can't get out of it fast enough."

"I suppose," agreed Shireen pleasantly. "I guess you think of what it means and not how it looks. Women are so silly about such things. They only think about how a man looks, and that's been one thing about the war. The men have all looked wonderful, at least." No, that didn't sound so good, either, so she went on quickly. "You won't want to wear your old clothes any more, of course, and this terminal-leave will give you time to have some made."

"I'll wear the old ones. There wasn't anything wrong with them."

"But, darling," she said sweetly, though firm in her intention to convince him and absolutely sure she would, because the possibility of not being able to did not exist. Her first quick thought was to give

375

the old suits away if he refused to get new ones and then he would have to. But she would try gentle persuasion first. "They were all right then, Ed, but now you can afford to wear really good clothes."

"I can't afford to, though. Let's not begin by kidding ourselves about that one."

She looked at him in astonishment. "But Ed—how are we kidding ourselves? You know we decided long ago that if I made any money we would consider it to be ours. You haven't forgotten that?"

"I haven't forgotten. But you must be able to see there's quite a difference between talking about it and having it."

"No. I don't. And I don't see why you should."

"Well—" He laughed again, and lifted his shoulders. "There is a difference, all the same."

"What do you propose to do, then? I've got this apartment and certainly we can't run it on whatever you'll make at whatever you decide to do. Not in the beginning, at least."

"Not ever, probably."

What was wrong with this man? She was getting nervous and excited, listening to him, for he was saying things she had never expected to hear.

Everything had been going along all right. She had her whole life planned, from minute to minute and day to day and practically from year to year. And now he was back and had begun creating problems where they did not exist. Giving her new things to think about when she had already thought it all out and knew where she was and where he was, too, and she did not want him to give her additional trouble. Things were bad enough as it was. Married to a man who might go back to his silly insurance business and be lucky to make five thousand a year for the next three or four or five years and leave her with the responsibility of writing another book or starting a business or doing one damned thing or another which could bring an income of a hundred thousand a year. Since she had to have that much at least to keep going, once the taxes were paid.

"But why do you say that, Ed? Why do you admit defeat before you even begin?"

"Did I admit any defeat?" he asked her calmly.

"Of course! You said you might not *ever* make enough to afford the way I live!"

"Well—I might not. Ninety-nine per cent of the men in America couldn't afford it. Are they all defeated?"

Shireen felt a little wave of tiredness and discouragement. Poor Ed. He was just back from the war. He had been through so much—things she could never know about or imagine. And she must be gentle with him. She must humor him. In time he would come to see things her way. She must not try to force him or make him uneasy or give him any worries. She must help him to get rehabilitated. That goddamned war, in one way or another, had been nothing but a nuisance to her ever since it had begun. Why didn't the world let people alone? Didn't they have trouble enough without all this outside nonsense coming into it?

She drew a deep breath and then answered him carefully. "No," she said. "Of course they're not defeated. Money isn't really important—it's just that everyone thinks it is. And you know I want you to do whatever will make you happy. But please, darling, promise me not to think of this money as mine. It isn't. It's ours."

She meant exactly what she said. He must think of it as theirs. So long as he never thought about spending it in any way she would not like or without consulting her.

"All right," said Ed. "I'll think of it as ours." But he sounded as he always did when he did not want to argue any longer; she could not be sure she had once convinced him of anything.

"Then you will buy some new suits?"

"Yes."

"Oh, darling. You're so sweet. I love you, Ed, I really love you! Please believe me." And perhaps he did. She couldn't be sure. At least he pretended to.

For two or three weeks Ed was around the house. Shireen asked him if he minded if she went ahead with her schedule, and he said that he wanted her to. So she did. She had no time for him during the day, and on the appointed nights there were guests, or they went out. But she kept asking him if he was happy and he kept assuring her that he was.

Both of them were conscious, though, that the lives they had shared when they were very young were gone and they would not get them back another time. For it seemed as if everything that had happened to her, all the new patterns in her character and personality, showed up now like an invisible ink subjected to chemical treatment.

It made them both sad to know that the young, trusting and trusted simple part of their marriage was gone for good. Though Shireen refused to acknowledge this to herself and kept hoping that some miracle would set things straight.

"Don't worry about Ed," she said to Georgia, when Georgia expressed some concern about his quietness and detachment. "He's still getting reconverted. Anyway, Ed's crazy about me. I'm his whole life —he couldn't live without me. Remember," she continued, bragging, "I've spent a lot of time learning to be as many things as possible that a man needs to bolster up his ego. I operate on the theory that every American loves a bargain."

She knew well enough what she meant to him.

The way it had begun didn't matter, the separate parts weren't important—until they had composed a whole. It had happened so gradually, little by little, in the repeated pattern of their life. And now she was part of his being, he wouldn't have been the same without her. There was no such abstract idea for him any more as woman. When he thought of women he thought of Shireen. When he thought of a woman, he thought of Shireen. There was no place where she began to exist in him, no place where she did not exist, nowhere that he could be sure of belonging only to himself.

She was every way he had ever seen her look, everything she had said to him, everything he had felt for her or because of her. And, if they separated, how much of this would go with her and how much with him? This was the real property settlement they would have to make. For she knew he was in danger of finding he had entrusted so much of himself to her that he would have very little left.

But she had no time to think about these things. She had so much to do. More than she could ever get done. And there seemed to be more every day.

After the first two or three weeks Ed was no longer around very much. He went out in the morning and came back at the time she told him to in the evening—for dinner, or to meet the guests she had invited, though she felt that he did not like her new friends or feel at ease with them.

Late one afternoon he came into the bedroom. She had finished her writing and taken a bath and was getting dressed. There were half a dozen people coming for dinner. He kissed her as she sat making up her face, reflected in the mirrors that lined the dressing room and re-reflected, hundreds and thousands of times, into infinity. They talked a little, idly, for nowadays they seemed almost wary with each other, like two strange animals thrown together, each waiting for the other to make the first move.

He sat down on a chair nearby and lit a cigarette. "Shireen—there's something I've been wanting to talk to you about."

"What's that?" she asked him carefully. If Ed had been thinking he might have come up with some new idea that was his and not hers and which would perhaps demand some reorientation in her life.

"I wonder—well—would you be very disappointed if I went back to the insurance business?"

Oh, was that all?

"Why, of course not, darling. Why should I mind? You know I want you to do whatever will make you happiest. I know what, Ed—Georgia knows a lot of people and—"

"Now wait a minute, please. I know your intentions are good and I appreciate the fact that you want to help me. But I don't need Georgia to find me a place. That's something I'll do for myself. I'll tell you why I mentioned it: I got a call the other day from a guy I knew in

378

the Navy and we were talking about setting up an agency together. We wouldn't do the selling—the brokers would come to us. It might turn out to be something pretty good." He was watching her, a little anxiously.

She turned and smiled at him warmly, vastly relieved to find this problem almost settled. "I think that's a wonderful idea, Ed. Who is this friend of yours? Is he someone of importance?"

"I don't know what you mean. He's a guy about my age. We'll have to make what we can of it together."

Shireen began to brush her hair.

Well—why should she have expected anything else?

Ed in a big office, as she had pictured him, making hundreds of thousands of dollars a year, powerful and awe-inspiring, seemed now completely ridiculous. She felt foolish ever to have imagined it could happen. Just because she wanted it to. Just because it had happened to her. She was a freak. Her whole life was a crazy kind of fluke. It was the American dream come true. But, as Dallas had said, it couldn't come true for many people. Not, very likely, for Ed Farrell. The kind of success she had had was no more contagious, Ed could no more catch it from her, than she had been able to catch his easiness and confidence.

And maybe that was the very thing that was wrong with him anyway. He was too easy, too happy—too goddamned well adjusted ever to amount to anything. She, after all, had been miserable all her life, and maybe that was what you needed to spur you out of complacency.

But now she got up and came and stood before him, her hands on his shoulders, looking down, and his arms went around her eagerly, holding her to him, his head against her breasts. He held her close and she stood there motionless, stroking her hands over his hair.

"Ed—" she whispered. "My darling—"

He tipped back his head to look up at her and he seemed pitifully young and helpless and in need of something she could no longer give, the kind of love she had felt for him once. "I'll do the best I can, Shireen—I promise." And she hated herself again. She closed her eyes. The guests would be coming. This was no time to cry; she moved away from him to finish dressing.

"I know you will, Ed. You'll do very well, I'm sure of that." But why was it he had always made her feel this sickening self-contempt? As if he represented someone she had once wronged, or everyone she had ever wronged. But who could it be? What was it she had done? Nothing she could remember.

And in spite of herself, as the weeks went by, she grew more resentful of him. Mary Carlisle would bring her the week's checks to sign and several hundred or a thousand dollars would be gone from the

379

bank account. Then she would wonder why she must be left to worry about all this herself.

Why do *I* always have to do everything? Why is it no one in the whole goddamned world has ever done anything for me? No one ever taught me anything. I had to learn for myself. No one ever gave me anything. I had to get it all myself. Why can't I once get a chance to relax? Why can't someone else look after me?

But there wasn't anyone. And maybe there never would be.

She would set her teeth and try to push these thoughts out of her head so that she could work, write, finish a book. Make some more money. Pay it out in taxes, most of it, but somehow have enough left to live the way she was determined to live.

And so, if a servant forgot to polish the silver he was fired. If the cook was not good enough, get rid of her and get another one. If there was dust on a lamp it was a serious matter. If anything was out of order—the magazines on the coffee table, the lamps on the end tables, the ashtrays moved from their appointed places, a picture frame tipped—she got nervous and anxious and wondered irritably why nothing was done right unless she did it herself. And she did not have much time to spend with Ed. How could she? She had to keep learning and working. She had so many things to do. Everything depended upon *her*.

But she was polite to him. Just so he never questioned her or tried to change anything, she was polite. She had no time for quarreling now. Her time was too important.

Images floated through her mind from time to time—while she was writing, while she sat reading or practicing the piano or going somewhere in a taxicab.

She saw herself as a newspaper owner, sitting at a big desk, dressed in a simple suit with a white chiffon blouse, surrounded by secretaries and telephones, with a great many respectful men hovering around— her employees—while she smiled and made decisions about what the public should think today. Or she was wearing a smart well-bred black dress, standing in the House of Representatives and making a speech while all the people (men, again) listened and watched and were amazed at such capability and such beauty in one woman. Or she saw herself playing Mary, Queen of Scots, dressed in crimson velvet with golden chains around her neck and an ermine-lined hood over her hair, her eyes shining and her lips parted in some love scene with the Earl of Bothwell, but only her own face showed in the gigantic close-up that seemed to move out and engulf all the people in the theater, and the people again turned out to be only men.

None of these achievements seemed in any way too ambitious or beyond her capacities.

She might go to Europe or the Orient, meet everyone of importance

380

and write definitive articles or books on international politics. She might write a play and appear in it herself.

And what would Ed be doing while all this was going on?

What kind of substance would be left to their marriage once she had removed so much of herself from it? She couldn't concern herself too much with that. Ed would have to find his own path in life, and once he found it they would either go along it together or they would not. And, since it seemed clear enough that she knew what she wanted and he did not, that made the responsibility his alone.

She felt a little easier, thinking of it that way.

Chapter 52

"It's amazing," Ed said to her, and he was lying in bed with his arms behind his head, watching her and smiling. "You get up in the morning and you look like hell. And then you slap on some of this and dab on some of that and after about an hour you look perfectly beautiful. I've got to hand it to you, Shireen—you're clever."

She looked at him with surprise and then quick embarrassment and suddenly she wanted to hide herself. She was tying the belt of her robe, her hair was tangled and her face bare of make-up, and all at once she felt incredibly ugly.

Automatically she glanced into the mirror across the room and grimaced. "I guess I'm getting old," she said apologetically.

"Twenty-eight isn't exactly old."

"It seems old. I feel old. I feel a thousand. Ed—tell me the truth. Have I changed much?"

She looked at him and waited for his answer, appealing to him for kindness and reassurance. She was hating him violently though she did not know it.

He was her enemy.

But she almost had him beaten. He wore clothes she had bought for him. He ate food she got for him. He was waited on by servants she paid for. She was better than he was, in every way.

Yet he had one power left.

He could lie in bed in the morning and tell her that she was not actually beautiful and reduce her to cringing abject submission. He had waved a wand, some magical masculine wand: We want women to be beautiful. Don't ever forget that. And if they aren't we reject them. Even now, when she had everything and he had nothing, he could remind her that she was not a natural beauty, that she was only able to create the illusion of beauty—and the implication reached out, like spreading circles in a pool after a stone has been flung in. She might turn to other men but they would find her out. They would eventually see her as she really was, without her mask, and they would reject her too. Ed could reject her now, but he was kind and she must be grateful for his kindness; it was more than she deserved. For her face, after all, was the reflection of her self.

Nothing anyone else had said to her—Johnny or Jack MacDonald or Paul Worth or any of the men in whose eyes she had sought a

382

reflection she could not find in a mirror—could be counted. Not while there was one man who told her it was not true. He was the man who must be right.

The one thing she had wanted more than all others was to be truly and undeniably beautiful, for beauty was the most valuable thing a woman could have.

But men knew nothing about that. They sat back in comfortable smug masculine superiority and laughed at women's hats and criticized their clothes and said among themselves and to their wives and sisters and sweethearts: Isn't it ridiculous the way you women spend so much time on yourselves? If you'd spend half as much learning and studying and accomplishing something, you wouldn't be squawking about being inferior. You waste your lives on frivolity. *They* didn't. They had simplified things for themselves more and more. Their clothes were virtual uniforms so that there was no need for learning about line and color and whether this or that was more becoming. They left their faces alone and clipped their hair short. While women sat in hair-dressing parlors or having their nails manicured and their bodies massaged or went scouring through the stores to find exactly the right handbag for a new dress, they were out upon the world's and their own business.

"You haven't changed at all, Shireen," Ed said to her, and it was as if he had ridden by in his gilded coach and thrown her a few coins. "Or, if you have—it's for the better."

She gave a deep heavy sigh and after a moment said: "Oh, Ed— I'm so *afraid!*"

"Afraid of what?" Perhaps he looked a little amused, but she couldn't be sure.

"I don't know. I'm afraid of everything. I'm afraid of dying and getting sick and growing old and poverty!"

"Darling, darling—come here."

He reached out his arms and she went and lay down beside him. Around them was her lavish bedroom. It was hers completely. It had been designed and planned as her background. Ed came into it every night like a stranger, like a man visiting his mistress. But now she lay there, held close against him while his hands stroked her hair and his voice spoke softly and reassuringly, as if she were a frightened child.

"There's nothing for you to be afraid of, Shireen. You've got everything. You mustn't be afraid, sweetheart."

She clung to him gratefully; some sense of comfort and security seemed to come from the warmth of his body and soak into her. If it could soak down deep enough perhaps she would be at rest. Sometimes it seemed to, but then she would find it had warmed only the surface and not gone deep, not down to where she was cold and frightened, cringing against some dark damp wall.

383

"Oh, but Ed, there is! There's so much to be afraid of! You don't know!"

How could *he* know? He was a man. He was safe. The world belonged to him. But she had to fight and fight and fight, and she was getting tired, more and more desperately fearful. There semed to be a growing sickness in her until she thought it would be a relief to slide, drift, let life dwindle away from her, and die. Her fear of death had become so great she was convinced she could only be free of it by killing herself, so she would no longer have to fear she might die unexpectedly.

"What is it you want, Shireen?"

"I don't know, I don't know," she moaned. "More of everything, I guess."

"You'll get it—don't have any doubt about that."

"But what about you?" she cried, and then lifted her head and looked at him. "Oh, Ed, I'm sorry. I don't know what I'm saying." She drew away from him and sat up, feeling like a drunk who has had a pail of cold water thrown over him. How had she ever said that? How had she let it slip? But maybe he wouldn't notice.

He did, though.

"I know," he said. "I'm not much use to you."

"Oh, but darling, you are! I meant—"

"I know what you meant. I've been thinking about it, too. And I'm afraid there's only one solution."

Her face brightened a little. Ed had a solution. He had found one. All this time she had been wondering what was the matter with him—why he left everything for her to do—he had been thinking, and now he had the solution. She felt a tremendous relief. Someone else had found it after all. She could quit looking.

"What is it?" she asked him softly.

"I think I should leave you." He did not look at her as he said it.

"*Leave* me?" she asked him incredulously. "But why, Ed?"

"You know why, Shireen."

"But I don't know why. I can't imagine why. Aren't you happy?" Aren't you happy, with everything I've given you? What more do you want, for heaven's sake?

Ed laughed, and it had a strangely different sound from any laugh of his she had heard before. "Happy," he said.

"Well? Aren't you?"

"Shireen, you've always been such a child. And you aren't any more grown-up now than you ever were. It's cute and appealing, sometimes, but it can't be much use to you in life. What in the hell do you mean by 'happy'?"

"Why—I don't know. Whatever it means. I can't say offhand. You must know whether you are or not."

384

"I know all right."

"And you're not?" she demanded.

She had never expected to find anywhere such appalling flagrant ingratitude. After all the things she had given this man. After all she had done for him. And now he wasn't happy. What had *he* not to be happy about? She was the one with the worries. She was the one who had to balance this apartment and the servants and their cars and expensive clothes on her head and somehow walk the tightrope without tipping the whole thing over.

"I don't know what the word means," said Ed. "Neither do you. Maybe none of us do. But I do know I'm getting more uncomfortable every day."

"More uncomfortable?" And here he was being given everything in the world a man could need to make him comfortable.

"Yes—more uncomfortable. Look here, Shireen, we keep on walking around this. Maybe we've been thinking that if we ignored it it would turn out to be like the pink elephant and just disappear. But this is no drunk we can sober up from, I'm afraid."

"What are you talking about!"

"Why pretend you don't know?" he asked her gently. He looked at her without animosity or resentment, like a small boy who has lost something important to him; and Shireen's heart began to hurt her.

She threw her arms around him, wildly repentant, miserable, confused. She had hurt him again. No matter what she did, it always turned out that she had hurt him. She must somehow make amends.

"Oh, darling, you know I couldn't get along without you! Oh, Ed, my poor baby! How can you talk that way? How can you think such things?" She was holding his face in her hands, kneeling beside him, and she began kissing him with quick anguished hysterical little kisses. "I do need you. I need you now more than I ever did! What would I do without you?"

He was leaning on one elbow, but his face was turned up and he was looking at her, wanting so obviously to believe that she meant what she was saying. "Do you?" he asked her. "Do you need me?"

"I do, darling. I swear I do! I promise you I do!"

But after a moment he looked away. "I wish I could believe it. I've kept telling myself to believe it. But it isn't true, Shireen. Oh, we could go on like this—maybe all the rest of our lives. But don't you see what's happening to us?"

She became cautious again. "No, I don't."

He doubled his fist. "Why do we have to talk this way? Jesus! Oh, I don't know what to do. Out there—my God, how I wanted to get back to you. I was sure nothing else in the world would matter once I got back. I was sure I could somehow make you keep on loving me —I believed it because I had to believe it." He shook his head. "We've known each other a long long time, Shireen. All our lives, it seems like."

"I know, Ed," she said softly. "It has been all our lives, I guess. And we hoped for so much, didn't we?"

"I suppose we did. It's hard to remember now. Out there, I used to think about how it was when we first met. The way you were then. And all the things we used to do—"

He was not looking at her but a reminiscent smile had come onto his face and he looked almost happy again. Something like the boy she remembered from such a long time ago, when she had made an idol of him and thought that if she could only have him she would have everything on earth she could ever need or want.

"Remember," he said, "how we used to go shopping for the groceries together? And the first thing you learned to cook was tuna fish pie and we used to have it until it was practically coming out of our ears? And remember the long walks and bicycle rides we used to take out in the valley on Sundays?"

"And talk about all the things we wanted to do," Shireen went on eagerly. "Remember the time you were away and I thought a burglar was trying to get in and I climbed out the bathroom window in my robe and was sitting there in the garage waiting for you when you came home?"

"You were always expecting a burglar." He laughed. "Remember the time we drove up in the mountains for the week end and carried the sleeping bags and all our gear up a stream and then found the road came right along beside it anyway?"

As they talked it seemed as if these things had happened a very long time ago, and maybe not to them at all. So much had happened to them both in the meantime, and their memories had piled up.

"And remember," she said, "when we used to go dancing at the Biltmore and all the girls would try to flirt with you and you never so much as looked at anyone but me? I was so proud of you, and of myself for having you when everyone else wanted you."

"Yeah," said Ed, and the light went out behind his face again. "Times have sure changed." He tried to pretend it was a joke.

"And darling," Shireen went on desperately, feeling that the bond of memories between them was slipping once more dangerously toward the broken present, "I'll never forget the first gift you ever gave me. Remember it?"

"That string of pearls? It cost me five dollars."

"But that was such a lot of money to us. I'm still wearing them. Only now I suppose people think they're real."

"I suppose they do. They wouldn't imagine Shireen Delaney would wear anything but real ones."

386

"I'm very sentimental about those pearls. They mean the first few months we were married—when we believed in everything."

"And now we don't." He looked straight at her again. "Do we?"

"Of course we do, Ed. We really do."

"No, we don't. We're not the same people. This is a lot of years later. It'd be nice if we could have stayed the same—you always eighteen and me always twenty-one. I guess we even thought we could—just by wanting to. But it gets clearer every day."

"No, Ed. You mustn't talk this way."

"Why not? You can't bring back something that's dead just by pretending it's alive. That's over, Shireen. Look at this place. It's yours. You worked for it and got it and paid for it and it's yours. I can't kid myself that any part of it's mine. It doesn't even look like me."

"But Ed! Don't you like it?"

"Like it? What's that got to do with it? It's beautiful. Only I've got no business in it, that's all. I feel like a stranger every time I open the door and come in. I keep expecting the servants to ask if Miss Delaney is expecting me."

"You mean you don't like to have them call me Miss Delaney?"

"Shireen, for cris'sake, I don't care what they call you. You're in love with your own name, and it doesn't make any difference to me—but now even that's different somehow. And your friends. They're not my friends, you know that. I'm your husband—Shireen's husband —so they're nice to me and polite and they ask me along but I got nothing in common with any of them. They don't give a damn about me. I don't even know what they're talking about, most of the time."

"Ed!"

He looked at her quickly. "What?"

"I will not have you talking this way! We have everything in the world that anyone could want. And we should be happy—I won't stand for us being anything but happy. Look at the millions of people who have nothing at all—and we have everything. We've *got* to be happy! It isn't right for us not to be!"

He smiled at her again. "Little Shireen," he said tenderly. "Still so sure you can make things what you want them to be."

"Little Shireen, nothing! It's the truth. Now, let's take a shower and get dressed and have breakfast and then we'll decide what to do. It's a lovely day outside and we have the whole world. Do you realize that we can do anything on earth that we want to today? Nothing can stop us! Why, we should be out of our minds with happiness!"

He was smiling as she talked, and then he kissed her, perhaps because it hurt him to hear her talking so eagerly about things he no longer believed were possible. Shireen, he knew well enough, would always believe what she needed and wanted to believe and she never

387

gave up anything without a tremendous struggle. He couldn't do it for her. She would have to learn.

He kissed her and she began to stroke his face, murmuring: "Darling, darling, I love you so much. I love you, I love you, I love you. I want you to be happy. Oh, Ed, you've *got* to be happy!"

He grinned at her, an expression he put on over some look of deep inner tiredness. "I know. You want me to be happy and you'll see to it that I am—if you have to kill me to do it."

Chapter 53

Shireen glanced at her watch. She frowned a little.

"I don't understand this at all. Seven o'clock. Ed's usually home by six-thirty, unless he calls me. I should have let him know you'd come, Mike."

They sat in the living room, Mike on one green and white striped love seat and Shireen across the black lacquered coffee table from him, sitting on the other. She wore a flowing gown of pale gray chiffon and lace, with a wide sash swathed around her waist and two big dark-red artificial roses stuck into the low neckline. Mike sat there looking solid and brown and healthy, with captain's bars on his shoulders and a row of ribbons on his chest. He was finishing his third bourbon and water and the ashtray beside him was full of cigarette stubs, for he had been smoking nervously ever since he had got there an hour and a half before and been let in by the maid. Shireen was dressing when he came.

She had swept in, her hair black and shiny, holding out both white hands to him, her red mouth smiling, and Mike had pretended to reel a little with the shock.

First they had gone through the house, Mike walking almost on tiptoe, as if he might jar something out of place, following her and murmuring: "Holy smoke, Shireen. It's terrific." After that they sat down and began to talk, but so far had not said anything that either of them was thinking.

They had not spoken of the last time they had seen each other—here in New York, two years and a half ago. They had not mentioned the letters they had written, or what either had done with them. They had not talked about the guilt they felt. Of how things were working out now that Ed was back after her whole life had changed. Whether her success had given her the thing she had been looking for, or what the war had actually meant to him.

Instead he had talked about his experiences overseas as if it had been one big fraternity initiation—and Shireen had taken the changes in her life as if for granted. They felt safe being together again, and returned to a time they must both have been longing for. She felt kinder toward Ed and closer to him than she had for a long while. She had been looking forward eagerly to his surprise and pleasure when he came home and found Mike there.

But now something had gone wrong.

Ed was late.

And this was unprecedented. Dinner was served at seven-thirty every night unless there was some very good reason to change it. And how would it look to Mike—Ed being late? He would see instantly, she felt sure, that things had gone all wrong between them.

She kept on talking to Mike, asking him if he wanted another drink, telling him to please have some more hors d'oeuvres, but she was slowly getting more and more angry.

How dared Ed do this to her? Embarrass and humiliate her, and before Mike, of all people? Let their friends see what their marriage had come to, in spite of everything she had done for him? Just wait until he gets here, she was thinking while she talked. He can't treat me this way—

"I can't imagine what's happened to Ed," she said, but her face seemed unconcerned and her tone was casual. "This isn't like him, Mike, you know that."

"Maybe he stopped off for a short beer." Mike was grinning, admiring her looks, and apparently had no interests beyond her and the drink in his hand.

"But why should he do this without letting me know? He never has before."

"First time for everything," said Mike. "God, Shireen, you look so damn beautiful."

"Do I, Mike? Thanks. That's very nice of you. But wouldn't you think he'd at least—"

"Shireen, for cris'sake, don't worry about it. The guy's old enough to be out alone, isn't he? What are you—his mother?"

"Of course not. I never try to run Ed's life. He can do as he pleases, you know that. It's because you're here." She glanced around as if she were looking for something to throw. "Oh, I wish he wouldn't do things like this to me!"

"Ed hasn't done anything to you, Shireen," said Mike quietly. "The guy's a model husband. I hope you know it."

"Oh, of course," said Shireen. But something in her voice and expression could have indicated that the model had been changed in certain respects since he had seen it last. "Ed's very sweet."

"He's the greatest guy in the world," said Mike, and finished his drink. He looked at Shireen, and there was that momentary blend of longing and desire. His face darkened with guilty embarrassment, and he glanced away. "Mind if I have another drink?"

Shireen was tapping her foot. "That's three you've had already."

"Three? Is that all?" He got up. "Y' know, I'll bet I've drunk enough bourbon in the last three years to float the whole goddamn United States fleet."

"Go ahead then. Drink some more. Maybe you can capsize it."

She wandered across the room, ran her fingers along the piano keys, and then sat down and began to play. She played a page or so of "Clair de Lune" and then, without clear intention, began playing "You'd Be So Nice To Come Home To."

For a few minutes she watched the keyboard, but then she looked across and saw Mike standing at the bar-table, his glass in one hand, a pair of tongs holding an ice cube in the other, and his face was as helplessly bewildered as it had been the morning he left her at the Cheshire House. She was instantly disgusted and angry with herself.

Mike was nothing to her and she, in reality, was nothing to him. Whatever he remembered, whatever she remembered, was of no consequence to either of them now. They had renounced each other without ever having discussed it—and there had not been anything real to renounce: an undercurrent infatuation which had existed between them for years and once, because the circumstances were right, had been expressed. But certainly that had nothing to do with this moment—so why should she want to call it back again?

Curiosity? The wish to assure herself that no man could ever completely forget her? Because she was angry with Ed for having failed to be the man she believed she wanted?

Of course, she could always tell herself she did such things because she needed to know them for her writing. Since life, if you did nothing but live it, seemed to her to have very little significance. Not what it cost to live. Experience acquired meaning only if she could interpret, recreate, and put it into some permanent form. Or it was lost and became an irrecoverable part of eternity, belonging no longer to you but to the impersonal forces of the universe to which all human experience consigned itself. She believed she had found a way to conquer this fatal flaw in living and that was to put it on paper before the jealous gods snatched it away and took it to themselves.

That was all the excuse she had ever had for the mistakes she had made, the harm she had caused, the pain she had suffered herself. She could not be quite sure if it was all the excuse she needed.

But still, someday it might be valuable to know how a man feels when he has made love to his best friend's wife and confronts her again in his friend's home. She had found that physical intimacy between a man and woman never perishes, for the knowledge remains part of bodily awareness and is communicable without a word being spoken. That was interesting, wasn't it?

But not for her, for someone else who lived inside her.

My other me, she told herself.

Shireen got up from the piano and gave a quick brush with the back of her thumb along the middle keys. It was a sudden jarring

391

sound and broke the quietness. Mike laughed, from a combination of relief and embarrassment.

"That was very pretty," he said, and strolled back slowly to sit down again. "I didn't know you could play, Shireen."

"I don't play very well. I've just been taking lessons a few months. But I enjoy it."

"You're amazing."

She sat down again, across from him, and lit a cigarette. "Why, for heaven's sake?"

"You work so hard at everything. It must be wonderful not to be naturally lazy."

"Wonderful?" Shireen repeated in surprise. "Sometimes it's pure hell."

"Then why don't you take it easy? If it's tough being energetic, just be lazy."

"You know better than that, Mike."

"No, I don't. I'm a lazy bastard myself, and I guess that's the way I prefer it. Oh, sure, when this thing ends I'll go back to the law and work like hell and maybe in twenty years make a fair amount of dough. But I'll never be able to kid myself again. Not after this last three years. The war is the greatest thing that ever happened to me. All the liquor you want. All the women you've got stamina for. You're never alone. There's always someone up above to tell you what to do and someone down below to take the rap. Hell, it's a great life. Not for the guys who got it, I know that, but I happened to be one of the lucky ones. People wonder why wars go on and why we keep getting into them every few years. Well—civilian life isn't all it's cracked up to be by a long shot. And with what most of us have to look forward to, no wonder war is a relief. God, I *must* be drunk. I'm saying everything no decent citizen is even supposed to think."

Shireen looked at her watch again. Seven forty-five. "No decent citizen is supposed to think," she said sourly.

If he doesn't get here . . .

"Think about what? You think too much, Shireen."

"I never think at all," she said firmly. "The one thing I avoid is thinking. It's *intolerable* to think!"

He looked at her in surprise and finished his drink. He shook his head. "Is my memory failing me, or have you changed these last couple of years? You weren't always like this?"

"Yes I was. I just didn't say it before."

"You seem different. You seem nervous and worried about something—I don't mean Ed being late. Something permanent. You're not very happy, Shireen."

"What if I'm not?" she asked defiantly, jealous of his comfortable bland easiness. "Who is?"

392

Was she the only person on earth who was constantly worried and nervous and troubled? Wouldn't anyone else admit it? It sometimes seemed she must be and it made her more lonely than ever. To be so different, not even to know anyone else who was so different. And the loneliness was growing unbearable.

Mike was looking at her sadly. "I always think of you, Shireen, as one of the luckiest people I know. And you are. But if you don't think so—then something's wrong. What is it?"

"Lucky!" Her face turned bitter. "What's ever happened to me that's been lucky? Is shutting yourself up for four years and working on something and never showing it to anyone and not knowing what will ever come of it *if* anything ever comes of it—is that luck?"

"But it was lucky it turned out the way it did. A lot of people work and work very hard and for more than four years and never get anything. Look at this apartment. Look at all the things you have. Even financial security—if you're careful—for the rest of your life. I don't know what more anyone could want. You've even got a good husband, a guy who's crazy about you."

"Ed?" Shireen asked, as if she was not sure whom he might be talking about.

Mike got up and went to pour himself another drink. "Of course Ed."

He poured the drink slowly, for he was drunk enough by now that he had to be careful or he might make a mistake. And then he came back across the room toward her. She sat and watched him, and her face had relaxed. She looked pitifully sad. It happened so often, whenever she forgot, just let her face go.

"Ed doesn't love me," she said, and the moment it was out she wondered why she had said it. But of course she knew. She wanted sympathy. She wanted Mike on her side. I hate myself, she thought, and went on: "Not any more, he doesn't."

Mike was now clearly uneasy. "Shireen, that's ridiculous. He's nuts about you and you know it."

Shireen smiled secretly. "Maybe he was once. But not now. In fact, he wants to leave me. He's said so several times the past few weeks."

"He wants to leave you! Now you know that's crazy. Unless he thinks *you* want him to. That would be the only possible reason. I know that as well as I know anything. What's happened to you two, anyway?"

"Nothing, Mike. I don't think we ever expected to stay married this long in the first place."

"Shireen, that can't be true. I'm sure there's some mistake about this."

"Well, really, Mike," said Shireen, and now she seemed perfectly

393

cool and detached. "I do know what goes on in my own life, you know."

Mike looked at her in bewilderment, as if he could not believe he had ever seen her any other way than sitting there immaculate and groomed and shining, dressed in chiffon and lace with her hair brushed smooth. He narrowed his eyes a little as he looked at her, as if trying hard to see behind and beyond the girl who sat opposite him fitting another cigarette into her gold holder. And then he shook his head, as though the image had refused to come and he would not try any longer.

"Ed," she told him, "simply has not been able to adjust himself to this kind of life."

"Well, give him time."

"He's been back eight months."

"It may take a lot longer than that. Maybe a couple of years. You'll have to be patient."

"Patient!" cried Shireen, and got abruptly to her feet and walked away from him, across the room. She stood for a moment with her back to him, looking through the windows at the lighted buildings. She turned around again, slowly. "I've been patient all my life. I'm tired of waiting!"

"Waiting for what?"

And then she gave a sudden despairing sigh. "I don't know."

Mike put his drink on the table and walked over to her. She raised her head and looked at him, helplessly. "Shireen," he begged her. "Don't be so unhappy. Oh, Shireen—"

She looked at him, waiting. And down underneath she was curious again, wondering what would happen. Men and women, she thought, haven't got much business together except when they're in bed.

He turned away. "I'm a goddamned fool," he said with soft fury.

"No, you're not, Mike. You're not at all, believe me." Something protective, reassuring, almost maternal had come into her face and manner and the sound of her voice.

Mike glanced around anxiously. "Let's turn on the radio. Let's do something! Let's stop talking."

"I'm sorry, Mike," she said gently, and with a deft movement drew back her skirts and stepped away from him, crossed the room and went into the library where she turned on the phonograph, leaving in it the pile of records she found there. She came back, smiling slightly, as if she had somehow been good and kind and considerate, helped him out of a dangerous difficult situation. At that moment the door opened and Ed walked in. She caught a glimpse of his face as he appeared in the doorway, guilty, almost fearful, and knew instantly that he had been drinking.

But almost before she had seen it the expression was gone and he

394

and Mike rushed toward each other. Shireen stood and watched them shaking hands, pounding each other on the shoulders, both of them grinning happily.

"Mike, for the love of God! I no more expected to find you here—"

"I got in today. Shireen and I thought we'd surprise you." He poked him lightly in the chest.

They went on talking, neither waiting for the other to finish a sentence, laughing and excited. Shireen watched them and was glad to see that Ed was genuinely happy. Mike had been his friend for so long and they understood each other and were comfortable together. Everything seemed to be all right again.

She walked toward them and as Ed glanced at her there was that guilt and strange half fear on his face again. "I'm sorry I'm late, Shireen," he said quickly. "I stopped off with—"

Shireen kissed his cheek. "Darling, it's all right. I should have let you know Mike was here, but I wanted to surprise you."

"Oh," said Ed, and looked relieved. He kissed her on the forehead.

Shireen turned then and linked her arms through theirs and stood a moment, smiling first at Ed and then at Mike. The three of them strolled toward the dining room and Ed and Mike began talking again. The elaborate apartment, the servants waiting to serve dinner, the complexities in each of them turned magically to stage props and papier mâché. Mike was here and everything was the way it used to be. Ed held Shireen's chair and she sat down, her face gleaming in the candlelight, bending forward a little and smiling at them with a beneficent flowing warmth.

"Isn't it wonderful for us to be together again?" she asked them happily.

Chapter 54

Mike's influence on Ed was not altogether a good one in Shireen's opinion. They both drank a good deal, and Mike apparently convinced Ed he was still student-body president and future conqueror of the world. By the time he had been there four days she began to think it would be just as well when Mike went away and Ed began to see things as they were again. But she felt pity, as well, seeing how eager Ed was to be reassured by his friend, and how he seemed to keep hoping that she would believe it too.

One night Shireen sat between them in a night club where they had gone after a play, and watched them drink and listened to them talk. When they weren't talking over old school escapades they talked about the war. After awhile she felt bored and jealous of the fact that nothing in their conversation included her; and she resented what seemed to her their mutual flight from reality.

"I think you men," she said, "have always fought against being civilized." They both looked at her in surprise, as if they had forgotten she was there.

"What?" asked Mike, as though he had come back from some-where and just caught the end of a conversation.

"Of course," she went on, "if it weren't for women, men would still be living in caves and eating raw meat and hitting each other over the heads with clubs. It's women who've taken you by the ear and made you stop being either little children or wild savages—which is apparently all you ever really want to be. And you resent us for it. Every so often you have to get away where you can behave the way you wanted to all along."

"Well—" said Mike, and he raised his eyebrows thoughtfully and looked down at his drink. "I guess I'd never thought of it that way before."

"Shireen's got so many theories," said Ed, and he smiled tolerantly, glad to have an ally. "She's got everything figured out. Absolutely everything. If there's anything you want to know about, Mike, just ask Shireen. She'll tell you."

Shireen looked at him coldly. "Not *quite* everything."

Both Mike and Ed glanced away, off at people sitting near by, pretending to have discovered something very interesting over there.

396

And Shireen felt ashamed of herself for she knew what had been in her mind and was sure they must know, too.

She reached out impulsively and took his hand. "I'm sorry, Ed. I didn't mean that the way it sounded. You know, sometimes I think that if I'd lived in another age, I'd have been completely impossible."

Ed glanced at her. "Have times changed so much?"

Shireen burst into shocked laughter. Usually he apologized for the things she did wrong. And she felt relieved that for once he had not been any kinder than she. She laughed as if it was one of the funniest jokes she had ever heard, and was almost grateful to him for not having been humble this time.

The two men, after a moment's surprise, began to laugh too. And the laughter seemed to establish once more a friendly equilibrium and put them at ease again.

"One thing about Shireen," said Mike, "is that she has a wonderful sense of humor. She can always laugh at herself."

"It's her saving grace," said Ed. "That, and the fact that she has good taste."

Mike grinned, as if he thought Ed was only teasing her. "Along with beauty and brains and talent and money."

Ed looked at his wife, rather carefully now, though his face had loosened a little from the liquor. He had told her often enough that she was his goddess, the woman he worshiped and loved and needed beyond everything else. This was the other side of it. He also disliked her, maybe even hated her.

She watched him, seeing the expression on his face, aware that she was relieved to know it, for it took some of the guilt from her. Thank God he was not completely a saint.

"She's got all that, all right," Ed said. "The gods were kind to her. But the only gift she really counts is money. Nothing else matters to her but her money. Isn't that right, Shireen? You could lose everything else, if you had enough money."

"I suppose so," she said irritably. She felt that he was attacking her out of his own disappointments, rather than for what she had done which deserved it. "What could anyone do without money, after all, the way life is today? It makes anything tolerable."

"Not quite," said Ed softly.

Shireen's eyes hardened and she stared at him steadily, but he was looking away from her, down into his glass. Mike had begun to glance nervously around again, and was drumming his fingers on the table.

"I'm sure I don't know what you're talking about, Ed," she said slowly and evenly. "My money has certainly improved life for you considerably. If a man ever came home to be rehabilitated in style— it's been you." Mike looked at her swiftly, his face horrified, and then he looked away, turned in his chair and began to signal for the waiter.

397

Ed gave her a glance that was almost vicious, but Shireen continued to stare challengingly at him, and he looked down at his drink again. Then abruptly he picked up the glass and finished it.

"How about another one, Ed?" Mike asked him, for the waiter had come and was standing there.

"Okay." Ed had slumped a little in his chair, one hand still holding the glass, the other in his pocket.

"You, Shireen?"

"All right, thanks."

She looked back to Ed but he refused to meet her eyes. And a quick scorn came up, for she knew he was afraid of her and of what she might say to him if she got angry enough. But though he had retreated from her again she was confident she could coax him out of hiding whenever she liked with a sweet smile, a brief caress, a few kind words. She always had. The magic had never failed yet. Ed loved her and she was convinced he would love her no matter what she might do or say to him. So, deciding to leave him where he was for awhile and let him suffer, she turned brightly to Mike.

"Where were we, anyway?" she asked, as if there had been only some mild digression from one conversational topic to another.

"Women," said Mike, and grinned maliciously, "are the civilizing influence. Wasn't that it?"

"Oh, yes!" She laughed now and it was a charming little laugh, easy and free, and her face had begun to flow and sparkle again. She looked at Mike and there was something open and intimate in her expression. Ed sat watching her with no apparent jealousy but only a painful yearning. He watched her covertly, as if from hiding, while she talked. She did not turn once to glance at him but talked directly to Mike, who sat with a look of stupefaction, listening to her probably, but absorbed helplessly by her beauty. He seemed momentarily to have forgotten that Ed was there.

"But that isn't the only reason," she said, "why men go to war. I think the whole thing has a sexual basis. The normal sexual expression for a man is a display of power, isn't that right?" She did not wait for anyone to agree with her. "And the ultimate expression of power is to inflict death. In war men are not only permitted but encouraged and in fact forced to carry out this urge for complete and final dominance—to the point of causing death. I know there's some roundabout connection with sex. There always is. But of course it's the sort of thing no one ever talks about." She opened her palms and shrugged lightly.

While she was talking Mike had snapped out of his trance and glanced guiltily over at Ed. Ed had sat without moving, slumped down, watching her. When she stopped he lifted his glass and took another long drink.

"Don't you think that's true, Mike?" she asked him.

Mike grinned again, self-consciously, but apparently pleased she had taken him into all this deep reasoning and made him her confidant in so esoteric a matter. "Could be. What about you, Ed? Do you think there's any connection between death and sex?"

Ed laughed, and the laugh was almost melodramatically short and bitter. "Of course there's the example of the female praying mantis and the male."

"That's beside the point, Ed," she said impatiently, disposing of him and his innuendo. "But everyone knows, who's had a thoroughly satisfying love affair, that at the end there's a kind of dying. A release from yourself and almost from life for a few moments, that spreads out into time and space. That's something we can't explain, isn't it?"

She looked at Mike and caught a momentary flicker in his eyes, a quick charge of memory that blazed an instant and went out. The two men now seemed thoroughly uncomfortable and attended to their drinking. Shireen was impatient with them. Hypocrites, she thought scornfully. What were they afraid of?

A few minutes went by and no one seemed to know what to say any more. They sat in a kind of stupor, both men somewhat drunk, Shireen proudly scornful of their drunkenness. She lifted her glass and sipped her emerald-green drink from two tiny straws spiraled with color like old-fashioned barbershop poles.

"It's sure hot in here," said Mike after awhile.

"Let's get out," said Ed.

"Which one's our waiter?"

"I think it's that guy over there. Hey—Almost got 'im. Nope, not quite."

"Why don't you wait a minute?" Shireen asked them softly. "The next show goes on right away."

And almost immediately the master of ceremonies walked to the small stage and the floodlights went up; the room began to shuffle with preparation for growing quiet. Ed turned his chair around to face the stage and Mike leaned forward on his elbows, lighting another cigarette. A girl with a careful sunburned mask painted over her face and white-blonde hair piled up like spun sugar, walked out and leaned against the piano. She shook out a scarlet chiffon handkerchief and looked bored, but well satisfied with herself.

"God damn," murmured Mike. Shireen looked at him, lifting her eyebrows, but he was intently watching the girl.

Then she looked at Ed and he was watching her too. She waited a moment for him to turn back to her and, when he did not, leaned forward and kissed him on the cheek. "Darling—" she whispered. "You're not mad at me, are you?"

The girl began to sing, very slowly and softly:

> "If I loved you—
> Time and again I would try to say . . ."

"Listen to the music," Ed told her, not turning his head.

"But Ed," she insisted. "Please don't be mad at me. I didn't mean to do anything bad. Honestly I didn't. You don't think I'm obnoxious, do you?"

He looked at her with a sad smile. "I suppose I do."

But she pretended not to believe it. She laughed and slipped her arm through his and then turned to watch the girl, determined to show them both that she was not afraid of her or even slightly jealous.

> "If I loved you—
> Words wouldn't come in an easy way,
> Round in circles I'd go . . ."

The girl still leaned there languidly, as if something had tired her too much to move, and as she sang she opened her red mouth and showed her teeth and looked ready to devour every male in the room.

On the day Mike left, he and Shireen and Ed had breakfast together and then Ed went to his office. Mike and Ed shook hands and told each other how good it had been to get together, wished each other luck, and somehow looked to Shireen—who stood watching them— like two conspirators. A world existed in their friendship that she did not know and could never know. And she was a little curious, a little jealous at realizing she was shut out.

Then she walked to the door with Ed, as she did every morning when he left for work, holding his hand. "How's everything going?" she would ask him, as if it were something confidential or even perhaps a little embarrassing, like asking a friend in a hospital how he's feeling after his operation. She knew very little about the work he did, for even when she asked him he did not talk to her about it much, and when he did she was not listening. Only pretending to.

Each time he answered the same way: "Fine. Everything's fine."

"That's good, Ed. I'm glad you're doing what you enjoy."

And then he would kiss her lightly and she would smile at him, like a mother sending her little boy off to school, and he would go out. That was when her day began. She would shut the door and turn and go about her business and he almost never entered her mind again until he came back in the evening; when she was usually a little surprised to see him, as if a stranger had turned up, or an old acquaintance she had not been expecting.

Now she went back, her blue morning robe trailing behind her, to where Mike sat at the white iron table out on the terrace, smoking a

400

cigarette and drinking one more cup of coffee. Shireen took the chair beside him and poured another cup for herself; Mike leaned over to light her cigarette and they both sat without speaking while the maid cleared away the dishes. The morning was hot and clear and felt as if summer had come to stay. When the maid left, Shireen sat silently a little longer, stirring her coffee, and then she sighed.

"I'm going to miss you, Mike. I wish you could stay longer." She always meant it when she said it. But when he went, of course she wouldn't. Probably she had never genuinely missed anyone in her life, and never would.

"I wish I could too." They were quiet again. Shireen felt there was something he wanted to say to her that he was having difficulty with, and she waited for him. He gave a self-conscious little cough.

"Shireen—"

She tipped her head and looked at him. "Yes, Mike?"

"Ed loves you a hell of a lot, you know that?"

"Yes," she said softly. "I suppose maybe he does. Oh, I'm sure he does. I don't know why I sometimes think he doesn't. I guess because I know I don't deserve him."

"Never mind that," said Mike. "The guy's nuts about you. But he's scared. He's scared as all hell."

"Scared?" Shireen asked wonderingly. "But why, Mike? What can he possibly be afraid of?"

"Losing you, of course. What else? He's been talking to me, you know, and I want to tell you this because I'd hate to see this thing blow up. And it will if you aren't pretty damned careful. A lot more careful than you've been so far."

"You mean I haven't been careful?" she asked him in great surprise. "Have I been doing something wrong?" She frowned a little, trying to think what it might be.

"I've known Ed most of my life, and the one thing the guy's always had was his own self-respect. You know that, Shireen. Nobody grew up with more reason to believe in himself than Ed Farrell. Everything: his family, the grades he got in school, he was always at the top. Out in the Pacific, too. Everyone's always thought he was terrific— and he is, let's face it. Now look at him. He's out of the war, even before it's over, through no fault of his own. And as if that's not tough enough to take, his wife has made a howling success and is rich as Croesus, living in a joint that looks like a movie set where not one thing was planned with him in mind—"

"Oh, yes it was," interrupted Shireen. "I told the decorator I wanted everything big enough so a man could be comfortable."

Mike smiled. "Okay. You told the decorator. But what have you told yourself? You're letting this slip away from you, Shireen. You're tearing the guy down, little by little. Oh, I'm sure you don't know

401

you're doing it—and I know you much too well to think you'd do it intentionally."

"I certainly would not!"

"But don't you see what's going on? You've got such a terrific respect for money you think nothing else in the world is important. And now you've got money and Ed hasn't—not enough to count as against yours, anyway, even if it is what the two of you lived on before. So you've lost respect for him. And it shows. I've heard the things you say to him. No great harm in any single one of them. But add them all up, day after day, week after week, month after month—you're giving him the Chinese water torture, Shireen. I mean it."

"Oh, Mike—I think you're exaggerating all this."

"I'm not exaggerating anything, Shireen. He goes around here like a guy walking on eggs and he treats you as if he's afraid you may blow up in his hands any minute. Ed's not like that—you know he isn't. What've you done to him?"

Shireen stared at him and the quick thought came that she could ruin their friendship, Ed's and Mike's, with half a dozen words. So how did he *dare* talk to her like this? But of course he knew she wouldn't.

"What have *I* done to him? I haven't done a goddamned thing. It's been like this ever since I've known him. He plays the part of a meek sweet mouse and makes everyone think I'm a terrible bitch! He's always done that! And he got away with it, too, until I made some money. And now he can still get away with it with his old friends—but not with mine. They know I'm not so bad and they wonder what's the matter with him. And you know as well as I do what it is. Ed's always been a bigshot. And now he isn't. That's all there is to it. Furthermore, I don't even think he wants to be any more. I used to believe Ed would be a great success, but either he never wanted to or now he's afraid to, for fear he won't ever be as successful as I am—no matter what he does. And he won't, either," she added in a mutter.

Mike was quiet a moment, thinking over what she had said. "Maybe he doesn't. Money has never been as important to him as it has to you."

"It never used to be this important to me! But I've found out that it makes up for everything else!"

"What else?"

"I don't know. All the things you think exist somewhere in the world, when you're young and naïve. No one ever knows what they are. Except that in time you realize you were only fooling yourself. They aren't anywhere. Money's the only thing you can count on."

"You know, I told Ed the other night I thought you were spending

402

your money too fast and he said he hoped you spent it all—and went broke. I suppose he thinks that would give you back to him."

Shireen's eyes narrowed cruelly. "Oh—he said that, did he? Well, I'm not surprised. But it wouldn't give me back to him, and I'll tell him so. The truth of it is, Mike, that Ed's jealous of me." When before I was jealous of him—his ease and confidence and popularity and the way everyone loved him.

But Mike laughed sharply. "Shireen, that's crazy. What man has ever been jealous of a woman? Don't you see what it is? The whole pattern of marriage has been turned upside down with you two. Now you're the one who supports him, you're the one people seek out, he tries to fit himself into the edges of your life and finds there isn't much room for him. And when you first got married it was nothing like that. He played the normal man's part for years—"

"The normal man's part!" sneered Shireen. "I suppose that what you're getting at is that women have no business being cleverer or making more money than men. Because whatever will the poor dears do then? They're not used to it, because it's their normal part in life to dominate and give a woman what they think she deserves—a house and clothes and whatever fragments of affection they have handy. And if that power is taken away from them then they're nervous and upset and begin walking on eggs! And isn't it pitiful! I suppose if a woman happens to have some kind of ability she should be thoughtful enough not to use it, because she might do better than her husband and that would make him unhappy! Is *that* what you're telling me?"

"That's about it, Shireen, whether you like it or not."

"As it happens I don't like it. I not only don't like it—I refuse to have any part of it. I don't have to any more. I can take care of myself and I've proved that and I'll never go back to where I was and what I was. Ed can either come along with me—or go his own way!"

"If you honestly feel like this, then you've got no business being married to Ed. Or anyone else, either."

"Don't I know it!"

She was shocked, at first, to hear herself say it. And then aware of a tremendous relief. There. It was finally out of her. Put into spoken words. And she felt cleansed of something she had carried, festering inside her, but which could cause no further damage now.

Mike looked at her with no attempt to conceal his disapproval and she suddenly despised him. She had upset his applecart, too, his belief in his omnipotence, which he had been talking about even while he pretended he was pleading for Ed. He had really been talking about all men.

The hell with them, she thought contemptuously. If they can't do

403

anything else they can always look smug and take refuge in the fact that they're male. But that isn't enough. If I'm ever going to respect a man at all he's got to be more than that. So much more. Anyway— I don't think there's any such man on earth and I'm not going to waste any more time trying to find him. I've got too much to do.

Mike stood up.

He paused for a moment, looking down at her, and her face as she turned it up to him softened now and began to plead for his kindness and trust: Don't hate me, Mike. I didn't mean any of those things I said. I'm not bad. I'm really good—I mean to be. And slowly she saw him respond, the yearning came into his eyes again, as if he wanted to believe her and was searching for that part of her he could believe.

"Anyway," he said, "you're sure pretty."

She smiled. "It's the luckiest thing that ever happened to me." He touched the side of her face briefly, and then turned away.

She walked with him through the living room and into the foyer, where his bags had been set against the wall. She had a reassuring sense of triumph, as if she had conquered him after all. There was always something she seemed to promise—and by that means she had kept them hoping, one after another, throughout her life. Ed and Johnny and Jack, maybe even Dallas—each man had hoped he might or could be the one to find a clear pathway to where that promise dwelt. But none of them ever had. And, if she could help it, no one of them ever would.

It would be the end of her self, if it happened.

Mike turned, with his hand on the doorknob. "Well—you know how I feel about you, Shireen. I think you're a wonderful girl. I always have, and I always will. But I thank God I'm not married to you."

Shireen shook her head. "You know, I can't remember a man I've loved or who's ever loved me, who hasn't said that sooner or later. Until I'm just about used to the idea myself." She looked away, frowning a little. "But I still don't know if it's something wrong with me—or with them."

Mike grinned, and apparently her implication of cowardice did not frighten him. "Good-by, Shireen," he said gently. He was completely free of her and looked as if he knew this and was glad to know it. She felt a little frightened by some premonition that this would always happen, sooner or later, with everyone. Ed, too.

They stood silently, reluctant to part, postponing it second by second. At last Mike drew a deep breath, bent down and kissed her on the cheek. "Take it easy."

"I will. You, too. Good-by, Mike."

He opened the door and went out, turned once and waved to her

404

and she smiled and waved back. Then she closed the door and walked into the living room, her eyes going over it carefully for reassurance, taking it to her like a balm to soothe her cut and ragged pride. It's so beautiful, she thought. And it all belongs to me. That must mean I'm worth something. After all, I didn't hurt anyone or cheat anyone to get it.

Or maybe I did. But *who*? I don't know.

But all the same I must be nice to Ed. For there had come up a sudden cold sad wind of fear at the possible thought of being alone. He's warm and comforting, at least. I won't hurt him any more. I'll stop doing and saying all those things. Maybe I need him more than he does me and if I'm not careful he might get up courage enough to leave me someday. I can't let that happen.

She sat down at the piano and opened her book of exercises. She and Mike had talked through half of the hour that she was supposed to spend practicing. She started the metronome and began lifting her fingers on the keys, one after the other.

Chapter 55

Ed stood at the terrace railing. Shireen, wearing a scant black linen dress, with bright green sandals on her feet, sat on a yellow couch behind him, smoking. Neither had spoken for several minutes, not since they had finished dinner.

She leaned forward, picked up her liqueur glass and took a sip of crème de cacao.

It was early July and the night was hot, wrapping itself around them, clinging, pushing them down. There was no slightest breeze and the city rose on all sides around them, oppressively close in the heat; the buildings seemed to crash in defiance at the sky. The air had a thick humming emanation from the millions of lives, like a taut wire set vibrating.

It was the first evening they had been home alone together in the four or five weeks since Mike had gone. And, it seemed almost inevitably, they had begun to quarrel.

Shireen had told him that Georgia was having some people at her farm over the week end and wanted them to come too, and Ed had said that he did not think he would; he suggested that she go, and he would stay in town and work. He had a great deal to do. She had told him he could do it some other time, that it would be nice in the country and horribly hot in town and she wanted a change and why in the devil didn't he ever want to do anything with her any more? And he had smiled but not answered. The finger bowls had come then and they left the table.

Shireen sat now and listened to the *Romeo and Juliet* overture, drifting out from the library, and waited for him to turn around and tell her he had changed his mind. She was sure that he would because, for so many years, he always had.

She looked at him contemptuously, thinking that he was as comfortable inside his own skin as a dog, and that nothing could get through to trouble him. That was part of what was wrong between them. She knew it now for sure. It seemed as if during all these years there had not been one thing Ed had really cared about. He had let her have her own way, not because he loved her and wanted for her the things that made her happy, but because of some deep indifference. It was, perhaps, directed toward the end of keeping her in need of him because he never crossed her. And so he had given up little by

406

little, given away piece by piece of himself, until she felt that the personality which had been emerging as Ed Farrell a great many years ago had been slowly sacrificed to her as a peace offering. She hated herself for having let it happen, and him for having given her that much power. She felt keenly responsible for everything which in her estimation he lacked. She had taken it away, deprived him, used it for her own ends.

So it was her fault, after all. You want life your way, she told herself, and only your way. Anything else terrified her, for she was convinced she could not surrender on one point without forfeiting the entire battle.

She waited awhile longer and then, thinking that after all she was stronger than he and could afford to be kind, got up and walked toward him. I'll be nice to him, poor darling. And then he'll want to go. It'll be good for him, as well as me, to get out into the country for awhile.

She came to the railing beside him and put her hand gently on his shoulder. He glanced down at her and she smiled. He looked at her for a moment, taking in the glossy texture to her summer-brown skin, the tropical fragrance of her perfume, her slender fingers with long plum-colored nails that matched the full shiny oval of her mouth. He looked as if he might be trying to see behind the smile, or to find something in it that was not there, and then he turned his head away.

"It's a beautiful night, isn't it?" she asked softly.

"Yes, I guess it is."

She reached out and touched the ivy that trailed from green-painted boxes along the railing. "This is growing very well, isn't it?"

"Yes, it seems to be."

Shireen sighed.

Then she turned and faced him. "Ed—please talk to me. Tell me what it is that's troubling you. I want to help you, if you'll only let me. Honestly I do."

He looked at her a moment and then shook his head. "No, Shireen. I'm afraid you could never help anyone but yourself."

"I don't know why you should say such a thing, Ed," she said, keeping her voice soft and reasonable. "Because it isn't true and you know it. I've tried very hard this past year to help you—and I'm not even ready to give up yet. If you'll tell me what I've done wrong or not done that you want, I'll do it."

"I know—I'm sorry. I've got no right to blame you. Something's gone wrong somewhere, I don't know what the hell it is, but I guess I'd rather put the blame for it on someone else."

Since he was not accusing or attacking her, she felt a warm rush of pity and sympathy. Poor Ed. Poor dear sweet Ed. How unhappy he was. And how sorry she was for him. She patted his arm.

407

"What do you think has warped you, Ed? Me—or the war?" It did not occur to her as at all funny that she could think of herself and a war as catastrophes equal in potential harm.

And apparently Ed did not think it funny, either; he answered her seriously. "I don't know," he said, in honest bewilderment. "I guess it's just that I'm warped."

"Well, then," said Shireen briskly. "Maybe we can think of a way to cure you. It can't be irrevocable, you know."

"But I'm afraid it is. I'm afraid that somewhere along the way I lost myself. I let my identity get away from me—don't ask me how."

"If that's all it is," said Shireen, "it's easy enough to fix."

"What?" Ed looked at her in astonishment. "Easy enough to fix? You sound as if I'm an engine that's burned out a bearing."

Shireen smiled. "Well, in a way maybe you are. Anyway, I know the solution."

"So do I."

"What's *your* solution?"

"Divorce."

"Now, Ed, you know that's nonsense. If you wanted to leave me you'd have done it or you'd do it—you wouldn't just keep on talking about it every time something makes you discouraged. You could never get along without me and you know it. Now, let's look at this thing sensibly."

"Your way, you mean."

"Don't be sarcastic, Ed," said Shireen mildly, like a mother speaking to a small boy who is not yet old enough to be very sensible and who must therefore be treated with tolerant kindness. "I don't mean that my way is necessarily best. But let me give you a suggestion— you certainly don't have to accept it."

"Okay," said Ed wearily. "Let's hear it. I'm at the point where any change would seem to be an improvement."

"Well, then let's look at it this way. Your problems are not actually very complicated, if we examine them carefully. The trouble is, we haven't. A little honest sensible discussion can usually correct anything, don't you agree?"

"Go on," said Ed impatiently. "Get to the point."

"You've reached a state, as far as I can see, where you're bewildered about things that are not in themselves bewildering. It's just that your attitude toward them isn't clear, and therefore you respond first one way and then another and you get confused and baffled and finally discouraged. Like the rat running through the maze when the experimenter keeps changing the door to the food on him and he finally gets so bewildered and hysterical he simply lies down and gives up. It seems to me, Ed, that you're suffering from a neurotic condition induced by coming back from the war and finding that while

408

you were away someone put in a whole new set of doors. Now, I know that you don't expect me to live the way I did before or to give up anything I've been able to get. So our problem is to get you adjusted to it—isn't that right?"

As she talked along, in a low crisp reasonable voice, like a secretary explaining that the paper clips must be ordered and some envelopes and then the office would function perfectly again, Ed began to smile. The smile came so slowly that she did not notice it at first; and then she saw that he was looking amused. She felt offended. She was trying to help him and now he was smiling as if she was being silly and as if he were, after all, superior to her.

"Well!" she said. "Is there anything wrong with that? You tell *me*, then, if you know so damned much about it."

"Only this, Shireen. Suppose I did get used to the new set of doors. That still wouldn't make *you* happy, would it?"

"Of course it would! I'd be all right if you were!"

"That's never true. Even I don't make the mistake of thinking I'd be all right, if you were. It's partly what's happened to you that makes me unhappy—but at the same time it's mostly me. Because if I saw clearly, as I think I do, that it's hopeless for us to go on living together and that we don't want the same things any more, then the obvious answer is for me to clear out. Go where I can get along. Here, I can't, and maybe I never can. To tell you the truth, I don't think I'm the guy for this life." He made a gesture, indicating the terrace and the apartment behind them. "And furthermore, I don't think I'm the man for you. Once, maybe—but we were kids then. I don't think you know how much you've changed, Shireen."

Shireen listened to him, tapping one foot and raising one eyebrow a little. If she had had any honest respect for Ed Farrell or his opinions, she would have been outraged. This was an attack on her, plain and simple. But he, poor man, didn't quite know what he was saying or doing or thinking, so she would keep on trying to be patient with him.

"Nonsense, Ed. I haven't changed at all. I just live in a different house and wear different clothes. But I'm exactly the same. I keep telling you that over and over. Now, if you'll try to keep your mind on what we're discussing and not keep wandering back to me and what's wrong with me all the time—"

"You're in this too, Shireen. Because if the money and success you've had had not affected you the way it did—"

Shireen took the cigarette from her holder and flung it across the railing. "Ed! This is completely absurd! I'm trying my best to help you and here you are—"

Ed shook his head. "No, Shireen. You may think you're trying to help me, but you're really trying to help yourself. You find I'm a nuisance to you this way and a source of embarrassment. I don't

409

always do what I'm told and I sometimes go around with a long face when you want to see a cheerful smiling one. I'm like a chair with a broken leg and you want it fixed so you can sit on it again without having to remind yourself that you mustn't sit down because it's busted. The truth is, Shireen, that you're not interested in anything but your own affairs. That's all right, if you want it that way. I don't believe you can help yourself. Shireen—I *don't* think you know what's happened to you."

"I've told you, Ed, that I'm no different."

"Okay. Suppose we agree you're not essentially different. But now you've got the chance to live life exactly your way and no one else's and you're doing it. You can afford now not to consider anyone else in the world. I just don't believe that I belong here any more. Everything in this new life is yours. Your ideas, your personality, and your money bought it."

"I thought we were never going to call it *my* money. If that's what's troubling you—"

"It isn't. Don't misunderstand me. Money isn't that important. It's you, Shireen. Oh, hell what's the use?"

"What's the use?" she cried. "Our marriage is going to hell and you say 'what's the use'! Do you know what's really wrong, Edward Farrell? I haven't wanted to tell you this, but I think it's time we quit pussyfooting around this thing and look it squarely in the eye. You're jealous of my success, that's what it is! You've been the big guy, all your life. At home your mother doted on you. In school you were captain of this and president of that. In the Navy you were Lieutenant Farrell and had medals pinned on you. You've lived on a diet of admiration since you were born. And now the tables have been turned. Someone else is getting the praise and admiration and money and you don't know what the hell to do about it. The only way you can figure out to beat me is to make a half-million dollars a year and you can't find out how to do that and there isn't any way to do it! Take my word for it, Ed. It can't be done! I'll probably never do it again no matter if I write myself blue in the face. So Ed Farrell finds himself being an ordinary guy, Shireen Delaney's husband, and it's tough to take! I hate to tell you this, Ed. And I never would have told you, only—"

As she talked Ed's expression had changed again, and now his face showed pitying incredulity, as if he could not believe she was saying what she was, but that if she was he felt sorry for her.

"Shireen," he said, pleading with her. "Shireen, for the love of God, stop and listen to yourself. If you knew half the things you say you'd never let yourself be caught saying them. It's not decent for one person to talk that way to another. No matter how you feel. Not now. I took a lot from you while things were pretty even between us—while I was supporting you and you were keeping house for me. But this is hitting below the belt. It's not nice, Shireen."

Shireen's face shifted from shame to defiance. What had she said? She wasn't sure, ten seconds after she had said it. But it couldn't have been anything so terrible. She had only told him the truth. And he was too goddamned cowardly even for that.

"You hate me, don't you, Ed?" she asked him finally, when there had been a long moment of silence between them.

She said it rather pitifully. She believed she didn't care if he left her or not, and that she had no false pride about whether he left first or she did. But she did not want him to leave hating her. She wanted him to lose more by their parting than she would, and he could only lose more if he took with him the memory of a sweet and warm and lovable girl he had not been able to hold. Not a hard bad-tempered vixen he was relieved to escape from. So she had flipped the coin and brought up the other side of her personality.

And Ed responded out of years of habit. His face softened as he looked at her. "No," he said. "I don't hate you. I love you."

"You must love me, Ed," she murmured. "You must. After everything we've meant to each other all these years. We have every reason to be happy together, darling. You know we have!" There were tears in her eyes and she was passionately convinced that she meant every word.

Ed reached out his arms and drew her to him and stroked her head and petted her as if she were a little girl who had skinned her knee. "Don't cry, darling. Please don't cry. I'm a goddamned fool. I know it's true, everything you said. I do feel I'm a failure. I want to be something myself and not just Shireen Delaney's husband and I'm such a jerk I don't even know how to go about it. I don't even like the insurance business. I don't think I ever did—but Dad wanted me to go in with him and I suppose I thought—Oh, the hell with it."

She had talked to him about that, years ago. But it was too late now. That was what he did, whether he liked it or not, and he'd have to make the best of it. But she despised him for that, too. It was inexcusable not to know what you wanted to do in life, to let yourself be persuaded and determined by other people. But she would not say that to him now.

She lifted her head and gave him a sweet childlike smile. "You'll get to like it in time, Ed. I'm sure you will."

"Maybe. I suppose it doesn't matter. I must have expected something different—I don't know what I expected."

"You expected to always be president of the student body. Just by smiling at people." Oh, she thought, dismayed. Why did I say that? He might as well know it, though. It takes work to get any-

411

where—hasn't he found that out by now? The damned fool. And she was contemptuous of him again.

"I guess maybe I did. But Shireen—you don't need a husband any more. There isn't one single thing I can do for you that you can't do better for yourself."

"You're a wonderful lover, Ed—"

He released her quickly and turned away, embarrassed. Now, she thought, what was wrong with that? He should have been complimented. The truth of it is, of course, one man's much the same as another, with slight variations, and the only thing that makes it different is how you feel about the guy. No matter what I say, it's wrong.

"For God's sake, Shireen. Do you think any man likes the idea of being nothing but his wife's stud?"

"I didn't say you were—oh!" She turned and started to walk away, ready to give up. Let him leave her. They would never get together on anything. This was all a waste of time. There was no cure for their relationship. But when she had taken a few steps she turned around again.

"I haven't told you what I think will solve our problems."

"What?" But he did not look as if he believed she knew.

"Your present trouble is clearly neurotic. And there's a cure for neuroticism. Go to an analyst."

"Me?" he asked her.

"Of course, you," she said, and now she seemed to be in good spirits again, half joking.

She had the feeling that she had proved something to herself. "What's the matter with that?" she demanded. "A lot of people do, you know. It isn't always possible for us to solve our own problems. That's nothing to be ashamed of. Do *you* think it is?"

All of a sudden and to her complete surprise, Ed laughed. "No," he said. "I don't. Only this is funny as hell. Because when I read that book—*Neurotic Personalities,* or whatever it was called—it struck me all through it that you're a perfect composite of all the neurotic traits."

"What?" asked Shireen, amazed. "It did?"

"Sure. Didn't you think of that?"

"Well," she said. "I suppose so. I don't know. Anyway, we're not interested in me right now. A neurotic does not function efficiently, that's one clear thing. And as I think you'll be willing to agree, Ed, I function pretty efficiently. So I'd say you're the one who could benefit by the analysis."

"Maybe I could. But I can't afford it and that would be one thing more I'd be spending your money for."

"Ed Farrell." Now she was his mother again, gentle, chiding, faintly humorous. "You know perfectly well that whatever amount of money

412

it might take would make very little difference to me and might save our marriage. Will you do it? Will you promise me?"

"Let me think about it."

"Why think about it? Why put it off? If that's what should be done, then there's no use delaying. And I know a very good analyst—the one Dallas went to. Why, as I told you, Dallas used to have those terrible headaches and—"

"Let me think about it, Shireen. For a few days."

She looked at him and would have gone on except that she recognized Ed had come to a point of stubbornness where he would stick and nothing she could say or do would move him. Well, then, let him think it over for a few days. He'd come to it in time—she would see to that. She had completely forgotten that when she had met Dallas's analyst she had considered that he knew a great deal less than she did about many things. Anyway, everything in her life indicated only too clearly how much more efficient was her functioning than even that of an analyst. So no doubt he could give Ed a good deal of help.

Chapter 56

Shireen gave him two days to think it over, during which she did not mention the subject. And then she began to bring it up again. He kept telling her to let him consider it a little longer.

About a week later they came home at midnight from a dinner party and Shireen sat on a couch in the living room and lit a cigarette. Ed stood with his hands in his pockets, waiting for her, looking at the painting over the fireplace. Shireen frowned. It was very hot and she was tired and irritable. If something wasn't done to make an improvement in her life soon, she felt that she would go out of her mind. And it was up to Ed to make the change.

"I think you must actually like to be the way you are, Ed," she said after awhile. As she said it she noticed that the maid had put the wrong crystal ashtray on the coffee table and she got up and changed it, straightening the end-table lamp slightly at the same time.

Ed watched her, amused. "This place is really driving you crazy, isn't it?"

"What are you talking about? I love it. It's everything I ever wanted."

"Too bad you can't enjoy it."

"I do enjoy it!" she snapped. "Damn that woman! Look at this candy dish! She hasn't polished it in two weeks, I'll bet. Just look at it! Tarnished!"

Ed sighed. "I'd fire her tomorrow, if I were you."

"I think I will." This was intolerable. The woman was getting careless. Well, there'd be no more of that. "But look, Ed—you know we're getting nowhere this way. You really should do something about yourself."

"I've just about made up my mind."

"Well, thank God. About time. Do you want me to call him for you?"

"Never mind. I'll call him myself."

"You'll forget. Or you'll put it off."

"For God's sake, Shireen!"

She looked at him in surprise. "What's the matter with you now?"

He hesitated a moment, then turned and crossed the room and she watched him, her eyes slanted and evil as a cat's, her foot tapping impatiently. When he had reached the entrance to the foyer, where

414

he would turn in a moment and be out of her sight, she jumped up and ran after him.

"Where are you going?"

He looked at her for several moments and she stared back. They faced each other like enemies, neither one willing to strike the first blow, each measuring the other to find his advantage.

"I'm going for a walk," he said. "I suppose you don't mind?"

"I don't mind if you go to hell."

Ed's expression sent an instant cold flash of fear into her. But then it was gone so quickly she could not be sure she had seen it.

He opened the door.

"I don't want you to go, Ed," she said, her voice low and even.

Ed did not turn or look at her or speak, but went on out and started to close the door behind him. She ran across the foyer and grabbed the inside handle, jerking it open. He was pushing the elevator button.

"I said—"

He glanced around. "I heard what you said."

"And you're going anyway?"

It seemed incredible to her that he should dare disobey. He never had before, even when he had had no economic right to command.

"I'm going anyway," said Ed. They could hear the sound of the elevator coming up from below.

Shireen stood and stared at him, her face turned ugly.

And then Ed smiled. "I wish you could see yourself. You'd never let yourself think whatever you're thinking, if you knew how it makes you look."

"I don't care *how* I look!"

But she kept her voice low, for the people in the apartment across the hall might be home and she did not want to be overheard. They knew her as the sweet and modest and charming *Shireen Delaney* who was so successful and yet so simple and unspoiled, who spoke to them every day in the pleasantest way imaginable.

"If you don't come back here I'll—"

"You'll what?"

The elevator was almost there. Shireen hesitated a moment and then shot at him: "Remind me to divorce you one of these days!"

The elevator stopped, the doors opened, and Ed got in without another glance at her. She started to slam the door—then remembered who she was nowadays and closed it quietly. She turned and rushed into the bedroom, locked the door and the French doors onto the terrace, and threw herself on the bed, sobbing violently. I hate you, Ed Farrell, she screamed inside herself. I hate you, I hate you, I hate you, I hate you. . . .

The next day she was ashamed of herself again. Ed had come home a couple of hours later and knocked at the door and she had heard

415

him but refused to answer. She supposed he must have slept on the couch in the living room and the next morning when she came out to have breakfast he was gone. She was full of remorse and called him at his office.

"Darling—" she said, when she heard his voice. "I'm so sorry about last night. I'm so terribly sorry."

He did not answer.

"Ed!" she cried anxiously. "Are you there?"

"Yes. It's all right, Shireen. Don't worry about it."

"Oh, but sweetheart, I was terrible. I don't know what makes me act like that. You know I've always had such an awful disposition."

"I know," he said. "It doesn't matter. Forget it."

"You're so sweet, Ed. I don't deserve you. I know I don't. And I'm going to change, I promise you—"

"Okay."

But he sounded tired and detached and it frightened her. She might be actually losing him.

"I mean it, Ed. Oh, please, darling, you've *got* to believe me."

"I believe you. I always have, haven't I?"

"But I mean it this time, Ed."

He hesitated a moment. "I went to see the doctor."

"Oh, darling, did you? That's wonderful—I'm so glad. I know everything's going to be all right now. And do you like him? Did he tell you anything?"

"I like him all right, I guess. I did the talking. He didn't say much of anything."

"Oh." She was a little discouraged, for she had hoped the doctor would instantly take him in hand, explain everything, change his character and personality. "Well, he will."

But even when two weeks had gone by she could not see any improvement. In fact, if anything, it got worse. He refused more and more often to go out with her in the evening. Sometimes she called his office during the day and he was not in and would never tell her later where he had been. Shireen began to hate the doctor, too. He should *keep* him from doing things like this. I'll call him up, she thought, and tell him he's got to do better than he's done so far.

She was paying for it, wasn't she?

One night she sat in bed reading and waited until after one-thirty for him to come home. He had called Mary and told her to tell Miss Delaney he would not be back for dinner and for her not to wait for him because he might be late. Shireen was furious. He knew better than to do things like that. He knew that it made her worry, made her lose sleep, and he knew how much she needed her sleep if she was going to work the next day. At last she slammed the book shut, threw the pillows on the floor, snapped out the light and lay down.

416

I won't think about him.

She began to think about Johnny Keegan, instead. She had not seen him now for a year and a half, but whenever she felt too lonely or lost or discouraged she turned to him for solace and comfort.

. . . There was a big party going on in a lavish house. She was wearing the white chiffon gown with a sari over her black hair and no other woman in the room was noticeable at all. Three men were talking to her and she was standing smiling at them, serenely aware that they were absolutely enchanted. Then she heard a voice behind her. "Hi—" She turned quickly and he was standing there smiling at her, tanned as he always was, with that look of happy expectancy on his face, as if he had just seen something wonderful, or been granted some vision no one else had had. That was what she remembered more than anything else, the look he always had of knowing about a miracle. She caught her breath as she saw him. "Johnny—" The three men had disappeared, not walked away but simply disappeared. She did not know who they had been anyway. "Why didn't you call me, Johnny?" He was still smiling at her and the smile had in it the quality of a caress, deep and intimate. "I was going to," he said. His hand touched her arm and they walked slowly out, looking at each other as they walked, through the crowds of people melting mysteriously away as they passed. Outside, he took her into his arms—the night was warm and tropical, familiar as a bath and all the summer nights of her childhood. He started to kiss her . . .

Shireen turned over, quickly and impatiently, annoyed with herself for wasting time on such fantasies. Life should be lived, not imagined —except when you got paid for your imagination. Then she got up and went into the bathroom and swallowed two sleeping pills. She had been taking them almost every night for the past three or four months.

One of these days, she told herself, I'll get my sleep back again.

She lay awhile, waiting, and finally her thoughts began to slip around, get out of her control, and dissolve through a series of images. There was a fish with his head caught in a floor radiator so that he stuck out at an angle; an old man sat down near by to eat dinner at a chess table. She saw a great darkness and streaks of water, like copious tears, rushing across it, pouring down continuously. And then she was descending interminable flights of stairs.

Sometime later she woke very suddenly. There had been a sound from somewhere—footsteps—and she woke in terror, not knowing where she was. It had come. Whatever she had been waiting for and dreading. It was here now, in the room with her. Everywhere around her, something huge and faceless and powerful, waiting to destroy her. She tried to scream but could not move or make a sound.

And then she realized that it must be Ed.

417

He must have come home and walked into the room from the terrace. Her fear turned instantly to anger. She reached over and switched on the light.

"It's me," she heard him say. "I didn't want to wake you."

And then, as she saw him beside the terrace doorway, she found a genuine reason for anger. He was drunk.

He stood looking at her and his face was stupid and blank. As if he had given up completely, accepted defeat, no longer wanted to struggle. He stood there, weaving slightly, watching her like a defiant little boy.

"You're drunk!" she cried accusingly. "Where have you been?"

"Oh," said Ed, as if it made no difference to him what she thought or how she felt or even how he felt himself, "I've been here and there."

"Who with!"

She was trying to control herself but each moment she grew more outraged, hated him more furiously. It had been several years since she had lost herself in an uncontrolled rage against him, when all the buried hostility had flown out of her like a gigantic angry bird taking flight. She was close to it now.

"A couple of guys," said Ed. "Friends of mine from overseas." He said "friends of mine" with a small triumph, as if he was glad to know he had something he could tell her about as belonging to himself, apart from her. Nothing she had given him. He looked helpless and lost and bewildered.

But that was not what Shireen saw as she looked at him.

She saw a man to whom she had given everything, for whom she had manufactured a life, who was now standing before her like a fool, his pride shuffled off somewhere and left like a fallen garment. She saw weakness and despised it. She saw a retreat from life she refused to take herself and it sickened her. She saw a being over whom she believed she exerted complete and absolute control, who had grown indifferent to her. She saw a man she hated.

"And why didn't you call to let me know what time you'd be home?" she demanded.

Ed sauntered unsteadily toward her. He took off his coat and threw it on the chaise and loosened his tie, flexing his neck muscles and thrusting out his jaw as he did so. Something that was purely masculine in the gesture broke the last of her self-control.

"*Don't* throw that down there!" she shouted. "Pick that coat up! At least you can pick up after yourself, since you don't do another goddamned thing to earn your living!"

He looked at her. "Shut up." His voice was low and sullen.

Shireen leaped out of bed. "Don't you dare say that to me!" she yelled, and rushed toward him. "I hate you, Ed Farrell!" And she drew back her hand and slapped him across the face as hard as she could. It gave an instant tremendous satisfaction and she wanted to hit him again. "I hate you!"

Ed rocked a little as she struck him and then steadied himself and looked at her. His face was white and his expression had turned ugly and dangerous; with the back of his hand he struck her quickly on the cheek. She made a sudden cry of amazement and pain and moved away from him.

"Don't ever do that again," he said.

Shireen held one hand to her face. He had not hurt her much but she had realized for the first time that he was no longer tame and docile, ready to accept whatever she did to him. He was capable of killing her now. She was astonished and outraged to realize that their years of living together had brought them to this moment. This was the end of everything. They could not live together after this. She was aware of some satisfaction as she thought that it was he who had done it, after all.

The responsibility was his, for he had done something to her which she could never forgive.

"I've always known," she said slowly, "that under that pretense of being so sweet and kind and good-natured you—"

"Stop talking. I warn you, Shireen, I won't be responsible for what happens if you go on like this. Go to bed now and be quiet." He looked at her as she hesitated, still trying to measure if she had any power left over him. "Go on. I mean it."

She turned and went back to bed, lay down on her back and pulled the sheet up; she lay there looking at him. He had the physical advantage and she must leave him alone for now. But that was not important. She could hurt him far more than he could hurt her, for once he had lost this false sense of power he had been given by liquor and anger, he would be completely helpless again. She began to feel a little sorry for him and her fury washed away. But a cold contempt took its place.

"It makes me angry to see you drunk," she said quietly. "I suppose I shouldn't mind it as much as I do. Come on—let's forget this happened. Get undressed and come to bed. I'm sorry I made such a scene."

And Ed's expression changed again. He stood looking at her with pathetic eagerness, grateful that she was being kind and gentle with him, almost beguiled into trusting her, since he needed to so much. But that look went too and he turned wearily and walked into the bathroom. Shireen switched out the light, after first glancing at the clock. It was three-thirty.

Goddamn him. Keeping her awake. Making her lose sleep. Upsetting her schedule.

419

When he came out and got into bed a few minutes later she pretended to be asleep. He lay there, far from her for the bed was wide, and he lay very very still. There was something trusting and frightened about the extreme stillness in which he lay. He's a fool, thought Shireen with disgust. A complete fool. And before long she fell asleep.

Chapter 57

Shireen sat at her desk typing, watching the words come out of some hidden recess in her head onto the yellow paper before her. When she heard a knock she got up in the middle of a sentence, walked to the door and unlocked it and saw Mary Carlisle. Mary, who did not exist while she was working, but whose face and the suit she was wearing and the sound of her voice was like a slap of cold water.

"I'm sorry," said Mary. "But there's a Colonel Keegan on the phone who absolutely insists on talking to you. I tried to put him off but—"

"I'll take it," said Shireen. "Thanks." She closed the door and went back to her desk and picked up the telephone.

"Hello?" she said. "Johnny?"

"Hi. What goes on with you, anyway? I had to give that dame a line that would have gotten me in to see the Pope before she'd even let me talk to you. How exclusive can you be?"

Shireen's laugh was a little shaky. "I have to work for a living, you know." She was wondering if that click had been Mary hanging up in the other room. She must be careful. If Mary ever got anything on her—Fine thing, to keep a mortal enemy as your private secretary.

"Working?" repeated Johnny. "Not writing another book? The girl who said she'd never write again as long as she lived?"

"I'm afraid so. Trying to, anyway. Johnny, where are you?"

"La Guardia."

"What are you doing here?"

"On my way west."

"West? How far?"

"Don't know. All the way, maybe. I can't talk much over the phone."

"Can't you come over here? You're not leaving right away?"

"In a few hours. I guess I could make it for half an hour or so. How's Ed? Everything's fine with you two now, I suppose. It should be. He's a great guy, Shireen."

You goddamned lying hypocrite. "Yes," she said. "Everything's fine. I guess you got my letter. We'll talk when you get here."

"Okay. See you in about an hour." He hung up.

She sat for a moment and looked at the sheet of paper in the type-

421

writer. The words looked strange and unfamiliar, as if they had been written by someone else, or by her a long time ago. She pulled the sheet out slowly, put it beneath the other pages she had written that day, opened the desk drawer and set it on top of the rest of the manuscript. It was four-thirty.

She thought of calling Ed and making up some excuse to keep him from coming home while Johnny was there. But then decided not to. Even if he did—she had a quick image of the two men beginning to quarrel over her, fighting, and herself going off with the victor— Johnny. You're out of your mind, she told herself, and crossed the hall into the bedroom.

She went quickly and automatically through the routine of bathing, making up her face, brushing her hair. And then searched through the closet for the dress he would like best—the one she hoped would most impress him with her desirability. She took out a dinner gown of silver-gray jersey and when she had it on it was molded and clinging, as if it had been wrung out and put on wet. She stood a moment and looked at herself.

Thank God, she thought. One way or another you're able to *look* like a beauty. Even if you aren't one.

She went into the living room and, as she got there, heard the sound of Mary's footsteps crossing the foyer. She started to go out, almost panic-stricken, but Mary had come to the door and now called her.

"Hey, look at you!" Shireen turned around, as if she had been caught. Mary was looking at her and smiling with faint pleased insolence. "That dress is terrific."

Shireen lit a cigarette. "Thanks." Then immediately she began to explain. "Colonel Keegan is an old friend of my husband's. He's coming over for a little while."

Mary shook her head. "A friend of your husband's. I might have known it. Everyone's so interested when I tell them I work for Shireen Delaney. They think you must live the *most* fascinating life. But I tell them you're the dullest woman I've ever known—and probably never so much as looked at any man but your husband in your whole life. Well—'night. See you tomorrow."

"Good night."

Shireen stood where she was and waited to hear the door close behind Mary: I've got to get her *out* of here before she drives me crazy.

Don't think about her! She's gone now. Forget she exists. Why let her bother you? She began to walk around the room, taking a few dead leaves off the roses, straightening the magazines on the coffee table, opening the cigarette boxes to make sure they were full. She kept looking at her watch. He should be here any moment.

She wondered why she was letting him come. As if she and Ed didn't have trouble enough. It had been Johnny, after all, who had first made her realize how little she had ever loved Ed. But she knew there would never be a time when Johnny would be where she could see him and she would refuse. No matter how many years went by— no matter how they changed or what happened to them—Johnny would mean to her what he always had.

As she wandered around the room, which was perfectly in order, putting it in order herself, she felt a mounting resentment of Ed. He was in her way again, standing between her and Johnny.

Once, out of all the times he had told her he must leave, she should have said to him: "All right, Ed. You've said this often enough, I guess you must mean it. So, since you're so sure you want to leave me—go ahead. It's too bad that it worked out this way but it did, so let's not have any hard feelings or blame anyone."

For a moment it seemed she had actually said that to him, that he was gone and would never come back and she and Johnny were free now to mean to each other whatever they could. And then she realized that she had been fooling herself again and felt embarrassed. Ed, in a sense, was her protection against Johnny. Johnny never gave her anything to plan on and, she suspected, never would, with or without Ed.

But after all, she reminded herself, he couldn't do these things if you didn't let him. You're as much to blame as he is. You've made every decision yourself your whole life, and if this is how you've finally wound up, then it's no one's fault but your own.

Other people aren't like this. Take a look at anyone you know and you'll see that they get along pretty well. They're not obsessed with fears and surrounded by hobgoblins, afraid of themselves and everyone else on earth, living beyond their means and worrying about how the hell they'll get along, messing up their marriages and not able to make up their minds whether they love this man or that one or no man at all. *Other* people aren't like that, she told herself.

Or are they?

The hell with it. Why doesn't he come?

The bell rang. Shireen ran across the room and into the foyer. The maid was coming through the dining-room door on the other side.

"I'll get it, Stella."

She opened the door and Johnny was standing there, holding his cap in one hand. And she thought again that there could be no other man in the world who had Johnny Keegan's smile.

"Hi." And all in one glance he took possession of her again.

"Hello, Johnny." She was trying to smile and look composed, but her legs were weak and she quivered inside. "It didn't take you long to get here."

She stepped back and he came in, glancing around. He whistled softly. "So this is where you live now."

423

Shireen laughed, self-consciously. "Come on," she said, and turned around and heard him following her. She walked several steps into the living room and then turned to face him again, waiting eagerly. "Do you like it, Johnny? Do you think it's pretty?"

"Sure," he said softly. "Of course I do. It's beautiful." He was smiling at her again and he looked pleased, as if satisfied to find she had accomplished all this by herself—the shy girl who had told him that first night that she was trying to write a book.

"How about Ed? Does he like it?"

"Yes. Of course he does." She did not want to talk about Ed or be reminded of him. "Johnny—wouldn't you like something to drink? It's so hot. It's been simply stifling for weeks now. It seems as if it's been like this forever. You must be miserable in that uniform."

"I don't want anything—oh, a coke, maybe."

She excused herself and went to the kitchen. When she came back Johnny was out on the terrace, standing with his back to her, looking at the city. The sky had darkened and the air felt thick and close, as if there would be a thunder shower. She paused a moment in the doorway, thinking of how they never met except to say good-by. They had never once seen each other without guilt and haste, the sense that they were stealing time and affection from someone else and would be punished if they let themselves be happy.

She walked over and touched him on the shoulder and as he turned she saw that he was smiling. He began to talk to her. The tone of his voice and the words he said made it seem as if they were casual friends who had seen each other a few days before and very likely would meet somewhere or other tomorrow. She watched him and listened and felt as if she stood apart from herself, looking at both of them. Why does he keep pretending and hiding, she wondered.

She asked where he was going.

"I don't know for sure. Something's cooking out in the Pacific. The Navy fliers are all saying the war's got to end soon."

"How long will you be gone this time?"

"Who knows? Maybe the rest of my life."

"Oh, please don't talk like that, Johnny! I can't stand hearing it. You're not going to die." There was a roll of thunder off in the distance and the sky seemed to move down closer upon them.

"It wouldn't make much difference."

"How can you say such a thing?" She wanted to shake him. There must be some way she could force him to stop playing games with her, stop romanticizing himself and take the risk of being whatever he was.

"I told you a long time ago, Shireen—I've had everything I want."

"No one's ever had everything they want."

"No? What about you? You've finally got everything the way you want it, haven't you?"

She sighed. "I suppose so." Stella came out with a silver tray and set it on one of the tables. There was a roar of thunder across the city. "It's going to rain," she said. She watched Stella leave and then walked back to pick up the drinks. Johnny followed her and she handed him one.

"You think about yourself too much, Shireen."

"I think about myself too much? Why, even if I wanted to, I don't have time. I'm busy every single minute of the day."

"It doesn't take much time. It's a habit you form early, and from then on you do it automatically. Everyone you meet, everything you see, everything that happens, you measure by just one yardstick—yourself. What does it mean to *me?* What can I use it for? What impression am I making?"

She was beginning to get angry. Why was he talking to her like this? What had she done to deserve it? Why wasn't there someone who would just be nice to her—when she was so tired?

"You seem to have me all figured out."

He smiled. "It wasn't hard. We're pretty much alike, you know."

"That's what I've always tried to tell you."

"Too much alike."

"So that's what you've been up to. One more way to tell me we don't belong together. That's what you've been looking for since the first day we met, isn't it?"

"It happens to be true. Shireen—why is it you still refuse to see this thing the way it is? I thought maybe this time it would be different."

"Like hell you did." She looked up and smiled as there was another roll of thunder; her face was suddenly mischievous, amused. She glanced back to him. "God's mad." But then she frowned and sighed a little and turned away.

"If you could understand just one thing, Shireen, we'd be straight. If I ever changed to be what you want, I'd be nothing at all. You'd lose the very thing you think you want, because it wouldn't be there any more."

She smiled slowly. "So you finally admit it."

"Admit what?"

"That you're afraid of me."

"Oh, Shireen, stop talking such goddamned nonsense."

"And how could you lose yourself? If you exist at all." She closed her eyes and made a quick gesture. "Let's not talk like this. Let's not have anything ugly to remember."

"It might be better if we did."

She looked at him helplessly, wondering what it was that made

425

them keep on this way, the last time they might ever be together. As if there were both a positive and a negative force between them, pulling them violently together, pushing them violently apart. Something apparently beyond the control of either of them.

They were quiet a few moments and then he asked her: "How about Ed?"

"Ed's all right. Why?"

"Is he happy?"

"Happy. Who in the name of God is ever happy? What a question."

"Ed should be. He deserves to be. I've told you before, Shireen— he's one of the very few guys I've known that I've had any real respect for."

"I remember." She was sitting down now, smiling at him. "And it must have proved something to you, having the wife of a man you honestly respected fall in love with you. You must have thought you were quite a guy, every time you got in bed with me."

His face changed so suddenly she was shocked. Red spots like stains appeared over his cheekbones and he looked angrier than she had thought he could. "I've warned you I won't listen to that goddamned analytic nonsense, Shireen. One more crack like that—and that's all, sister."

She looked at him in dismay, and then she was crying. She bent forward, covered her face with her hands, and began to sob uncontrollably, as if these were the tears she had been longing to shed all her life and at last they had come. After a moment Johnny sat beside her and took her into his arms. He held her and let her cry, while one hand stroked her head, and then he began talking to her softly. "Darling, darling, I'm sorry. I had no business saying that to you. Don't cry any more. Please don't. You haven't anything to cry about. You've got everything there is in the world."

"I haven't, Johnny. I haven't anything at all. Not even Ed, any more."

He raised her head and wiped the tears away. "That can't be true, Shireen. You know it isn't. You mustn't say such things."

"It is true. He doesn't love me any more." They looked at each other. Then after a moment he got up and left her, walked a few steps away and turned around again.

"I've got to tell you something, Shireen."

Now, she thought, he's going to say it after all. Her tears had produced the magical effect. "Yes, Johnny?" Her voice rose to a light expectant delicacy.

"I'm getting married."

Her face seemed to break apart. "You—can't. I don't believe you."

"I am, though."

"Who is she?"

"What's the difference?"

"I want to know. Is it someone you've known all along? Did you just meet her? Johnny, you can't do that to me!" He smiled a little then and she leaned forward. "You're not in love with her?"

"I'm going to get married—that's all."

She got up and walked over close to him. "You can't, Johnny! You can't leave me!"

"I won't leave you. We'll always mean whatever we do to each other. Shireen—if you've been thinking about divorcing Ed, get that idea out of your mind. It won't do any good."

"It won't do any good, because you'll be married?"

"That's right."

She turned away. "I wish I'd never met you. The whole thing's been a waste." She said it bitterly.

"It's given me some of the happiest times of my life. And I'd like to think the same is true for you." His face was serious now and he watched her carefully as he talked. "You know, Shireen—if we'd been lucky enough to have met a few years earlier, we might have made something pretty wonderful out of this. At least we can always think so. Or maybe we wouldn't. Maybe we'd have loused it up, like people always do. Perhaps we're luckier than we think."

She felt a sudden disgust. She was conscious of the terrible heat and could feel sweat on her forehead and arms and running down her bare legs; she turned weak and sick, as if she might be going to faint.

"I've got to shove along," he said. "Guess I'll miss Ed. But will you promise me something, Shireen?"

"What." Her tone was perfectly flat.

"Promise me you'll try to make a go of it with Ed. You'll be sorry all the rest of your life if you hurt him."

They stood a moment and stared at each other and then she turned and walked back inside. She wanted him to leave, go away, never come back to her again. She wanted to forget she had ever known him. Something was waiting—something important which she must do and which he was keeping her from doing. But she had no idea what it was.

He followed her in. "Shireen, try to look at it from his angle. Think of what it must have meant to him to come home and find everything changed."

"I know," she said with weary impatience. "I have thought about it. I've thought about everything you can possibly say."

"Have you thought of this? Considering someone other than your-self—*first*?"

For an instant she had an image of herself slapping him, and the look of dismay and surprise it would bring to his face. She turned her head, as if to conceal it from him. "I've thought of that, too."

427

"Try it then, instead of just thinking about it."

She swung around suddenly. "What did you come here for? To tell me what's wrong with me? To make yourself think you're a hell of a fine guy coming to show me my sins—so you can feel easier about your own? I've got trouble enough, Johnny Keegan, without listening to your goddamn smug sermons! Why don't you get out?"

He smiled at her, as though in pity. "You don't mean what you're saying, Shireen."

"Oh, yes, I do! And I know what you're up to now! You want to win me back again—not because you want me, and not because you care how unhappy I may be if you do! But so you can leave me behind you—someone else who loves you and will miss you and keep you alive inside them if you should get killed! Get out of here, Johnny Keegan! Get *out!*" She turned and ran through the library, across the hall and into her bedroom, slammed the door behind her and locked it. Then she rushed to close the French doors, for the curtains were blowing and it had begun to rain hard.

Chapter 58

Half an hour later Shireen came back into the library. It did not seem possible now that Johnny had been there. She looked around and found it surprisingly empty, as if it had always been empty. That was comforting. He had left no trace. It didn't matter.

That's one thing about me, she thought. All my life I've been able to turn around and close the door—and forget who was on the other side.

And anyway, I'm not so bad. More people would be like me if they could get away with it.

She stood awhile and looked at one of her paintings. She kept glancing at her watch. Ed was late again. She moved along, looking at the book titles.

When it was fifteen minutes past the time Ed was supposed to be home she turned abruptly and went to the desk, opened the telephone book and dialed the number of La Guardia Field. She asked to have Colonel John Keegan paged. She had stopped thinking, but was nervous and tense and felt that the most important thing in the world was to speak to him again, just for a moment—just long enough to tell him she was sorry. She waited, drumming her nails on the desk top, watching the door and hoping Ed would not come.

After more than five minutes a woman's voice spoke to her. "I'm sorry. We haven't been able to locate Colonel Keegan."

"Will you try again, please? I'll wait. It's very urgent. He'll be there any minute."

"Do you want to leave your number and we'll ask him—"

At that moment Ed came through the door, smiling tentatively, as if he was testing her out first; she put the telephone back in its cradle.

There he was, and suddenly it seemed she had known him much longer than ten years. She had known him all her life, and he had played the same role from the beginning. He had taken love away from her—he had been good and made others think she was bad. She looked at him now with faint surprise and curiosity.

"Hello," he said. "How's everything?"

She was sitting with her arms on the desk and her hands folded in front of her. "Fine," she said softly. "How's everything with you?"

"Fine. It's been hot today, hasn't it? Good thing we had that rainstorm."

"Yes, I guess it's a little cooler now. Would you like a drink?"

"Good idea. I'll fix it. Do you want it in here?"

"No. Let's go out on the terrace. Maybe there's a breeze. How was your hour with the doctor?" She got up from the desk, looking back for a moment at the telephone, and then walked out.

"All right, I guess."

Shireen went to the terrace and sat down. The servants had taken the cushions in when it began to rain, and then put them back again when it stopped. She waited for Ed to bring her the drink. If he had come ten minutes later, she would have been able to talk to Johnny and explain that she was nervous and upset and had not meant what she said. In everything that had happened between her and Johnny, there had been Ed—standing between them, making them despise themselves and, by the fact of his existence as her husband, accusing them by implication of a crime which should have been no crime but great happiness. She blamed Ed entirely and forgot that he knew nothing about it.

He came out and handed her the drink. She thanked him and he sat down across the coffee table from her in one of the bright blue-green chairs. She leaned forward and lit a cigarette but did not speak to him. He was quiet and she thought with scorn of how he had always waited for her to make the first move, never initiating anything himself, but merely responding to whatever came from her. And she saw that he was unhappy. Well, let him be. He should have learned by now that you have to make some effort for happiness or anything else you want. It didn't come by waiting. Nothing had come to her by waiting—and she was through letting him wait for her to give life to him.

She got up and walked to the railing, to escape the sense of him watching her. The maid had come out and was setting the table for dinner at the other end of the terrace. It had begun to grow dark but the air was still and wet and bore down heavily upon them.

She stood looking out across the treetops of the Park, and it seemed that she realized clearly for the first time that Ed had cheated her all these years. He had lived a long way from her—at whatever distance was necessary to let him keep his comfort. If the climate was right he had lived close by, but if it got too hot or too cold or a storm came up, then he had moved away. Back into his cave. Some secret cave she had not known he had and could not locate, so that she couldn't follow him in there and grab him by the ear or stand with her hands on her hips and demand that he come out and face her. He had not risked anything on her and she despised him now for having protected himself.

She heard his voice. "Are you tired, darling?"

"Yes, I guess I am. It's been hot for so long."

430

"Yes," he agreed. "It's been hot."

Is that all we're ever going to say to each other, for the rest of our lives? The ivy's growing nicely, isn't it? It's been terribly hot, hasn't it? How was your hour with the doctor? How's your work coming? Isn't the soup good?

Was there nothing at all left of what had been there once?

...if we'd been lucky enough to meet a few years earlier, we might have made something pretty wonderful out of this...Or maybe we wouldn't. Maybe we'd have loused it up, like people always do...

But surely it would have been different with Johnny? *At least we can always think so.* Perhaps that was the valuable thing Johnny had given her, after all—one illusion neither of them could ever spoil. For she had no more essential faith in their chances than he had: different beginnings, coming to the same end. And if he hadn't destroyed it, she would.

I suppose the closer you get to any mirage, the more you see of the desert.

She walked back toward Ed and he sat very still, looking at her. There was something begging, pleading, in his expression. If you will only love me, he seemed to be saying. But love him for what? He isn't the man I want. I want someone else. Something else. I want—

Oh, I don't know what I want.

Her head was aching dully and she wondered how that could be; she could not remember having had a headache before.

I just want to be let alone. I need a chance to be quiet, not have anyone demanding of me or pulling at me. I need a chance to think things out and get it straight. Whatever it is. If I could have a little peace—I might be able to do it then.

"You've been working too hard, Shireen."

"Maybe. But I have to, after all."

Ed looked away. "I know. I don't earn enough to be any use to you."

She did not answer. If she began to say what she was feeling it would be one more bitter quarrel between them. And there was no use in that.

"We're only putting it off," Ed said.

She looked at him swiftly and her eyes were hostile. Well, then, why don't you go? Do I have to *tell* you to leave? Do I have to have that on my conscience along with everything else? Can't you make the decision and take the responsibility if it turns out wrong—just once?

"I don't know why you keep saying that, Ed."

"You don't want me any more and you know it. I don't think you know what you want—maybe a combination of Clark Gable, Einstein, and Henry Luce." He smiled.

431

"Don't be silly."

"Dinner is served, Miss Delaney."

Shireen glanced around and gave her an automatic smile. "Thank you, Stella."

She and Ed sat down at the table, beautifully set, with a bowl of yellow roses and tall blue candles burning along one side. I won't think about anything, she told herself, taking a cracker from the plate Stella presented. Thinking has never got me anywhere yet.

"My doctor said—"

"Let's not talk about your doctor!" said Shireen sharply. "If you ever want to leave—you'll leave. And that will be that. So let's cut out all this talk. I'm sick of it."

Ed had been looking at her down the table and now he picked up his spoon, bent his head, and began to eat. It was a submissive gesture, as if he had given up again, and that angered her. Damn him anyway! Why couldn't he make up his mind? What was he waiting for? What would it take to make him leave her? The fury came boiling up again. She felt as if she had been closed into a small room and must somehow break her way out.

They finished their soup and Shireen pressed the buzzer with her foot. Stella came and took the plates and she and Ed were silent during the rest of dinner. Once in awhile she glanced at him and he was sitting there like a dutiful worried child.

When dinner was over they walked back to the couch and sat down to drink their coffee. "Would you like a liqueur?" Ed asked her.

"No, thanks."

They sat and looked at the night. After awhile they began to talk about the news. Ed had had a letter from Mike that day, and Mike seemed convinced the war would end sooner than people expected. Well—that would be a relief. At least she needn't feel so guilty about the things she had, if the world was at peace.

A few minutes later Ed got up. "I think I'll go out for awhile."

She looked at him in amazement, finding it impossible to believe such an idea could even occur to him—on the night she had lost the last few hours she might have spent with Johnny. Because of him.

"Where?"

Ed shrugged. "I don't know. A movie, maybe. Or maybe I'll take a walk."

"I should think you've covered Manhattan pretty thoroughly on your walks these past few months."

Ed smiled guiltily, like a small boy who knows he is misbehaving and will be punished for it but does not care. Wants to be punished, in fact.

"Not quite," he said, and went through the French doors into the bedroom. She sprang up and ran after him.

432

"I refuse to let you go!"

Ed looked at her with mock surprise. "You refuse, Shireen?"

"I do! I—" At that moment Stella came to the door and Shireen, seeing her, stopped quickly and composed her face. "You don't need to bother turning down the bed, Stella. I'll take care of it later. Thanks." Stella left and she waited a moment for her to get far enough away. She could not bear to think of the servants overhearing a quarrel between them. "I *can* stop you! I *will* stop you! I forbid you to go! God damn you, Ed Farrell, you can't keep doing this to me! You *can't,* do you hear me? I won't *let* you!"

Then he laughed. It was the first time in months she had seen him grab command of himself and exert it triumphantly. "Shireen," he said quietly, "for once in your life, you're licked." He turned and went out. She stood where she was and stared after him, her body taut and stiff and her fists clenched. Rage battled inside her as if it would knock down the walls of her body and break her to pieces.

I'll kill him when he comes back. I'll kill him!

She went into the bathroom and rinsed her face in cold water, combed her hair and repaired her make-up. Then she began to move around restlessly. She called the airport again, but they could not locate Johnny. He had probably gone by now and there was no way she could find him. By tomorrow morning he might be flying out to the Pacific on that last trip he was always expecting to make—and she had destroyed whatever it was they had had together. She called Georgia, with the vague idea that if she could go over and talk to Georgia, Georgia would straighten everything out for her. But the hotel operator said that Miss Marsh was not in and, when she recognized Shireen's voice, told her she had gone out earlier that evening with Commander Harrington.

She wandered around awhile and then picked up a book and tried to read. Each time she found that her eyes had merely strayed across a sentence like a sheep nibbling and not cropping its grass, she went back and cropped up each word meticulously. And she kept smoking, one cigarette after another, until her mouth was dry as a carpet.

When Ed came in at one o'clock she was still sitting there. She heard him and kept her eyes on her book, but when she felt him standing inside the library door watching her she felt a little frightened and that made her angry again. She looked up.

The look on his face instantly reassured her and increased her rage against him. He was back, humbly, and he was prepared to stay.

"Well?" She put down her book and lit a cigarette.

"I've been thinking—"

"Congratulations." She blew out a cloud of smoke, staring across the room at the rows of books.

"I can't keep it up any longer, Shireen. I've lost all the respect I

433

ever had for myself—and now I'm losing respect for you, too. We're no good for each other any more. We've gone on already long beyond the time we should have stopped."

"This isn't exactly a new thought."

"I know. But this time I'm doing something about it."

"No—" she drawled, and smiled at him. "Are you—really? And what is it you've decided to do, Ed?"

"The only thing I can. I'm leaving."

"When!" She snapped it out, as if she would not give him time to change his mind.

"Tonight."

Chapter 59

They looked at each other a moment longer, Shireen staring at him as if she dared him to go ahead and do it, and then he walked past her and out the door. She sat there. He's going, she told herself, as if she had discovered something she had been looking for a long long while in a place she had never thought she would find it. He's finally going. This time he means it.

And then she jumped up and ran after him. This was the middle of the night. It would be better if he left in the morning.

But she must make him think she was doing something for him.

As she came in she saw that he had taken three suitcases out of the closet and laid them on racks. One was filled already and several drawers stood open. She watched him for a few minutes, thinking that it might be best if he finished packing first. So that when he woke in the morning he would see the packed suitcases and be reminded of his promise to go.

She went over into one corner of the room beside the open doors and sat down in a green and white striped satin chair. He went on packing without looking at her or indicating that he had noticed her enter the room. He closed that suitcase and began to fill another.

After a few moments she said to him: "Don't forget to take the camera I gave you last Christmas."

He did not glance up. "I don't want anything I didn't have before."

"At least take your new suits," she said sweetly.

They're much better than any you're likely to have for a long time. "You can give them away."

"Don't lose all sense of proportion, Ed. Just because you're going. Take along whatever you can use. You'll be glad you did, later."

Ed didn't answer. He continued moving quickly around the room, as if he must get this done and get out before he had quite realized what he had done. He had closed the second suitcase now and the last one was half filled.

Shireen stuck a cigarette into her holder. "Wouldn't it be more sensible, Ed," she asked him in a casual conversational tone, "for you to leave in the morning?"

"No. It wouldn't be. I'm leaving now."

"But where will you go? You know what it's like trying to find a hotel in New York nowadays. You'll be on a park bench. Look, darling, I'm not trying to persuade you to stay. I simply think you'd be—"

"Don't worry about me. I'm not your problem any more." He closed the third suitcase. In a few more minutes he'd be gone. He was in the bathroom now, taking his shaving equipment out of the cabinet. She'd be alone. And it was so long until morning. She stood up and confronted him as he came through the dressing-room door.

"But Ed, honestly, I don't think this is sensible. Just stay until morning."

He went past her, opened the suitcase again and put the small shaving kit into it. "What good could that possibly do either of us?" He straightened and looked at her directly for an instant and smiled. "What's the matter? The bogy-men crawling out of the wall already?" He closed the bag. Shireen ran to place herself in front of him.

"What are you going to do?" she demanded anxiously.

"I think I'll go back to L.A."

She had not been expecting that and it made her angry. What right had he to go back there? She looked at him scornfully. "Coward!" she said.

"I don't think so. New York isn't the only yardstick for measuring yourself."

What was she going to say to that? Oh, yes it is, too! It is for me so it must be for you!

He was going back to where he would feel safe and secure, where his family and his friends were; where he had been Ed Farrell and not Shireen Delaney's husband. Back to the first years they had known each other when she had looked to him to create a life pattern for both of them. Back to where he had believed in himself.

And what did he think that would get him?

He could go back to the place, but not the time. He couldn't undo the years. He couldn't change what had happened! And she hated him for wanting to recapture some part of what he had once had and what they had had together. Didn't he know it was impossible?

What right had he to that kind of forgetfulness, or any of those illusions? They had all been taken away from her.

Ed had picked up two of the suitcases and walked out of the room. Shireen started to follow him but then stayed where she was, waiting for him to come back. This wasn't really happening. It couldn't be happening. It was in her own imagination and, when the dream got too uncomfortable, she would wake up. Something or someone would save her.

Ed came back and picked up the other bag. He did not speak and she realized that if anything more was to be said between them it would be she who must say it. He started out of the bedroom and all his movements were now mechanical, as if he had managed to turn off his thoughts and feelings, as though he had found an escape

436

out of the painful present. And Shireen hated him for being able to detach himself and leave her to feel alone the impact of what had happened to both of them.

"Are *you* going to divorce *me?*" she demanded.

"I don't know what difference that makes. You get the divorce if you want to."

"How can I?" she cried, throwing up obstacles in some frantic half-formed desire to keep him there a little longer. "*I* can't leave New York, you know that!"

"Get it in New York, then. They have divorce courts here."

"I will not! I'll go to Reno! I'll be damned if I'll get it on grounds of adultery!"

His smile broadened. Shireen wondered if he knew about the other men and all at once she wished she had told him. That would have hurt him more than anything else. She could still do it. She could still destroy the last thing she had left him.

"Anything you like, Shireen," he said.

And she knew that even that wouldn't hurt him now. He had put himself beyond her. He was no longer vulnerable. He turned and went through the doorway and she waited a moment, trying to force herself not to follow him. Let him go. She'd live until morning somehow.

Then she rushed after him. He was out in the hallway and had set two suitcases beside the elevator. She watched him come back for the third one. As he bent to pick it up he glanced at her. She was standing with her hands clasped hard together, her whole face stricken with terror.

"Don't leave me now, Ed," she pleaded softly. "Not now—not in the middle of the night."

He looked at her a moment longer, and then shook his head. "Shireen, you poor little girl. You'll have to find some way to face yourself alone at night—or any other time. I can't stay any longer. You don't want me and you know it. You're afraid I'll go, but you're even more afraid I'll stay. And I don't trust myself. If I stayed until morning—" They could hear the elevator coming up.

"No, Ed!" She grabbed hold of his coat lapels. "In the morning it'll be different. I *can't* be alone at night. I can't!" She made one last desperate try. "Ed, this doesn't need to happen! We can work it out someway—I know we can!" She was so terrified that she scarcely knew she was lying to him. "Ed—I love you!"

"No, you don't, Shireen. There's only one person you've ever really loved."

She stared at him. Then he did know about Johnny.

"Who!"

"Yourself."

The elevator doors opened and Ed set two of the bags inside. The

437

operator took the other one. Shireen turned suddenly, without looking at him again, went back inside and closed the door and locked it. She stood there for a moment with her hands over her face—and then she went slowly back to the bedroom. She began to walk around it, mechanically closing the drawers he had left opened, thinking somewhere underneath that with him gone there would be more room for her own clothes . . .

She woke at eight, when Stella knocked on the door. It had been after four when she had fallen asleep, and the two sleeping pills had not worn off yet; it took her a few moments to remember that Ed was gone. She felt tired and dizzy and wanted to go back to sleep again. But, after a moment, she got up, impelled by the feeling that there was something very important she must do today. She had no idea what it was.

She went into the bathroom, ran water in the tub, and got in while it was almost too hot to bear. She lay there for several minutes, her eyes closed. My life's a mess, she thought. And it won't get any better. It's only going to get worse. She was filled with intense self-pity, for she knew that it could not be her fault.

Someone had done it to her. She had tried, but she had been tricked.

And then all at once she was sick of herself.

You've done nothing your whole life but think about yourself. What in the hell is the matter with you, anyway? Taking everything so goddamned seriously. It's no big tragedy, after all. It's nothing cataclysmic, or even dramatic. I'm probably never going to jump out of a window or kill someone.

I'll just go along the way I am, and to other people things must look as if I'm pretty lucky. It's nothing that even shows. Probably no one knows it but me.

So it's nothing to get *this* upset about.

She stopped there a moment, considering.

That's all it is—just the slow, gradual destruction of my life. My only life, as it happens. But I've still got no business taking it too hard, because no individual counts for much these days. Who cares what happens to only one person? It has to happen to a hundred thousand before it gets important.

Or maybe it is happening. How do I know? Maybe it isn't only me. It was my mother and father and their parents and almost everyone I've known. Maybe that's why—maybe *that's* what it is that's going on everywhere. I can't be so different—we're all alike.

But that makes it even worse!

If everyone's as unhappy as I am, then no wonder!

Oh, I won't think about it. I'll get dressed and go talk to Georgia. I've got to talk to someone. She started to get out. But she was reluctant to leave the heat and peace of the tub and as she stood up felt an almost overpowering need to climb back in, as though something inside her was striving to bend her body, make her roll herself into a small private ball and return to the security of the water. She forced herself to step out of it.

She dressed quickly, in a black linen suit, made up her face and then, carrying a wide-brimmed yellow straw hat in her hand, walked out. Stella was in the living room dusting.

"I've got to go somewhere, Stella. Don't plan on lunch today."

"Yes, Miss Delaney. There are some guests for dinner tonight."

Shireen stopped a moment. "Oh. Are there? I'd forgotten. Well— I'll call you later in the day." She went quickly, before Stella should remind her of something else.

And when the elevator doors opened there was Mary Carlisle.

"Well!" said Mary briskly. "What's happened to the schedule? Aren't you supposed to be practicing your—"

"You're fired!" said Shireen.

"What?"

"I haven't got time to talk about it. You're fired, that's all. Get your things and go home. I'll send you your check."

She stepped into the elevator and the doors closed. Her stomach seemed to be shaking and her hands were wet; her heart pounded wildly, as if she had just escaped from a terrible danger.

Thank God, I'm rid of her.

But the next moment she began to worry. She'll probably talk to the servants and turn them against me and I'll come home and find no one there and I'll have to start all over again.

Well—the hell with it. Everything else has to begin again, so that might as well, too. Anyway, I won't worry about it now. I've got more important things on my mind. As she walked outside the sunlight struck up at her from the pavement like a blow. She smiled and said good morning to the doorman and he handed her into a cab. She gave Georgia's address and sat back and lit a cigarette.

So Ed was gone.

Even now she could not quite believe it.

But then she thought: What difference does it make? Other men will fall in love with me. Whenever I want a man I can get one and I can get whichever one I want, too. That's one thing I've learned. And it's so ridiculously simple. You just fool them enough. Find out whatever it is they want and give it to them until you're tired of them —and then you quit and you're rid of them. And the better you fool them the more they're hurt when you're finished with them. So it pays to be everything they want—and I am.

Only I'm not.

I'm nothing of what they think I am, if they knew me. But they

439

don't. They can't find out what you hide if you hide it well enough. I can go on like this—a long time yet. As long as I'm pretty. And when I'm not—well, maybe I'll die first. I can always kill myself. That's one power no one can take away from you. If it gets so I can't stand it any longer, I can die. And no one can stop me. So I can never be trapped. There's always a way out.

In Georgia's office building she smiled at the elevator boy as if he was the one friend she had been waiting to see. His greeting reassured her that she still existed, still had an identity recognizable to other people.

"Is Miss Marsh in yet?" she asked him.

"Yes, she is. I took her up a few minutes ago. And how's everything with you, Miss Delaney?"

"Everything's fine. How are you?"

"Can't complain much. Been working you pretty hard, have they? Haven't seen you around in a long time."

"Yes, I've been working pretty hard."

She got out and smiled at him again. She walked down the hall and into Georgia's office. Georgia was standing in the reception room talking to her secretary, her hat on as usual. She looked at Shireen in surprise.

"What? What's up?"

"Can I talk to you, Georgia?"

They went into Georgia's private office and Georgia, closing the door behind her, looked at Shireen seriously. "What's the matter?"

Shireen tossed her hat onto the couch. "Ed's gone." She and Georgia looked at each other a moment and Shireen shrugged.

Georgia went and sat behind her desk. "He'll be back."

"No, he won't. He's gone for good."

She sat down on the couch, and realized to her surprise that she was feeling much better, because she was with someone she knew liked her and believed in her.

"Are you sorry?"

"I don't think so. I think I'm glad. He had to leave sometime."

Georgia shook her head. "It happens every time. They always get divorced."

"Who always gets divorced?"

"People like you. The old husband never seems to carry over into the new life. Well, what are your plans?"

"I haven't made any yet. He only left a few hours ago. I suppose I'll have to go to Reno. I fired that goddamned secretary this morning on my way out."

Georgia smiled. She had begun drawing doodles on a note pad marked at the top with her name in big blue letters. She drew dollar signs, five-pointed stars, and a spiral that she thoughtfully made

440

larger and larger. Both of them were quiet a few minutes and then Shireen said:

"I had a dream last night. I dreamed you said to me: 'Events that are going to happen, tap windows behind us.' And as you said it I had the feeling that you meant something about arousing old senses of guilt. But then I woke up before I could ask you." She smiled. "What was it you meant, Georgia?"

"I wish I could tell you."

They were silent. Shireen remembered something that seemed to have happened a long time ago.

"I saw Johnny yesterday afternoon. He was on his way out west. That's finished, too."

"You're tying all the strings on all the packages at once, aren't you?"

Shireen laughed. "You know me—always burn my bridges before I come to 'em."

Georgia went to look at herself in the mirror, powdering her face and smoothing on more lipstick. "Let's go have some coffee. Have you eaten breakfast?"

"Not yet."

"I'm going to a cocktail party this afternoon that's being given for Bill Egan—the guy who wrote *The Lucky People*. Why don't you come along? You can't possibly work today. Anyway, you might as well meet him. From what I hear he's kind of terrific. Seems to me he got divorced not long ago."

Shireen put up one hand. "No, Georgia. I've had enough of men. I don't want to meet any new ones. I'm not even going to think about men. I'm just going to work."

"For the rest of your life?" Georgia was smiling.

"Maybe. I don't know. Men have never been anything but trouble to me."

"It's been mutual, sweetie." She turned around and they walked toward the door. "I hear he's bright as hell and very good-looking."

"I hate good-looking men. They're even worse than the other kind. You have to treat them like lap dogs. I don't want to meet him."

"Okay."

Walking down the hall to the elevator Shireen was quiet a moment and then asked: "You say he's divorced?"

"That's what I hear." Georgia rang the bell.

"Anyway, I'm never going to get married again."

"You don't have to marry him, Shireen. Who said anything about that? How do you know if you'll even like him?"

"I know all right. I know I won't like him. I don't already." The elevator stopped and they got in. They went down several floors in silence.

441

"Well—I may as well go, I suppose. Otherwise I'll just sit home and mope." Or cut my throat.

"God forbid."

They glanced at each other, and then all at once they both began to laugh.